# The Sun Walks Down

*Also by Fiona McFarlane*

The Night Guest
The High Places

# THE SUN WALKS DOWN

FIONA McFARLANE

sceptre

First published in Great Britain in 2022 by Sceptre
An Imprint of Hodder & Stoughton
An Hachette UK company

This edition first published in 2023

1



A CIP catalogue record for this title is available from the British Library

Hardback ISBN 9781529389821
Trade Paperback 9781529389838
eBook ISBN 9781529389845

Printed and bound in Great Britain by Clays Ltd, Elcograf S.p.A.

Hodder & Stoughton policy is to use papers that are natural, renewable and recyclable products and made from wood grown in sustainable forests. The logging and manufacturing processes are expected to conform to the environmental regulations of the country of origin.

Hodder & Stoughton Ltd
Carmelite House
50 Victoria Embankment
London EC4Y 0DZ

www.sceptrebooks.co.uk

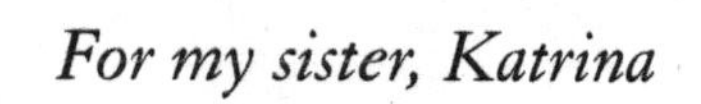

*For my sister, Katrina*

Three hearty cheers for the flag, the emblem of civic and religious liberty, and may it be a sign to the natives that the dawn of liberty, civilisation, and Christianity is about to break upon them.

JOHN MCDOUALL STUART, PLANTING THE BRITISH FLAG IN THE CENTRE OF AUSTRALIA, 1860

Now is so small a part of time.

OODGEROO, 'THE PAST'

The province of the poem is the world.
When the sun rises, it rises in the poem
and when it sets darkness comes down
and the poem is dark.

WILLIAM CARLOS WILLIAMS, *PATERSON*

# AUTHOR'S NOTE

The Flinders Ranges and the Willochra Plain are real places, but Fairly, Undelcarra, Thalassa and the Axam Range are inventions. The locations in which this novel takes place would, if they existed, overlap with two Aboriginal nations: the Nukunu Nation and what is now known as the Adnyamathanha Nation. I respectfully acknowledge the land's traditional owners and my novel's debt to them. Sovereignty of this land has never been ceded.

# THE COLONY OF SOUTH AUSTRALIA, SEPTEMBER 1883

The boy met a god by the hollow tree.

'Go away,' said the boy, and the god, formless, passed on in the direction of the red hill. Then the boy was free to hunt in the scrub for roosting hens. When he came upon the hens they flapped up as if they could fly, and he gathered their eggs in a basket. The boy was six years old and thin, with a vivid pointed face. He wasn't pale, exactly—his skin browned in the sun—but the visible veins at his wrists and ears suggested a delicacy that the people he knew associated with pale children. There was so little of him. When his mother held him, his heart felt near. Light hair, lifting in the briefest wind. And not so delicate, in fact—a strong boy, a good runner. The name people called him was Denny, and he answered to it.

The boy was gentle as he settled the eggs in the basket. Then his mother wanted him close—he knew this, even though she hadn't called his name. Nobody had ever told him about his mother's deafness; she was simply his mother, which meant she heard little and spoke less. But the boy knew when she wanted him to go to her. She had finished hanging the sheets on the line behind the house, and the boy went to give her the basket of eggs; she took it, bent down to him, and pressed her face against his neck. Today she belonged to him entirely—all his sisters were at a wedding in town and his father was out planting parsnips.

The boy and his mam were alone and loving among the sheets. Then quick as a blink she straightened, turned her back and went into the house, which always ate her up. The boy, following, wanted to help her churn the butter, but she made him put his boots on, she laced them tight, and she sent him out with a sack to gather grass and bark and twigs. He liked to collect things for the fire, and he liked to please her. The black dog, Mopsy, woke from her nap in the sun and looked as if she might come with him; but she heard Mam start the butter churn and went to supervise that instead.

The boy walked away from the red hill, although it was from behind the hill that his sisters would come home from town. The country he walked into was red and brown—desert country—but there was a haze of green over the top of it, because it was spring. At this time of day, the surrounding hills were white and yellow and green. A shrub scratched the boy's shin and he followed, for a while, the deep course of a dry creek. He kneeled on its stony bed and saw ants carrying a large dead fly. The word that came to him was 'housebound', maybe because he'd heard his mother use that word about Mrs Baumann, who had large eyes, like a fly, and clean, folded hands, and sat in a chair with wheels on it as if she had neat grey wings tucked behind her. But the boy didn't think of Mrs Baumann exactly; the word 'housebound' just dropped into the boy and went away again.

He rounded a curve in the creek and surprised a kangaroo. He knew the story of the kangaroo: once upon a time, it argued about food with its cousin the wallaroo, so now it stayed here on the dry, flat plain while the wallaroo lived up in the hills. The boy's heart was big with sorrow for the kangaroo, which crouched very still and looked at him. It seemed to be waiting for something to happen. Then it turned and flew from the creek bed and the boy climbed out to follow it for its dung, which also burned. Really, he followed it because it was fast, because the boy was also waiting for something to happen, because he was six years old.

Soon, things would happen. Men would call his name in the night; there would be blood on a handkerchief, and fire on the red hill.

The boy looked north and saw a high dark wall over the ranges. The wall was moving towards him. It was made of dust, and when the dust reached him it hid the sun. The sun was there, the boy could see it through his narrowed eyes, but it was brown now, and silly: only as bright as a lamp or the moon. The dust rolled down from the north in secret colours, very soft, until the wind came up behind it. Then it stung. The boy held the sack across his face, as his father had taught him to do when the dust storms came, and he turned around and began to walk, and that's how he got lost: trying to walk home in the dust.

When the storm had passed, his mother went out into the yard and spat red onto the red ground. She looked for him in the direction he had gone and saw no sign.

# FIRST DAY

The dust storm rose up in the central deserts. In order to reach the boy and his mother, it passed over the ridges, valleys and gorges of the northern Flinders Ranges. These ranges were laid down, long ago and slowly, in layers of rock: limestone, for example, sandstone, quartzite, also other types of rock that exist only here, in the arid middle of South Australia. They were laid down by time and water, folded into great peaks by the movement of the Earth, and in the aeons since then have been worn by time and water back to stumps. The European settlers, who came to the ranges in the 1840s, sometimes refer to them as hills, but this is too reasonable a word for the serrated ridges and startling inclines of this dusty, dry country. These are ancient mountains—so old that they've collapsed in on themselves, as stars do.

This particular storm contributed to the long, slow erosion of the Flinders Ranges by picking up more dust from the kicked surfaces of the sheep and cattle stations, then pouring over the jagged rim of Wilpena Pound. From there, it rolled down into the narrow northern neck of the broad tableland known as the Willochra Plain; it rolled on into the bristling wheat country, where it hid Denny and sent his mother running for the freshly washed sheets. That work done, the storm now continues south across the widening Willochra, which is surrounded by ranges on every side. The dust flows over the plain like a beery tide until it reaches the town of Fairly, where Denny's sisters are attending a wedding.

Fairly is used to these vast dusts. Its sharper edges blur, its few trees tremble, and the polish of its windows dulls a little, but even under dust it's active, alert and eager with proprieties. It boasts a neat school, four trains a week, a debt-free church and, in that church, a new harmonium. There's also a discreet German prostitute who keeps a piebald donkey and is tolerated because she is known to sleep only with white men. Fairly has huddled under storms like this one for the eight years of its existence. It was itself tricked up out of dust. The whole town, with its grid of ten streets, seems to turn away from the north, where the storms come from; it draws its shoulders up and looks south, as if Adelaide, three hundred miles away, might be visible over the crest of the next hill.

The dust, engulfing Fairly, could ruin Minna Baumann's wedding ceremony. When the first gusts start, Minna's brother unhitches the pony from the wedding wagon and leads it into the church. The storm lowers the light, batters the iron roof and makes a fine grainy sound against the windows; but all of this ends up increasing the solemnity of the occasion, at the centre of which Minna burns in her ivory dress. The pony snorts with fright, Peter Baumann quiets it, and even this seems reverent: after all, as Mrs Baumann will later remark, there was at least one donkey present at the birth of Christ. The vicar, Mr Daniels, does have a coughing fit, but he's known to have trouble with his lungs.

By the time the ceremony is over, the storm has moved on, bringing some spitting rain behind it. The dust sweeps across Thalassa, the last big sheep station in the wheat country; it throws itself south, as if it's determined to travel all those miles to Adelaide. But it's only, after all, a minor storm, and the Willochra Plain becomes so broad and flat the further south it goes that the dust spreads, tumbles, meets other winds and weathers, and eventually blows itself out.

When Minna Baumann steps out of the Fairly church and sees the red dust gathered on the road, against the few gravestones, along the arms of the young trees and among the garlands on her wedding wagon, she chooses to feel as if it's been offered to her as a gift. Her hair is tight at her temples. People press against her and take her hands. Mr Daniels has informed every one of these people that Minna and her husband are now one flesh. Her husband has found a handkerchief—not his own—with which to dust the seat of the wagon. He's dusting it for her. He, Mounted Constable Robert Manning, First Class, with his red hair and freckled face, is turning to her and laughing; is helping her into the seat; is going to drive her the few minutes to her mother's house so that Mrs Baumann can see her married daughter arrive in a German wagon covered with flowers. Minna is eighteen and ready for the world to be larger than her mother's house—but not too much larger.

'Well,' says Robert as they drive from the church. Children follow after them, yipping and shouting like dogs, as if they know what it all means. Robert says, 'Well,' again and clears his throat. 'Wasn't that a lovely storm?' Which Minna likes about him—the way he calls things lovely that aren't. He only means it was a good example of its kind.

Minna pulls petals off the roses that cling to the wagon. 'Let's go now,' she says.

'Go where?'

'To your house—where else? Alone.'

The wagon tilts in the road.

'Little Minnow,' says Robert. He holds the reins with one hand and puts the other on Minna's leg, just above her knee, and squeezes. She leans her head against his shoulder and it's as if they've been married for years and are coming home from the wedding of some other girl. Cheers rise from the people behind them. Robert puts his arm around her—more cheers. She misses his hand on her knee.

'It *was* a lovely storm,' she says.

Robert begins to hum, and Minna feels the hum pass from his body into hers.

Minna's mother is waiting for them on the verandah; her maid, Annie, has swept it clear of dust and pushed the wheelchair out. Mrs Baumann is dressed as usual in her glossy blacks, all complicated pleats and stiff corsets, so that, propped in her wheelchair, she resembles a fussy umbrella. She's issuing further instructions to Annie, who will have been opening doors and windows, shaking dust from the trees and chasing it down the front path with her broom.

'Annie,' Mrs Baumann says, 'you will go now and change your apron for a fresh one.'

Mrs Baumann kisses her son-in-law and shoos him inside to wash the reins off his hands, but she has questions for Minna. The first thing she wants to know: was the Swedish painter at the church? Minna expected this enquiry. The Swedish painter has preoccupied her mother since he appeared in town a week ago.

'No, Mama, I told you, they've already left for Wilpena.'

'The wife also?'

'Yes, both of them.'

'Psh,' says Mrs Baumann. 'And what are they going to do out there in the desert?'

'Paint, I daresay,' says Minna. She looks down at the top of her mother's head and feels the urge to kiss it, but Mama would shrink from that kind of affection.

'What about the storm?' asks Mrs Baumann.

Minna says, 'He promised us he would be all right.'

And she'd believed him. The Swedish painter had dazzled her the way an angel might, wandering into a village and asking for a meal and a place to sleep, seeming ordinary, complimenting someone on their bread, and leaving the next morning in a cloud of light so that everyone could see his wings. The enormity of the angel would humble the village; they would worship it and be glad to see it gone.

'Drowned in the dust,' Mrs Baumann says, abandoning the Swede to his fate with a shrug. 'But at the church, I was meaning—how was the storm at the church, Hermina?'

The guests are arriving. They gather at the gate to make way for each other. The men clear their throats into their fists and the women lift their skirts away from the red dust on the ground.

'Peter brought the pony inside.'

Mrs Baumann nods. 'Well, what else was possible?' she says. She reaches up and takes Minna's hand in her own, which feels furred and soft, like an apricot. If Minna had married in a Lutheran church, her mother might have made the effort to leave the house. The way Mrs Baumann holds Minna's hand, laughs, and says, 'What else was possible?' communicates all this: no pony would have been allowed into a German house of God. But Mrs Baumann is a long way from Germany. She and her husband left that fine, green country in their youths and came blazing into the Australian desert. Minna has heard the story many times. She is the result of it, and so is her brother Peter, and this house—the first in town with wooden floors. The wooden boards hide spiders, dust, lost needles, beads, which Annie must ferry out with her long broom. Other houses have wooden floors now, but the Baumanns' are important, because first. Minna has seen her mother summon strength from the wooden floors. She's insistent that they should never show the tracks of her wheelchair.

'Tell me,' says Mrs Baumann, 'did the Axams show their faces?'

When Minna says no, there were no Axams at the church, Mrs Baumann shakes her head, unsurprised. She closes her eyes and opens them again, and Minna knows that in that moment her mother has equipped herself for battle: her long, tedious battle with the Axams, who have insulted her by having good breeding behind them, property, sheep, while Mama (whose father owned a draper's shop, a substantial one, in Dortmund, but was not, you understand, a Jew) rolls in her chair over the wooden floors.

'So, you are now married,' Mrs Baumann says. 'My *Liebchen*. To a constable!' She glances at Minna's stomach, which remains flat beneath the ivory dress. 'And all things will be well.'

Mrs Baumann settles her skirt over her knees and turns a cordial face towards the gate, so Minna goes into the house to look for Robert. She finds him sitting on her bed with his elbows on his knees, his hands and head hanging so that she can see the slight thinness of his topmost hair. He seems almost dainty from this angle, despite his bulk and the size of his hands. She loves his hands. They look as if they've been baked, or as if he coated them in pink clay one day and it stuck. It has only recently occurred to Minna that men can be beautiful—during the Swedish painter's visit, in fact. She wouldn't call Robert beautiful. He's something else. He's desire itself.

'Hello, Mr Manning,' she says.

Robert lifts his head and smiles at her. It's a real smile—tired and loving. 'Mrs Manning,' he says. He puts his hands on his knees and stands, slowly, so that she sees him in thirty years, an eternity away, creaking up from a chair. He's so much larger than her bed, this room, the house. But not larger than the town. The size of him, next to her: just large enough. And red, white, pink, brown: the colour of local rock.

'Put your arms around me,' she says.

Robert hesitates. 'Your dress. And this, here, I don't want to squash it.' He points at the spray of orange blossom on her bodice.

'It's just wax.' Minna unpins the blossom and throws it on the bed. 'Shall we climb out the window?'

This makes him laugh. 'Too late for that.'

But it's early. Minna says, 'Now we'll never have to be apart again.'

'Sometimes, Minnow,' Robert says, smiling. 'Sometimes we'll have to be apart.'

Minna sees herself and Robert in the mirror on her wall. 'Look at us!' she says, and when he does she kisses him.

⁂

All five of the Wallace sisters have left their mother washing sheets, their father planting parsnips and their brother Denny collecting eggs in order to travel the few miles to Fairly for Minna Baumann's wedding. They've been allowed the use of the old mare and the spring-cart, which Cissy—who is fifteen, and the second eldest of the girls—drove to the church. Once there, she pushed her sisters into a pew and shushed them when they giggled at the entrance of the pony, and now she's making them all go to Mrs Baumann's for the wedding breakfast. She herds them through the gate and up the path in a dingy cloud of calico. Not even Joy, the eldest sister, is offered a cup of tea.

Cissy eats a slice of tongue while her sisters huddle under a pepper tree. She watches a lizard slip into the house through an open door and follows its example; then she's in a room full of oblong mirrors and intricate chairs. The wooden floor is silken with wax. Minna's wedding presents are laid out on a table, but Cissy won't lower herself to look at them. On another table, Cissy sees a silver bowl with silver palm trees rising from its rim. Each palm tree is attended by a turbaned Indian, and in each tree there's a silver monkey, and in each monkey's arms a candle. Cissy touches one of the candles, which is firm and smooth, and through a doorway she sees Minna Baumann pressed against the constable. Minna is covering her husband's face in a flurry of kisses. How ridiculous, to kiss his cheeks and nose like a baby's, or a puppy's! Especially when it seems to embarrass him. But then he begins to kiss her back with some force, lifts one foot, and uses it to push the door closed.

Cissy, disconcerted by the slamming of the door, goes outside to her sisters. They're a drab clump under the bright pink berries of the pepper tree, all of them wearing dresses cut from the same blue cloth. The youngest sister, Lotta, is crying, and the vicar squats beside her, holding one steadying finger against the ground. Mr Daniels and Lotta have the same coloured hair: yellow like hay, but dry hay that won't shine. He's talking to Lotta, and pauses to cough. He coughed in the church when Peter Baumann brought the pony in, but Cissy was grateful for it then; it covered the sound of Ada and Noella giggling. Now, joining her sisters under the pepper tree, Cissy is irritated by the vicar's fussy cough and consoling manner.

'I'll bring you another,' he's saying to Lotta, and Cissy sees a spoiled sandwich in the dust by his finger.

'It has a special sort of ham,' Noella says mournfully, eyeing the sliver of pink on the dirty sandwich, and Lotta gives the heaving sigh that means she will now stop crying.

The vicar stands up too quickly, which seems to make him dizzy. He holds a hand to his forehead and blinks; then he smiles at Cissy and says, 'Your brother is missing the fun.'

'Ha!' Cissy says, stroking Lotta's hair. 'Denny!' She lifts Lotta to her hip.

Mr Daniels looks as if he expects her to say more, but Cissy knows you can stand all day just talking for no reason, and then the day is lost.

'Did you enjoy the wedding?' he asks.

Surely he knows it's the finest wedding she's ever seen. Why bother asking? If the vicar ignored her she'd despise him; because he's courteous, she considers him a fool.

Ada tugs on Cissy's sleeve and says, 'Should we take Lotta home?'

Cissy pulls her arm away. 'You,' she says, 'were the one who insisted on bringing her in the first place.'

The vicar, who also looks as if he'd like to go home, says, 'I did promise your sister another sandwich. Why don't I secure a plateful? Some nourishment for you all before your journey.'

Before Cissy can reject this offer—if her sisters want to eat, they should be brave enough to approach the food themselves—Mr Daniels presses one hand to his chest and looks at Cissy with a stricken expression. She watches the colour drain from the top of his head down to his stiff white collar. He's swaying slightly, but before anything can be done about it, Mr Daniels collapses to the ground, hitting it with an unseemly, 'Oof!'

Cissy, who has waited all her life to be part of a catastrophe, so that she might take some decisive, swift action for which she will always be remembered, looks down at the fallen vicar, who appears to have fainted; then she looks up at the other wedding guests, all of whom are now aware of the pepper tree, the Wallace sisters, and the vicar lying in the dust beside them.

Adults approach, offering hands and handkerchiefs to the vicar, who has regained consciousness and whose face has now flushed entirely red. Cissy finds herself unable to move until Joy calls her name; then she herds her sisters out of the way as the vicar is helped to his feet. The only feasible course of action is to leave immediately.

Cissy, hurrying her sisters to the gate, is both mortified and furious. She wants people to say, 'There goes Cissy Wallace.' But why should they, when she did nothing but stand there in witless surprise? They're all looking at the vicar, who is being led into the house with a patch of red dust on the seat of his pants. Cissy wants to stay and hear what people say about him. She wants to hear about the handsome Swedish painter and his wife, and to get close to Mrs Baumann's wheelchair, which people say is made of Indian reed; Cissy wants to know what's so particular about Indian reed. She'd like to see if the Axams of Thalassa turn up, because she despises them for being the kind of people who are referred to along with the name of the place where they live. She'd like to see and hear everything so that she can tell Miss McNeil, the schoolteacher, all about it—Miss McNeil, who isn't at the wedding because she claims to be busy. Busy with what? Cissy wishes Miss McNeil were here in order to be angry alongside her. Angry at Minna Baumann's complicated dress, the frailty of the vicar, the size of Constable Manning's hands on Minna's waist, the width of the plain they all live on, the stupidity of planting wheat that will either dry up or be eaten by grasshoppers, the dust storm that may have damaged that stupid wheat, and at the extravagance of growing roses for no better reason than to put them on a wagon at a wedding.

Angry at store-bought candles and silver bowls with silver palm trees growing out of them. Miss McNeil should also be angry that Cissy has taken the time to darken her boots with lamp-black and to trim her nails and brush her hair, and angry that she would like to stay and be talked about. Cissy is longing for someone to be angry with her.

But here are these sisters, blocking the gate, and the terrible responsibility of loving and looking after them. And there will be chores at home—the whole house full of dust, no doubt, and Mam left to look after it, and Denny, all by herself.

As Cissy drives them north out of town, Noella asks, 'What part did you like best?'

'The dress,' says Joy, her face raised to the sky as if expecting God or rain.

Cissy would like to whip the mare and send it flying. The dress, the dress! As if the dress is anything. 'If I get married,' she says, 'even to a tiny jockey, don't you *ever* bring a horse into my wedding.'

Her sisters laugh. They drive past other small wheat farms like their father's: past Britnell's and Jutt's, who have committed to at least one more harvest, and past Swinborn's, who have already given up, and past Nead's, who are about to. The wheels of the spring-cart roll softly on the thickened road. Joy, Cissy and Ada sing; Noella claims to like the gritty feel of dust between her teeth. The afternoon is warm, and flies sleep on the girls' matching hats. Lotta fusses until, about a mile from home, she vomits over the side of the cart. Then she sleeps and her sisters stop singing. But Ada continues to hum.

Here is their mother, Mary Wallace, moving in and out of the house that Denny thinks of as eating her up. The house is made of mellow red stone stained occasionally with white and yellow. It has an iron roof and, nailed to the northern eave, a snakeskin to keep the swallows from nesting. Inside: a clay floor that must be swept morning and evening, limewashed walls that must be repainted every spring, a stove under a dark hood that spits heat all day, one big room that's both parlour and kitchen, two neat bedrooms and, at the end of the verandah, another room, a lean-to built of clay and native pine, where Mary's husband sleeps. The house could be dark—small windows—but isn't; the door is always open, and in the main room a large chiffonier of fine mahogany gleams with mirrors that throw out light. On top of the chiffonier, a porcelain bowl of porcelain flowers. The other furniture is the right scale for the house and more obviously serviceable. There are cushions, the kind you might kneel on to pray, meticulously needlepointed with Bible verses by Mary's stepmother. And in the corner of the parlour there's space for failure to crouch, open-mouthed, larger or smaller depending on the day, the weather and the harvest. Mary cleans that corner just as thoroughly as the rest.

Behind the house, baking in the continual blast of desert sun: a garden planted sensibly with cabbages, and the privy beyond it; an iron washhouse and a bread oven built of bricks; a tank for the rain that may or may not come; a path and gate to the road, and another path and gate to the yard where the goat and cow spend their days, and the hens, too, when Mary keeps them in. The house and garden are fenced to keep animals off. Cats come, naturally, wanted or not. And rabbits. Also, in certain seasons, long, fat carpet snakes, which coil beneath the boards of the verandah and keep the rats down.

Beside the garden: Mary's washing line strung up on two thick poles, the closest things within the fence to trees, and Mary with her arms full of the sheets she rescued from the dust. She's hanging them out again, the black dog at her heels. Her long brown hair is wound in a coronet around her head. Mary is up before everyone in the morning and still up after they're all in bed at night. The day opens and it closes and Mary is making beds, cooking meals, feeding animals, brushing hair, mending dresses, sweeping floors, writing letters, washing shirts, wringing sheets, churning butter, dressing children, straining milk, clearing tables, knitting socks, fetching water, hoeing the garden and darning stockings. Now she's pegging the sheets to the line. Every time she finishes hanging a sheet she turns to look out over the yard, the plain and far into the hills, hoping to see a walking boy.

When he doesn't come she goes out to the edge of the yard and calls his name, making an effort to raise her voice. His name—Denny—disappears as if some other mouth is waiting just beyond hers and has swallowed it. She calls with more effort, and Deniston this time, as if the plain will respect his full name; she thinks of the name Deniston as formal, because it's her father's. If Denny were to call out in response to her, she wouldn't hear him: Mary, a sufferer of persistent ear infections, lost most of her hearing by the age of twenty-two. So, when she calls her son's name, she looks to see if anything moves in an answering way.

Not even the cat comes to her. It sleeps, full of rat, in the shadows of the cowshed. Mary thinks to try the shed—Denny might have run there when the dust picked up. A well-built cowshed should be dense and dark, should shuffle with the sleepy lives of many animals. This shed is empty. It's built of bark, it leans, the lime between the slats is crumbling, so Mary can see at once in the mottled light that Denny isn't there. The goat comes tottering in from the yard, expecting food, and the dog yaps at it.

Mary looks for Denny in the horse yard, the stable, the pigpen with no pig in it, and all the other sheds that have grown about the place as they've been needed. She doesn't find him in the water tank or any of the troughs, on the roof or under the house, or in the hollow tree that stands between the house and the red hill.

There's no need to worry, Mary tells herself. He'll have found a spot to shelter and fallen fast asleep. Or come across his father, and they'll appear together at sundown. Or he'll have walked along the road to wait for his sisters and they'll have seen him there by the roadside, a little stump, and lifted him up into the cart. Or he won't have filled his sack yet and is staying out until he does, and it's just the storm that makes her miss him.

But branches fall and snakes bite. There are sudden drops and steep gullies, dams and waterholes. There are strangers in the desert: natives, hawkers, swagmen, stockmen, teamsters, Chinese labourers and Afghans with their camels. Denny might meet any of these people—or he might meet no one at all, which could be worse. Mary remembers, though, that the Englishwoman is out there with her husband, the Swedish painter. They stopped at the house on their way north; the Englishwoman came to the door while her husband held the horses at the gate. She asked for a 'wand of aloe'. Her speech was clear—she spoke loudly, as if she already knew of Mary's deafness—and what she meant was a piece of the aloe vera by the gate, which Mary's family calls the lettuce plant. The girls have scratched their names in its green flesh: Joy, Cissy, Ada, Noella. One of them wrote Lotta and Denny in, too, and Mary carved her own initials, also her husband's, and those of her oldest son no longer at home, and since then she's been afraid for the plant, as if it means more than it should. On the rare days she goes out of sight of the house, she looks for the aloe first on returning. It would disturb her less to see the house gone than the plant.

So that it might have hurt her to give a piece of it to the Englishwoman. She worried that it would, but anyway said yes. 'Only,' she said, 'mind the part with writing on, if you don't mind.' Then felt ashamed of having repeated 'mind'.

The Englishwoman promised that she would do as little damage to the plant as possible. She'd use a freshly sharpened knife. There was something green and cool about her. Her forehead gleamed with sweat, but it looked as if she'd just stepped out of a green, cool river. Her hair was dark and her husband's light; when she reached the gate, her smooth head shone next to his tawny one. Cutting the aloe, the Englishwoman was careful with the knife. Her husband watched her, and when she finished, he lifted his head and gave Mary a formal wave. Mary raised her arm to repeat the gesture, and it was as if they'd saluted each other across a battlefield, which seemed to make the man smile. It felt like a transaction; as if he'd given Mary something just by smiling, and now she was in his debt.

When the older girls and Denny came home from school—what day was this? Only yesterday? The day before?—they were thrilled to hear the news of the Swedish painter's visit, except for Cissy, who responded with a dismissive snort. Even so, Cissy went down and lingered by the aloe, rubbing its raw edge, and Denny followed her. They stayed by the gate, looking out along the road. Mary, thinking of this and of the Englishwoman and of the aloe wand, feels as if she has sent a piece of her own self out onto the plain and that Denny—not that she should worry, he'll be home soon—Denny will find it if he needs to.

Mary returns to the house. She fetches a broom and sweeps the dust out of the house and onto the verandah; then she sweeps the dust from the verandah to the yard. She uses the broom to swat the flies from around the door, to sweep the chickens through the yard, and everywhere she steps the ground feels yielding. She sets out with a kerosene tin for the pump, hears Mopsy barking, and looking south she sees a manageable cloud of dust moving along the road: the girls are nearly home. She fills the tin with water and carries it back to the house without spilling a single drop. Before the girls arrive, she changes her dirty apron for a clean one.

The girls, talking all at once, begin to pull off their Sunday clothes as soon as they're inside. They step bare and freckled out of their blue dresses with the ease they always have when men aren't present. Mary made the dresses, made the identical red bloomers, and trimmed their hats with the same blue ribbon.

The girls speak loudly and Mary stands in the middle of the room in order to hear the things they say. Denny isn't with them.

Cissy hasn't changed out of her clothes, although she's taken off her hat, and she's in a stir. This always happens: she makes her sisters go with her to things like weddings and Sunday school teas, and when she comes home she stalks the house and yard in an obscure fury, flinging tea-leaves on the garden, snapping dishrags and kicking at the chickens.

'The vicar fainted right in front of me,' Cissy reports, taking the tin from her mother and pouring water from it to fill the kettle.

Little Charlotte, who is rarely separated from Mary, hangs among her skirts. Mary strokes Lotta's warm head and leans down, intending to ask her if she's seen her brother.

'Lotta dropped a sandwich,' says Noella.

Mary straightens.

'They didn't offer us anything to drink,' says Cissy, rolling up her sleeves.

Noella, scratching behind Mopsy's ear, says, 'The sandwiches had a special sort of ham.'

'There was nothing special about that ham,' says Cissy. 'And riding off in a wagon full of flowers! Would Minna sit in an old wagon any other day? Roses, Mam! Roses from where? Pure sentiment is what it is.' She talks like Miss McNeil at the school. 'And nothing to drink, not even for Joy.'

'We never went up and asked, though,' counters Ada. 'We never even said hello.'

Mary clears her throat and says, 'Denny.'

Cissy, poking at the stove, says, 'Peter Baumann brought the pony in from the storm, right into church. What about Denny?'

'He's gone. I don't know where he is,' says Mary. The girls look at her then, all but Lotta, who's still wound in Mary's skirts. Mary finds herself smiling, though she can't imagine why. 'He was out when the storm came through. I sent him out for kindling.'

'But that was hours ago,' Cissy says.

'Yes.' Mary looks at the clock on the mantel, her mother's clock—it came from England, and though she knows the secrets of a wound-up clock, she sometimes struggles to believe that the time it tells is not the time in Norwich. She says, 'I thought he might have met you on the road.'

Cissy, muttering something Mary doesn't catch, lifts the singing kettle off the stove.

'I called his name,' says Mary. It sounds so feeble. 'I looked everywhere—the sheds, the stable.'

'He does sleep in the cowshed sometimes,' says Ada.

'I thought he might have gone to meet your father.'

Cissy is tightening her hair, she's pressing an arm against the doorframe as she checks the sole of one black boot. She doesn't bother to say, 'I'm going out to look for him.' They know she'll go out to look. Mary has been waiting for Cissy to come and do exactly this: make the gestures that mean she's preparing herself to go out and find Denny. Cissy might be capable of standing at the gate and hauling the whole plain in like a net. Trees and fences will come with it, flocks of sheep, paddocks of wheat, the railway, and also Denny—Cissy will catch him up and bring him in. Mary would like to step across the room and press her forehead against her capable daughter's shoulder. But Cissy doesn't like to be touched. She's ready to go, having tapped the boot hard against the side of the doorway—she always complains of stones lodged in the soles of her boots—and taken a drink of water.

'Which way did he go?' she asks.

Mary points.

Ada hands Cissy her everyday hat, which is an old one of Mary's: it has a tiny hole in the crown and no ribbons.

'I'll come with you,' says Ada.

But Cissy is issuing instructions: Ada to the dam, Noella to the creek. Mary hears Cissy say, 'Joy, you climb the red hill,' and Joy, who is always reluctant to climb the hill, says, 'He won't be up there.'

Cissy huffs and says, 'Probably not, but you can see for miles.' She turns to Mary. 'You and Lott will be here when he gets home.'

Cissy squares the battered hat on her narrow head. It makes her head seem separate from her body, which is still dressed in its wedding clothes.

'Your dress!' says Joy.

'My dress, my dress,' says Cissy. She steps onto the verandah, marches down the path, opens the gate and closes it, and strides across the road. Mary watches Cissy walk onto the plain. She seems to sail over the thorny ground, with nothing to stop her step or catch her skirt. It's as if there's nothing there but Cissy—no plants or rocks or flies, no sun or temperature at all, and Mary is proud to have made this girl, this daughter, who will find Denny and bring him home.

The Axams of Thalassa do come to Minna Baumann's wedding breakfast. First up the path come the two Axam boys (only they aren't boys, they're men in their thirties, shortish, squarish, with high surprised foreheads): George and Ralph, without their wives. And after them their mother, Joanna, her hair the kind of white that was once blonde, and all of her upper body covered in a cashmere shawl of fine navy so long that at the back, where the shawl dips to a point, the fringe almost touches the ground. Joanna Axam wears the shawl to hide her left arm, which she injured a year ago in a riding accident. Because she considers the shawl a kind of disguise, it's the most beautiful she could buy in Adelaide. Otherwise, Joanna favours practical clothing in grey and brown; small, tight hats for her small, tight head; sensible hairstyles; and sturdy shoes. Even to a wedding, she wears clothes that make people think of horses.

The Axams come to the breakfast, although they weren't in church for the service—shearing starts next week, protested George Axam, what do they expect, we don't have all the time in the world for weddings. And his brother Ralph said, we'll go for an hour. George's wife approved of this (she's only at Thalassa because the Swedish artist came to stay, she'll leave as soon as possible, they should convey her regrets but please not make her endure a policeman's wedding), and Ralph's wife's opinion is irrelevant: she's pregnant and in Adelaide.

Joanna thinks they should have been in church. Otho Baumann was an enormous help when he came to Thalassa as overseer after Joanna's husband died, and it would be right to honour Otho's widow and daughter by attending the entire wedding. Joanna pointed this out to her sons, to no effect. Since her accident, they seem to have decided that all she needs from them is to be asked about her health. Having enquired, and made a modicum of fuss, they can withdraw. It's been quite startling to Joanna, in fact, to hold so little sway in her own household, and so suddenly. Where once she would have marched her sons to every minute of the Baumann wedding—in memory of Otho Baumann—she can manage only an hour of the breakfast now.

But heavens, what an insufferable bore Otho Baumann was, what a German, always riding about on enormous horses like a fat medieval knight, the skin under his eyes sagging so much that the bright red of his inner eyelids showed. It made looking at him a kind of violence. Joanna hadn't been surprised to learn of his death from heart congestion—had felt some satisfaction, even, because her own husband died young, and since then she has understood that marriage includes death, a fact that people ought to acknowledge sooner. She does pity Wilhelmina, Otho's wife, in principle. But then you visit the Baumann house—today, for example, arriving for the wedding breakfast—and you see Wilhelmina swathed in her permanent mourning, as if she thinks the privileges of grief should be accorded to her forever, and she makes one of those graciously apologetic gestures from her wheelchair to remind you that she can't rise or walk or come to greet you, and that you must come to her. Then Wilhelmina is hard to pity.

Joanna remembers the young Willie Baumann as an agile woman, if somewhat colourless. Now she's enthroned in her immobility, so that Joanna Axam and her sons are required to walk to Wilhelmina, adjust their faces, bend down towards her frizzed forehead and accept her proffered hand. Her hands have always been lovely, as if they've never touched wood or water, and on her right ring finger she wears a large red opal. Wilhelmina claims it's a Hungarian death opal, one that will lose its fire as soon as its owner dies. Joanna admires the opal, would like it for herself, and she suspects—this is fanciful, yes—but she's almost sure she's seen the opal flicker in her presence, as if it's prepared to switch allegiances.

Already the maid is hovering with a chair for Joanna, and the two widows sit side by side on the verandah. Joanna leans in towards Wilhelmina (who since taking to the chair speaks in a deliberately quiet voice) and the guests looking over at them see their companionable heads, their dark dresses and their dogged persistence. They see how old we are, Joanna thinks—everyone ages at a wedding, while the bride and groom grow young. If Willie and I died tomorrow, the newspapers would call us 'relic of the late Otho' and 'relic of the late Henry'. She makes sure to shoo the flies from her face without sending them to Wilhelmina.

Minna Baumann brings her policeman groom to be introduced. Apparently Joanna has met this Robert Manning before; well, she thinks, I've met most people. Minna has found herself a husband with good square shoulders (her sons' slope)—look at his whole wide permanent face, each freckle as dependable as a brick. This one, thinks Joanna, will be a long time dying. She approves, but then she's always approved of lively, pretty Minna.

Joanna's sons wander through the crowd, drinking and laughing. The boys often resist coming to this sort of occasion, then find themselves surprised by pleasure. Certainly they're enjoying this more than they enjoyed the visit of the Swedish painter, Mr Rapp, who intimidated them—they'd preferred

Rapp's wife, who'd asked about maps and routes and permanent water sources. Mrs Rapp's questions gave George and Ralph the opportunity to approve or alter the Rapps' intended path north to Wilpena Pound; they could give advice and argue with one another. They warmed to Rapp once he expressed his enthusiasm for river red gums that have been toppled by floods and now lie with their roots exposed. George and Ralph sent him out to some excellent specimens, perfect for painting, and Joanna saw in them a pride that a man like this, an artist, required their assistance and admired their big dead trees; this also made it possible to laugh at him.

Joanna's boys are used to spending their days with station hands, shearers, teamsters and shepherds; as a result, they can be uneasy when encountering their peers in Adelaide. But their manner at Wilhelmina's is just right. The people here care as they do about the time of year, the shearing or the harvest, about the weather, and often when they meet the Fairly men it's on the cricket field or at the races, when Thalassa and the town compete, so there's an elastic kind of rivalry between them, amiable, robust—it generates conversation, it gives them gestures and phrases, it provides. At present, George is holding forth in a circle of blacksmiths, bankers and shopkeepers, and he's flushed with the gratification of it.

Wilhelmina Baumann is speaking in her quiet voice, folded as neatly as her hands. 'Such a pity to have missed the church,' she says, and Joanna says, 'The storm, my dear, the dust.'

In fact, it wasn't the storm that kept the Axams from the church, though it did delay them—they hadn't left for Fairly until it passed. They'd all been ready, too—dressed, the horses harnessed to the carriage—when it came pouring down from the north, and they'd had to take shelter in the stable. Ralph filled his pipe, despite George's ban on smoking in that particular building, and said nothing more than, 'It's come up pretty sharp.' George paced back and forth, fretting about the sheep, threatening to abandon the wedding altogether.

'A storm like this could go on for hours!' he cried. It lasted thirty minutes.

But when Wilhelmina says it was a pity to have missed the church, she's speaking of herself, apparently—of the fact that she couldn't be present for the ceremony. 'I always thought,' she says, 'to see my daughter married.'

Wilhelmina says 'my daughter' in a way that also sounds like '*meine Tochter*'—speaking, as she often does, somewhere between two languages so that no one can forget her facility with both. Or perhaps she does this only with Joanna, who Wilhelmina knows to be one-quarter German and unable to speak a word.

'She makes a lovely bride,' Joanna says, looking over at Minna.

Minna is talking with Ralph, the youngest Axam son, whom Joanna—and no one else—calls by his childhood nickname: Bear. Minna is very animated—well, it's her wedding day—and Bear is leaning in to her pretty ear, saying something that makes her laugh. Minna's laugh is genuine, and poor old baffled Bear goes quite red, and for the first time it occurs to Joanna that Wilhelmina Baumann might once have hoped for some connection, through her daughter, with the Axams; that she's disappointed in Minna's constable, who will prove so steadfast. But oh, Joanna wants to say, my sons are entirely unremarkable.

Wilhelmina looks appraisingly at Minna. 'Mr Rapp wanted to paint her.'

'Mr Rapp paints landscapes, not portraits,' Joanna says.

'A charming man. We had a most pleasant day when he came to dine, and to speak my own tongue with such a one—what pleasure.'

Joanna has grown tired of the Swedish painter's charm, is glad he has left her house, and dislikes talking about him. 'Mrs Rapp also speaks German,' she says. Joanna considers Mrs Rapp far more impressive than her handsome husband.

'Well enough,' Wilhelmina allows.

'And French,' Joanna says. 'I believe they met in Paris.'

Wilhelmina glitters in her chair. 'You know, I trust, that Mrs Rapp's father lost the largest textile mill in northern England, and a fortune along with it.' She lowers her voice further. 'A player of cards.'

Other guests approach before Joanna can convey that she is indifferent to this gossip; now she must sit silently, smiling and nodding, to make sure that Wilhelmina is given her due as hostess. The Axams have missed, apparently, the shocking collapse of the vicar, who seems well enough now, if a touch moist at the hairline. Mr Daniels comes to Joanna's side and speaks at length about the constant expense of the kerosene with which he lights the church. Finally, George steps up and whispers into Joanna's stifled ear, 'We must get back.'

Wilhelmina says goodbye with excruciating grace, and Minna with real affection, and even Minna's constable waves them off so that it almost feels as if she, Joanna, is the one who's just been married and is leaving her own breakfast. No one speaks much on the way home, but when the setting sun is so red on the western horizon that it looks like a fire come to consume the world, Joanna lifts her veil and says, involuntarily, 'Oh.'

'What's the matter?' Bear asks.

'Nothing at all,' Joanna says. 'Don't fuss. I simply noticed the sunset.'

George peers up at the sky without interest.

Bear says, 'That's the dust from the storm still in the air. Makes the sky red.' He yawns and shifts his trousers over his knees. His wife, nearing the end of her first pregnancy, has been instructed to delay giving birth until the shearing is over and done with. What kind of father will Bear be? Joanna wonders. What kind of man have I made him? Loving, noisy, impressed by his own achievement. The kind who answers questions no one asks.

Mathew Wallace, Denny's father, has spent the day sowing parsnips with his one hired hand, Billy Rough. They've sown in half-mile rows, and at the end of each row one of Mathew's big Shire horses—stubborn, moody Treat—insisted on stopping to sniff at the ground; precious time was wasted in coaxing him to move his enormous, feathered feet. During the dust storm, which they weathered in a dense brace of mallee, the other horse in the pair spooked and had to be calmed. Now that they're knocking off, both men and horses are irritable and covered in dirt. The men loosen the horses out of the yoke and walk behind them until they're near Billy's hut. Mathew says, 'Get on and give yourself a wash. You look like you've been ate and spewed up again.'

Billy laughs, sings out, 'G'night', and peels off.

Now Mathew is alone on his land and he likes this feeling, especially when the day is ending and he's about to leave home for a while. At this time of year—shearing season—he always takes a dray and team of Shires into Fairly, picks up stores of flour, tea and sugar, and carries them to the stations in the far north of the plain; he loads up bales of wool at those stations and brings that wool back to the railway. He plans to leave for these rounds the day after tomorrow. He'll spend the next two months going back and forth with stores and wool, station to railway, one station to the next, while the shearing goes on and after the shearing; he will rarely sleep at home. These are the crucial months in which Mathew's wheat will thrive or fail and there's nothing he can do but cart wool and pray for rain. People at the stations always welcome Mathew Wallace and his high horses. Wallace will bring up the chaff! Wallace will get away the wool! Wallace will drive his team down the sloping passes, shouting, 'Tell the wool to get off and walk!' His surefootedness comes right out of the East Anglian fenlands. One of his ears blooms, puffy and misshapen, from the side of his head. He believes there's a power with which he can bargain in order to make everything turn out right.

He's only had one pair of his big Shires out today, and they know the way home: they follow a familiar track towards the red hill that stands beside Mathew's house. Mathew has named his farm Undelcarra, which means 'under hill' in the language of the blacks—though Billy, who is black, says it doesn't, or that it depends which language, or that it just depends. Undelcarra is forty times larger than the Huntingdonshire smallholding on which Mathew grew up. Half of his four hundred South Australian acres are under wheat; the rest is saltbush and dry soil and every fly that ever bothered God.

From Billy's hut, it takes Mathew half an hour to walk to the red hill and the house beneath it. He thinks, as he walks, of various habitual gripes and satisfactions—a gelding with a hoof abscess, what he's likely to be paid for this year's carting, the decent price he got on the parsnip seed, how soon until they can afford to keep a pig again—all of which are minor proddings at major fears: that he'll default on the mortgage, the principal of which is due next year; that with a more lively wife he might have got on better; that five is a lot of daughters. He walks alongside his wheat, which is knee height and green enough, and doesn't look too knocked about by the dust storm. The winter has been wet; now they need a good wet spring. The last two harvests failed. The sky is bright as a burning field.

As Mathew approaches the house, he sees light at the windows. He built that house, hauled the stone for the walls, split the flagstones for the hearth, burned the lime and cut the planks of wood for the deep verandah. He pulls out his pipe as he walks with the horses, pleased with what he sees: the red hill with the sun behind it, the lone cypress pine growing on top of the hill, the house in the hill's shadow and the light in the house's windows. He likes knowing that his wife is inside with the children, and that, without him, there'd be no house, no kids, and kangaroos would eat dry saltbush where Mary has her garden. This makes the light of the house seem stronger.

Mathew has faith in the knowledge of the body, which is full of ancient memory. He trusts in the customary shape of things, assuming that children and marriages and farms grow into their ordained forms, just as plants and animals do. If his faith wavers—and it does, at times, in this dry country—he reminds himself of certain truths: that he was meant to hear, in a church at Ely, a preacher crying out, saying, 'Act now, change everything, trust God, and prepare yourself to work!' He was meant to go with that preacher to South Australia; to work alongside him and his followers in the settlement at Encounter Bay; to propose marriage to the preacher's daughter. Her father was unsure—Mary's hearing was poor, she wasn't meant for the fields, was brought up only to light work; the preacher wanted to wait and seek God's will. But who knew how long that would take? Mathew reminded the preacher that his father, back in East Anglia, owned the land he farmed; he promised that Mary would never step foot in a field. There was no refusing him. And now the house is built, the girl is married, the babies are born, and Mary's father lives hundreds of miles to the south.

Mathew pulls at his pipe. He senses movement behind him—it might be a rabbit or a rat, but it turns out to be Cissy.

'Dad,' she says, and he squints hard to see her. She's a dim shape in the last red light and carries a lantern, which is shaded, and he thinks that if a girl can get this near without his hearing her, he's getting old. She stands beside him, and the horses nod and grunt. 'We've been waiting for you.'

Mathew looks towards the house. Mary's silhouette appears on the verandah; she's holding one of the younger ones, either Lotta or Denny.

'Well, old girl,' Mathew says.

'We can't find Denny,' Cissy says. 'He's lost. We thought he might've gone to you in the storm.'

Mathew's first thought is that the boy is playing a trick. He's not a devious boy, but he gets silly fancies and little frights. He likes surprising people with gifts and games.

'I've not seen him.'

'We've looked all round,' says Cissy.

Mathew's next thought is that he has no time for this: he has work ahead of him in the stable tonight, preparations to make tomorrow, and a promise to be in Fairly with the dray and team the day after. The boy, Mathew thinks, can stay out all night if he wants to, and he says, 'Walk on,' to get everyone moving again. Part of him believes that he will get to the house and find his son safe inside it.

'I need to get these two put away,' he says, dipping his head at the horses.

Cissy seems about to say something, but she stops herself; she runs back to the house, her lantern swinging. She meets her mother at the gate, they speak with their faces close together—Lotta's face between theirs—and by the time Mathew reaches them he feels a tug of fear.

'You can see as I don't have the boy,' he says to Mary. He's ashamed of not having Denny with him, and his body knows that, of all things, shame is the worst. 'I've come from up Snake Paddock and never seen him.'

Mary looks at Mathew, as she often does, as if something has confused her. He knows she finds him hard to lip-read, though in her presence he tries to keep the fen out of his voice, along with any phrase she might consider common. But this expression isn't the one she gets when she hasn't heard him: it's her more general look of bafflement at having found herself here, in this place, with these people. As always, her confusion undoes him; as does the fact that, to make sure she hears him, he must lean in to her left ear, which smells of powdery violets. He says, 'Ah, you're worried, Mary. But he'll have got caught up, is all, and be back by teatime. Look, the sun's not down yet.' He points towards the shrinking sun.

Mary doesn't look at the sun. 'It isn't like him,' she says.

Mathew disagrees—he knows his son to be a daydreamer—but doesn't contradict her. If I remain calm, he thinks, she'll not be worried; and if she's not worried, there's nothing to fear. 'If he's not back when I'm finished with the horses, I'll go for Billy and we'll look.'

'Yes,' Mary says.

'We can look after the horses,' Cissy offers. She turns to Joy, who is standing on the verandah, and yells, 'Put on your apron, we're feeding the horses.'

Joy shrugs and goes inside.

'These two here need cleaning up,' says Mathew.

'I know that,' Cissy says. 'We'll do it.'

'It's careful work,' he says. 'It's cold nights, so—'

'Don't wet their bellies,' Cissy recites. 'No water above the knee.'

'It's careful work.'

'What about the constable?' Cissy says. 'I could fetch him.'

'You'll stop home with your mam,' says Mathew. Mary isn't looking at him; she's looking out into the dusk. What does she see out there? Another life, in which none of this is happening? Lotta sighs as if deeply bored. Mathew turns his back on them and calls out, 'Denny!'

Cissy says, 'When that shepherd was lost last summer, they went out with a tracker. The police did.'

Mathew calls again, 'Denny! Show yourself now, Denny! I'll count to ten!'

'We've been calling for hours,' Cissy says.

Mathew calls, 'One! Two! Three!', and when Mary says, 'Hush now, hush now, darling,' he turns to her in anger; but she's bent her head to Lotta's and is quieting the child, who's crying.

The black dog, Mopsy, comes tearing up the path with her strange whinny, more like a foal than a bitch.

'She wants her supper,' Mary says, and then, to Mathew, 'You'll need food to take out with you.'

'A bit of bread would do it,' Mathew says. He thinks of his oldest child, his first son, who said one day that he wanted to join a stock drive north into unknown country, and Mathew told him no. Did Joe obey his father? Certainly not—he was young and knew his mind, or thought he did. And Mathew, fuming, drove him off.

Cissy leads the horses into the yard. 'Not a drop above the knee,' he calls, though he's about to follow her, to saddle his riding horse. Mopsy gives one demanding yap.

Lotta, blinking, looks up at him as if she's just noticed the dark and the presence of other people.

Mathew turns to Mary. 'Keep a lamp burning overnight.'

Mary nods. If Mathew were at the supper table and felt this surge of love, he would reach over, fluff someone's hair and say, 'Sit straight.' Now he'll ride away on Bonfire, chewing on Mary's bread; he'll collect Billy and tonight they'll find Denny. Then the carting will pay well, they'll have a wet spring, the wheat will thrive and the principal will be paid on the mortgage. When he rides home again tonight with Denny safe, Mary will smile at him and say, 'You've done well, you're a good man, I was right to marry you and I'm content.'

---

When the sun had almost set, the boy found a rock that formed a kind of seat and sat on it, his legs outstretched. This was the time of day when the sun touched the red hill and the gods came creeping out of it—out of the sun. They parted the branches of the cypress tree and stepped with care over the rocks at the top of the hill. They ran like water down the hill, and their footsteps were like water around the corners of the house. Denny was aware that these were not the only gods. There was also the Bible God, who loved him. Sometimes his mother read aloud from a book of old stories about many gods from olden times, who roared and thundered. They each had jobs to do, like men, and were in charge of things like the sea and music, but those were not the boy's gods. His gods took charge of nothing. They watched men work and laughed at them. His gods weren't good or bad. But they spoke of him, he thought, with special care, though he had never heard them speak. And he hated the red hill.

He hadn't cried yet. He wasn't a boy who cried much, but when he did, it was in loud gulps. Other boys had called him 'sissy', but Cissy was the bravest person he knew. He had, earlier, wet his boots when he piddled, and after that they'd felt much heavier. But he couldn't take them off by himself, so they'd stayed there on his tired feet, laced tight. Sitting on the rock, he tapped the toes together. He didn't like wearing boots; but he did it, when he had to, to please his mother.

He had his knife with him, the one Dad was teaching him how to skin possums with. He could use his knife to cut the laces from his boots but Mam wouldn't like that. He'd done it once before, and then she'd had to talk to the hawkers when they came to the house selling shoelaces. The hawkers had quick, showy hands. The boy liked them, especially the one who pulled his wagon with a team of goats, but Mam didn't. So he decided not to cut his laces. He thought of other uses for his knife. He could make marks on trees, as his father had told him to do if he was ever lost. But was he truly lost? Or was he like a glove or spoon that someone couldn't find; they'd call out, 'I've lost it!' and Cissy would say, 'It isn't lost, you just don't know where it is.' He wasn't sure what being lost felt like. The way he felt reminded him of seeing the moon shining in a cup of water, and when someone moved the cup, the moon was gone.

The light had almost faded, little rat things rummaged in the grass, the last crows flew towards the dark. The air grew colder and the boy was hungry. The sky looked as if someone had sprinkled sugar over it, shaken the sugar, then crushed it in. The boy walked up into the sky and tasted the sugar; he walked across the sky and found himself on another rock in another part of the plain. He was somewhere else, but this rock looked the same as the first one he'd sat down on. There was dust in his teeth, his nose, his fingernails and the roots of his hair. He was thirstier than he was hungry. When he closed his eyes, he saw his mother walk away from him into the house and lock the door behind her. The boy still had his sack. He laid it out across his legs and waited for the morning.

# FIRST NIGHT

The Swedish painter's name is Karl: Karl Rapp. His English wife's name is Elizabeth, but he calls her Bess. On the night of Minna Baumann's wedding, they lie by the embers of their campfire in the hills north-east of Fairly and Karl says, 'There's a light I want, I haven't seen it since that morning with the crows—like green glass coming down. It's a morning light.'

And Bess, who is also an artist but for the time being works only in black ink, says, 'The first thing to do tomorrow is find the waterhole.'

'Then the green glass.'

'We might need rain for that.'

'And for the waterhole,' Karl says.

Bess closes her eyes. He has a minute or two left with her—soon she'll fall asleep and enter the room she lives in without him, and Karl will be alone in the cold hills. In an attempt to keep her for another moment, he says, 'The dust today.'

That afternoon, they'd watched the dust storm advancing over the wrinkled plain: a russet cloud with a froth of light on top of it. He and Bess both sketched the cloud and half hoped it might reach them, but they were high enough, or far enough away, and were spared.

Bess says, 'I kept waiting for it to open up and Moses to come walking out.'

'Yes,' says Karl, but he was waiting for something else: for the dust to plunge him into darkness. After all, this is the desert—a prophet should meet the Devil here. But a true prophet, Karl acknowledges, wouldn't undertake his pilgrimage in spring. A prophet wouldn't bring his wife with him (or, for that matter, be ordered on the pilgrimage by his wife, who has arranged the sale of an album of desert drawings to a list of valued subscribers). Is it possible to turn a desert into a house? It is, for Bess. Lying beside him, she builds four walls, a roof, a door that has a lock in it, lamps lit and soup on the stovetop. She makes things comfortable, but not by fussing; it's that she's so practical. More than practical, which sounds dull. How to explain it? Wherever she goes, a room comes with her, and that room contains everything necessary to a proper, useful life. Sometimes Karl joins her in the room. Other times not: the door is locked. It seems to Karl that Bess, unlike other people, goes on living her palpable life when no one else is present.

Bess yawns and says, 'Goodnight.' Then she says, 'But every night is good. No flies.'

Which makes Karl laugh, and the horses stir, but she responds to neither sound: she's said goodnight and is in her room. The door is locked. Bess sleeps deeply—deeper than other women he's known. He can push his blankets off and stand up, he can walk down the slope and piss, and none of it will wake her. He can stand by the horses and smoke, leaning against a shabby tree. He can sing a Swedish lullaby that the horses seem to like; the packhorse in particular rubs against Karl when he sings. So Karl stands and walks and smokes and sings, and he watches the sky, which he doesn't trust.

He first became suspicious of the sky just after they left Adelaide—that charming, airless town. He and Bess had both been glad to leave it. They travelled first through the green wine valleys by coach, and when they stopped to pick up horses at Wingaree, a sheep station north of Clare, the late afternoon produced an unusually multicoloured sky: white at the horizon, grading into orange; above that, apple green; then a large band of rose, blending into crimson. Above that: a true blue. Above that: olive green, then lavender. As sunset approached, the sky turned such a vivid red that it looked as if a smokeless fire were burning just over the horizon. Men were sent out from Wingaree to investigate. They came back and said it was only the sun. Only the sun! The sun come to devour the stars—the cannibal sun. The sky remained bright and heavy for about half an hour; its pigments, if Karl were to paint it, would have been ochre and Indian red. Then the sun disappeared below the horizon, but the sky didn't grow dark—there was still red in it, diffuse and radiant, like a steady flame seen through waxy paper. Above this red, Karl saw a swarm of green lights. The waxy red faded, then the green; the twilight turned a violent purple; and when the moon rose, it was blue.

Karl didn't sleep that first night at Wingaree. Instead, he sat beside the window and watched the bruised moon. Bess woke early, as she always did, and asked what he was waiting for.

'The sun,' he told her.

Bess laughed. 'Do you think it might not come?' She kissed the top of his head and went to wash and dress.

When the sun finally rose, Karl thought he saw a ring around it. The ring was blue, with a russet outer rim, and the sun itself was faintly tinged with lavender. That evening, the sky again turned an apocalyptic red, but this time—knowing there was no fire—the residents of Wingaree went about their ordinary business, and seemed surprised by Karl's continuing interest in the phenomenon. Once something has happened twice, can it be called extraordinary? So he and Bess were left alone to watch the sunset, and just after the sun disappeared they witnessed a strange and brilliant cloud that Karl thought was new. It spread out above the horizon like the last wash of a wave onto a beach, thin and rippled, and it appeared to produce its own grey light.

'Maybe it's just a local kind of cloud,' said Bess. 'A native cloud.'

But Karl was certain that God had just invented it. The new cloud faded as the second wave of red flooded the sky, with the green light above it and the lilac clouds above that; these colours drained into the purple twilight; once again the moon was blue and, the following day, the sun wore its halo. Karl and Bess left Wingaree on their borrowed horses, heading for a property called Thalassa, where they had an introduction. They travelled north, towards and through and beyond Port Augusta, over the Pichi Richi Pass and out onto the Willochra Plain, and every evening the sky turned this livid red and the moon shone blue. One night, when they were staying at Thalassa, Karl saw the new cloud again: long, sheer and luminescent. So, he's concluded, the sky is changing its colours and its forms, and he doesn't know what to do with it.

Karl is a painter of filtered sunlight, subtle effects and tonal harmonies—in Stockholm, his humid pastels were considered 'unduly French' by at least one patriotic critic—but this disastrous South Australian sky makes demands of a more emphatic kind. It says: I've arrived, like history. It says: you have no choice but to paint me. Yes, you—a painter of stippled shade and blurred horizons—you're going to have to think in red. The sky has chosen Karl for its own mysterious reasons. Why else would he be here, now, in this unlikely place? Who else is going to record this calamity? Certainly not Bess, with her black ink.

But Karl dislikes demands. He prefers things to come easily, knows this about himself, and tries to disguise it. His biggest fear is that, as an artist and a thinker, he is lazy, superficial and incapable of seriousness. Pleasures tend to arrive in his life, and he tends to enjoy them; this has, he suspects, limited his capacity for hard work. Years ago, a peevish lover speculated that a fairy godmother had granted baby Karl talent and beauty but overlooked enterprise and persistence.

He knows he is a good painter—even a very good one. Is he good enough for the sky? He might be. He could, he supposes, lay everything aside and learn new forms, colours, tones, resemblances; he could pay attention to new vibrations of the sun. The red sky's demands are simply light making its rightful claim upon him. He has, after all, spoken passionately about the supreme truth of light—has stated more than once, drunk among his friends, that light is his religion. I love it more than beauty! I swear to devote my days to its worship! Karl is superstitious about breaking public vows of this kind, but finds private excuses for doing so. Bess (whom he married, in part, for her capacity for seriousness) tells him that, having agreed to emigrate to Australia, he must adapt himself to painting Australian subjects. But no Australian subject (is there such a thing?) has interested him—until this sky, the thought of which exhausts him.

So, on the night of Minna Baumann's wedding, Karl leans against a tree in the foothills of the Flinders Ranges, smokes, and sings his lullaby designed to put the sky to sleep. When it's awake, the sky makes him think of ways to paint it, and he isn't ready yet. He doesn't trust it and he doesn't trust this country, which claims to be a desert. But there are trees, grasses, flowers. On this particular hill, tonight: trees resembling pines, my God! As if this were a scraggly outpost of the Schwarzwald. Bess, worried about his lungs, insisted that he leave Sweden for a warmer climate—fine. But they might have gone to the ochre streets of Rome, or to the Holy Land, to paint wan pictures of palms and ancient walls. Yet here he is, so far south that he'll soon fall off the Earth and pass through the skies of Europe like a comet. No, it's emphatically not Palestine, though there are, as it turns out, camels here. Which stink and scare the horses.

Karl finishes his pipe and kisses each horse goodnight. He looks down at the Willochra Plain; he can see a few faint lights, and he thinks that if he lived here he would make every effort to leave. He would be capable of working hard at *that*. He opens

Bess's pack to look at what she's worked on today: every sketch is skilful, tense and limited, as if under obligation to someone. She's far too careful. But Bess, sleeping neatly on her bedroll, has made so many things possible: hard work, good health, this desert journey. She's the gift of enterprise and persistence. She's like a cloud that shines without the sun behind it. Thank God for Bess, thinks Karl, lying down beside her, but he turns away so as not to see her sleeping in her room, without him.

Billy Rough, Mathew's hired hand, lives in a shepherd's hut. The hut is a remnant of an earlier time, when the whole northern part of the plain was parcelled out among vast sheep and cattle properties. For years, hooved animals trampled the Willochra, until the South Australian government decided that the area would be better under wheat. It was arid land, yes—the Surveyor-General said so—but everyone knows that rain follows the plough. Most of the big properties were broken up and their parts were leased as smallholdings, like Undelcarra. Billy remembers those pastoral days, and the days before them. He was born on this country fifty years ago. He's left it many times, but he always comes back.

Billy's hut stands in a grove of she-oaks just over a mile from the red hill. It has a three-legged camp oven in one corner, a bunk, a perch on which there is no bird, and here Billy's happy, here at the end of the day he can tend his own fire. He's boiled his tea and eaten his supper. Often Billy has visitors, people passing through, some of the Thalassa mob—he never knows who might appear. Tonight is quiet, though. He can hear the sound of the fire, the faint hush of the she-oaks, and Virnu walking with a whinny in the yard. The fire jumps and spits.

On his way outside to relieve himself, Billy tests the muscles of his arms and shoulders. Then, on the clear ground in front of the hut, he takes three long, deliberate, springing strides. To anyone watching he might be dancing—but he isn't dancing, his right arm is straight behind him and it windmills over his shoulder, there's nothing in his hand and he sends nothing ahead of him like a small, hard ball. Every movement is so controlled—the run, the trajectory of his arm, the forward motion after opening his hand—that if there were a small, hard ball, a cricket ball, it would travel just as Billy willed it. There's no need to stop and watch where and how the ball lands: Billy knows where and how it lands, and that there is no ball. But he stops anyway, because he can hear a horse approaching.

It's Mathew on Bonfire, and he calls out from beyond the trees with a long, loud whoop, which is his way of saying: it's me, get ready, I'm coming. Billy can see Mathew's lantern among the trees and, a moment later, the lift and roll of Bonfire's big head. Mathew is talking as he appears, saying Denny was out when the dust came up, hasn't come home, and was last seen heading north-west. So Billy sets the fire to smoulder and not blaze, saddles Virnu, and the men ride out into the night.

Cissy got as far as Fairly Creek on foot, so they ride to Fairly Creek, shouting for Denny all the time. They leave the horses there, then follow the creek north-west, searching in dips and gullies, calling Denny's name down the washouts that open up across the plain. They turn off into the creek's tributaries and search along their banks, behind their boulders, among the roots of their trees and in their few pools of water. Billy says that if they haven't found any sign by daylight he'll go to the camp at the Thalassa ration depot and bring back a tracker.

'A good one,' Billy says.

Mathew says, 'Aren't you all good?'

Billy is surprised; Mathew rarely refers to his blackness. He seems generally to operate on the principle that the less he acknowledges it, the more likely it is to go away. Billy says, 'Some are better.'

'If nothing's turned up by morning I'll go to the police.' Mathew swings his lantern, calling, 'Denny!'

When Billy was a boy in camp, he knew not to go far from the fire: take care, there are men out there with trackless feet. His mother used to sing him a lullaby about a girl carried off by an eagle, and he knew that if he walked too close to the edge of a cliff he might be pushed over it by a spirit. But Denny has his own ways of being frightened—Billy has noticed Denny's watchful way of being in the world, his dislike of sunset, the way he speaks to invisible things, and his fear of the red hill. Denny has a gift for fear, and along with this gift comes courage, which is required of him in the world he knows. Billy approves of this: yes, be frightened; yes, be brave. With Denny's fear and courage in mind, Billy changes the way he calls out in the night.

'Denny Wallace!' he calls. 'It's your dad and it's Billy! It's us two all alone looking for you, Denny!' He and Mathew drop down into a creek bed and Billy calls, 'It's us two only! It's Billy and your dad!'

Mathew grunts. 'Who else would it be?'

'Nobody else,' Billy says, but he continues to call this way, identifying himself and Mathew, and Mathew goes on calling, 'Denny!' They rarely exchange words, but this isn't unusual; they've worked together for years now, first when Mathew was head stockman at Thalassa, and then when Mathew employed Billy on Undelcarra, and they're comfortable with silence. They climb out of the creek, call, go back to the creek bed and call again. They startle kangaroos, scatter lizards out from under saltbush clumps, turn to peer at fleeing dunnarts, and, lifting the lanterns, they see corellas and galahs sleeping in the branches of the gums. Billy would like to whisper in Denny's secret ear: nothing but us two searching you out, nothing coming for you, nothing looking at or thinking of or paying attention to you, just us.

They follow Fairly Creek over the plain, splitting up sometimes—Billy takes the land north of the creek and Mathew the south. They always come back together. This is easy enough to do, what with the lanterns and the shouting. Billy doesn't think Denny could have made it this far from home, but he waits for Mathew to signal when it's time to return. Mathew does this, finally, by standing beneath a red gum with his hands on his hips, looking around, nodding his head and clearing his throat. Then they follow the creek back to their horses and reach them at the earliest sign of light. The air is cold; there's a crack to it as they breathe. The cold may not be the source of Mathew's trembling.

'To town, then,' Mathew says.

They stop off at Undelcarra on the way, and Billy waits while Mathew goes inside. The first fly of the day hovers at Billy's left eye. Cissy already has the Shires in the yard and is mucking out their stalls with a passion that suggests they have done her some personal wrong. Mathew returns with food and tea, and Mary comes out to stand on the verandah. Billy looks at her and touches his hat; she gives a slight nod in return. Mary has always been guarded with him, but she's courteous.

On the way to town, Mathew says, 'Couldn't hurt to go on to Thalassa and see about that tracker.'

Billy nods. He's going to Thalassa; he always is. Thalassa is home.

The sky is lighter when they part in town, but still quite dark.

Minna Baumann turns in her tender bed. Her husband breathes against her shoulder; he's tired, but he kisses her when she asks him to. They haven't slept yet. Tonight is their first time in a bed together and the fact that everything is permitted excites them. They're used to being discreet, so they're delighted by noise. They keep the lamp lit and study each other, touching what they see. When Robert gets up for water, Minna studies his knotty shoulders, the three dark moles like a lucky constellation on his upper thigh and the whiteness of his backside. And when, later, she gets out of bed to stoke the fire, she makes sure he's watching her. This is her first night in her new house, which has the added piquancy of being attached to a police station. She prowls naked through the bedroom, touching objects that now belong to her. Robert falls asleep.

Robert has so few personal possessions: his clothes, a mantel clock, a few books, a blank postcard from the Riverina, his guns and sword and, propped in one corner, a long, thin native spear. His clothes are neat—except for the suit he was wearing today, which she kicked beneath the bed at some delirious point. It's his uniform that interests her. The first time she saw him, not long after he arrived in Fairly, he was wearing his uniform and he made her think of a field of ripe wheat: dark ground, bright head. But the pinkish mottle of his skin also brought to mind her mother's stories of the golem, a creature made from clay that might be good or evil. It had seemed imperative to know, and quickly, whether Robert was good or evil.

When Minna was twelve, a friend of her father's—staying for one night on his way further north—had come into her room and touched her growing breasts. Sometimes, afterwards, she thought about it with curiosity: the way he pursed his lips, didn't look at her, and breathed loudly through his nose. She imagined a boy in his place, which interested her more. She knew she was pretty. Her mother would inspect her and say, 'I knew my children would have looks,' but if Wilhelmina were in a bad mood she'd say, 'Even the Devil was beautiful when young.' Minna's mother still talks a lot about the Devil; they're old acquaintances, and Wilhelmina has a proverbial mouth, which she says is true of Germans. She speaks of the Devil's preferences—his favourite piece of furniture, his favourite food, his favourite kind of girl—and these are all allusions to things Minna shouldn't be or like. Mama knows endless tales about him, which Minna as a girl used to ask for until every sound at her midnight window was Mephistopheles. Then the thorny German script on the wall that said 'A mighty fortress is our God, a mighty shield and weapon' seemed to confirm the dangers of the world.

Robert reminds Minna of a picture she used to love of Faust and his poor Gretchen. Robert is Gretchen: not because he's slim or girlish, but because he has the same red hair and paper-coloured skin. The printing of the picture was a little heavy-handed, so that pale Gretchen was hatched with pinkish red in all her shadowy places, and so is Robert. He flares up in the sun, as if he's in some never-ending fever. His good humour, the size of his hands, the way he settles down into a chair and stretches his legs out, his uniform, and the fact that he's a man of the law: all this made Minna feel from the first that nothing she did with him could be wrong. She was the one who convinced Robert, out in the garden one afternoon, to put his hand beneath her skirt. It wasn't far from there to everything. She loves to hear the whimpers she can tear loose from him.

And now he's sleeping, right there, in his bed, and she has every right to be in this room and to see the way he's spread himself out, naked. The room is hers, the house, the bed, the sleeping man. All of him: his dark armpit, his softened cock. His uniforms are hers now, and she's allowed to lift the trousers and pull them on just to see the way they feel, to roll the cuffs and wrap the belt twice around her waist, to pull his boots on and stuff the bottom of the trousers into them, and to swim through the wide sleeves of the shirt. She buttons the jacket of itchy wool and shuffles to the long mirror in the hall to look at herself in what light there is—the sky is brightening, the first birds are calling out. Her reflection is ridiculous. She's reduced by the uniform—by its size—and at the same time has played her own trick by turning it into something silly. She wonders if Robert, seeing her, would be angry and accuse her of being disrespectful. But would he mean it?

Then there's someone beating at the front door and a man's voice shouting, 'Manning! Manning!'

Robert told her to expect urgent calls at any hour, but surely not on their wedding night? She steps into the kitchen and, after Robert hurries down the hallway on his way to the door, she runs to the bedroom. Her heart is very loud.

It's Mathew Wallace at the door—she hears Robert call him Wallace. He's saying that his son is missing. And this seems unjust, since Mathew Wallace has so many daughters and his oldest son is off somewhere, no one knows exactly where; or perhaps Minna's mother hasn't told her everything. You can't trust Mama to have told you everything. And the Wallace girls were at the wedding; apparently they even came to the breakfast and stayed three minutes and left as soon as the vicar had his fainting spell. Now their brother is missing in the desert—he might as well be on the moon. Minna listens, but Mr Wallace has lowered his voice.

'Only one thing for it,' Robert says and, a few seconds later, 'I'll raise the lads.'

Minna feels that in any catastrophe Robert will always know the 'one thing for it'. How helpful that would be: to know the one thing, always, and to do it. Now Robert comes back into the bedroom, already holding his constable's cap. He's shirtless, but has pulled on his crumpled wedding trousers.

'What in God's name?' he says when he sees her in his uniform, but he isn't angry, he's laughing and says, 'Name and rank, constable?'

'Constable Manning, Eighteenth Class,' Minna says, also laughing, trying to remove a boot and failing. Robert kneels on the floor in front of her and pulls the boot away. Minna begins to laugh harder, then covers her mouth and whispers, 'Is he outside?'

Robert shakes his head. He's removed the other boot. He's still kneeling and he rocks back to rest on his heels. His hands drum at his thighs.

'How awful,' she says, but can't help smiling. 'His poor little boy.'

'You're my little boy,' says Robert. He pulls at the trousers Minna's wearing until she slides down to the floor with him and climbs into his lap.

## PRAYER OF THE GERMAN WIDOW

I thank you, Heavenly Father, through Jesus Christ, your dear Son, that you have blessed me so graciously on this day of gifts and marriage. This day I sent my Minna out, strong and wise, to meet her bridegroom. Minna, my trimmed wick. For into your hands I commend myself, my body and soul, and all things, as Luther said each evening while he prepared for bed. By all things he meant the mountains and hills and rivers not only of Eisleben, but also South Australia, and all that's in between, all that's above and below, the angels and devils, the hearts of men—all things. I commend them to you, I commend my married daughter, I commend my humble self.

For a time, I thought that I was born for missionary work. I had in mind the trials, the dangers, the lines of black children outside a small white school, the husband raising his voice up in the church, the happy holy heathen, the grace of God. Then I thought that I was born for Otho, who chose me and then chose South Australia. We worked and worked, we were workers in the vineyard, the great trees fell, the sun mellowed, the sun bit, the grape grew on the vine. One year of blight and we lost everything. I thought then that I was born to suffer. I suffered coming north; I suffered at Thalassa among the animals and the men; I lost one baby, then another and another, and thought I'd grown too old for children. All while Otho spent his days consoling Joanna Axam for the death of her husband, and working to keep her rich. Then, when her sons grew up, she cast us out.

But that was all right, it could be endured. Otho was clever—he'd bought into the Blinman mine and had started to earn money, and I had my healthy baby twins. Then I thought that I was born for children, for Peter and for Minna: the sweet milk of their mouths, the endless need when they were sick, the calling of my name into the dark. There is selfishness in children, it can't be helped. They all insist on growing. Peter grew self-important, a true German, full of restless longing, and Minna too obliging with the men. I saw her kiss that painter in the garden, just days before her wedding. And now she's married to a policeman because she's carrying his child. I did have hopes for her. Ah, but she has a pretty waist, at least for now. I had one once myself. And her father did indulge her.

Poor Otho, who was born for work—he dreamed in silver, he dreamed in copper; he grew thicker, darker, hardly there, windy and long-winded, a funny old machine with money in him, that he made and gave and lent and lost and made and lost. And here was missionary work at last: Otho's sickbed. The boiling of the sheets, the bowls of blood, the doctors like hopeful suitors, the reading in the morning from the prettiest parts of

Scripture, the wading late at night through his darkest fears and shames. The parade of children, friends and debtors; the clutched hands; the forgiveness; and the death. Thanks be to God.

Peter already busy in the world, fussing at the mine, away from me—he wouldn't even stay tonight. And Minna married, so that's the last of it. The flawless nights ahead, the house intact, and everything decided. Nobody to need me. I'll be left to shrink. But that's not so—there's Minna's baby on the way. It will need and need. *Ach*, the warm scent of its heavy head!

But that's to come. Tonight, if I could stand, I'd walk across the room and open every door and shout until they ran to me: Otho, Peter, Minna. I would tuck and peck them, I would look and look. If you offered me one hour, just one minute, I would spend it young, and Otho young, with my face in his neck. Hide not thy face far from me. Oh Lord have, Christ have, Lord have mercy, and Lord now lay me down to rest.

## SECOND DAY

Billy, riding to Thalassa, meets George Axam on the road. George is driving his wife north towards Fairly in a smart dogcart. The wife is dressed for train travel. Billy slows his horse; George slows the dogcart. The plain rolls out on either side of them, studded with occasional trees.

'Morning, Billy,' George calls.

His wife lays one gloved hand on his arm.

Billy stops beside the cart. 'Morning, Mister George,' he says. 'Morning, missus.'

George's dislike of Billy is palpable, as always, but they're involved in each other's lives in ways that won't allow them to pass on a road without speaking. Billy's sister Nancy used to be George's nursemaid; what a fat, pink baby George was. Nancy would carry him about wherever she went, and Billy would use a single piece of string to tell him dozens of stories. He'd play out Thumbkin on George's fingers: *virdnaapanha*, *ringwaitanha*, *wawarriwartanha*, *nuininha*, *thumbkiniha*. But this former tenderness is forgivable. What's unforgivable to George is that, when he was five, his father died, and Billy saw it happen.

George says, 'On your way to our place, I hope? And planning to stop? There's a deal of work to do.'

'It's a madhouse,' says George's wife, then laughs, as if surprised at having spoken.

Billy's horse moves under him. 'I can't stop,' he says.

George raises his eyebrows. 'Wallace keeping you busy, is he?' He shifts forwards in his seat. When people refuse him—which rarely happens—George becomes alert and aggrieved. It's bad enough that Billy chooses not to live and work at Thalassa, although the native camp is full of his relatives and his sister runs the kitchen. Really, what Billy chooses to do or not to do is immaterial to George; what affronts him is the fact that Billy is free to make choices.

Mrs Axam presses her husband's arm. 'The train,' she says, then smiles—not at Billy, but at something behind him.

'It's the Wallace boy,' Billy says. 'Six years old. Been missing since the storm yesterday.'

Mrs Axam takes her hand away from George's arm and presses it to her mouth in horror. A lost child is the thing white people are most afraid of. It's the one cost of settling on this country that they consider unreasonable.

'That's no good,' George says. 'Has Wallace looked for him?'

Billy resists the urge to say, Of course. 'Been out all night.'

'Has Wallace gone to the constable?'

Billy tips his head towards the town. 'There now,' he says.

'Excellent,' says George, lifting his hands and the reins in them; he's preparing to move the cart on. That's just like George—trust in the authorities and spare yourself the worry.

'Be good to have Tal out looking,' Billy says.

Tal, who lives most of the time at the Thalassa camp, is the best tracker in the district. Also the best rider, swimmer and hunter. He refuses to work with sheep but condescends to handle Thalassa cattle. He can get cows and horses safely over creeks in flood without a sound from any animal. He can shoot fifty rabbits in an afternoon and track any dingo. He can brand a half-wild steer before you even notice he's brought it to the ground.

George lowers the reins. 'Now, Billy,' he says. 'I can't spare Tal. Another time of year, you know, I wouldn't hesitate. But the shearing . . .'

'Tal's a cattle man,' Billy says.

'Yes,' says George, 'and he's butchering the bullock this morning.'

Mrs Axam returns her hand to her husband's arm.

'Look'—George raises the reins again—'the constable will sort out trackers, trained men. If he doesn't for any reason, I'll send Tal.'

'Tal knows the country,' Billy says, but the dogcart is moving.

'You'll let me know?' George calls out. 'And tell Wallace how sorry I am, won't you, about his boy?'

As the dogcart moves down the road, Billy turns and sees Mrs Axam's maid sitting in the back with trunks and parcels. The maid looks at Billy with her mouth set straight in her long, white face. She lives in the house in Adelaide, and is the sort of maid who is referred to by her surname, which he forgets.

Billy had been planning to head another mile down the creek to the camp by the ration depot, but if a bullock is being killed this morning, Tal will be at the slaughter yard, which is part of the station headquarters. A Thalassa bullock is killed before the shearing every year and Tal always takes charge. He's strong and neat. He can kill a bullock before it begins to cry out and roll its eyes; he can be that fast with it. He knows a word that puts the bullock in his power. And the hides seem to fly off, whole and even, under Tal's sharp knife. So Billy rides down into the river valley where the Thalassa homestead sits among its outbuildings and fences and gardens, its pens and yards and sheds and tanks. It's shaded by gums and palms, and busy as a little town. *Yura* women, bending over tubs of laundry, call out to him in greeting as he passes.

Billy rides through all this activity knowing his sister is here somewhere. His mother, too—old Pearl, who has otherwise retired from formal duties—has probably come up from the camp to help. He remembers this valley before the house was built; he remembers camping here at the permanent waterhole in the river. Billy was a child, around Denny's age, when Henry Axam settled at Thalassa. One day not long after Henry first arrived—before the house and depot were built, before George was born and Joanna came north—Henry sat beneath a tree and watched the children of the camp play a game with bark shields and hunting sticks. Billy in particular excelled at this game: he loved to stand in front of a crowd of boys, holding his shield tight to his chest and using it, as he pivoted on nimble feet, to send each *wirri* glancing left or right.

A few days later, Henry came with a cricket ball and a roughly carved cricket bat suitable for Billy's size, and he taught Billy how to bowl one and hold the other. After that, Billy spent time with Henry Axam almost every day, learning how to bowl and bat and field. Henry included the other children at first, but Billy was singled out for his uncommon talent; as a result, a new world suggested itself to him, in which one person was distinct from another. Billy came to understand that there were more divisions than those between his father's people and his mother's people, the hot and cold winds, the orange tree and the bullock bush. There was also the division of brother from brother, gelding from stallion, wheat from chaff. The world, with its endless distinctions, wasn't a place you lived inside of, as he'd thought; instead, you walked and ran and bowled upon it, individually, as Henry did. The most important division, Billy came to feel, was that between talent and mediocrity: a boy was either good at cricket, or he wasn't.

Later, once the house was built, Henry provided trousers, a shirt and a jumper, all in cream, along with a striped blazer, tailored in Adelaide to Billy's exact dimensions, and a thick wool cap that absorbed perspiration. Whenever guests arrived at Thalassa, Billy would dress in this uniform and wait to be summoned. He would demonstrate his skills on the bare ground behind the house, or on the cricket pitch by the woolshed, while Henry explained his plans to take Billy to Adelaide, to Sydney, and finally to London, where the boy would be recognised at Lord's as the world's finest player. Then, Henry would say, try telling me the Aboriginal is a natural sportsman but lacks stamina! Look at his footwork: it's perfection! After this speech, Henry would take his visitors away to see Thalassa's other wonders—the Greek temple or the biblical garden—and Billy would stay on the pitch, swinging the bat and running between the wickets until one aunty or another called him to be useful.

Henry also taught Billy how to ride a horse, how to muster cattle and how to sing a number of filthy songs in European languages. These, said Henry, were the kinds of skills Billy would need in his life at Henry's side. When Billy was taken by his elders—'kidnapped', according to Henry—for his first initiation into sacred law, Henry was furious. On Billy's return from the ceremonial ground, weeks later, as a Vardnapa man—no longer a child, but not yet an elder—he learned that all further initiation ceremonies had been forbidden, as had the use of language. When, a few years later, Henry drowned, there were no longer enough qualified men left to perform Billy's second initiation, the one that would have made Billy an elder himself; the older men had been killed, imprisoned, or had died of disease. It was then that Otho Baumann came to manage Thalassa and the ration depot; he came with his whips and rules, and Billy learned how dangerous it was for a man like him to be extraordinary in any way, to be singled out. So Billy left the ranges for the first time; he spent the Baumann years droving up and down the Queensland stock routes. Riding into Thalassa now, decades later, means, for Billy, remembering a proud boy in cricket whites, swinging the bat while Henry promises him glory and Lord's.

Billy skirts the homestead and heads straight for the slaughter yard. When he arrives, Tal has already killed this year's bullock and is lifting the caul fat out in white nets. A boy holds a dish beside him, waiting to rush the fat to the kitchen. The animal, half skinned, lies steaming on the stone. Tal moves surely above the bullock with his knife, finished with the caul now and working on the windpipe, and soon the carcass is ready to hang. Men heave it up while Tal directs. He struts in the yard, sometimes nodding and sometimes shaking his head. Billy is struck, as always, by the commanding heft of Tal's body. His handsome face is open, smiling; he takes pleasure in his work and in his pleasure. Billy felt the same way when he played cricket. Skill gives you power: you can see the future because your skill will make it happen. To watch Tal strip the last of the hide and lay it out is to see the way a thing should work. Then, when he's finished, Tal turns and swaggers, arrogant and ordinary in a way that Billy recognises, because he used to do the same whenever he proved his superiority at cricket.

Tal is washing his hands at the pump when Billy approaches and says, 'Hard at it.'

'Big one this year,' Tal says, shaking the water from his forearms. 'Biggest yet.'

'Good hide,' Billy says.

Tal looks across the yard towards the hide as if it poses a delicate problem, invisible to anyone but himself. He always performs his modesties with a flourish.

'Good eating in that one,' says Billy, and Tal nods, solemn; he's serious when it comes to food. But having washed and been complimented, Tal is now finished with the bullock. He's looking for something else with which to prove himself: he straightens up, lifts his chin, surveys the yard. He rolls his head to stretch the muscles of his neck.

'There's a job for you,' Billy says. Billy leans down to work the pump and takes a long drink. 'A missing boy.' He wipes his wet mouth with his upper arm.

'What boy?' asks Tal. '*Utnyu* boy, is it?'

'Yep,' says Billy, though he's aware that Tal already knows the answer to his question. If the missing boy weren't white—if he were Nukunu or Yadliawarda—Tal would already have heard about it. 'Little one, six years old.'

Tal nods. He seems indifferent to the news, but this is his usual way with any proposition.

'You're the best tracker hereabout,' Billy says.

Tal accepts this as his due. Billy waits.

'You a manager now, eh?' says Tal. 'Big boss handing out jobs?'

Billy swats at the flies that crawl under the brim of his hat and says, 'You want to do it for no pay, that's all right with me.'

Tal raises his eyebrows.

Billy says, 'There's a pound in it for you if you find him.'

Tal whistles appreciatively. But Billy knows that, although Tal hates sheep, he likes shearing season. He likes to challenge the shearers to trials of strength. Billy understands that Tal won't want to be out tracking on his own when he could be at Thalassa with an audience. And Billy knows Tal doesn't want to do it when Tal says, 'I better check with old Georgie.'

'Saw George on the road just now,' says Billy. He pushes at the dirt with the toe of one boot, looks past Tal towards Thalassa Creek; this is how business is done, this nonchalance. 'He says no. Says he can't let you off work.'

Which has the desired effect: Tal throws his head back, hoots, and slaps one powerful thigh at the thought that George Axam, who relies on Tal's many skills, has any real authority over him. If George says no, Tal will say yes—this is what Billy hopes for.

Here's Billy's sister Nancy coming down to inspect the bullock. She's girlish, Nancy, though she must be nearly fifty; well-padded, with just a trace of grey in the curls that show at the front of her headscarf, and Tal acts up to her, as he always does. Tal's twenty years younger than she is, but he likes to tease certain women, and Nancy is one of them. So he laughs louder.

'That's a big laugh for an early morning,' Nancy says. She reaches up to touch the hair that curls—in exactly the way that hers does—above Billy's right ear.

'Georgie's trying to boss me,' Tal explains. 'And this man here is trying to boss me.'

'It's a funny old world,' Nancy says; this is a favourite phrase of Bear Axam's, and Nancy always uses it in a tone that's both affectionate and mocking. 'What's he bossing you about?'

Tal jerks his head at Billy and says, 'Wants me to find a lost boy.'

'Denny Wallace is missing,' Billy says, and Nancy's smile disappears.

'Since when is he missing?'

'Dust storm yesterday.'

'But Georgie says no, I can't go,' Tal adds, no longer laughing but still amused.

Nancy, who maintains an essential belief in the goodness of George—his secret, perpetual infancy—shakes her head. 'He won't say no.'

'He already did,' Billy says, and then, seeing her dismay, adds, 'Unless the police don't bring trackers. If the police don't bring trackers, Tal can go.'

'Police' is the wrong word to have used. Tal shakes his head. 'None of that business,' he says, and it's as if he's just packed himself up, his own bag of tricks. 'None of that,' he says.

Nancy puts one warning hand on Billy's arm and together they watch as Tal walks backwards, turns at the bullock hide, then goes into the smithy, where steam pours from the door. They both know Tal has no interest in working with molten metals, but he likes to prove to the smiths that he can endure the heat.

⁂

The vicar, Mr Daniels, is due to leave town this morning. He's often away from Fairly for weeks, because his parishioners are spread out over the northern plain and on into the hills, and he goes to preach in their hot iron churches, their stuffy parlours and their one-room huts. The people of these outer places welcome the young vicar: he's an event, he's company, and he brings news. Most of Daniels' flock are Methodists, but they demonstrate a genial pity for this stray Anglican, the latest in a long line who've been sent north because Henry Axam built an Anglican church and attached a living to it, as if the Flinders Ranges were annexed to the Home Counties. The Methodists have their own lay preachers, but they are nevertheless Daniels' parishioners and they turn to him for official business: he marries them, baptises their children and buries their dead. He's never intimidated anybody with the thunder of God's justice—no one but himself. From the pulpits—often just kitchen tables—of the Willochra

Plain, Mr Daniels preaches the grace, rather than the wrath, of God.

Although Daniels is almost unbearably lonely in Fairly, he dislikes leaving town on these pastoral journeys. He dislikes any revelation of his own fundamental fixedness: he goes, he comes, he goes, but he's only ever Thomas Daniels, a little too Low Church to be High and a little too High Church to be Low, with his wheezy lungs and his second-class Cambridge degree. His Methodist parishioners have told him that after a soul's conversion comes the second blessing, which registers in the body as the unmistakable presence of God. Daniels has never felt anything like that. He wonders if he'd like to. Can a spiritual transformation be felt physically? And should it? All he does is come and go; he never changes. But other people change while he's away on these short trips: men grow sadder, wives access new stores of complaint, marriages collapse or heal, babies arrive and girls turn into women. A girl like Cissy Wallace, say—at least fourteen. She has a secret sort of face. In two years or so, it might open up.

So Mr Daniels is leaving Fairly today, although he's woken up feeling quite unwell—still shaky from his spell at the wedding breakfast, no doubt—and would prefer to stay in bed. He plans to lead the morning service, eat his dinner, set out on horseback with a bag of chaff and a bushel of bran, and be in the town of Wilson in time for an evening prayer meeting. Then news comes that Denny Wallace is missing. In church, Daniels preaches briefly on the Parable of the Lost Sheep, acutely aware that many of his congregation saw him fall on his backside yesterday. Then he sets out for Undelcarra in order to bring comfort to Mary

Wallace, as is his duty. He imagines comfort, sometimes, as a pudding wrapped in linen, a little spongy and steamy and warm; a gift he carries wherever he goes, which should float in water but has a tendency to sink.

He can bring comfort to Mary Wallace, and surely he can be of help, too, with the search for Denny: he's used to travelling and knows the roads. Sometimes they're boggy with mud, or long snakes lie across them in the sun, or something on them alarms his horse—something Daniels can't see. Sometimes, his asthmatic lungs squeeze so tight that every breath has to burrow its way through to his throat. Last winter, on his way home from a baptism at Hookina township, he fell asleep and tumbled from the saddle, hurt his ankle, and lay for days—it felt like days, but was actually overnight—until rescue came. He lay by the road with his crooked ankle and looked at the bleak, beautiful country spread about him, with shadows on the hills and scaly lizards hissing in the grass, and understood it to be the book of God's glorious revelation. He thought this might be the second blessing, but then the sun set and he was left to shiver in the moonless dark. Now, every time he rides out of Fairly, Daniels lifts his eyes to the brim of his grey hat, as if it's the one thing separating him from God, and prays, 'Father, test me.' And another voice always comes, unbidden, which adds, 'But Father, keep me safe.'

Daniels isn't alone on the road out to the Wallace place. Some men ride and others walk, or drive carts and gigs. Women carry baskets on their arms and in their laps. They call out when they see him.

'Good morning, Mr Daniels,' say the women, although many of them have already shaken his hand this morning.

'Bad business, eh?' say the men.

'Poor, poor Mary,' say the women.

'God bless you, Father,' says Mrs Daly, a Catholic.

Daniels greets them all, then touches his horse with his whip and passes them by. When he's behind them, they seem to be in flight from some disaster, and he's touched by the slowness of their passage and the calm, sad way they take it. Once he passes, he feels as if he's leading them, and remembers what may have been the defining lesson of his schooldays: that Roman generals, parading through the imperial city, were attended by a slave who held a crown above the general's head while whispering 'memento mori'.

He reaches the edge of town, where Sammy So's vegetable gardens lie up against the creek in orderly rows. Then the road turns away from the creek; the country flattens, and all along the road out to the Wallace place you can see the surprising hill beside their house. The way it erupts from the flatness of the plain seems so unlikely, as if some tired prophet passed by once and God made a hill to give him shade. Denny Wallace is somewhere out beyond the hill. This place has swallowed up whole bullock teams, distinguished men of science and families in houses—how likely is the survival of one boy? Daniels lifts his eyes to the brim of his hat and prays until he reaches the Wallace farm.

Constable Robert Manning stands at the gate, more convincing in today's uniform than he was in yesterday's wedding suit. When Daniels arrives some men are teasing the new bridegroom. 'You get a wink of sleep last night, Robbie?' they ask, and laugh, and jovial Robert claps them on their shoulders. Then they see the raw-boned vicar and laugh louder. Manning shushes them with a reproving look at the house; the men organise their faces before moving off.

The constable shakes Daniels' hand. 'The women will be glad to see you,' he says.

'However I can help,' says Daniels. 'With the family, obviously, but I'm also prepared to search.'

Manning nods. His eyes are already on the next arrivals.

Women sit on the verandah of the house, watching the vicar as he approaches. They're all busy in some way with their hands. Some have children sucking corners of their skirts or sleeping in their laps. These are the friends and neighbours who always visit an expecting mother, a new baby, and any house with sickness in it; they attend all births and deaths. The Sussex vicarage in which Daniels grew up was often occupied by its own phalanx of these women. He's never been entirely sure how they know when to arrive and when to leave.

As Daniels steps onto the verandah, one of the women calls, 'Mary!' into the house's open door. Another hushes her and says in a low voice, 'She'll think it's news,' and another says, 'She won't hear anyway.'

Mary Wallace doesn't come to the door; Cissy does. She seems taller than she did yesterday, but then the Wallace house is built on a different scale from Mrs Baumann's.

'Mam's inside,' she says. 'Dad's already out looking.'

'On his own?' Daniels decides to interpret the fact that she hasn't greeted him as familiarity rather than contempt.

'With Billy. We couldn't stop him.'

Lotta peers from behind Cissy's legs and Daniels says, 'Hello, Charlotte.'

Lotta says, 'Denny went.' Her solemn face shines. Yesterday he'd seen it blurred with tears, but now, in all this hubbub, it's crisp and sharp.

'Yes, and he'll come back,' says Daniels, and sees Cissy press her lips together in disapproval. She stands aside to let him pass.

The vicar ducks to enter, although the door is high enough—Mathew Wallace, after all, is a tall man himself. Daniels feels rather dizzy—he nearly trips over a dog—and suspects he may be coming down with something. At the kitchen table, Mary Wallace pauses at kneading dough to say, 'Thank you for coming, Reverend.' She looks the way she always does: like a woman settled deep into effort. Her hair is wound in a braid around her head. She looks strong and reconciled enough to be a nun. He knows her father is a man of God; also that she can read some Greek. People of every sort end up out here with their hands in a mound of dough—he likes that about this wide-open place. He walks to her side and, lowering his hat, says, 'My prayers are with him, Mrs Wallace.' Which he had planned to say as he rode along the road and is satisfied by the sound of now.

Mary Wallace rubs at one cheek with her forearm. Perhaps she'll pray with him. But she begins to knead again; she hasn't even heard him. Before he can repeat himself, a woman comes through the door shouting, 'I've brought more butter, Mary!' The time for prayers has passed.

There are flies in the house, of course—the small, brown, soundless kind but also one big black blowfly in a corner, and this one trapped fly battering its corner sings loud enough for all the rest. The stove burns very hot, and women crowd over it. One woman at the other end of the table makes parcels of salt meat while another carves fresh mutton from a fatty leg. Among all this busyness the vicar stands with his hat, the sole man in the room and essentially invisible. So he leans close to what he knows is Mary's better ear and asks, 'Is there some way I can help? Any way at all?'

Mary is quiet, kneading, and then she says, 'Lotta needs changing.'

This seems like a request for anyone in the room other than Mr Daniels—but Mary spoke so softly that no one else could have heard her.

'Lotta?' he repeats. Now a man pushes his head in at the door and shouts, 'Morning, Mary,' and a name—Ned—is relayed through the room until it reaches Mary's better ear, distracting her, and Mr Daniels' having said 'Lotta' seems to have summoned Lotta herself, who stands at his knee and looks up at him. So Daniels crouches beside her as he did yesterday at the wedding breakfast, when he offered her a sandwich and she dropped it in her eagerness to accept.

'Your mother says—' he begins, but finds it hard to finish.

Lotta watches him with keen attention. A smell seems to stain the air about her. So changing Lotta does mean what he fears—but surely Mary doesn't expect him to be the one to do it? He holds Lotta in his arms and stands, thinking that this might bring her to someone else's attention, and says, 'She needs changing.' But no one notices. Someone announces, loudly, the arrival of Ruth Jutt, which registers as a subtle shift of the arrangement of women, so that one of them steps away from the stove and another dusts her hands and walks outdoors, where she sneezes. The blowfly still animates its corner. The smell of Lotta is nearer, it's darker, and she leans into his face and says, 'I did one.'

Mr Daniels knows, with the futile vanity of the ordinary-looking, that he's turned red; he feels the flush of blood among the roots of his hair.

'Very well,' he says, and steps through the nearest doorway. He did, after all, ask the Lord to test him. Here's a neat white bed, here's a chequered blanket on the bed, so he lays Lotta down on the blanket and, as he does, he says to her, 'God is my strength and refuge. And yours as well, Lotta, let me assure you.'

Lotta lifts her dress and underneath it is a napkin wrapped around and pinned in place. It's easy enough to unfasten and unwrap the napkin, and the smell, released, seems healthier for being in the open. He keeps his eyes averted, though; bare Lotta and the brown mess are items he must navigate without inspection. Looking away, at the wall above the bed, he sees a photographic portrait of an elderly man with thick white hair and eyebrows, sitting in a chair with one leg crossed upon a knee. His sombre expression is at war with the merry roundness of his face. Daniels leans in closer—still holding the cloth—to read the name beneath it: Mr Samuel Deniston. And it comes to him that this is Mary's father—the celebrated Samuel Deniston, Reformist, who led his family and flock from England to South Australia, who survived shipwreck and fire and famine, who built towns and chapels and spread the word of God. They call him, in the newspapers, 'the Southern Shepherd'. *This* is Mary's father? And Denny must be named for him: not Dennis, as Daniels had assumed, but Deniston Wallace.

Daniels is looking at the portrait when Cissy comes in saying, 'Lott-Lott?' He turns to her and sees how her grandfather is the secret of her face. Like the Southern Shepherd, she is called to something, and this makes her both luminous and unyielding. Daniels stands with the soiled napkin in his hand and Cissy snatches it off him. She doesn't speak; nevertheless he hears her say, 'Are you of any use to anyone?' She gathers the four corners of the napkin together and carries it away, leaving Daniels, leaving Lotta, who lies blinking on the bed.

'Sorry,' he offers Lotta, who seems resigned to apology, as if she often hears it. She's absurdly like one of the old women in Daniels' congregation, whose men drink and whose faces say, at all times and not without compassion, 'Ah yes, human folly.' The loud blowfly has made its way into this room and hovers at Daniels' ear.

When Cissy returns with a fresh napkin, Mr Daniels leaves the house. The men are gathering in the yard. They've brought gear with them so that if Denny isn't found today they can camp overnight and start the search again in the early morning. They'll do this for days, if necessary. None of them can spare the time but they still come, and Mathew would do the same for each of them. These men will search all day, and Mary and the women will spend all day feeding them.

Daniels wonders why he's thinking in terms of days when Denny could be found this morning. He suspects he has a slightly elevated temperature, but it may just be that the day is growing warm. He wonders if he could walk across the yard and join the men, become one of them, go searching alongside them, and knows he can't. But he has a plan. He thought of it when Cissy didn't say, 'Are you of any use to anyone?' He'll go out himself, alone, to a high place, and see what can be seen. His lungs are faulty, but the Lord gave him excellent eyesight. He'll stand in a high place and see what's revealed to him, and he'll pray and be tested.

Mr Daniels greets the men, takes his horse, leaves the Wallace farm, and knows that no one wonders where he's gone.

---

The boy was walking in the dry creek beds. There were two kinds of bed the boy could choose to walk along: the sandy and the stony. The sandy ones were all white forwards and backwards, and hard for the boy to walk on. The stony creeks tired the boy's legs less, but he had to watch his feet in case he stumbled. And all the creeks—there were so many, but no water in any of them—had a hundred trees along the sides. Some of the trees were alive and reared up over the creeks, they were big dusty gums. Some of the trees were dead, and the boy had been told that their branches could drop at any moment and crush him.

The boy chose to walk in the stony creeks. He was careful to look between his feet—in case of tripping—and at the trees—in case of falling branches. There was no breeze. The sky had turned white and hidden the sun so he wasn't sure of his direction, but he knew he needed to hide, probably in the hills. He was too frightened to set out across the open plain, and the sun was strong now, so he stuck to the creeks because he thought one of them would lead him to the hills, and might have a bit of water in it. He was thirsty and it hurt to swallow.

As the boy walked, it occurred to him to pray the way he did at home before bed, but the prospect worried him. Usually when he prayed he was in the house, and the house was in the centre of the yard, which was beside the road, which led to town, which had the railway, which went south to the sea and on to Adelaide, where you could buy anything you wanted. So the boy was worried that, hearing his prayer, the Bible God might look for him in his bed and not see him, might look with enormous eyes out over the land to find him, might spend time that way when there were other things for God to do: stir monsters in the deep, tear the sea in half, send angels out on errands and comfort babies. God was always busy. The Israelites were, to the boy, still slaves in Egypt, the bush still burned, the city teemed with frogs, the slaves walked always in the desert, trumpets sounded, walls continually fell, golden statues were thrown into the fire, at every minute the Israelites found the promised land, had found it, were about to find it—there was no time when these things weren't happening: burning, falling, walking, finding. Everything happened always, all at once. The sun was always shining, here or in some other place; but only when it set above the red hill could the gods step out from it.

Last night the gods had carried fire. Long ago, when he lived with Mam in a house, the boy had been afraid of the embers going cold in the fireplace at night: surely a cold fireplace meant the gods could creep down the chimney. More recently he had come to understand that the gods, who after all lived on the sun, weren't afraid of fire. He also realised that the gods had no interest in the house or the people in it—it was when people came out of a house that the gods paid attention, and usually that was a lazy kind of attention, a just-in-case kind. The gods would see the boy looking for hens in the saltbush, but he could tell them to go away and they would go. They didn't like people to be on the hill, so they sent out warnings: a falling rock, a shaking in the ground, a crow in the cypress pine. But in the last few days the sun had been so red when it set that the boy thought the gods must be angry; and last night they'd seemed to know that he was far from home, and had come looking for him with fire in their hands. He'd seen them: two lights burning, sometimes together, sometimes apart, stopping and starting and calling his name. They were hunting him. He'd crept away from them in the dark.

As he walked, the boy thought of things he liked to eat: salty bread and dripping, treacle sandwiches, potatoes baked down in the ash and plums pulled out of pudding. He thought of oranges and licked his lips, which stung. He walked for a long time before he found some muddy puddles with a kind of crust on them, so he knew to take a stick and dig nearby for water. He dug but didn't find it, so he tried to drink the funny water in the puddles. Tiny bees hovered about, but they paid no attention to him. They made him think of a song he knew, 'How doth the little busy bee improve each shining hour.' Ada often sang it to him. Can an hour shine? The boy sat in the bottom of the creek and was afraid that there might be a flood. He knew all about the sudden floods that washed through the creeks and over the plain, killing people and sheep and trees. How much water could he drink while being swept along? He was afraid, too, of the Hooky Man, who his father said waited in water to drown children.

The boy's boots were heavy, his toes felt puffed and wet. The boots had been his brother's once. He knew he had a brother, much older, tall and leaning—he leaned on fences, against walls, he propped his feet on things, his hair was dark and the freckles on his face were like the drops of water Mopsy shook from her fur onto the ground. The brother used to throw the boy into the air and catch him. But the brother went away and now the boy had only sisters—so many sisters, who cried and fought and sang, who wore their hair in long thin braids and knew things (not Lotta, though, she was a baby), who took him for picnics on the red hill. He was frightened of the hill, but he followed the sisters up its stony side, or Joy or Cissy carried him, and they sat on top under the shade of the big cypress tree while the air trembled around them. From the top of the hill the house looked very small, and if his mother came out to dig in the garden or go to the pump she was smaller still. Her shadow jumped and buckled, like a cat. And his father, too, if visible at all, was often no larger than a fence post.

The boy sat by the puddles and drank more grubby water. His feet were itchy in his brother's boots—he couldn't stand them for another minute—so he cut the laces with his knife and pulled off his socks and there they were, his feet, with blisters on them and some drying blood. The smell was strange, as if someone had lifted a wet old leaf to see what hid beneath it. He pulled the laces all the way out of the boots and put them in his pocket, thinking he could tie them back together so Mam wouldn't have to speak to the hawker with the goats. He soaked his socks with water and stuffed them in his pocket as well. He walked a while carrying the boots, but they were too heavy, so he hid them among the roots of a tree and continued along the creek.

✦

At Undelcarra, Cissy climbs the red hill in order to watch the search parties fan out over the plain. Constable Manning—she almost thinks of him as Constable Baumann now—has sent more men north-west than in any other direction, because that's the way Mam says Denny went. But does Mam know, really? Other mothers beat their children, shout and pinch, nag, meddle, drink, run away, get sick, die; Mam works and smiles. She's a good mother to young children. But children grow and she doesn't seem to. It's as if she went walking down a road one day and someone came up behind her, put one hand on her shoulder and held her there—and she was willing to be held. Was perhaps relieved, since the road was long and tiring. Cissy knows that Mam should be loved and looked after; but can anyone be sure that when she says north-west, she has it right?

Cissy watches the search parties. She would have joined them if there'd been a horse available, but Dad took Bonfire, Billy has Virnu, and even slow old Merry—who walked them to Minna's wedding yesterday—has gone on loan to Sammy So. Nobody rides Dad's Shires. Cissy stands on the hill and wants a horse. Her father has a phrase: 'Let's be up and doing.' Cissy wants to be up and doing. She was made to do. No one, says the Bible, lights a lamp and puts it in a cellar. Not true, thinks Cissy—the world is a cellar, and I am lit.

Cissy sees Joy come out of the house and wave up at the hill with both of her arms. The black dog, Mopsy, follows at her heels. Cissy would like to ignore her sister, but a summons like this is irresistible. Cissy is needed, Cissy will *do*. When Cissy is halfway down the hill, Joy shouts, 'Mam wants you!' She stays to watch Cissy descend. Mopsy runs forwards, cropped tail wagging, and tries to sniff between Cissy's legs. When Cissy reaches her, Joy inhales—preparing to speak—and Cissy finds even this simple noise intolerable. No one should live so close to other people that they're forced to hear them breathe and eat and sleep. Cissy can stand the sight and even the smell of other people, but not the intimate racket of their mouths and noses. And what's Joy saying? Something about poor Minna Baumann having to give up her husband the day after her wedding.

Cissy snorts and says, 'If you're going to feel sorry for anyone today, it shouldn't be *her*.'

'I feel sorriest for Denny,' Joy says. 'Then Mam.'

'No one asked for a list.'

'I still think it's hard on Minna.'

'It will do her good,' Cissy says, not really thinking of Minna at all. They approach the house; Cissy eyes it, as if to size it up before a fight. The day has reached its hot, inactive middle, and the women sitting on the verandah snooze, swat flies, and rarely speak.

Joy turns to Cissy with her face screwed against the sun and says, 'Don't you like people to be happy?'

What a question! Cissy isn't interested in happiness. 'I'd rather they were useful,' she says. 'Happiness won't find Denny.'

She goes into the house—lit, lit. Joy follows as she always does, slower than Cissy, so that you have to pity her. And pity, too, the way the family begins to move when Cissy enters, as if they require her presence in order to do anything at all. They've been sitting in tense silence: Lotta on Ada's lap, Noella with her feet wrapped around the legs of a chair, Mam by the stove where the big pot steams. When she sees Cissy, Mam stirs the pot; Ada bounces Lotta on her knee; Lotta begins a subdued song; and Noella unwinds her feet and sneezes. Even the women on the verandah have more vitality than any member of Cissy's family. But all these women with eyes and legs who could be out looking for Denny and aren't—what's the point of that? When they could *do*.

Cissy goes to Mam, who rests one hand on Cissy's wrist. Mam's hands are always cool. She calls them 'pastry hands', and this phrase has given Cissy a distaste for pastry.

Mam says, 'I need you to go to town.'

Cissy's heart leaps. She'll walk there—miles of moving, reciting poems to herself all the way, each step in time with the poem's rhythm. But Mam says, 'Mrs Daly is driving back.' Which means company and chat. Mrs Daly is perfectly fine, but to sit beside her and say things, to be polite when the sun is pouring down and the flat red road stretches ahead, will be a waste. Cissy will feel, talking to Mrs Daly, that she's a pail in which there is a tiny hole, and through that hole the best of her will trickle out, unnoticed.

Mam fishes in her pocket and produces a handkerchief, knotted, with money in it, and a piece of paper. She says, 'You're to go to the post office and send two telegrams.'

Cissy looks down at the paper and sees two names there: her grandfather's and her older brother's, with addresses for both. So Mam knows where Joe is—a station, apparently, in Victoria. The messages are simple: 'Denny lost two days. Police search.' For Joe, she signs off 'Mother'; for the Reverend, she signs off 'Mary Wallace'. Cissy wonders at Mam spending extra money on her surname, as if worried her father won't know her by her first.

Now here is smiling Mrs Daly, gathering things together—basket, bonnet, Cissy, kisses from Mam and the girls, licks from Mopsy—and saying how pleased she is to have company on the road, linking her arm with Cissy's, promising Mam prayers and her famous seed cake tomorrow morning. Cissy wonders at the energy required to produce all of this goodwill. But as she helps hitch the pony to the trap, she sees that Mrs Daly may actually be as cheerful as she seems—she's been made cheerful, possibly, by the novel activity of the morning, and Cissy wonders at herself: am I the same? Pleased that something is happening, at last, more important than a wedding or a harvest? The thought of this, held against her fear for Denny, subdues her. It makes her obedient to the rules of talking with an adult; makes her reverent towards Mrs Daly's confessions of nothing, helps her produce her own; so that by the time they arrive in town and Cissy jumps from the trap, Mrs Daly leans down to her and pats her cheek with a warm hand—Cissy closes her eyes for a moment at this intrusion—and says, 'You're a good girl, Cissy, very good.' Which isn't true.

Mr Blake in the post office wants to see the money before he'll send a single telegram. Then he taps out Mam's messages on his telegraph machine, giving no indication that he knows or cares about Denny being lost. His neutral face is shaded by a green visor.

'How long will it take?' Cissy asks.

'It's already finished,' says Mr Blake. He has a slight lisp.

'But how long till they reply?'

Mr Blake's face twists under the visor. The white hairs of his moustache are tinged with green. 'Wouldn't that be nice,' he says, 'to be all-knowing,' and Cissy says, 'It *would* be nice—you could tell me where my missing brother is.' Then she leans over the counter of the post office and looks Mr Blake in his green eyes and doesn't hiss, exactly, but presses her tongue against the roof of her mouth and blows air at him. The sound she produces is more startling than a hiss.

Mr Blake's eyes open wide. 'Miss . . .' he says, and Cissy says, 'I'll be back in an hour,' and leaves the office.

Mid-afternoon in Fairly. The heat raises sweat under Cissy's arms, on her forehead, and in the small of her back, but there's no natural shade under which to shelter. There aren't any public trees in Fairly, unless you walk down to the creek, where there are young willows, planted by Mrs Baumann as a service to the community; apparently there are many more trees in Germany. But Cissy has been told not to go to the creek alone: that's where the Afghans stop when they pass through with their camels, and it's also where you're likely to find any natives who've come into town from the Thalassa camp or elsewhere.

Away from the creek, the only deep shade is to be found on the verandahs of the three public houses: the Transcontinental, the Sheaf of Wheat and the Imperial. These stand in a row across the road from the railway station, their iron roofs all painted in the same green and white stripes. She walks past each of them, ready to glare at any man she sees loitering in their shade—loitering when they could be out looking for Denny, when they could be *doing*. The large main entrance of the Sheaf of Wheat is propped open by a chair, a man sits sleeping on the chair, there are flies on his shoulders and a grubby rag over one knee, and he's so tired, even asleep, that Cissy forgives him, approves, thinks: he has *done*.

Each hotel has a smaller door with a sign above it saying 'Ladies' Entrance'. As Cissy passes the Imperial, its ladies' door opens, a bell tinkles from the shadows behind it, and Miss McNeil, the schoolteacher, steps into the street.

'Hello, Cissy,' says Miss McNeil, as matter-of-factly as if she expected to see Cissy in the street; as if she's always stepping in and out of the ladies' entrance of the Imperial, and possibly she is. But surely I would know, thinks Cissy, miserable at the thought that anything about Miss McNeil has escaped her. Miss McNeil is wearing the dress Cissy likes best, the olive-green one; when the hem gets red with dust she looks like a Christmas bonbon.

Now—and this is unusual—Miss McNeil is gathering Cissy into her arms; no-nonsense Miss McNeil, whose flinty metal brooch presses against Cissy's breast.

'You poor dear,' says Miss McNeil. 'Your poor dear brother.' Her hair smells clean. She draws away to look at Cissy and shakes her head with a faint cluck; she holds Cissy by the elbows and says, 'How is your mother? What brings you into town?'

'I sent telegrams,' Cissy says, her arms straight by her side, Miss McNeil still holding her elbows. What will happen now? Will they dance right here in the middle of the street? Cissy feels dizzy, as if she might faint exactly as the vicar did, and Miss McNeil seems to know this and says, 'You need water, a drink of water,' but Cissy mishears—'a drink of winter', she thinks, as Miss McNeil guides her through the ladies' entrance and into the gloom of the Imperial. The ladies' bar is empty, but a man's head appears at a window in the wall.

'Back so soon?' says the man, and he winks.

Miss McNeil smiles, and there! There are her dimples! She seats Cissy near the man's window. 'This young lady needs a reviving drink,' she says.

The man withdraws, humming, and Miss McNeil touches the back of her shining hair. 'This will help,' she says to Cissy. 'You must all be so very worried.'

Cissy has imagined various situations in which she would require consolation from Miss McNeil. All of them involve an opportunity to press a thumb to Miss McNeil's dimples; none of them include a statement as bland as: 'You must all be so very worried.' This is Miss McNeil, who daily declares at school that her students shouldn't speak unless they have something worthwhile to say! Cissy hates the dim heat of the Imperial, the polished wood, the potted palm and dead flies in the window, the smell of boiled meat; she hates the way Miss McNeil sits with her head cocked, waiting for the return of the man.

He reappears, calls, 'Hey ho!', and pushes through a tray with two mugs on it. 'On the house,' he says.

Miss McNeil accepts this offer with a gracious nod of her head. Cissy thinks the man will leave the window, but he doesn't; he leans further out of it with his forearms pressed against the sill. Cissy drinks from her mug, expecting water, and tastes something else—maybe ale, she isn't sure. She doesn't like it. Miss McNeil smiles, but the smile is private: it knows something Cissy doesn't. Miss McNeil has said to Cissy before: 'Cissy, you are too fixated on *knowing*.' What a thing for a teacher to say! Cissy has a strong feeling that she knows a great deal, that she knows things Miss McNeil can only guess at, but she can't put them into words.

Miss McNeil is smiling at the man in the window. 'Mr Lewis,' she says, 'this is Miss Cecily Wallace, a student of mine. Cissy, this is Mr Lewis.'

The man nods at Cissy and says, 'Happy to meet you, Miss Cecily. And are you one of the clever ones, or one of the dim ones?'

Miss McNeil laughs at this cruelty and says, 'Cissy is extremely clever. If I had my way, she'd be off to Adelaide, to the Training College, to become a teacher.'

This is the first Cissy has heard about the Training College. Her immediate thought is: but Miss McNeil isn't in Adelaide.

'A scholar, then,' says Mr Lewis, and he winks at Cissy, but she knows the wink is for Miss McNeil.

Mr Lewis has dark skin but he's a white man; he has a high wrinkled forehead and is balding, but he's not particularly old. He's an ordinary sort of man, and undistinguished: he isn't wearing a jacket, his rolled-up shirtsleeves reveal raised blue veins, and he's young and strong enough to be out looking for Denny. But he's here in the Imperial with the palm and flies and ale, and Miss McNeil is saying, 'Cissy isn't like us—she's a true Australian. She was born right here in South Australia. Weren't you, Cissy?'

Cissy isn't sure whether to be proud or ashamed of this allegation, or if she's supposed to point out that they're all British subjects, no matter where they were born. Uncertain of the correct response, she gives none. This seems to disappoint Miss McNeil—this version of Miss McNeil, anyway, who enjoys pointless speech and who now prompts, 'Well, Cissy?'

'Yes,' Cissy says, sullen, bewildered.

Mr Lewis smiles; he's looking at Cissy, but the smile, like the wink, is not for her. 'A clever citizen and someday teacher,' he says. 'I expect you've learned almost all there is to know.'

'I know some things,' Cissy says.

'Such as?'

Miss McNeil waits for Cissy to speak, and when she doesn't, Miss McNeil says, 'She knows poetry, don't you, Cissy? Tennyson in particular. Dozens of poems by heart.'

But Cissy won't speak. She has closed up the way some flowers do at night.

'I know a few poems,' Mr Lewis offers. 'Shall I recite one?'

'Please do,' says Miss McNeil. 'There's nothing like a Welshman's voice for recitation.'

It's awful, all this saying, it's hideous; Cissy refuses to believe in a single word. It seems impossible to be talking like this while Denny is wandering out in the desert.

Mr Lewis pushes his shirtsleeves higher above his elbows. He clears his throat and lifts his chin and says: *'Down from the ranges and on into Fairly, the desert behind me, the sea far ahead—a pretty girl waiting all rosy and curly—yes, that's where you'll find me: in Fairly, in bed.'*

Miss McNeil, dimpling, scolds him. 'Not that kind of poem!'

Cissy stands and walks to the door of the Imperial and, when she opens the door, is further humiliated by its little bell.

The street outside is still long and hot, but the sky has begun to redden in a way that seems unwarranted. Cissy sees Miss McNeil's horse at the trough on the other side of the road. Beyond the horse, she sees the train tracks, and after them the flour mill, and after that nothing but stunted scrub with the ranges in the distance. Everyone Cissy knows lives here in this bowl of mountains. It may be that the train tracks go to the other side of the mountains and simply stop—there's nothing beyond the ranges, the train is pretending, her parents and Miss McNeil are pretending, there's no Wales, no Adelaide, no Training College, no sea. How stupid to send telegrams into nothing! At this very minute, Denny may be climbing into the mountains and finding the nothing on the other side of them; he may step into that nothing and never come back.

Miss McNeil has followed Cissy onto the verandah. Once upon a time, whole weeks ago, she told Cissy that she—Miss McNeil—would only ever fall in love with a man who was also in love with ideas.

'You're not offended, are you, Cissy?' says Miss McNeil. 'Mr Lewis—'

Mr Lewis! 'Who is he?' demands Cissy.

'He's Mr Lewis,' says Miss McNeil, placid, pleased, as if that's enough.

'What ideas is he in love with?'

Miss McNeil inclines her head to one side and smiles. 'Kindness,' she says. 'Joy. Work. Play. The body unfettered. A man and a woman.'

That's too many ideas. Cissy would like to burn with one idea, one true and important idea, but she doesn't want to choose it—she wants to be chosen. She wants her whole self to be so full of this idea that looking at her is like looking at the idea. No one she knows burns with one true idea like this. Until today, she thought Miss McNeil might have.

Miss McNeil is still speaking. 'I'll tell you something, Cissy, that will save you time. A woman like me, and you're like me: we don't wait for our hearts to decide anything for us. We don't *fall* in love—we stride into it. We choose.'

'And you've chosen Mr Lewis?'

'I have,' says Miss McNeil.

'When?'

'Do you know how unlikely it is,' says Miss McNeil, 'that he and I, that you and I, should all be here, not just in this particular place but at this particular time?'

Cissy would rather not be here. She would like never to have seen Miss McNeil step out of the Imperial Hotel. She would like never to have heard of the Training College or Mr Lewis. She says, 'I just came to send telegrams.'

'Cissy,' says Miss McNeil, in her teacherly voice now, 'you have no idea how big the world is. You have no idea how *long* the world is.'

'My brother is lost,' says Cissy. 'Don't you care?'

'Of course I care,' says Miss McNeil. She looks at Cissy with an expression she often wears for younger students: puzzled and fond.

'I can't join the search because I don't have a horse,' Cissy says, 'so I'm going to take yours. I'll bring her back when Denny's found. Mr Lewis can see you home.'

'Very well.'

Cissy gives a terse nod and turns away. She's both offended and buoyed by Miss McNeil's willingness to hand over her horse.

'Well,' says Miss McNeil, 'and what do you think of him, of Mr Lewis?'

Cissy looks back at her. 'What do I think? I think! I think! I think he looks like he'll snore.'

Miss McNeil laughs on the verandah. She says, 'Denny is lucky to have such a formidable sister. You'll find him, Cissy, I'm sure of it.' Then she opens the door and disappears forever into the tinkling dark of the Imperial Hotel.

Cissy stands for a while with Miss McNeil's horse, waiting to see if the ladies' entrance will open again. The horse is a bay mare, red as a new penny. Her name is June. Nobody goes into or comes out of the Imperial, so Cissy leads June to the post office.

'Nothing yet,' says Mr Blake, and he seems contrite, or perhaps just nervous.

Cissy leaves without speaking. Through the window she sees Mr Blake remove his green visor, which leaves a thick pink mark on his otherwise pasty forehead. It's just about time to close for the day. Soon, Cissy knows, Mr Blake will lock the door and go into the room behind the post office, which is where he lives, and he'll wash his face and hands and pour himself tea, and he'll be alone for supper. Mr Blake's wife is dead, his children live elsewhere; he'll be alone all night, and when he wakes up in the morning, he'll go on being alone. Cissy wonders if Mr Blake knows how long the world is, and suspects he does.

Cissy rides June towards the edge of town, heading north. She passes the house Minna must now live in with her constable; its windows are bright with the red west. She passes the unclaimed lot, marked at its corners by grubby flags, which optimistic women persist in believing has been bought by a milliner. She passes the last house: that of the reclusive German woman who Cissy has been told in hushed tones is a seamstress, and who keeps a donkey tethered to the native peach tree outside her cottage because, Cissy assumes, the donkey will bray if anyone tries to steal the peaches. Then come Sammy So's gardens, crowding the creek; then Fairly ends. Cissy is startled, as she always is when leaving town, by the decisive arrival of not-Fairly, which has existed since long before the houses and the railway and the Imperial Hotel, although Cissy finds this hard to imagine. Just outside of town, an emu runs over the plain with his striped chicks following behind him; he runs away from the sun and into the twilight shadow that's creeping across the Willochra.

The road to Undelcarra is completely flat, but Miss McNeil's horse insists on taking it sedately, and Cissy acquiesces to this pace. She recites her favourite Tennyson in time to June's slow rhythm. Cissy loves Tennyson for his reliable music; she responds to the sound of him more than the sense. '*Twilight and evening bell, and after that the dark!*' she chants. '*And may there be no sadness of farewell, when I embark.*' How would it feel to embark for the Training College? Her family would never manage without her. And might it be possible *not* to love Miss McNeil? The sky is red and the shadows are turning a thick, sooty pink.

A mile from home, a man appears on the road, riding towards her. He's singing, and Cissy identifies him as Constable Manning: who else would be singing on this road today? He's singing his way home to Minna. He sees Cissy and stops his horse and says, 'I know you. You're a Wallace. Which one are you?'

'I'm Cecily.'

His face swims in the velvet light. 'It'll be dark soon.' He looks concerned but in a routine way, as if concern is simply part of his duty as a policeman. 'Not out looking for your brother, are you?'

Cissy sits taller in Miss McNeil's saddle. 'I had business in town.'

'Business?' says Robert Manning, and when he smiles she sees the blush of his mouth and throat beyond his teeth.

She says, 'Have you found my brother yet?'

Robert leans across from his horse and puts one hand on her shoulder. 'Not yet,' he says. 'But no news is good news, and there's a sergeant on his way from Port Augusta.' His voice is so low and his hand so warm on her shoulder that Cissy looks up at him, at his broad bully's face, and she does as Miss McNeil says she must: she chooses. She chooses to be in love with this Robert Manning. She watches as he rides away, waiting to see if she feels any different. She doesn't. But by the time she reaches the gate with the lettuce plant beside it, she thinks there might be something very slightly altered in the region of her heart.

Bess and Karl reach the waterhole two hours before sunset. Bess knew they would find it today; she's good at finding things, is in fact delighted by the challenge of this landscape with its pleated hills and endless scrub and deep sandstone gorges. The waterhole lies in one of these gorges, which itself runs through a steep, compact range on the north-eastern edge of the Willochra Plain. The walls of the gorge are striped in shades of carmine and ochre, and these stripes, uniform in width, run along the rock at an unlikely forty-five-degree angle, as if a colossal finger has tried to prise the range out of the ground but given up before the job was done. The floor of the gorge is sand, as befits the bottom of a river. Bess takes note of all these things because they are useful to her, both practically and artistically—this is always the nature of Bess's looking.

The waterhole itself is, as promised, sizeable; it seems to seep up out of the sand, and is shaded by large gums whose smooth pale branches emerge from wrinkled grey trunks, like geese rising out of an elephant. The sun is hot, so Bess and Karl swim, and as they swim they drink, and the gorge rises up around them with its red, striated sides. Half in shadow, half in sun. The waterhole is cool and deep and on either side of it the dry riverbed looks like a narrow white road through the trees.

After swimming, they decide to camp here for at least a day, although they're both impatient to reach the marvellous vista they've been promised, and for which they've made this trip: the ridged walls of Wilpena Pound, a natural amphitheatre in the ranges north of the Willochra. Karl, naked, sits on a big, flat rock. He's the colour of a honey made by happy bees. But here—in these shadows, beside the red walls of this gorge—Karl's colour is less dazzling than elsewhere.

'What's this place called?' he asks.

'Neville Spring,' says Bess. When they were staying at Thalassa, she asked for the native name and learned it from Nancy, the housekeeper; she wrote the name on the map but has forgotten how to pronounce it. There was a story, too, about an ancient snake who lived in waterholes—Nancy called him the Akurra. 'Take care with them holes,' she said. 'You better not wake him.'

'Neville!' scoffs Karl. 'A boy who needs to blow his nose. Not a name for a place like this.'

'What shall we call it, then?'

'This place,' Karl proclaims, 'is called Two Red Men. The first one's there above the pool—look at him twisting like a devil. He's the Politician.' He points at a vertical ridge of rock that juts out from the hillside. 'The second is behind you, he's the Tax Collector. Look at him rubbing his hands together.'

'*Three* Red Men,' says Bess. 'You're sitting on the third.'

'That's true. And what is he?'

'The Art Critic,' says Bess. 'When it comes to you, he takes it lying down.'

Karl laughs at this, filling the gorge with sound.

As soon as they arrived in the Australian colonies, having spent weeks on the ocean with nothing nameable between Weymouth and Brazil, Bess and Karl began to play at naming things. Sometimes their names were grandiose: Valley of the Eastern Sun (for the dingy laneway behind the first rooms they took in Melbourne) or Stream of the Seven Sorrows (Karl upset a pail of ripe pears into a gutter—eight pears, only one retrieved unharmed). Sometimes they liked to glorify the funny Australian names of things, like 'creek' and 'paddock': Robes of Heaven Creek, Parnassus Paddock. Sometimes, exasperated, they named a Dog's Arse Boulevard, a Fleatit Bottom or a Shitboot Lane; one shabby house, which always had underthings drying in the garden, they called the Parthenon. In this way, the unfamiliar streets of Melbourne were made for them, in secret, and every place spelled out some private message for the Rapps.

Bess and Karl Rapp: with Melbourne behind them now, and those weeks on the heaving ship, and before that Stockholm, Paris, London, Leeds, all of Europe, the low skies of family; all of that behind them now, and here are the Rapps, alone at a waterhole in the red rock country of central Australia. In debt, certainly, but Bess has become accustomed to a life without money in it, and is full of plans to make some. She didn't expect Australia, but she'll make use of that, too, as she does of other things—she'll make something out of it. She's thinking of a children's book, which she'll both write and illustrate. She takes out a pencil and paper and begins to sketch the waterhole as a child would see it, a child of seven or eight. The sandstone of the gorge takes on fantastic patterns. She adds kangaroos resting in the shade and parrots in the trees. In the water she draws a swimmer's shadow. What kind of child would ever see this pool? The child of one of the big sheep or cattle properties—a lonely child, she thinks, who makes an unlikely friend. What kind of friend? A native man? A native child? A kangaroo or emu? And together they have adventures. Children, tucked in nurseries, like illustrated escapades. And illustrations of this kind suit the black ink she works in; until they can afford more materials, she'll leave colour to Karl, who can't be without it.

Karl, cursing flies, jumps back into the pool and for a long while stays underwater. Bess holds her breath until he comes back up. Every movement he makes creates waves against the waterhole's little beach, and the smallest sound of him echoes down the gorge.

'Shall I dive down and try to touch the bottom?' he calls.

'Better not,' says Bess, remembering Nancy's warning about the snake; nevertheless Karl tries and fails and comes up spluttering. Then he floats on the surface and she can see his whole exquisite body. She never thinks of it as belonging to her, but then she doesn't think of it as belonging to him either. She wishes, sometimes, that his body would step aside and leave them be. He waves at her, then turns and swims until he's out of sight behind the Art Critic.

Bess goes back to her sketch. She draws an enormous snake coiled around the perimeter of the waterhole. What if the child made friends with the snake? She could give it a trustworthy canine face. Bess experiments with this—a devoted, drooling snake—but finds herself producing elongated gargoyles. When she looks up again she sees a plump grey wallaby coming down to the waterhole to drink. Karl is watching it. He's silent, just a pale head above the water. The wallaby's tail is striped, it has yellow feet. It's slightly larger than a cat. And it seems to be two different animals: one when it's moving and another when it's still. It takes wary, shuffling steps forwards and waits, comes forwards again, and again, and waits.

Bess leans over their packs and takes up her rifle. She loads it, opens and closes the breech, and waits for the wallaby to come nearer the waterhole. When it's close enough, she pulls the trigger, and the sound is so loud in the gorge that she has to shut her eyes. When she opens them again Karl is rising, streaming, from the pool. His arms are raised, he's shouting, but all she can hear is the echo of the shot. It's as if there's a battle taking place around a corner, or a clumsy ambush.

They meet at the body of the wallaby. Karl crouches to stroke its snout. It has such tiny paws, entirely black. He's saying something about not having killed it outright, but she says, 'Of course I did,' and she did: the wallaby is dead.

Now Karl sulks. 'You might have warned me,' he says, but he knows as well as she does that warning him would have scared the wallaby away, so she doesn't reply. She just stands beside him as he strokes the wallaby's head. The fur on its cheeks is white.

'Look at the eyelashes,' says Karl. 'How could you kill a thing with such eyelashes?'

Bess says, 'We won't eat the eyelashes.'

Karl closes his eyes and his own lashes sit lightly on his cheeks. Then he stands up and dusts his hands against his thighs. 'I won't eat any of it,' he says.

Bess lifts the wallaby into her arms and it feels nothing like a baby, but she thinks of a baby. Not her own—she has no baby, never has had, but she once held a baby that was dead and now anything she holds that's roughly baby-sized makes her think of it. The wallaby is all long feet and tail and furred ears, and the flies have already found it.

Bess says, 'We haven't had fresh meat in days.'

'We haven't had fresh meat,' says Karl, imitating her voice. He leans over to wash his hands in the waterhole. 'You were drawing,' he says accusingly. 'You were working.'

She's still working, in fact: taking note of the thickness of the stripes on the wallaby's tail. A wallaby with a striped tail would make an excellent companion for a child's adventure. She knows it annoys Karl that she was working—that she can work anywhere and at any time, that in the middle of the work she killed the wallaby, and that if she wanted to she could leave the wallaby on the ground and go back to work, and the work would be unchanged. And yet here he is, full of grief for the wallaby, washing his hands like a woman who's just finished dressing a corpse. If he were to pick up a pencil now, if he were capable of working after such violence, then every line and shape and colour would be the death of the wallaby. So she says, 'Just a sketch. I want to remember this place.'

He's pulling his boots on. 'I'm going to walk,' he says, and makes his way down the gorge towards the plain. He's going to watch the evening's lurid sunset, dressed in nothing but his boots.

Bess lays the wallaby out on the Art Critic and does some quick sketches of its face and paws. Then she builds a fire and skins, cleans and butchers the wallaby, much as she would a rabbit; the blood runs down to stain the sand and the flies form a fuzzy cloud. Karl often teases her about her proficiency at shooting and skinning, which he considers particularly English; she allows this because she pities his having grown up in a city. His childhood nickname was Lada Katt because he caught rats with his bare hands: rats in the kitchens and alleys and attics and stairwells of Stockholm. She roasts the meat, boils water for tea, checks on the horses, and when Karl comes back he kneels beside her, smiling, and oh, he's beautiful, and happy now, as if he met some woman out there in the sun, some desert nymph—he's so pleased with himself.

He kisses her and says, 'My huntress. My Diana.'

'What news from the sun?' she asks.

'Redder than ever,' says Karl, but he is the sun; and he says, 'Look!' One hand is clenched shut. When he opens it there's a shining beetle on his palm: a green beetle with a horned head crawling on the pink of Karl's hand.

'This is the green light I wanted,' he says, angling his hand so the beetle walks off it and onto a leaf, then under the leaf.

They sit to eat by the fire. She gives him the best parts of the wallaby and he eats them all down to the bone.

# SECOND NIGHT

Just before sunset, Mathew Wallace and Billy Rough make camp by a dam. Mathew doesn't want to stop, but they haven't slept in two days and are struggling to stay upright in their saddles. The country here is low and flat, largely grassless thanks to the animals that come to drink at the dam, and the trees are red gum and native pine. Mathew, clearing space for a fire, notices a fresh cut in one of the gums—a gash made by a small knife. He calls Billy over.

Billy looks at the cut and says, 'It wasn't Denny.'

'He has his knife with him,' Mathew says.

Billy steps forwards and mimes the cutting of the tree in order to demonstrate that it was done by someone taller than he is.

'I told him to make marks on trees if he got lost,' Mathew says.

Billy nods, and Mathew remembers that Billy was probably there when he gave Denny those instructions, or Billy gave them to Denny himself. One of them, maybe Billy, said to Denny, 'If you're ever lost, then you look for water, you make big tracks, break branches and stomp in the dirt, and when you find water you stay with it. Make it easy on us to find you.' Surely someone had given Denny that advice. But they haven't found broken branches or boy's footprints, and here is this mark in the tree. It was made in the last day or so, and is very noticeable in the smooth upper flesh of the gum.

Mathew says, 'He'll have climbed up to get above the lumpy bark and make the cut where I'd see it.'

Billy looks around the tree, and Mathew looks with him. There's nothing nearby on which Denny could have climbed. And still there are signs, to Mathew, that Denny made the cut: something about the length of it (it's deep but short, as if made by someone whose strength ran out); the way it faces towards Undelcarra; the fact that Mathew saw it before Billy did; and its proximity to the dam. How likely is it that someone else has been out here in the last day and cut this tree?

Billy says, 'A man's been through here a short while past. A tall man leading a lame horse. He went that way.'

'Blackfellow?' Mathew asks.

Billy shrugs. 'He's wearing boots.'

'Maybe he's seen something,' Mathew says, and they leave their gear at the dam and follow the tracks of the tall man and his horse.

As they walk, Mathew can't help thinking of his horses back at Undelcarra. Is Cissy watering and feeding them properly? Is she mucking out their shit? Who's carting water to the big tank by the stable and filling the troughs in the yard? Who's being careless with candles in the straw shed? Who will cart the stores to the stations and the wool to the railway, and who will pay the principal on the mortgage? If we find Denny, thinks Mathew, none of that will matter. He offers God the horses and the harvest and every inch of the farm.

Once the sun sets and it's too dark to see the tracks with any certainty, Mathew and Billy are forced to return to the dam. While Billy prepares supper, Mathew takes his lantern over to have another look at the cut in the tree. All day he's been afraid that he's missed Denny because he's chosen one creek bed over another, looked west when he should be looking east, gone one measly mile in the wrong direction. Mathew, running his fingers over the cut, feels that it confirms his course. It seems to swell with urgency up out of the tree, as if the trunk has split itself open in order to expel something. The tree's dark, secret life swarms deep inside. Mathew takes his knife and makes another cut next to the first one—its exact twin—so that if Denny comes back he'll know Mathew was there.

Now Mathew and Billy do what they always do when they're camped out away from home: they eat, and then they fight. Mathew began the tradition; his father trained his boys in bare-knuckle boxing, and Mathew used to fight with his brothers when they worked together as watermen on the fens. At night, while travelling, Mathew often gets a brimming feeling in his limbs and finds it hard to sleep—then only a fight will calm him down. Mathew would never fight a man who wasn't equal to it, or hit anyone who couldn't hit him back.

His fights with Billy are always the same. They know the steps and repeat them, feinting, waiting and trading blows until Billy tires, as he always does. After all, he's older. Tonight is no different: they keep the tempo even, they know each other's weaknesses, one-two punches from Mathew, strong compact shots from Billy, Mathew feints but Billy won't be led, Billy is lighter on his feet, Mathew waits to hear Billy breathe through his mouth rather than his nose. A straight punch to his left cheek and Billy's down. Mathew waits a moment before extending a hand, which Billy always takes. Then they begin another round. Mathew is stronger, but Billy is faster. They shuffle and dance in the dirt while the horses graze just beyond the firelight, and Mathew takes note of every chance he sees to inflict real damage—he finds himself wanting to hurt Billy for being so sure that Denny didn't cut the tree. But he holds himself back.

After two rounds, they settle by the fire. Mathew falls asleep immediately, but is woken in the night by the sound of cattle coming to drink at the dam. Many of the heifers are in calf. They seem strangely dainty as they step down to the water, and the moonlight turns their hides silver. The cows are sure-footed in the dark. Mathew wants to chase them off, but that would be dangerous. He's left to watch as their hoofs churn the ground, knowing that, by morning, there will be no sign of the tall man's tracks.

---

The sun has not yet set when Joanna Axam calls her whippet, Bolingbroke, and goes out to tend to the Thalassa garden. She disapproves of the garden, which is thirstier, more beautiful and more expensive than it has ever been in the forty years since Henry planted it, but she's never been able to bring herself to let it die. Henry wanted a biblical garden, not because he was devout but because the idea tickled him. He'd visited the Holy

Land and said that the dryness of Thalassa was something like it, and he planted olives, roses, pomegranates, lilies, figs—Judas Iscariot hanged himself from a fig tree, which was, apparently, a reason to have four in your garden.

Henry had been full of this kind of harmless perversity—mostly harmless. He liked to drive out to dry salt pans wearing a boating blazer; he filled the dining room with an enormous musical cabinet called an orchestrion, which shook the house whenever he played it; and he built a mock temple that he dedicated to Clio, the muse of history. By moonlight, when the gum trees almost resembled willows, the temple looked like something painted inside the lid of a harpsichord. One year, he ordered two dozen date palms, and they came from Melbourne via Adelaide as fledglings: frondy, stumpy things strapped to the sides of camels, and the gait of the camels—left and right and left and right but moving forwards all the same—set the fronds waving in an undecided wind. It was certainly a triumphal entry, with the shouts of the Afghan drivers, the swaying of the baby palms, the camels rumbling out their frayed complaints and, behind them all, a little dog, holy in his hairiness. Henry called it Palm Sunday (it was a Tuesday in September). Even now, kneeling by the iris bed with slender Bolingbroke sniffing at her feet, Joanna can hear the barks of that delighted dog.

Joanna was twenty years old when she married Henry Axam, and twenty-six when he died. He commissioned a portrait of her in her wedding dress: a shining buckle at the tiny waist, a stick of orange blossom in the buckle, endless white buttons, lace at the throat and wrists, her face rigid, and the lobes of her ears peeping out from her light, looped hair like plump pearls. This portrait hangs in the dining room at Thalassa. Only the blue shadows beneath her eyes are human.

Joanna married Henry because of his plans for a pastoral property on the Eyre Peninsula; because he promised she could breed racehorses; and because she admired his determination to make the world in his own image. And she loved him. He was the surplus third son of an earl, and when he was upset his voice let slip the Lancashire accent of his favourite nurse. She has wondered, now and then, how tired she might eventually have become of his capacity to find absolutely anything interesting.

Henry set out to establish himself as a pastoralist as soon as he and Joanna were married. Hearing troubling reports of Aboriginal resistance to settlement on the Eyre Peninsula, he chose to go north instead. He took men and seed and cattle and three thousand sheep, and he wrote to Joanna in Adelaide with news of the land he'd chosen. 'There are fields of grass,' he wrote, 'for mile after mile; anyone would think the land was farmed, except that there's no one here but the natives, who I expect to be no more than an annoyance and possibly quite useful.' Joanna wanted Henry to call the property Mulla Mulla, after the velvety silver-pink flowers that grew there in spring (he sent her a cutting, which she pressed in the pages of her grandmother's Bible). In typically contrarian fashion, he called his desert station Thalassa, after the sea. Perhaps it was just as well; within two years of Henry bringing sheep and cattle to the Willochra Plain, there was no mulla-mulla left on Thalassa.

Henry was at Thalassa when George was born. He sent his pocket watch down to Adelaide and commissioned a portrait of his wife and child to be painted on it. There were no enamellists in town so Joanna made do with an indifferent watercolourist; the resulting portrait didn't resemble mother and son so much as a truncated swan cradling nine pounds of swaddled bacon. Henry wrote that he was delighted with the watch and that he was building her a house. He promised that the house would be sensible.

When his son was six months old, Henry appeared in Adelaide, kissed the rosy bundle that was George, and took them north to their sensible house, which was long and low, with stone walls eighteen inches thick and a pitched slate roof. The house lay always in the shadows of its deep verandahs. It stood beside a river in which were to be found several permanent waterholes, and Henry had plans for a garden. Around the house, the Thalassa headquarters were laid out like a small town. There was already a cemetery and a cricket pitch. Dingoes were a nuisance, but there was less native theft of stock than on other stations; Henry claimed this was because he had the good sense to provide the local natives with flour, blankets and the occasional ram, which he distributed from a depot a mile down the river. He apologised to Joanna for the temporary lack of racehorses, but here was a stud of Spanish ponies ready for breeding and exporting to the Indian Army.

For two years, Joanna oversaw a series of white housekeepers and their handyman husbands—each of them lazy, ingratiating or sly, and some so talented as to be all at once. Then, with the opening of the Victorian goldfields, every white worker left Thalassa for the diggings, and Henry had no choice but to replace his stockmen and shepherds with natives. Joanna needed a cook, so Pearl arrived from the depot camp, and Pearl brought her children: young Nancy, who became George's nursemaid; and Billy, who, with his cricket bat, was already Henry's shadow. The girls in the Aboriginal camp made passable housemaids, and would work for rations. Pearl managed them; Joanna managed Pearl. Ralph was born, made miniature growls, and they called him Bear. George was always simply George. He cut his teeth and walked and spoke and ran among the dogs along the creeks. The cattle raised the dust with their hard hoofs, the sheep sang in the saltbush. Joanna rode in the hills above the station where the rock was sometimes yellow, purple, sometimes red.

Henry died crossing a creek in flood. Billy was with him and told him not to cross, but Henry did as he wanted and went in on his horse. He was thirty-three: the age of Christ. He would have called that poetry. Henry died, and the horse survived; the name of the horse was Barabbas, which might also qualify as poetry. But Joanna is of the opinion that, outside of books, there's no such thing as poetry. There had been talk of killing Barabbas, but he was perfectly sound and Joanna wouldn't hear of it. She rode him for years afterwards. When he was too old to ride she pastured him near the house and visited him every day. She continues to respect the way he remained indifferent to her until the end of his life.

Joanna has strong opinions about horses. They're what kept her at Thalassa after Henry died, although her horse-breeding days largely ended with the droughts of the late sixties. If her sons, as boys, wanted to ride, they had to catch one of the calm old horses from the homestead paddock, ride it to the stable bareback, and saddle it themselves. She's always insisted on the American method of breaking horses, much kinder than the British way of choking with a noose; she used to be skilled at this, too, and oversaw it all herself. She wouldn't allow any Thalassa horse to be struck. It's not that she was indulgent or soft-hearted; her methods made them, she maintained, better horses, better for human purposes. She used to be something of a tyrant about it all. Then, one ordinary day last year, she went out for her usual morning ride and, an hour in, found herself folded on the ground, bleeding, with one arm caught beneath her and no memory of how she'd got there. She'd fallen, obviously—from her own horse, which she'd trained herself—and presumably had hit her head; what she hated was not knowing whether she'd caused the fall herself. What mistake might she have made—she, who never made mistakes? Nobody crowed or scolded, but she saw her authority evaporate until she became the thing she'd always dreaded: the wife up at the house. And, even worse, a wife without a husband.

So that now, while everyone is busy preparing for shearing, while even the sheep are busy, Joanna has little to do. But she must work; therefore, the garden. Kneeling by the irises, which are showing signs of rot, she can hear men shouting in the stable yard; a boy drives a flock of goats along the other side of the garden wall. Joanna bends over the irises with sharpened scissors. Bolingbroke noses among the roots of an olive tree.

From the garden, Joanna has a clear view of the main road into Thalassa, and she keeps an eye on it as she works. When she sees two men in police uniform riding up to the house, one on an excellent horse, she stands and watches them, shading her eyes against the glaring redness of the sky. Shortly afterwards, Nancy appears in the garden with the news that the visitors are policemen from Port Augusta come to look for Denny Wallace, there'll be four of them in all who need a bed for the night—two white policemen, two native trackers—and where should they be put? The trackers are easy but Joanna must decide what to do about the policemen, one of whom is a sergeant. The house is busy, they aren't prepared for guests, and she's tired. So the officers are, via Nancy, consigned to the bachelors' hall, and Joanna returns to the irises.

Ten minutes later, straightening above the purple beds, she sees two more mounted men on the road—these must be the native trackers. One of them sits well in the saddle but the other is visibly uncomfortable, possibly because of the heavy cloak he's wearing slung over his left shoulder and tied under his right arm. Despite his discomfort, there's something proud about the way he carries the cloak. Beneath it, he appears to be wearing a police uniform, just as the other tracker is. The cloak is made of some kind of fur but the tracker wears it with the pale hide facing out, and there are dark marks across the skin. It falls to the horse's belly and conceals the man's left arm; no part of this arm is visible, it may be perfectly whole or it may be missing altogether, but Joanna can tell from the care with which the man sits in the saddle that the arm is incapacitated—perhaps in the same way as her own. Whatever has happened or not happened to the tracker's arm is private and, at the same time, advertised by the cloak, and this seems honest to Joanna, so that she finds herself wanting to inspect the cloak—not to know what's underneath it, necessarily, but to know what the cloak is made of, how it's made, how thick the fur is, and what it feels like to wear over a damaged arm.

Joanna goes inside and calls for Nancy, whom she instructs to invite Sergeant Foster to her sitting room, to come and light a fire half an hour after his arrival, and to prepare a simple supper on a tray, which Joanna will eat as soon as she's rid of her guest. She goes to her sitting room, where she sits in her armchair and arranges her blue shawl so that it drapes over only one shoulder—hiding her injured arm, but leaving the other free. Bolingbroke curls up on the floor beside her feet.

The sergeant, when he arrives, is no longer young, but he's trim and strong-featured—he makes Joanna think of a Roman senator, but the sort whose recent speech has been ridiculed by someone smarter and less kind. He's a man who pushes the air about when he's in a room. Henry was like this, too, but the effect in Foster is different: less good-humoured, somehow persecuted. Joanna knows, from long experience, that he's the kind of man who must be cultivated, reassured and pandered to, and that all this must be done in secret—he should never be aware of it. He would, Joanna sees, be quite glorious in his grudges. They would be like love affairs for him. He has done nothing more than greet her and sit in a chair, and already she dislikes him. But she's also convinced by his solidity—he's just the man who should arrange the search for the Wallace boy. His whole manner seems designed to telegraph that he considers this invitation to meet with her his natural due. That convinces her, too. He'll go to the Wallace farm, and if the boy can be found, this man will find him. This man and, let's not forget, his trackers.

It's the trackers she wants to speak with him about—the one tracker's arm and cloak, specifically—but she'll take her time to get there. Otherwise she might as well remove the shawl and throw her injured arm at him. So: the pleasantries, the chat. He's stationed at Port Augusta, spent years up north, and then, and then, just as she's nodding at how inevitable it all is—his career, promotions, experience of the land, previous encounters with lost people of all ages, his courtly petulance which has turned, under her questioning, into calculated modesty—he surprises her by saying he's an author.

'I wrote about your husband in my second book,' says Sergeant Foster. 'You may know it? *Forging the Path* is the title.'

What astonishes Joanna more than anything is that she does know his book and that she—who rarely reads—has even read it. Read it, of course, because Thalassa is in it, and Henry is in it, and seeing Henry's name in print feels to her like a recognition; like something reaching up through the absence of Henry to say, 'Yes, he did exist.'

'*Forging the Path*,' Joanna says. 'I believe we have a copy. How marvellous.'

Now Foster gloats in his chair like a man who's sprung a trap. This makes it seem conceited of her, somehow, to have read the book—as if someone has walked into a room and found her studying her face in a mirror.

'Let me say how much I admired your husband, Mrs Axam,' Foster says, 'and all the men who opened up the interior. It takes a certain kind of man to be a pioneer.'

'I suppose it does,' Joanna says. She remembers now the way Sergeant Foster's book depicted these pioneers: as hardy men with fearless dreams, capable of anything, just and provident—the gravity of it all. Foster's Henry was the bold and optimistic son of an earl, astute and physical; his death was dramatic, full of melancholy irony. But surely Foster knew about the pomegranates in Henry's garden? The Greek temple? The elaborate plans for ostrich farming? If Foster's pioneers had actually existed and were gathered in a room, Henry would have snuck out to a different party. She sees now that Foster, here in her own sitting room, knows this to be true and expects her to be grateful for his having invented a more prudent Henry. A heavy Henry. She's reminded of the marble slab Henry's sisters sent from England, which weighed so much that it took six months and an inordinate amount of fuss to get it from Adelaide to his gravesite at Thalassa. At her feet, Bolingbroke gives a brief, rough cough.

Foster is speaking, still, about the pioneers, and he's elegiac, calm, as if a great age has passed—the real work, he says, is ongoing further north. He gives the impression that the harder the country was to subdue, the more it honours him to have served there. What does Joanna have to do with a man like this? What did Henry? Foster speaks as if the history of the country depends on him entirely; at the same time, there's the delicate suggestion that he's been inadequately rewarded for his efforts. He has, after all, written three books! And, he's saying now, a lecture on Abraham Lincoln, the 'Martyr President', and another on the synthetic philosophy of Herbert Spencer. And he's just published an article, well received in the cities, on the need to annex unclaimed Pacific islands to keep them from becoming French penal colonies. Oh, his concerns are international. He pushes and pushes the air. Joanna sees that she underestimated the sergeant when she thought he'd need constant reassurance. He merely requires her presence in the room.

But soon Nancy will come to light the fire and that will be Foster's cue to go, so Joanna summons a social smile with which to interrupt him. It works; there are advantages to having been married to the son, no matter how belated, of an earl. She says, 'You're accompanied by native trackers, or so I hear.'

'Yes, two men,' says Foster. 'Of the better sort.'

'And one of them, I'm told, wears a distinctive kind of cloak.'

'Of course,' says Foster, evidently pleased by Joanna's interest, 'of course, you won't have seen anything quite like it this far north. They're curious, these blankets, there's real skill involved. This one is typical of its type. It's made of possum pelts, forty-eight animals in all, but I've seen cloaks have over sixty pelts, truly remarkable. They're sewn with kangaroo sinew. They punch the holes with a sharpened fibula, that's a bone of the leg, the kangaroo leg, and the sinew of course comes from the tail. And in Victoria—'

'He wears it to conceal an injured arm?'

Foster, no doubt unused to interruption, pauses. Then he says, 'I'm told a shark attack, but I couldn't say for certain.' He clearly rues this imprecision.

'My husband had an interest in native cloaks,' Joanna says. This isn't true, but, she thinks, it could have been; if Henry had known there were such things, he would have been interested in them. Costumes of any kind delighted him. 'I'd like to inspect it.'

'The skill I spoke of may not be obvious to an untrained eye,' Foster warns.

Joanna inclines her head to demonstrate her resignation to this lamentable possibility.

'Very well,' says Foster. 'I'll have it sent in here, if that suits you?'

'Thank you,' says Joanna, in a way that indicates their conversation is now over while also suggesting that he's the one who brought it to a close. Foster, more malleable than expected, produces those active, anticipatory noises men make before they stand to leave a room. She wishes him the best with the Wallace boy and he winces at her wishes, as if he doesn't require them. She remembers that his book includes a chapter on the heroic women of the bush, who sigh with loneliness in the eerie twilight, as if the sun is always setting and the trees are always dense and straight and in a violet haze. He surveys the room as if he's just entered it, he makes a chivalric gesture of farewell, and finally he leaves.

Someone is out on the verandah closing the shutters of the bedroom windows; by the time they reach Joanna's sitting room, Nancy will have come. And here she is, Nancy, with her succinct knock and her sleeves pushed up to her elbows. Joanna has long given up asking Nancy to dress more neatly. She carries a lamp and with it lights other lamps; then she kneels at the hearth to build the fire.

'Billy came this morning,' Nancy says, and then, as if recognising that Joanna will be slightly saddened to think that Billy didn't come to say hello (and she is), adds, 'Not to the house. He went to Tal about the lost boy—wants Tal to look for him.'

Joanna hasn't thought much about the Wallace boy. She's worried for him, naturally, but he seems, to her, already gone forever, like a hundred other boys who aren't her own. 'George won't like that,' she says. This is merely an observation; how many times has she made decisions for Thalassa in which George's preferences were immaterial?

'George said no,' says Nancy. 'So that's the end, Tal's not going.'

And Joanna thinks: surely, in the matter of a child, someone might have consulted me? She sits high in her chair before the fire, not huddled under a shawl like a withered crone but as a queen, with just one martial shoulder draped in blue. The blue of the shawl leaps in the firelight, the fire leaps, her back is straight, her visible arm is firm and white, her feet are smooth and strong. But her court is one whippet with a chronic cough, one black housemaid—who loves her, who condescends—and a garden full of palm trees. She, who was mistress of a thousand sheep, of magnificent horseflesh, of a moonlit temple, of an extraordinary man. Who desired her. Who bent down to her ear and whispered, 'My darling.' Who signed his letters Pup and called her Puss (this less queenly, admittedly—but still!).

'I'll speak to George,' Joanna says. But will it make a bit of difference? The queen appears calm, but she would like to step outside and grieve with her head in the dust.

Nancy stands and wipes her hands on her apron just as the shutters are pushed closed from the outside. She locks the shutters and draws the curtains. She says, 'I'll fetch that supper tray.'

Nancy leaves, and Joanna watches the blue parts of the fire until she hears Nancy's returning knock at the door. Joanna stands to open it, as she always does, because Nancy with the tray can't open it herself, and there at the door is not Nancy but the tracker's possum-fur cloak. It's still attached to the tracker. Joanna thinks of a story Henry used to enjoy, about an ancient prophetess who asked a god for eternal life but neglected to ask for eternal youth along with it. Henry found this story funny; if he'd lived longer, Joanna thinks, it would have depressed him.

'Well,' Joanna says. 'Did Sergeant Foster send you?'

The man says, 'Yes, missus.' He's wearing the cap of the native police; he removes this now and holds it against his side. His hair is parted quite severely above his left eye. Joanna finds it hard to judge the age of natives, but he looks younger than she expected, no older than George, although his moustache is greying. He gazes at a spot on the floor to the left of her skirt. She won't invite him into the room, but it's perfectly all right to speak to him from the doorway.

'What's your name?'

'Jimmy Possum, missus.'

'Where are you from, Jimmy Possum?'

'Long way off,' says the tracker. 'Close up Encounter Bay.'

'Did Sergeant Foster tell you that I wanted to see your cloak? I find it beautiful.'

Is it beautiful? She thought it might resemble a patchwork quilt; now, this close, there's no comparison. A quilt is pretty, a bed with a quilt on it looks like a bed of flowers. Spreading this cloak on a bed would be like dragging a mountain into a room. The tracker—Jimmy—strikes her as shy, but the cloak bristles and spits. It's a greyish tan and ragged at the edges, but these edges don't look unfinished—they look inevitable. Some of the pieces of hide are decorated with dots and larger circles, others with diamond shapes, long sinuous lines or crosshatched shorter lines. Some show figures that look like people, and on one hide towards the front Joanna sees the unmistakable outline of a shark. How must it feel, she wonders, to own such a thing, to wield its authority, to wear it as a shield and trophy? No one wearing this cloak would be assumed to have contributed to their own disastrous fall.

Joanna lifts her right hand. 'May I?' she asks.

The man is silent, which Joanna interprets as assent. She reaches forwards and touches the cloak where it falls over the man's shoulder. It's warm with the quick, beating life of a living thing. She feels how the patterns have been scraped and dug and burned into it. She feels the thinness of her own blue shawl.

A cry comes from the end of the corridor, down which Nancy advances behind her tray. 'Get, you bugger!' she snaps at Jimmy. 'Go on! Get, you!'

The man doesn't seem startled, as Joanna is. He looks at Joanna's face for the first time, as if to confirm something. Then he steps back and walks up the corridor, past Nancy, who says, 'Go on! Get!' Nancy ushers Joanna into the room, where she deposits the tray on the table.

'What was that one doing here?' she asks.

'I wanted to see his cloak. I didn't expect him to come along with it.'

Nancy shrugs. 'He never takes it off.'

'Sergeant Foster failed to mention that.'

Nancy lifts the lid from the tureen and waves away the rising steam. 'Hot,' she says, as if daring Joanna to claim otherwise.

Joanna says, 'I want that cloak.'

Nancy tilts her head back as if she can only see the room adequately from on high. She may need spectacles, Joanna thinks, as she has thought before. Henry didn't approve of women wearing spectacles.

'I'll pay well for it,' Joanna says. 'You can tell me what would be fair. Will you talk to him?'

'Oh no,' says Nancy. 'No, missus.'

'Why not?'

'You don't want that old thing. What for?'

Joanna sits in her chair. 'That's none of your business.'

Nancy raises her eyebrows and replaces the lid on the tureen.

'I'm not hungry,' Joanna says. 'Take it away.' Refusing to eat is one of the few remaining ways she has to defy Nancy, who Joanna knows to be immovable once she's refused to help.

Nancy leaves the tray where it is. She crosses to the door and stops with her hand on the doorknob. 'I like that shawl that way you've got it,' she says. 'Over the side that way. Looks very good.'

Nancy hums as she closes the door, and she hums as she moves down the hall. Joanna rubs the rim of the tray with one finger. She draws the blue shawl off her arm and throws it into the fire.

---

Mary goes to bed early at the insistence of all the women filling her house. 'There's nothing more for you to do today,' they say, and send her and Lotta into the room with the white bed and the portrait of Samuel Deniston, pulling the door to without closing it completely. Mary unwinds her braid mechanically, and sprinkles the four inches of loose hair at the end of it with violet-scented powder. Her mother taught her how to make the powder, and it would never occur to her to sleep without working it through the end of her braid with her mother's boar's-hair brush. Lotta, drowsy in the bed, watches as Mary brushes. At one point she jumps, as if she's heard a scary noise. What kind of noise? What made it? And did Denny hear it too? But it's nothing—it's Lotta's limbs jumping as she sinks into sleep.

Mary climbs into the white bed and Mopsy jumps up after her, turns once, and settles down, peering at Mary over her curved tail. The look is conspiratorial: Mathew doesn't allow Mopsy on beds or chairs, but Mathew is away from home. Lotta presses her face into her mother's shoulder, but Mary lies awake. By sending her to bed, the women have left her with one task: to look for Denny. She looks for him as she looks for all her children – by feeling out along the threads that bind them to her. Here's Lotta's thread, the shortest of them all, and a thread each for the older girls, still in the parlour (though Cissy's thread is slack; Cissy who came home tonight with her teacher's horse). The telegram Mary sent to Joe is a thrumming thread all of its own. Denny remains tethered, but his thread is fraying. Where is he now? Is he crying? Is he sleeping?

Above her, Mary sees the portrait of her father. Truly, she's always aware of his presence, in much the same way that a child, forced to wear a tight bonnet, never forgets the strings at her throat. But he seems changed to her tonight, stern and loving on the wall. Did he ever lie awake in his bed, tugging at the threads that bound him to his own children? Did he feel them loosen from him, one by one? She pities him, and mourns his losses. From her tangled bed, she imagines him saying, 'Thanks be to God! May His will be done, for He works in all things to the good of those who love Him.'

Mary is used to God's will, which is not to be resisted. It was God's will that her father should bring them all to South Australia, that Mary's mother and the twins should die on the voyage out, that Mary's sister should die of scarlatina a year after their arrival, that her brother be trampled by a horse the following spring, and that Mary herself should lose most of her hearing by the age of twenty-two. Over each of these events Mary's father presided, saying, 'God is good.' God asks, and Mary gives. She has never bargained or accused. She has rejoiced with her father for the dead in Heaven.

When Mathew proposed marriage, Mary was reluctant to leave the Reverend alone. Then she realised that her father was preparing to marry again himself: a younger widow, childless, who, visiting the house, was kind to Mary, spoke louder and more slowly than required, and talked at once of a new colour for the curtains. Mary relinquished all her claims to the Reverend's household. From her pending stepmother, she learned of Samuel's worry that no man would wed his poor deaf Mary. She accepted Mathew's proposal as God's will.

Aside from her ear infections, Mary has been blessed with robust health. Her legs are thick and long, her braid swings from her head like rope, her hands are strong, and yet she can, if required, play the piano, paint flowers in watercolour and say grace in French. The piano, flowers and French are never required. There's another life in which they might have been, but it was taken from her so long ago that she would hardly recognise it now. Occasionally she sees glimpses of that other life—the clock on the mantel, the mahogany chiffonier, the violet-scented powder—but they don't fill her with the longing she knows Mathew thinks they do. In fact, she expects little from life: she was raised for death. Death is the joyous destination, the longed-for prize, the soul's sweet home. Mary's time in the world, her father has taught her, should be full and keen and useful, which requires a healthy body; to that end, he has inculcated in her a belief that bodily wellbeing is linked inexorably to the regular movement of the bowels. That takes care of the body, which is temporary. The soul, however, is eternal.

Still, Mary's heart beats, her hair swings, her fingers sink into cool soil and pull up turnips and spinach, the sun draws out the freckles on her dry, bright cheeks, and she bears child after child. Her children are rarely sick; none has ever died. It's her lot and duty to be content, so she's wary of both great joy and sadness. She sows and reaps and then, because she thinks she must, takes all her harvest and stores it for the life to come.

Mary, looking up at her father as she lies in the white bed, holds Lotta's sweaty hand in order to remind herself of the reality of her earthly flesh. Childbirth and the weeks following it are the closest she's come to fully occupying her body, and Lotta was her hardest labour and recovery. The itchy agony of those haemorrhoids! About which, of course, she never complained. Mary tries to see her children as belonging to God: only borrowed. She and Mathew have agreed, finally, that there will be no more of them. He built the room off the verandah to sleep in; Mary hung the portrait of her father above her bed. Mary was taught that humans prove their superiority to animals by regulating their desires. Does she still desire Mathew, and did she ever?

Love and duty are so bound up together, and Mary is willing to leave someone else to puzzle them out.

The door opens and Mary closes her eyes as the older girls tiptoe through her bedroom and into their own. Is Denny cold? Has he found food or water? Is he with Mathew now, and coming home? She tugs at his thread, but it doesn't answer.

Mary prays 'Thy will be done,' and waits to feel as if she has passed a heavy object over to a person more able to carry it. She lets go of Lotta's hand. Still heavy-laden, Mary falls asleep.

Sometime in the night she wakes to the sound of a child sobbing and—strange sensation—it fills her with hope. But it isn't Denny crying to be let in. It's Lotta, who's wet herself and is sniffling into Mary's left ear. Mopsy, unimpressed by this disturbance, jumps down from the bed and goes out to sleep in her basket by the stove. Mary changes Lotta, tucks her back in, kisses her hair and smooths it, and feels the kick of Lotta's chilly feet. Then Lotta asks for a song, so Mary sings her mother's favourite hymn. '*Love divine, all loves excelling*,' she sings in her low voice. Lotta burrows into Mary, her breathing slows, Mary stops singing the words and hums the melody until Lotta's mouth opens and her breathing against Mary's neck becomes long and messy, sticky with sleep. Mary rests her chin on Lotta's head, feels how warm it is, how tiny, and chases away the dreadful thought that if she'd been told two days ago to sacrifice one child—that it was God's will and there was no avoiding it—then she might have chosen this one, the youngest and another girl.

The boy stopped before the sun set. It wasn't a decision; his legs simply became heavier and heavier, until he couldn't move them. He tried to sit, and was surprised to find the ground so quickly. It just came up. There was an acacia tree beside him—had it always been there? His head ached and he thought he might be crying, but when he wiped at his face there were no tears. His tongue sat hot and heavy in his mouth, but his legs were cold—they felt like wood. Sometimes, when he ate a lot, his father told him he had hollow legs, and now he felt the truth of this: his legs were hollow, his tummy, and his arms. His eyes were hollow. He closed them and, when they opened again, the sun was gone. The sky was high and cold through the sparse leaves of the acacia. He was lying on the ground now, and felt something scratch against his neck on many legs—when he brushed at it, he found the rough edge of the sack. It took him some time to remember why he had a sack at all. His thoughts rocked back and forth, not settling, until he recalled the socks in his pocket. They were still a little damp, and he sucked what moisture he could out of them. Then he slept without agreeing to, and woke without knowing that he had. He just slept and woke and slept and woke. That night, if he'd heard the gods call his name, he might have gone to them.

---

Minna waits for Robert in the house attached to the police station. She's quite amused by this idea of living in a police station, although it horrifies her mother. Minna knows Mama hoped for a more prestigious son-in-law than Robert; her resistance to the match didn't dissipate until Minna implied that she was pregnant with Robert's child. Minna is not, as far as she knows, pregnant with Robert's child. But she is now married to him, and he need not be a constable forever.

Meanwhile, he and Minna will live in this house, which is meant for a family; Robert has really occupied only two of its rooms. When Wilhelmina toured it for the first time, she said, 'Obviously the kitchen is too small.' It's true that all the domestic arrangements will have to change. Robert had a woman coming in to cook and clean, and she took his washing with her, but she prefers to work for bachelors, so Minna's mother has offered to pay for a maid. Until they've found someone suitable (which may take some time—good domestic staff is scarce this far north), Annie Bell can come from Mama's house to help. Together, Annie and Minna are undertaking an inventory of the wedding gifts and household goods. When this list is made, Wilhelmina will decide what other things are needed.

When Annie visited earlier today, Minna was afraid that she might talk about Robert's mouth and fingers, about the sounds he makes when he's inside her. Which should be private, she understands. But she's giddy with delight. She's holding herself back from laughter at all times. She can't help but feel that Denny Wallace, by disappearing, has made her rightful joy seem immoderate, and that this is a kind of theft. So she was falsely gloomy with Annie: 'Poor little thing, it's all too dreadful.' And then optimistic: 'Oh, they'll find him.' Then she made excuses and hurried Annie out. Minna wants to wait for Robert alone. She wants to walk through all the rooms in the house and press herself against each surface. This, at last, is what bodies are for: binding yourself tight to things and people. One day she *will* be pregnant with Robert's child, and this idea excites her.

When she hears Robert's horse outside, Minna goes to meet him at the door. He picks her up and swings her about, and she likes the secret feeling of his hands in her armpits. She serves him his tea, though he says he's eaten, and she asks him how things are with the Wallaces. He sits on a chair that belongs to Minna now, eats from Minna's plate, and when he speaks, his words become Minna's as soon as he says them. He's tired and dirty. He doesn't look like the Swedish painter, but perhaps he's beautiful after all, with the red high in his cheeks. He's like a man who's fought his way through a battle to deliver an urgent message. Minna's whole body beats for him. He belches unashamedly and they laugh together; it's understood that nothing about their bodies is private any longer. Robert grins like a boy.

'What's kept you busy today, little Minnow?' he asks.

'Busy? All I've done is sleep.'

'All you've done is sleep?' Robert leans forwards and pulls at her chair until their faces are very close.

'All day,' says Minna.

Robert blows gently against her forehead and she watches the movement that his lips must make to do it. That's more thrilling to her than the feel of his breath against her skin: to see his body move to please her.

'You came home to me tonight,' she says.

'Didn't I say I would?'

'Will you come home tomorrow night?'

'Would you be lonely if I didn't, little Minnow?' Robert kisses the corner of her mouth.

'Promise you'll come home.'

'All right. I promise.'

'What if you're out in the hills and you can hear the lost boy crying? And you can see him up on a cliff? And you could rescue him if you stayed? Will you still come home then?'

'Yes,' Robert says, trying to claim her mouth.

'And what will you do when you come?'

'I'll do this,' says Robert, and they go to bed.

It isn't like their wedding night: Robert is more single-minded. He smells in the bed, and Minna likes it—he isn't a bridegroom, he's a husband, and she desires him even more. But he's tired, and after he's spent they lie with legs entwined and talk at the edge of Robert's sleep. Minna asks him questions. 'Do you love me?' she asks, and the answer is yes, yes. 'Will you always?'—and the answer is also yes. But yes isn't enough, she wants more, not more 'yes' but more of the him he was while they were apart.

'What did you eat today?' she asks and, when he tells her, 'Who made it all?'

'Dunno,' drowsily, then, 'Mary Wallace, I s'pose.'

'She's deaf, you know.'

'She can still cook, can't she?' Robert says, tickling Minna's waist and tweaking one nipple. 'There's other women helping. And one of her girls made milk pudding.'

'Which girl?'

'I don't know their names.'

'Was it Joy? No? Cissy?'

'Cissy,' Robert says. 'That sounds familiar.'

'Cissy Wallace made blancmange?'

'Milk pudding,' says Robert. 'Bit on the watery side.' He jiggles Minna's breasts with his big red hands.

Minna kisses him. The watery blancmange delights her. But she thinks of Mary Wallace and all that cooking and says, 'Wouldn't Mrs Wallace want to go looking for her boy? Instead of cooking all day?'

'Who's going to feed us, then?'

'I'd want to go out looking, if I lost my baby.'

'You'd go out looking, would you?' says Robert, stretching his arms in a way that says: sleep now, no more talking.

Indignant, smiling Minna: 'Isn't that natural in a mother?'

Robert traces one finger up Minna's arm. Minna would like to feel it inside her, it doesn't matter where; but the finger promises nothing—he's so near to sleep. He says, 'If she was looking in the first place, maybe he wouldn't have got lost.'

Minna considers this. It seems an unkind thing to have said. 'But how could she have known about the storm? And she was all alone.'

Robert rolls in the bed and says, 'Mmmmm.'

Her constable is leaving her now, for hours of sleep, and tomorrow she'll be alone for hours waiting for him to come home again. Minna considers the Wallace family. Mrs Wallace was alone because the girls were all in town at Minna's wedding. So who is at fault? Mrs Wallace for not watching, the dust for rising, or Minna for getting married? Minna has been blaming the little boy, she realises, for wandering off alone. Now she sees the part she played in the disaster.

'I'll take the food that's left from yesterday,' she announces. 'Annie says there's piles.'

Robert makes an indulgent growl. He's burrowing into the bed. She sleeps soon after he does, and dreams so many times of Robert waking her to say goodbye that in the morning she isn't sure which of them, if any, was real. Either way, he's gone.

# TALES OF THE YADLIAWARDA AND IRISH HOUSEMAIDS

## I

My name is Arranyinha. I'm called Nancy. My brother's called Billy, my mother's Pearl. Our family name is Rough. My mother used to work for a family called Roughley—that's why. You want a story for your book? This one here's a story I used to tell George and Bear when they were kids. I'm thinking of this story with that boy lost out there.

This story happens far from here and a long time past. Some people live beside a river, they're comfortable and there's good food, their place is rich. But there's trouble: rats everywhere, eating all their food and everything. So they get together and the boss—now he's a fat one—the boss says we'll sort this out, we'll give a big reward to anyone who kills those rats. A man turns up and says he'll do it, he wants that big reward. Now he's a clever one, the man, he has a magic pipe. He plays the pipe and those rats come out, they follow the man all the way into the river. All those rats drown. That's why that river is choppy now and dangerous—river's full of rats. The man with the pipe says, Where's my big reward? But the boss won't give it. Everyone laughs at the man with the pipe and he goes away. Everyone's happy now because those rats are in the river.

A night goes by, maybe another night. The man comes back with his pipe. He plays that pipe and instead of rats coming after him, it's kids. All the boys and girls in that place hear the pipe and follow it. He doesn't take them to the river. They go along dancing to a big hill. The boss and the people say: Those kids will have to stop at that hill! It's too big to climb! But the man plays his pipe and there's a loud noise and the hill opens right up. The man with the pipe walks in and the kids follow him and the hill closes again. All the kids are gone, stolen by the man. After that there's a big crack in the side of that hill. Just one boy was left behind—he wasn't fast enough. But I'd say to George that all I needed was one boy, and when Bear was bigger I'd make it two boys who escaped. I'd say, Two boys is all I want.

I had my own girls later. Their skin was light and they were taken from me.

One time old Joanna heard me tell that story about the rats and wanted to know where I learned it, and I said, You told me. She said, When? One night when it was storming, I said. We hadn't lived at her house for too long. I was still such a skinny one. Old Joanna was scared of the storm, so she sat with me and George and said she'd tell a story. Now I'm telling it to you.

## II

Surely you scientific gentlemen have better things to do than pester me for stories? All right. I'm Anne Catherine Bell. People call me Annie. I was born in Sydney, New South Wales, but Mother and Da were born in London and in Dublin. I don't tend to put that round—smells of convict, which they were, bless the pair of them. Also sounds Roman Catholic, which Da were, but I keep that quiet too. Mrs Baumann wouldn't like it. I know she'd prefer to keep a German girl, but she says I'm better than a black. Not that she minds the blacks, she always says, only they're unreliable—once she had a girl who was good at her work but when it got too hot she'd walk off somewhere cooler, and if she took offence with something Mrs B said or did she'd vanish for a day or two, then come back like no one could have missed her. They only want discipline, says Mrs B. I wouldn't know.

It's all right here at Mrs Baumann's. I get every Sunday afternoon free, don't I, and Cook's not lazy like some are. She passes wind, though, something chronic. The best thing about Mrs B is that her chair means you always know just where she is. She can't creep up.

Now, this is terrible about that missing boy. When I were little I were that scared of the bush, I thought any kid within three yards of it was lost forever. One time Mrs B were out visiting at Thalassa and took me along with her. I went into the kitchen and got talking to the cook there, fat old Pearl. She were talking about being a girl. When I were a girl, she said, but in that funny way they have, I can't do it. So Pearl's a girl, and she's sitting by the fire and she sees a light shining up on top of a hill, looks like a fire. But there's no people up on the hill to build the fire. Her mam says to her, 'Don't be frit, that's just the spirit cooking damper for her lost little ones.' I don't know what sort of spirit. A ghost, maybe? This spirit was a mother whose kids went off, a boy and girl, and the spirit thinks she'll cook damper so the kids'll smell it and be hungry and come back.

But they don't come back, so the spirit makes a hill and she climbs up to listen for them crying. When she's climbing she's singing a song—a song about a bird, I think it was. There was a song for the boy and another one for the girl, and the mother found them. She found the boy first; she followed the sound of the bird and he was at the end of it, or something like. Though if she's the one making the song, how can she follow it? Maybe I'm remembering wrong. I forget how the girl was found. It took a long time, I know that much. What matters, I suppose, is that she found her. The finding is what matters.

They're funny, mothers, how you lose them. And you never think you will. They say you recover from it in time, though I'm still waiting. You wanted a story? Well, I told you one, and it'll serve.

## THIRD DAY

Sergeant Foster orders his men out of bed well before sunrise and makes sure they raise a respectable amount of noise, waking Thalassa dogs and more than one rooster. Foster likes to make noise in the morning and sees no reason, on this occasion, for restraint: he's annoyed not to have met the men of the family; not to have been offered a room in the main house for the night; to have been fed with his subordinate, Constable Wooding, Third Class, in a makeshift dining room (although the madeira was excellent); and then to have found his native trackers sampling the same madeira in the kitchen. The morning is cold enough that the breath of men and horses comes out white and cloudy. Any colder and there'd be a frost.

Foster and Wooding leave Thalassa before the trackers, who know to wait half an hour before setting out: Foster always rides ahead of his trackers, in part because he dislikes the fuss that is sometimes caused by the sight of Aboriginal men in uniform. It's getting light by the time he's on the road, though still a way off from sunrise. This is the period Foster calls 'piccaninny dawn'—an excellent time of day. Foster has seen the way a camp of natives stirs at this greyish hour, and he admires them for their industry. He's willing to refute anyone who claims that the Australian native is indolent and childlike. On the contrary, he'll say—'they're quick and crafty, very skilled; certainly the desert blacks, who aren't blessed with the fat fish and rainfall of the coasts. You simply have to turn those qualities to the good.' Foster often feels disheartened by the difficulty of this task, but never at this hour of day, not as long as he's already up and on his way somewhere, as he is this morning.

The country between Thalassa and Fairly is flat and treeless, except for the usual rows of river gums that grow along the many creek beds of the plain. The road runs beside the railway tracks, which have been built above ground level on banks of earth and rock. Foster knows that, with heavy rain, this part of the Willochra is subject to sudden floods, and approves of the railway's raised construction. It was a flood that killed Henry Axam; Foster snorts in his saddle at the thought of such a fop pitting himself against the elemental waters. The morning has that brilliant, mineral quality he loves in early spring out bush: clear sky, the rising sun burning off the night's chill, each tuft of grass distinct, the ranges rising green and red on every side and, to his left, six or seven mallee ringnecks skimming the saltbush. He thinks, as usual, about how he might describe all this in prose: 'vast, rolling plains' occurs to him, but he dismisses it at once as far too obvious; he prefers 'the radiant sheen of the ringneck parrot' and 'the indolent spiralling of the omnipresent eagles'. Foster observes Thalassa fences strung along the road,

Thalassa troughs and windmills; looking ahead, he sees the chimney smoke of the distant town. Everywhere he looks, he sees evidence of order. The ride into Fairly and beyond it, to the Wallace farm, gives him considerable satisfaction, and he and Wooding reach Undelcarra by nine o'clock.

The sergeant is happy to meet the constable who has, until now, taken charge of the search operations. Foster has heard good things of this Manning, with one exception: as a young policeman, it appears, he turned a blind eye to some card sharps at a race meet; seemed, in fact, to accept money from these sharps in return for his blind eye. Upon questioning, Manning mounted some credible defence involving the intention to stop payment of a cheque, and the matter was allowed to rest. Foster's informant did discover that, soon after this incident, Manning distinguished himself in the capture of two inveterate cattle thieves, one of whom he shot and killed—a man held in such low esteem by his own people that no reprisals came from the natives. Foster remembers this episode because he alluded to it in his most recent book, *Customs of the Central Australian Aborigines.* Foster judges a man by his deeds, as he hopes to be judged himself: some are good, some are ill-advised. The key lies in the balance, and he considers Constable Manning's ledger squared.

Certainly Foster is pleased by the set-up as he rides into the Wallace farm and sees horses saddled and men assembled. Manning's waiting at the gate. He looks younger than expected, broad-set and ginger.

'We had word late last night,' Manning says, once Foster has introduced himself. 'There's signs of the boy north-east.'

'What signs?'

'A trail. Footprints.'

Foster nods. 'Is this common knowledge?'

'No, sir,' Manning says. 'I thought it best to wait for you.'

Foster approves of this. In these situations, he prefers to keep general hopes high and specific expectations low. Manning says he'll take Foster to speak to the mother, who he mentions is hard of hearing, and leads the sergeant up the path towards the house. This building, like the others scattered around it, is dwarfed by the expanse in which it's settled. A black dog watches them from the verandah.

'Where's Wallace, then?' Foster asks.

'He's out already, sir, with his black boy. Been out since yesterday morning.'

'We're not looking for him as well, then, are we?'

Manning seems to find this neither funny nor tasteless; it's hard to know if this neutrality indicates obedience. Either way, he may turn out to lack initiative. And yet the card sharps, and the capture of the cattle thieves—it's possible that this is just a bigger operation than he's used to, and he's out of his depth. Foster comes to a sudden stop. This is an old tactic of his; he likes the agitation it produces in the man he's walking with.

Foster says, 'Any reason to suspect ill-treatment?'

'You mean, was the boy ever thrashed? Not beyond the usual, I'd say.'

'What kind of man is Wallace? Any talk about him?'

'Nothing out of the ordinary,' Manning says.

'Nothing out of the ordinary,' Foster repeats, as if confirming a long-held conviction of his own. Then he begins to walk again, and reaches the house ahead of Manning.

The interior of the house is exactly what Foster expects to find on one of these failing northern wheat farms. There's always one good piece of furniture that looks out of place, an emissary from a better life—in this instance, a fine chiffonier. The harvests fail, the mortgage looms, but no one ever forgets to polish the mahogany. The mother, Mrs Wallace, appears to be sensible and tidy. Unusually tall, perhaps, but Foster approves of tallness in women; it suggests ambition of the right kind. In cases like this it's the mother you look out for—if she should get overexcited, you'll have problems. (It goes without saying that fathers can be tricky too: defensive of their turf or, like this Wallace, determined to play the hero.) But Mrs Wallace seems to be in control of herself. She looks at Foster's lips and not his eyes, and holds her head in such a way that he concludes her left ear's best. There's food ready, and a big girl, presumably the eldest Wallace daughter, hands him a pannikin of tea. He likes the look of her. Nice wide hips. There are other girls—younger sisters—wandering about. One child yawns against the mother's leg. Another girl pokes with some vehemence at the fire in the stove; the black dog yaps at her feet.

'Please sit,' says Mrs Wallace.

'I'm sorry,' says Mrs Wallace.

'The smoke,' says Mrs Wallace. She seems inclined to start sentences with no intention of finishing them.

The girl at the stove says, 'The smokestack's coming loose again.'

Foster hadn't noticed any smoke but now that she's mentioned it, there is a whiff in the air. If anything, the girl at the stove is encouraging it into the room. He sits in the armchair he's offered—it'll be the father's chair, you can see where his boots have smoothed a groove in the hard-packed floor. Foster has learned to accept the hospitality of these good, simple farming types without fuss; they offend easily. He remains conscious all the while of the oldest girl, the one with the hips, who stands quite still but gives the impression, nevertheless, that she's revolving to give him a look at every part of her. The mother sits in a less comfortable chair and draws the yawning child onto her knee. Manning, the young constable, remains standing.

Foster sits straight in the paternal chair. 'I have a good deal of experience with lost children,' he says, 'and there are certain predictable behaviours.' He once heard adults described, in a joking tone, as 'lapsed children'; he disapproves of this. It suggests the puerile possibility of return, and to what? He was never more stupid than when he was a child. 'Now, an adult, if he's lost, or she, will walk himself in circles looking for a way out. That's if he doesn't have the sense to know his way by the position of the sun or stars. But children when they're lost have a tendency to walk in a long, straight line'—here he thrusts his arm out and squints along its length—'and nothing will induce them to turn back. Nine times out of ten, children fix on one way and they follow it to the death.' A slight stir in the room suggests that 'to the death' might have been too blunt. He adds, 'And that's how we find them. It's quite routine, quite ordinary.'

The girl at the stove lays the poker down as if it's a loaded weapon she can't quite trust and says, 'Denny isn't ordinary.'

So the child is either ill or mental, which could complicate things considerably. This is the kind of information he should have had before leaving Port Augusta.

Another girl, from out of the blur of sisters, says, 'He's delicate.'

'He's not sick or anything,' says the girl at the stove. 'Miss McNeil says he's sensitive.'

'What I need to know,' says Foster, 'is his height and weight, the colour of his hair, what he's wearing, and the kind of shoe if any.' The girl by the stove looks as if she plans to object to something, so Foster raises one finger and his voice: 'In addition,' he says, 'any identifying marks, any difference in foot size, any turning in of the feet, any limp or favouring of one side—anything *out of the ordinary* of this kind, I certainly need to know.'

The girl by the stove raises her voice to say, 'Oh? Is there another lost boy out there, and you're afraid you'll mix them up?'

'Cissy,' admonishes the mother.

'He drags his left foot,' someone says—it's the older girl with the hips. 'But only when he's tired.'

'He doesn't!' says the girl by the stove.

The girl with the hips ignores this; instead she takes a few steps towards Foster, dragging her left foot almost imperceptibly. By God, she's a lovely lot of flesh.

'He doesn't,' repeats the girl by the fire, but she looks unsure.

'He comes to here,' says the big girl, indicating a spot just above her right hip. 'Fair complexion, fair hair—this colour.' She points to the hair of the child sitting on the mother's lap. 'He has a red mark, strawberry-shaped, behind his left knee.'

One of the smaller sisters pipes up to say, 'It's because Mam wanted strawberries when—'

The big girl hushes her. 'He's wearing short grey trousers. Boots with laces and a light shirt. No coat.'

'No hat,' adds Manning. The girl by the fire looks at him as if surprised, and Manning notices and turns a smidge defensive. 'Mrs Wallace told me yesterday no hat.'

Foster looks back at the spot above the big girl's hip. 'And nothing else with him?'

The girls all look to their mother. 'Mam,' says the big one loudly, towards her mother's left ear, 'what did Denny have with him?'

'A sack,' the mother says. 'He had a sack.'

'Thank you,' says Foster gravely, rising from his chair. Manning and even the girl by the stove take a step backwards. The big girl, though, stays where she stands. He turns to the mother and leans in. 'I'll speak to the men now. We'll head out as soon as my trackers arrive. I'll do my best for you, Mrs Wallace, and your son. There's every reason to believe we'll find him safe and well.'

He thinks of the boy he found in a river, neck snapped; the other in the well at Blinman; the girl in a sand dune whose skull was uncovered by dogs; the Daylesford three in the hollow tree; and the boy with the cricket bat who tried to eat the leather of his braces before he died. Foster knows that unless this Denny Wallace is found within the next day, he'll almost certainly die of thirst, exposure, exhaustion, or all three—if he isn't dead already.

'What's more,' Foster says, taking Mrs Wallace's hands in his own, 'it's the season for native peaches. He does know, doesn't he, about the peaches?'

'Of course he knows,' says the girl by the fire, and the dog yaps as if in agreement.

Mrs Wallace bows her head over Foster's hands. He allows this, then extracts them with deliberate care. He makes sure to look at the girl with the hips, who doesn't blush or squirm. Before leaving the cottage to speak to the men assembled outside, he consults his watch, smiles, and gestures at the clock on the mantel shelf. 'Your clock,' he says, 'is slow by seven minutes.'

Joanna Axam decides to visit Mary Wallace. She calls Bolingbroke and he comes, mournful, on his reedy legs—the strangest, calmest whippet she has ever owned, who lives for heat and sleep and silence, and rarely stretches into a run. But when he does run, he flies more beautifully than any of his predecessors, and so she has a soft spot for him, for her brindle Bolingbroke, so long and loyal. His cough worries her, but he seems resigned to it.

Joanna's husband presented her with her first whippet not long after they married. She called that dog Golden for his tawny coat. He was magnificent at first, supple, shining, but Henry overfed him until Golden would only eat from Henry's hand—treats all day, that Golden came to beg for. Then, when the dog grew fat—who ever heard of a fat whippet?—Henry complained of Golden's gluttony until Joanna said, finally, 'Have you never thought that he overeats to please you?' After that, Henry left her to manage her own dogs. Joanna likes to take a dog when she travels about alone.

In reality, she no longer travels alone. Less than two years ago, she would have driven herself to Fairly and on to the Wallace farm; now, unable to control a horse or vehicle, she must wait for someone else to take her. She requests the services of a polite boy she thinks of as a nephew of Nancy's, although she has no idea if they're actually related, but George informs her that this boy has been put to work constructing sheep pens. George tells her this with his mouth drawn down as if he regrets the inconvenience on her behalf, and goes into the complicated possibilities of who they can spare (nobody) and for how long (no time at all). He's already deflected her questions about sending Tal to look for the Wallace boy. Then Bear says, 'I'll take you—I need to go to town to speak with Beller,' and George mulls this over, too: is this the best time for Bear to be away, all things considered, with the first sheep coming in this afternoon, washing starting tomorrow, and so much left to do before the arrival of the shearers? Bear lets his brother talk, says, 'All the same, I'll take her,' and goes out to the stable to hitch horses to the gig.

Now they rattle up the road to Fairly, Joanna with Bolingbroke sleeping in her lap. The dog opens his eyes occasionally, and it's as if his eyebrows have risen of their own accord and carried his eyelids with them—his eyes always look startled, as if he didn't expect them to open, but he doesn't seem to mind. Bear speaks at length of Beller, whoever that is (at one time Joanna would have known and spoken to Beller herself), and then of wool prices and what they can expect this year, and then of the poor Wallace boy. That subject gets Bear pondering his impending fatherhood. Oh, Bear, who's convinced that horses report to each other on all that's happened while they were apart, who will travel an hour out of his way so as not to hear the cries of sheep caught in a drought-boggy waterhole, who saw an opera once—Handel's *Serse*—and thoroughly enjoyed it (the women in disguise! the king singing to a plane tree!) and now considers himself relieved of the burden of all music. What he talks about now, as they near Fairly, is his excellence in a stock drive—he knows all the routes, never loses an animal when he takes sheep to the railway, to the back country or the outstations, or over creeks, and he confesses to his mother that he thinks these skills will translate into fatherhood, especially if he were to have a child who, God forbid, got himself lost. Then Bear returns to the subject of Beller, who is, apparently, a decent man, and some kind of stock agent.

'Why don't you stop in at Willie Baumann's while I see him?' Bear says and, having suggested this idea, considers it decided.

Joanna submits, but insists that Bear take Bolingbroke; she has heard Wilhelmina comment more than once on the whimsy of keeping a whippet that has never so much as run after a rabbit.

Pausing at the Baumanns' front door, Joanna prepares herself for Wilhelmina. She wonders how it would feel to walk into Willie's parlour wearing Jimmy Possum's cloak: like carrying a shield, she thinks, in the manner of a warrior queen. Having burned her blue shawl last night, Joanna is wearing a much less gorgeous green one. It's too flimsy to provide any kind of barrier between her arm and the world.

The Baumann house has recovered from the wedding. Here's the maid opening the door with a cheerful face; the hallway is filled with the smell of recent baking, and the parlour with bowls and vases full of Minna's wedding roses. Wilhelmina, lustrous in black, is as gracious as ever from her chair, which leaves Joanna clumsy and contrite.

'I must apologise for bursting in on you like this,' she says. 'I'm on my way to visit Mary Wallace.'

'Poor soul,' says Wilhelmina, smoothing her skirts.

Joanna says, 'Ralph needed to stop in town, so I thought: I shall look in on Wilhelmina.'

'Naturally I'm grateful for callers, Mrs Axam, whatever their reasons.'

Joanna allows a stiff silence. Then she says, 'Well, the weather is holding. We can be thankful for that.'

Wilhelmina nods knowingly. 'That is a mercy, with the shearing just beginning.'

Joanna considers insisting that she's thankful for the weather on the Wallaces' behalf, not Thalassa's (the weather *does* worry her, though, at shearing time); she decides not to bother. 'We had Sergeant Foster of Port Augusta stopping with us last night,' she says. 'He's to lead the search.'

'So I heard from my daughter. We are not, as you know, unconnected to the police force.'

They could spend the whole morning this way, with Wilhelmina glinting in her chair like a rigid star. But something makes Willie bend, because she leans forwards and says, 'My maid saw him pass with his men. One white man and, following after, two blacks.'

'Native trackers,' Joanna says. 'So now we can be sure the boy will be found.' Joanna has absolute faith in native tracking; she's seen it succeed so often. She's been told by one of the Thalassa shepherds that her tracks have changed since her accident. 'You been walking round different way,' he said, imitating her new gait with one arm held tightly to his side.

Wilhelmina shakes her head. 'Uncanny, isn't it, the way they find things? My old nursemaid used to say that whenever a long-lost thing was found, a demon had showed you the way.'

'Oh dear,' Joanna says. Is this a Lutheran notion? She often suspects Wilhelmina of parading the most lurid bits of Lutheranism as punishment for Joanna's neglected German quarter.

Wilhelmina continues. 'Naturally, I don't say that it's demons. We can only pray.' And then, perhaps thinking prayers too insubstantial, she adds, 'My daughter has gone to Mrs Wallace with food this morning, the last of her wedding breakfast. She has taken my buggy and my two bay mares. Mr Manning has no buggy at present. Hermina is looking, also, for a maid, but there are no girls who want to work.'

What Wilhelmina means is that there are no white girls who want to work. Joanna, whose own house is largely staffed by native women, says, 'How kind of Minna to take all that food. And more than the food—she's lent her husband, too.'

Wilhelmina raises one graceful hand. 'I was ready to send them on a wedding tour. I offered Europe, London, the waters of Karlsbad, but Minna won't go if I don't also. She has uncles all over Westfalen! But she is devoted to me. It seems now that it's just as well, with her husband needed. He is, you know, a remarkably capable young man.'

'My sons speak highly of him.'

'*Genau*,' says Wilhelmina, 'exactly,' as if that confirms it, as if Joanna accepts the opinion of no one but her sons.

Joanna turns her head to clear her throat and sees, on a shining table, the bowl of Indian silver she gave to Otho years ago, to thank him for having steered Thalassa through the drought. She always finds it strange to see the bowl here at Wilhelmina's, with its palm trees and its monkeys, crowned by candles that have never been lit. Henry gave it to her for her twenty-third birthday—one of many gifts. She reaches out with her good hand to give the bowl an affectionate stroke, but stops herself before Wilhelmina can fault her for smudging the silver. Besides, the bowl no longer responds to her. Joanna, rational in every other way, can't help believing that objects, by changing hands, transfer their loyalties between owners.

Wilhelmina, with disconcerting acuity, says, 'I see that today you are without your beautiful blue shawl.'

How like Wilhelmina to not only notice the absence of the blue shawl but draw attention to it. If Joanna had the loyalty of the possum fur cloak, she might have the courage to say: Willie, do your legs hurt you? Do you feel as if they're still a part of you? Teach me, Willie, how to mourn a limb.

Annie arrives with tea and says, 'I'm that sorry, Mrs Baumann, but Miss Minna took every bit of food with her; Cook says we've nothing left,' and Wilhelmina lifts her hands to her face—the opal in her ring startles with its rich red vein—and says, 'That girl! *Sie ein Herz aus Gold hat*. And yet we starve! But not even any plum cake? You know we had two in tins.'

Annie says, 'Miss Minna took the plum cake and all.'

Wilhelmina purses her lips. 'You should, I suppose, say Mrs Manning now.'

'I am more than satisfied with a cup of tea,' insists Joanna.

Annie continues to apologise with a slight wail in her voice, and Wilhelmina to scold while at the same time praising the kindness of her daughter, daring Joanna to object. The tea is poured and drunk, Annie goes back to rattle in the kitchen, the silver bowl shines in the heavy room, and Bear arrives with Bolingbroke to say that Beller is out after all, looking for Denny Wallace.

Wilhelmina, sharply: 'I could have told you that. They've all gone: the town is now deserted.'

'Quite right,' says Bear, flustered.

Joanna, rising, says, 'We'll leave you in peace and join them.'

Bolingbroke steps forwards, his ears folded in towards his eyebrows, and places his narrow head on Wilhelmina's knee. Every rib shows through his mottled coat.

'Oh,' says Wilhelmina, and lays a hand behind his ears. 'Oh, my darling.'

How strange to hear Willie speak like this, with so much love. Her tenderness appears to fluster Bear further, and he says, 'What a funny thing. He never gives me the time of day.'

Wilhelmina looks at Bolingbroke, stroking his stylish head, and Bolingbroke looks back with his eyes rolled up beneath those quizzical brows. You, thinks Joanna, are in complete control of those eyebrows, aren't you? Her devoted Bolingbroke, who has never once interacted with Willie in this way. They seem, Wilhelmina and the dog, to be conversing with one another, until Bolingbroke coughs. Then Wilhelmina laughs—a short, high, rapping laugh—which breaks the spell. Bolingbroke, that sage old viscount, turns away and trots to the door to await its opening. He looks more than ever like a miniature horse.

'How charming,' Wilhelmina says. She has withdrawn into herself again.

Driving out of Fairly on the way to Undelcarra, Bear says, 'She's a funny old stick. Just think of Boley doing that. Like he loved her.'

Joanna feels a sharp, possessive pain and tugs at her inadequate shawl. 'If you hurry,' she says, 'we'll catch Minna. She's taken what's left of her wedding feast out to Mrs Wallace.'

Bear does nothing to change the horse's pace. 'This is decent road out here,' he says. 'You'd expect more ruts, wouldn't you, from the cartwheels? I forget how flat this country is. Level as a cricket ground.' Dust rises from the road and settles as they pass. Then Bear says, as if he isn't sure, 'That was kind-hearted of Minna, wasn't it? To take food out to the Wallaces?'

'If you have to ask,' Joanna says, 'I haven't raised you well.'

Bolingbroke sleeps with his head on Joanna's lap. She doesn't swat the flies from around his face, but none of them disturb him.

---

Cissy is irritated with Miss McNeil's horse. She's trying to keep up with Sergeant Foster and Constable Manning (now that she's in love with him, she calls him Robert to herself; out loud she avoids calling him anything at all), but June isn't used to country like this. She was fine on the road yesterday and set out with confidence this morning, but now she's making daft decisions, becoming skittish, and at the same time showing off. Cissy, embarrassed by this nervy prancing, has mentioned at least four times that June isn't her horse. Foster and Manning pay her no attention, except that once Robert nods at June and says, 'She's certainly on her toes.'

There are six in their group: Foster, Robert, Cissy, the tracker with the fur cloak and two men from town, one of whom looks permanently surprised and the other as if nothing in the world could startle him. They're riding out to the place where the perpetually surprised man claims to have seen, plain as the nose on his face, a set of child's footprints that lead to the base of a large flat rock, then vanish. The man saw the footprints late yesterday afternoon and told Robert about them this morning. There seems to be some disapproval associated with the fact that Robert went home last night rather than staying out at Undelcarra: the surprised man has said, at least three times, 'I would've told right off, if the constable had been about.' Apparently Foster has chosen to keep news of the footprints quiet so as to produce neither excessive hope nor alarm.

Robert says, 'It's not much to go on.'

And Foster says, 'If it's enough, it's enough.'

June throws her head about and Cissy resists the impulse to disown her again. Cissy had been so bold back at Undelcarra, armed with June and approaching Foster and Robert, insisting that she be allowed to come along with their party, but neither Foster nor Robert nor anyone else seemed to care one way or another. Finding insistence unnecessary, she grew shy. No one seems worried about causing her needless alarm with this story of footprints, and actually she isn't alarmed, because children don't climb up onto rocks and vanish from them—that simply isn't something a child can do.

It's begun to occur to Cissy, however, that she may not know what Denny can do. She didn't know, for example, that he dragged his leg when tired. It makes him seem like someone else's brother. But he's *her* brother, and she knows him: he's the Sensitive One, just as Joy's the Lazy One, Ada's the Maternal One, Noella's the Greedy One and Lotta's the Little One. Cissy knows herself to be the Bossy One. Beyond these distinguishing characteristics, which are necessary in a large household, Cissy proceeds on the understanding that she and her family are all more or less the same person. Surely they all feel as she does, think as she does, and are only prevented from acting as she does by politeness, or weakness, or fear. If Joy were to come to Cissy and say, 'Denny is frightened of the red hill,' Cissy would think, What rubbish, it's just a hill. If her mother were to say, 'Living is a mystery to me, I was raised for death,' Cissy would think, How can living be mysterious when it's all we do?

Just ahead of Cissy, Robert is happy. She can see it in the way he rides. He and his horse know this pocked, scrubby country and jog over it with ease. He's big and red in the saddle, and his buttons and shoulders and sword turn the sunlight silver. He's full of one idea: his idea is Minna. This idea will, eventually, burn itself down until it becomes one of many. Cissy knows this because she has a low opinion of other people's capacity to love with steadfast devotion. A man is probably not capable of it. At Robert's side, Sergeant Foster has one idea: himself. This is acceptable to Cissy, because his idea requires him to find Denny, and so he will. The surprised man is eager with the idea of the rock and the footprints, the glory of discovery; he's saying, 'It's close, it's just ahead.' The unsurprised man leans back in the saddle as he rides, holds the reins with one loose hand, and yawns at the prospect of finding the rock. If an idea presented itself to this man, he would swat it away.

This leaves the Aboriginal tracker. He rides a little way behind Cissy and she gets the sense that he's staying back to watch over her, that he's concerned about her horse. She turns to look at him and he dips his head in a way that might be a nod. His fur cloak looks hot. It looks like it would smell. There are flies at all their faces but it seems to Cissy that there are more at his. She can't begin to imagine what idea he might have and, finding this disconcerting, prefers not to think about it.

When they reach the rock, dismounting and approaching it on foot, it looks completely ordinary: just a low, flat rock about ten yards from Marsden's Creek. But apparently there really are footprints. The tracker says so, Foster agrees, and the tracks are right for a boy in boots, though not necessarily one who drags his leg when tired. The surprised man swaggers about as if no one had believed him, and the unsurprised man chews at his cheek, still bored. Foster and the tracker cross the dry creek and walk out to a bluff beyond it, where they talk and gesture. Out here, the plain begins to rise into the hills. Robert shifts on his horse and Cissy feels keenly that he's been outranked. When he looks at her, she turns her head away too quickly.

Now Foster is walking back, but the tracker stays by the cliff. 'There are some indications,' Foster says. 'I'd say he's headed north-east, probably into those hills.'

'The Druid Range,' says Robert.

Cissy feels that she should be elated by this news, but isn't. It seems unlikely that Denny was ever here, was ever headed for the Druid Range. It must seem unlikely to the surprised man, too, who says, 'I never saw footprints leading off.' It suits him, actually, this genuine surprise, and Cissy likes him better. But she can't believe that Denny was here, standing on this lifeless rock. Why would he travel this way, to this unremarkable spot? This was sheep country before the government broke it up; it's been set aside for wheat but no one's farmed it yet. The acacia are Denny-sized. The ants are busy in the saltbush. The Druid Range is currently in shadow, and it crouches under the sky like a long, mauve beast.

'But why?' says Cissy, and when all the men look at her she feels that she and the horse are the one same trivial being, they are clumsy steppers on the plain of consequence, and for this reason Cissy speaks louder, raises her chin, throws the fact of herself out, and asks, 'Why would Denny go to the hills when he knows our place is on the flat?'

'Higher ground?' offers Robert. 'A vantage point, to see the lie of the land?'

Foster mounts his horse. He says, 'This is a boy of five years.'

'Six,' says Cissy.

'There is no value in assuming he will make any kind of useful deduction, any kind of concerted plan. A child in his situation will behave erratically.'

'I thought they always walked in a straight line,' says Cissy. 'And my mother said he was going north-west.'

'He'll have got turned about in the storm,' says Robert. 'Happens to the best of us.'

Foster draws himself up in his saddle. He seems to wear a crown of flies. 'There are tracks,' he says, 'leading towards and away from this rock. There are scuff marks on the rock to suggest he spent some time here, possibly slept the night. My tracker and I will follow the trail and you, sir, and you'—he nods at the men from town—'will come with us in order to relay messages. Manning, you'll go back to the farm and call the other parties in—the complexion of the search will alter now. Keep on the men you think particularly competent. I need my other tracker out here, and Wooding, who I believe went due east with three men. There will be someone waiting at this spot an hour past sunrise tomorrow—unless, as is entirely possible, we have found the boy already. Assuming'—and now he turns to Cissy—'this is acceptable to all present.'

June steps sideways, stupidly. Cissy says, 'My father should be told.'

'He will be,' replies Foster, 'when he decides to make an appearance.'

Robert adjusts his cap. 'I daresay he'll be in tonight, when he's found no sign of Denny.'

'Somebody should go to him right away,' Cissy says. 'He went north-west. I'll go to him.'

Foster looks at her, then says, 'See to it, Manning, that there are no more children lost out here by end of day, or I'll hold you personally responsible. And help her manage that horse.' He and the other men move off.

Cissy, mortified, feels that her eyes are growing wet. She tilts her head back to conceal any tears and, as her weight shifts, June sets off in a jog. This might be useful of her, except that it's in the wrong direction. Cissy, yet again, attempts to correct her, but what has Cissy ever ridden, really, but old mares and every now and then a pony? Robert follows and takes June by the reins; he makes this seem easy, but Cissy sees the flex of muscle beneath his uniform. His horse stays steady and ignores June's nips.

'I've a bit that would do her good,' Robert says, when June is under control.

Cissy feels this as the kindest thing ever said. 'Well,' she says, and gestures north-west, 'I'll start this way.'

'Oh, now,' says Robert. He's still holding June's reins. 'Don't you want to go back and tell your ma about the tracks?'

'What can she do about it? My father needs to know.'

'I wager he'll be in tonight and you can tell him all there is.'

Cissy sits higher in the saddle. It's one thing to have decided to be in love with Robert Manning, and quite another to listen to what he has to say.

'It can't wait,' she says. 'I'll go to him directly.'

Robert lifts his cap and scratches at his head. 'How old are you?' he asks.

'Fifteen.' What has that to do with anything? I am a true Australian, Cissy thinks. I'm smart enough to be a teacher.

Robert settles his cap again. 'Wish I'd worn a hat,' he says. 'Today's a roaster. Listen, how's this? You come with me to your ma, and after that I'll go out looking for your dad myself.'

'You don't know where he is,' says Cissy.

'No more do you.'

'I know they're headed north-west. And they'll want to keep close to water.'

'For all we know,' says Robert, 'he's at your place already. And wouldn't you like to give your ma the news they've found a trail? Won't she be glad?'

Cissy concedes that Mam will be glad. But Cissy isn't interested, right now, in Mam's gladness, which will make no difference to Denny. Telling Dad that he's looking in the wrong place feels much more urgent. The only thing worse than *not doing* is *doing incorrectly*. But Cissy's reluctant—she would never admit this to Robert, or anyone else—the truth is, she's reluctant to set out alone on a skittish horse to find her father. She wants more water with her, and more food. She wants Constable Robert Manning with her.

'So,' he says, 'we'll go back to your place, you'll see your ma, and I'll head straight off to find your father.'

Cissy says, 'I'm coming with you.'

Robert laughs. 'All right then, we'll go together.'

Cissy makes him promise, though she can see he doesn't mean it. Then she takes June's reins back, and they set out for Undelcarra.

⁂

Bear Axam is a gossip. His mother recognised this early and tried to train him out of his instinct for discussing the lives of his friends and neighbours, which comes from his desire to be liked and his fear that he won't be; 'nobody likes a telltale,' Joanna would say, from her great height, to little round Bear. Nevertheless, the adult Bear often finds himself caught in corners, pressed for tidbits, and asked for opinions on the behaviour of others. And he *is* liked. He's widely considered good-natured—if being affable and well intentioned is to be good-natured. Bear has been blessed by the gift of contentment. As he goes about Thalassa in dusty boots, he doesn't long for Adelaide and its clubs; as he plays cards in Adelaide, he doesn't dream of Thalassa and its freedoms. Since his marriage, he's only visited Fairly's

German prostitute, Inge Schmidt, three times. He brings treats for her donkey.

So the consultation with Beller was a disguise for his actual desire, which is to be at the Wallace house and see everything for himself: he has a true gossip's need to be eyewitness. He believes that if it weren't for the shearing, he'd be searching for the boy; driving towards Undelcarra, he imagined several versions of a triumphant scene in which he arrived at the Wallace farm carrying the rescued child, much to Minna's admiration. Now he and his mother are sitting at a table on the verandah of the Wallace cottage, which huddles against the ground in the tended, inevitable manner of a vegetable. The house is full of women, all of whom have greeted, and then hidden from, his mother. Minna sits across the table from him, smiling from her shaded seat, radiant with the virtue of having donated the remains of her wedding feast. A girl pours tea—a Wallace daughter, presumably. Bear presses his whip against his foot. The trouble with a crisis is that ordinary conversation seems inadequate, possibly even insulting, and Bear has no other kind. His mother knows what to say and is saying it to Mrs Wallace, who looks as if someone has tied her down to her narrow chair. Despite her height, she gives the impression of someone whose feet don't reach the floor. The Wallaces' dog sniffs experimentally at Bolingbroke's arse, and Bolingbroke ignores it.

Minna speculates aloud on the direction in which her husband went and taps one foot against the table in a way that moves even the hair against her forehead. She's in a hopeless fug of longing. Bear recognises this state because he's felt this way about his own wife, who can be cold or shy or just resigned, but also sometimes pliant, warm and very, very sweet. After a bit of time with the tea he suggests walking with Minna a short way to watch for Constable Manning, a proposal of which his mother clearly disapproves; but allowances must be made for the fact that Minna is now a married woman, and can therefore be alone with a married man. He offers his arm, Minna takes it, and Joanna is left on the verandah with Mrs Wallace, who anyone can see is too exhausted to speak. When Bear looks back one last time at the table, his mother lifts her chin at him. His theory, shared with his wife, is that his mother expects too much of him because he looks exactly like his father; his actual fear, shared with no one, is that she simply finds him ridiculous.

Minna was beautiful on her wedding day. Bear believes all brides are beautiful; if pressed, he would admit to finding himself beautiful at his own wedding. But Minna is even lovelier now, out here at Wallace's. There's something blurred about her, as if a painter has slipped with his brush and found a new effect. Bear is quite proud of himself for thinking something so poetic, and would like, if given the opportunity, to repeat it to Rapp, who paints just that sort of blurry picture. Bear leads Minna across one corner of the Wallace yard; in the other, a cow and goat stand in unusual communion. The animals look out at Bear from lowered lids. Because they require nothing from him, not food or water, not pity or affection, he feels judged by them. He's happy to open the gate and usher Minna through it, although this means she's no longer holding his arm. He offers chat—'Watch your step, Mrs Manning,' and, 'Thank heavens for a clear day,' and, 'Those are handsome horses'—but Minna is distracted and only produces short responses accompanied, sometimes, by smiles.

The further they walk from the house, the fewer edges Minna seems to have. There are no fences after the yard, and the wheat stands thin and green in the unmarked fields. It might be grass.

'Wallace's crop looks a little backward,' Bear says.

'Does it?' says Minna, who plainly doesn't care.

'He needs a good rain. Once the boy is found, of course.'

Minna says, 'Of course,' and Bear feels the panic of finding something to say that will win her true attention.

'I'm part German, you know,' he says.

'Is that so?' Minna looks out over the plain. 'Which part?'

Now Bear feels exactly like a schoolboy: his most terrifying master has just rapped him across the knuckles and said, 'Axam will never have Latin, but then, Axam will never need it.'

'Which part? Oh. Well. Oh,' stammers Bear, and Minna turns to look now, her face blank, her gaze level, her expression not unlike those of the goat and cow in the paddock. 'My great-grandmother,' he says. 'On my mother's side.'

Minna is still looking at him, now with an indifferent smile. It's quite devastating to Bear, although he's often the recipient of smiles like this one. What did I expect, when I am merely me? thinks Bear—thinks Ralph Axam, who objects to the use of his childhood nickname (his mother excepted) but in his own secret heart refers to himself by it. Minna walks out into the wheat. This distresses Bear—if it were his wheat, he wouldn't want Minna crushing it. Nevertheless, he follows. The wheat is so green—unnaturally so in this dusty place, where green is usually muted; it's quite obscene, and Minna is ravishing and edgeless in it, shaded under a wide hat. Bear's wife often complains that he never notices what hat she's wearing, but the hat she's wearing, Bear protests, never notices *him*.

'My parents were and are German,' says Minna, and these two tenses make her parents seem like deities, who *were* and *are* and *always will be*, 'and it doesn't matter, it makes not one bit of difference to anything.'

'How can it make no difference?' he asks her.

'Once you're married,' Minna says, 'you're reborn.'

Bear laughs at this.

'I suppose,' she adds, with rueful sympathy, 'it's not that way for everyone.'

'Who is it that way for, then?'

'All women, certainly.'

'Because women take their husband's name?'

'That's the least of it.'

Bear is on precarious ground; this is not an ordinary conversation. He has never felt himself entirely born, let alone reborn, and he entered into his own marriage with expectations of a domestic bliss that would require absolutely no change in his outlook, habits or behaviour. Now, he decides that the best strategy to take with Minna is a sort of fond worldliness. He says, 'How long have you been married?'

'You think I'm silly.'

Conviction always sounds silly to Bear, possibly because he hasn't any; he's unsettled by evangelists of any kind. He shakes his head. He feels much older than she is, much more wise, and would like to both shock and impress her. He smiles and says, 'You may not always feel this way.'

'Which way?' asks Minna.

'You may find,' he begins. And stops. 'You may find, well, that you don't feel at every moment as you did on the day of your wedding, or the days immediately following. So giddy, I mean.' Her face doesn't change. 'What I mean is, that's quite natural. You mustn't—well, rebuke yourself.'

'Of course it's natural,' says Minna, and clearly means it; her voice is a little shrug. It's as if he's offered her a sip of sherry and she's produced a cup, already full, of her own much stronger liquor, and is now drinking it down in front of him.

So Bear must draw on something else, some larger claim that will surprise her, and he thinks of an extraordinary night he spent with his brother and Karl Rapp. They'd been drinking in George's office, and Bear had been trying to goad Rapp into spouting the sort of ideas you'd expect from an artist: free love, universal pity, beauty, truth, and so forth. Rapp sat drinking, smoking, his face and hair reflecting the red-gold colour of the fire (in the weirdest way, like some sort of devil), and very smug—Bear dislikes good-looking men unless they seem either completely unselfconscious or appropriately apologetic—and all Rapp would talk about, and for a bloody long time, was the damn sunset.

Finally, though, the talk turned to the subject of wives. Bear always likes to know how people came to meet their spouses, especially when a match involves a discrepancy of any kind: in this case, Mrs Rapp seems such a blessedly unremarkable sort of person for a man like Rapp to have married (though, thinks generous Bear, she does have a fine complexion, like most English girls). But having raised—tactfully, he thought—the question of unlikely unions, Bear found himself listening with astonishment while his brother laid bare his own marriage as if Ellen weren't sleeping forty feet away. George spoke for a good ten minutes: at first about ordinary complaints (dress bills and petty servant squabbles), but then the torture of an attractive wife, of being away from her for weeks, of intercepting looks and making guesses, of never knowing but suspecting—all this while drinking, smoking, his voice rising and falling while Rapp nodded at him, his eyes all liquid pity, inviting confidences by saying nothing, until finally Bear's loyalty, his embarrassment for his brother, overcame his natural curiosity and he said, 'For God's sake, George.' And the spell was broken. A brief silence, followed by a minute or two of urgent talk about a troublesome heifer, until Bear yawned and stretched to indicate that it was time to sleep.

Then, just before retiring—to the arms, presumably, of his mousy wife—Rapp turned in the doorway (not at all well dressed, and yet everything he wore seemed to fall lovingly on his body, whereas Bear and even his finest clothes have always been engaged in constant negotiation) and said, 'Here's what I think, if you would like to hear it: love contracts a man and it expands a woman. When you, a man, fall in love with a woman, you see it as an end of possibility. When a woman falls in love with you, she also falls in love with every other man there is. And you must let her. Because when it starts, she sees you in every one of them, but if you stop her, she'll only see the part of them that isn't you.'

'You can't mean,' said George, 'that you allow your wife to be unfaithful?'

'My friend, you haven't understood me,' said Rapp, laughing. And off he went to bed.

Can Bear say all this to Minna Baumann? Or does it require a European accent and an artistic reputation? Minna is still standing in the self-sufficiency of having said, 'Of course it's natural.'

'Love,' says Bear, and clears his throat—just the word 'love' has a promising effect; Minna is looking at him properly now—'love contracts a man and expands a woman.'

Minna's smile becomes more private. 'Mr Rapp said something much the same,' she says. 'He said that when women fall in love with one man, it's with all men.'

Bear, looking for something to do with his hands, removes his hat; then he thinks of the sticky band of red the hat will have pressed into his brow, and returns it to his head. Of course Rapp has been spreading his gospel far and wide, and of course—the devil—he got to Minna first.

'What on earth can he mean by it?' Minna wonders, turning away to look across the plain, one hand held up to shade her eyes, although her hat seems adequate to the task; her hat, he thinks—disloyally—looks like a jellyfish run over by a train.

Bear, too, has been thinking over what Rapp could possibly mean when he says that women fall in love with all men. 'It's something like,' he says, and clears his throat again, 'looking at a mountain and thinking of God.'

'But why of God?'

'I mean a real, European mountain with snow on it, a snowy peak. You look at it with admiration and you think: God is the author of all things, including this mountain.'

'But you don't worship the mountain,' says Minna. 'You worship God.'

'Precisely,' says Bear, who fears that the analogy has got away from him. And also, he senses something behind him, something coming towards him through the wheat—fast and low and invisible; he doesn't know what it is, just that its purpose is Bear, its intent is all Bear, it has no knowledge or desire outside of Bear, and before he has time to turn and see what it is, what fury or demon has been sent after him, it's against his back and on his shoulders. He can't help but stumble forwards and throw out his hands, and Minna can't help but take his arm to steady him.

The thing at his shoulders breathes and shoves and licks, and he realises that it's Bolingbroke, suddenly active, suddenly playful, like one of those grandfathers you hear of who in their dotage begin to sing the bawdy songs of their youth. Minna is laughing, and all Bear can do as he tries, frantically, not to be pushed by Boley into the wheat, is take hold of her hat, so that he drags it from her head and she cries out. Then, in one glorious manoeuvre, he turns, takes Boley by the front paws, and calms him into a crouch. Minna, regrettably, observes none of this; she's holding one hand to the side of her head, and when she brings the hand down to inspect it, it's clear that there's blood on her fingers and in her hair. She looks at Bear and says, 'I think my hatpin has scratched me. It's come loose from its cap.'

Then comes the flourishing of Bear's handkerchief, Minna's acceptance of the handkerchief, a dabbing of the head and a wiping of hands. While this happens, Bear sees that he might reach out and touch the triangle of skin behind Minna's left ear, as if the blood has travelled there. He does, and Minna is so soft that Bear realises, not for the first time (though it feels like the first time), that soon he'll have a child; that he'll be a father, despite being merely Bear. They step away from each other. Minna offers Bear his handkerchief, on which there is some blood (it's remarkable, he thinks, how much blood can be produced by one trivial scratch); he indicates that she should keep it. Minna fusses with her hair, replaces her hat, adjusts it so that there's no sign of any disturbance, and slides in the pin. Boley inserts himself between Bear's legs.

'Such a beautiful dog,' says Minna. 'Does he belong to you?'

'No,' says Bear. 'To my mother.'

There's nothing then but to take her arm and walk without speaking back to the house.

---

In the early afternoon, one of Mary's telegrams finds its recipient: her father, Samuel Deniston, the Southern Shepherd. He sits in his study in Goolwa, three hundred miles south of Fairly, writing a strongly worded letter about the proposed steam railway that will connect his district to Adelaide; it's so strongly worded that, by the time his wife comes into the study to give him the telegram, he's short of breath and feels a feverish buzz in his temples. When he sees her in the doorway, he throws down his pen and says, 'Well, Muriel, Bayliss is dead.'

His wife, who tends towards the imperturbable, hands him the telegram.

'Mary's boy is missing,' he says, reading it. 'The younger one.'

His wife, Mary's stepmother, who has already read the telegram, answers, 'Poor lamb.' Then she looks at what Samuel's been writing and says, 'You'll tire yourself.'

He adjusts the woollen blanket on his lap. Here he is, the Southern Shepherd: this courageous figure, who brought his flock to South Australia, who sang and starved alongside them, preached to them and prayed for them; this tyrant, loved and loving, walking bruised and barefoot through the Promised Land, whose strength and whose sacrifice overwhelmed them all. He's got old. What little hair remains to him floats about his head in a gauzy white halo. He's always cold, keeps a vigilant watch on his bowel movements, and, having the sense that the world has begun to move too quickly, would prefer to hear no more than one new piece of information a day. He's already had news about the railway today, so the arrival of this telegram would agitate him no matter its message—and this message is so distressing.

And yet. Samuel's position on his daughter is that she, by going into the north country with her husband, must accept everything that follows, including a lost child: good or bad, commit it to the Lord. He's lived so long by this doctrine of God's sovereignty that it brings him genuine comfort, and he expects it to do the same for Mary. Nevertheless, he grieves for her, and worries for the boy, whom he has never met; he'll put aside all thoughts of Bayliss's steam railway and dedicate himself solely to considering his response to Mary's telegram. Why has she sent it? She's never sent a telegram before. She must need something from him, although the message contains no request. Does she want money? She's never asked for money. He looks out the window at the river and sees a barge sliding past, on which two men are fighting. It's hard to tell if they're playing or not. Mary won't want money; she must want prayer. He will pray for Mary and the lost boy now, and also this evening and when he wakes in the morning, and every morning and evening until he has more news, and will send Mary a letter to tell her so. She knows the true value of prayer. He takes a new piece of paper and begins the letter.

'I'll have this ready for this afternoon's post, my dear,' he says.

'Aye,' says his wife, and leaves the room.

As Samuel writes to Mary, he reflects that he's already corresponded with her this year: a letter on New Year's Day, as always; at Easter; and on his birthday. Age hasn't affected his memory, and he enjoys writing the names of his grandchildren in the order of their birth: Joseph, Joy, Cecily, Ada, Noella, Deniston and Charlotte. He's only met the two eldest. He's never been to the town of Fairly, and as he writes the letter it occurs to him that Mary might have sent the telegram because she wants to see him—she wants him to travel to the Flinders Ranges. He considers the possibility of going to see his daughter. He knows that there's a steam railway straight from Port Augusta to Fairly—he knows all about this railway, how many men are at work further north to extend it to Government Gums, exactly what rate the line is worked at and what the profit would be if the Goolwa railway were worked at the same rate. He's firmly opposed to the Goolwa railway. But if there were such a thing, he thinks, he could conceive of travelling to Adelaide, from Adelaide to Port Augusta, and from Port Augusta to Fairly, all by train. As it is, he's too old and unwell to make the journey. Just the thought of a carriage to Adelaide stiffens his bones.

As Samuel writes, telling Mary that he will hold her in his prayers—and he will, dearly; prayer is serious with him, he's both generous and disciplined with it—he imagines her standing in a neat room, surrounded by her children. The room has blue walls. All the children have light eyes and brown hair, just as little Mary did, and they gather around her like cherubs at the Virgin's knee (an image he dismisses promptly as too High Church). The buzz in Samuel's temples clears. The Lord didn't bless him with offspring from his second wife, so Mary is his only surviving child. For a moment, his longing to comfort her and meet her young ones leaves him breathless. Well, why not go? And if it kills him, it's the Lord's will. He's finished the letter, but he no longer needs it—instead, he'll send a telegram to say he's starting immediately for the north.

Samuel calls for his wife, who opens his study door.

'I shall travel,' he says, 'to Fairly. Book me a ticket on tomorrow's coach to Adelaide.'

'Are you quite sure?' asks Muriel, solicitous as ever, but obviously approving; he knows her to have a childless woman's reverence for family.

Samuel hears a male voice resounding in the front parlour. 'Who's come, Muriel?' he asks.

'Mr Bayliss.'

'Bayliss!' cries Samuel, standing; the woollen blanket falls to his feet. His wife kneels down to retrieve it.

Samuel is delighted at the thought of another debate with Bayliss, who would happily run a railway through his own mother's dining room. Bayliss is laughing with the maid in the parlour. There's a smell in the hall of beef and pastry. Outside on the river, the men who were fighting on the barge shout merrily at one another; gulls answer them. Samuel can no longer see Mary's blue room or the light eyes of his unknown grandchildren. Instead, he feels the tug of the wide, green river. A pelican struts among the bankside rushes, dressed as a clergyman. Bayliss guffaws and the buzz returns to Samuel's temples.

Samuel gives his wife the letter for Mary—the one that promises to pray for her, but doesn't mention making the journey north. 'Address this for me, will you, my dear, and have Jenny send it straight out with the post.'

Muriel Deniston looks over the letter. 'No ticket, then?' she asks.

But Samuel is barely listening. He runs his spread hand down his beard, squares his shoulders, and turns his face towards the sound of Bayliss laughing in the parlour.

---

Karl sits in the afternoon sun by the waterhole writing a letter to his friend Alström, who is also a painter. He's shirtless and shoeless and can feel his skin burning, but that's as it should be: he wants the sun to hurt him. It has claimed him, after all. Soon the gorge will be in shadow. The red gums around the waterhole are motionless, and so is the water; but every now and then, the surface of the pool makes a slight movement, as if something is stirring slowly far beneath it.

Karl doesn't know why he continues to write to Alström, who, on learning that Karl was emigrating to Australia, sent a letter saying, 'My dear Kalle, there is, for us, no meaning to any artistic achievement that doesn't grow from the soil of Sweden.'

More recently, Alström has achieved considerable success with new work inspired by the Norwegian coastline.

Karl writes: 'The sunset picture feels fated—what else could have brought me here to witness this sky? I have, until now, been scornful of painting sunsets—even the stupidest person finds them beautiful. But these are no ordinary sunsets. You won't understand me—you can't conceive of these skies without seeing them. Turner and Constable would be stiff with delight. Why, do you suppose, have the English specialised in sunsets, while we Swedes stick to pastel clouds and trembling aspens? We share their northern sun, don't we? This southern sun, however, is a different star—I'm sure of it. There's no way to describe these skies in words. If I had to try, I would say that they are light shipwrecked by dark.'

Would 'light capsized by dark' be better? Lord God, thinks Karl, what am I talking about?

'So, I have set myself quite a task. I'll admit I have resisted the project. I'm reminded of the prophet Jonah, who fled God's summons and was swallowed by the whale. The sky is my summons, the picture is my whale. Yes, I've struggled, but I've been swallowed, and the sky and I must come to an arrangement.'

Must we? wonders Karl, peering up at the sun. What does it matter? If he does manage to paint the sky, Alström will almost certainly never see the picture. He could say anything in this letter. Karl looks over at Bess, who's deep inside her room, working in charcoal. Bess, if she had been summoned by the sky (and she would never call it 'summoned'), would decide immediately on form and colour, take up a pencil and brush, and get to work. Her picture would be excellent, and, most importantly, it would be finished. But would it be the truth? Can Bess see the sky from inside her room? There must be, thinks Karl—as he has thought before—some way for an artist to live that is both housed, as Bess is, and out of doors, which seems to be his fate. This is the sort of thing he and Alström would once have discussed while deep in their *snaps* at the Freden. Karl returns to his letter.

'The picture, as I see it, will be square and exactly the length of my arm. I want a high horizon, a tilted plane for the ground, and a dwarfed figure over which the sky broods. The sky, you understand, will be allowed the smallest part of the picture—but it will dominate the scene, so that every contour, every mood and aspect of the ground and vegetation is altered by its rays.'

No—the sun produces rays, not the sky.

'Is altered by its searing glare. This dusk will be brighter than noon. The reds here are simply unimaginable, dumbfounding, the purest I have seen, as if fire itself has caught fire. Not to mention the deep purples, which are almost poisonous—when the sky turns red, the hills look bruised. I seem to be describing hell. But how to explain that, rather than infernal, the whole scene is sublime?'

Karl remembers that sublimity is going out of fashion.

'In truth, there is no sign of God in this red immensity; nor is there any sign of humanity, and yet I have never felt more like a man. Perhaps it is perverse to add—I am quite sure you won't understand me—that I have never felt more like a Swede. We Swedes are, after all, barbarians, and this is barbarian country. It is truly primitive.'

Karl doesn't think he believes any of this. He's also worried that he may have gone too far, so he writes, 'I would need to stay rooted to this spot for three years to paint anything worth looking at.'

He reads over the letter and a picture does begin to form in his mind. Oh, why not—he could at least make a sketch or two in pencil. He often has to trick himself into working. All right, here's the high horizon—here, the tilted ground. So, look, the plain rises to meet the lower slopes of the ranges—but be sure to show that the ranges are the stubs of mountains, the shoulders of mountains, they're so worn down. Exhausted by the sun. The rhythm here is horizontal—fallen mountains, fallen trees. Long lines—like this. Only the sky is vertical. The sun lifts it. A low horizon, then? No, he likes the idea of a small sky that nevertheless crowds everything else—it feels true. How else to express the feeling of standing on this empty country, knowing how big it is because you've travelled weeks from the sea and haven't yet reached the centre? (God, what he wouldn't give to paint—or eat—a fleshy little oyster!) And then this sky comes along and flattens you, overwhelms you, but without ever making the country shrink. The sky pulls the land up to it. It *involves* the land. How to get this feeling out and onto paper?

He begins another sketch. The horizon is more emphatic in this one, and a sentence occurs to him: 'The horizon participates.' He makes a note to ask Bess, later, if English has more than one word for horizon, as Swedish does—there's the simpler '*horisont*' and then the larger word, '*synranden*', which implies the act of looking, the very edge of seeing. Similarly important: the sun doesn't set in Swedish, it walks down. So much more activity in his first language: seeing, walking! Ah, the continual flawed translation of the world. The horizon *participates*. In what? He's close to something. Felled trees. An empty riverbed, with no beginning or end, mirror to the horizon. And what about the figure he mentioned, the dwarfed figure? A struggling figure, like this? Or is the struggle over? Or is there no struggle at all, but a unity between the figure and this bright red world? The sun sinking, holy, over the ruins of nature. The holy sun burning the cathedral of nature.

Karl throws down his pencil and, knowing that Bess will be irritated by the theatricality of this, picks it up again (he does look to see if Bess has noticed but, as always, she's busy with her own work). He's dismayed by how quickly this new picture of his has turned into an idea. That's all his friends talk about—ideas. All their paintings are ideas: what is Sweden, what is art, what is man, what is woman, what is nobility, what is nature, what is the life force? They call a painting of a winter field *Solitude*; Karl would call it *Winter Field*. He wants to do what comes easily to him, which is to be a body encountering the world. He wants sensory experience first, then emotion, then intellect (actually, that's quite good, quite lucid—he'll write it down). He wants a painting of a field under snow to feel like a field under snow. He wants a painting of the molten sun to burn. Why does he care what his Swedish friends think? To hell with Alström and his Norwegian coastline.

Karl begins a third sketch. The same forceful horizon, the same dry river. The dull teeth of the ranges. This should be simple, almost medieval. The picture's form begins to take shape: pines to the left, an ancient forest, which draws away from the figure in the right foreground. No, remove the figure, substitute with one of those huge skeletal trees—the viewer can't delegate the act of looking to a figure. The viewer is the figure; he participates in the picture, in the horizon. The viewer looks, the sun walks. The tree should seem to be burning (it won't be burning). And the sky is unbearable. Yes, that's it—I'll paint a sunset so awful and so beautiful that no one can bear to either look at it or look away. Is this possible? It all depends on the red.

Yes, the red! You have, thinks Karl, made your old mistake of beginning with form when you should begin with colour and with tones. Let the land provide the form: perhaps he'll find it in the vista they've been promised further north, the famed Wilpena Pound (he and Bess will have to find another name for it). He needs Wilpena Pound. It's too late to leave this camp today, but he'll have them up early and on the move tomorrow. Karl is trembling. The urgency of Wilpena! Meanwhile, he'll think in red. He'll consider the emotion of the picture—its occasion. He makes a note: 'both claimed and exiled'. He's not sure what that means, but it feels important. This is only a beginning, but he's on his way. He understands that this picture is the one that counts. It's the beautiful vessel he's been waiting for, into which to pour his true skill and feeling.

A big red ant, slightly translucent, hurries across Karl's sketch and he brings his fist down fast to squash it. Now the ant is a sunset. This feels auspicious: maybe he *has* reached an arrangement with the sky. He looks up at Bess, who's deep inside her room, working, working, and feels a tug of doubt. The picture will require a lot of him. Is he prepared for it? Yes, he's almost certainly prepared. He's willing to give up anything and everything for this picture—he'll give up Sweden, youth, happiness. He'll give up other women, which means that the pretty German girl, Minna, will have been his last kiss from a woman who isn't Bess. He'll give up anything at all, as long as he gets to have this picture. It will make him brave enough to face his own talent, which others have frequently described as so immense, so full of potential, as to be startling. Do you hear me, sky? That's our arrangement. I'll visit you this evening, I'll let myself participate as the sun walks down, and tomorrow you can take me to Wilpena.

Bess's dark head is bent over her drawing. He won't give her up. But that's all right—she's on the side of the sky. She brought him here, after all. She wants him working, and she makes work possible.

Karl is suddenly extremely hungry. He calls out to Bess—he has to call twice before she raises her head. She peers at him as if waking from a deep sleep.

'What is there to eat?' he asks.

'Yes,' Bess says, and puts her work aside.

Once Minna and the Axams have left Undelcarra, Joy goes out to hoe the northern wheatfield, over which she has been given responsibility. Ada and Noella have been sent to school in clean Monday pinafores. Lotta, who isn't old enough for school, is sorting her collection of bird feathers into coloured piles. Cissy, who always has to be involved in everything, has gone out searching with the men. This leaves the wheat to slow, lazy Joy.

Joy isn't slow or lazy—not really. She's full of subterfuge, but it's not malicious; only self-interested. She intends to endure. Joy's heard herself compared to a cow, but she thinks of a bull instead: her size, her strength. At night, when she dreams of sex, she rides on top. She cultivates her languor, which by now she's been forgiven; it's a way to conserve strength. Other girls her age have been sent out to work, but she's kept home to help Mam because—she knows this—no employer could be satisfied with her, unless all they needed was heavy things moved from one place to another, and not too many of those. As it is, Cissy is the biggest help to Mam, and she still goes to school. Cissy is rather old, in Joy's opinion, to be wasting her time on something as unnecessary as school, but Mam had a lot of schooling and wants that for her girls, where possible. What use will it do her, thinks Joy, when six months from now Cissy will be a maid at a hotel in Quorn, or housekeeping for some scabby farmer with wandering hands?

Joy is saving her strength for the man she'll marry and the children she'll bear. She can already feel herself carrying child after child. She wants a husband with nothing, so that she can make something for him. She'll look ridiculous in a wedding dress with ruffles and buttons and satin bows—it doesn't matter. They'll leave the church on foot if need be, walk out into the bush; she'll take her dress off to make a tent, they'll sleep beneath it while they build a house. She'll use the satin bows for bandages. The worst thing had been childhood—that was needless. Now she's ready.

None of the men in Fairly is fit for what she has in mind. She's interested in the solitary men who come and go, the hawkers with their carts full, the swagmen who trim their beards with lighted sticks, the shearers, the railway men, the workers on the Telegraph. She's interested in what Sergeant Foster would have been thirty years ago: ambitious, ready, but unfixed. She could, if necessary, have picked up the chair with Foster in it and carried him into the ranges. It wasn't necessary. She was practising on him because she saw how he appreciated her bulk.

Joy is casual about working the wheat. She runs the hoe over the top of the soil so that it looks disturbed. She pulls some of the larger weeds by hand; others she buries with the toe of her boot. She's connected only lightly to this land and will leave it soon enough; when she has land of her own, however, she'll break her back for it. If Denny were her child, she'd walk the Earth for him. Let Cissy finish school and be the one to play at mother's helper—Joy was made large for the large world.

When she finds a bloodied handkerchief in one corner of the field, Joy doesn't think of Ralph Axam and Minna out here two hours earlier: she thinks of Denny. She thinks, too, that the handkerchief is an excuse to stop hoeing and go back to the house. Only incidentally, while walking, does she look for a monogram; she doesn't find one. When she's close to the house, it occurs to her that another girl might be made squeamish by the blood, so she pinches one corner of the handkerchief and holds it away from her body. This is how she's first seen, carrying the handkerchief—by Lotta, who for some reason has abandoned her feathers and is squatting tearful in the garden.

Inside, the women fall on Joy—what've you done, are you hurt, what's this, what's all this? And then, where did you find it? Whose is it? They look for the monogram that isn't there.

They look at the quality of the linen and feel for the amount of starch, then conclude that it's a man's handkerchief. What's more, a gentleman's. Someone raises the possibility of Joanna Axam's boy, who walked in that direction with Minna Baumann earlier today, but Joy hasn't told the entire truth about where she made her discovery: she shouldn't have reached the corner in which she found the handkerchief as quickly as she did, so she's said she found it deeper in the wheat, where Ralph Axam would never have been.

The women are full of speculation, much of it delivered in low voices with their hands held up to their mouths so that Mam won't hear or be able to read their lips. One woman says, 'There's not so much blood, not really,' and another, 'I'd say it's a child's.' Joy doesn't see how it's possible to tell. Mam touches the handkerchief where someone has laid it out on the table; then she goes to the door and stands there so that Lotta knows to come inside. Lotta comes and Mary picks her up. Lotta's bare feet catch at Mary's skirt so that Mam's red flannel petticoat shows. Because of the handkerchief, the red of the petticoat feels shocking in the room—as if all instances of the colour red are further proof of something. Of what? Nobody will say, exactly. Mopsy cowers in her basket. Lotta's sweaty face looks pleased above Mam's shoulder; she wrinkles her nose at Joy, who feels chastened for bringing bad news home. But at least nobody expects her to go back out with the hoe.

⸻

After almost an entire day of searching, Mathew and Billy have picked up the trail they saw yesterday evening, then lost again: the tracks of the booted man and his lame horse, which were trampled by the cattle coming down to the dam to drink. Mathew, more sensible than he was yesterday, has conceded that the footprints belong to a man, but he persists in thinking that Denny made the cut on the tree. He's formed a theory—an awful one: Denny is with the man, but he's left no tracks because he's been put on the horse. Mathew is reluctant to share this theory with Billy, as if saying it aloud will make it true.

As soon as they start following the trail, it's clear—even to Mathew—that it makes no sense. The tracks take the most difficult path over rocky outcrops, loop back on themselves, swerve unexpectedly, and pause to make strange scuffling dances. After an hour of this, Mathew halts Bonfire, spits in disgust, and says, 'Whoever we're following is thick as two bricks.'

Billy, stopping Virnu, shakes his head in agreement.

Mathew says, 'It's a madman we're after.'

'Could be.'

'Is it blackfellow business?'

Billy's face registers the unlikelihood of this. He asks, 'You want to keep on?'

Mathew fears that he's reached one of those crucial points at which he'll make the wrong choice. He looks back along the route they've come, and then ahead. The tracks are leading them towards the western edge of the plain, where the striped ranges rise in overlapping saw-toothed ridges. It's a scorching afternoon—his wheat will be drying out. You would assume, looking across the plain, that not even the smallest soul could get himself lost on it: it appears flat from east to west, with only a scattering of hillocks. The scrub is low, the few trees are thin.

But the plain is pleated with furrows and channels where water's had its devious way, and Denny could be hidden in any of them. Also, a haze rises from the hot, flat earth, and looks sometimes like smoke, sometimes like an expansive lake; it drowns distance. The fens were like this too—deceptively flat and good for hiding in. But much wetter. Mathew wants water for his crops, but he's grateful to be looking for Denny in the dry. On every side, the ranges pile against the sky, red in sun and purple in shadow.

'We'll give it another hour,' says Mathew. Another precious hour of wasted time, if he's made the wrong decision.

They go on without speaking—Billy ahead and Mathew behind, crackling through the saltbush. The trail keeps on with its tricks, but Mathew can't bring himself to give it up, even when they've gone longer than an hour. Then Virnu stops abruptly. Billy dismounts, inspects something, points. There, beside a witchetty bush covered in scratchy yellow flowers, sits a pair of boots. Mathew dismounts to see for himself, and yes, they are, they're Denny's boots, with the laces missing.

Mathew is reminded of an early morning in his childhood when a man came to the door with the news that Mathew's father, drunk, had fallen into a dyke and drowned. Little Mathew wondered: if no one had been home to hear the man's news, would that mean his father hadn't fallen into the dyke? Adult Mathew would like not to be at home to the news that Denny's boots are sitting empty beside a witchetty bush in the middle of the Willochra Plain. They've been set down tidily, just as at night they're always lined up beside the bed Denny shares with Ada and Noella.

'Why would he take his boots off?' Mathew says, thinking that without his boots, Denny seems—if this is possible—substantially more defenceless.

'Could be they hurt his feet,' says Billy. They both know Denny hates wearing boots. Mathew is sympathetic to this, but shoes are one of the many minor battles he has ceded in his marriage: genteel Mary believes children should always wear them.

Mathew runs a finger over the empty eyelets of one boot. 'He can't manage the knots on his own. Can he manage the knots?'

Billy shakes his head.

'No,' Mathew agrees. 'But he has his knife. He's cut the laces out.'

Or, Mathew thinks, someone else has untied them for him, then taken them for some reason, and left the boots here. What would make them decide that Denny wouldn't be needing anything on his feet? To mask his rising panic, Mathew squats close to the boots. An ant explores the left one's tongue. He had them resoled last year and really they're in fair condition.

'The tracks keep on,' Billy says.

'And we'll follow.' Mathew picks up Denny's boots, shakes them free of ants, and stows them in his saddlebag. It's better when they're out of sight. In the saddlebag, they can't conjure quite so readily the exact size of Denny's feet.

From this point, the trail leaves off its meandering: it heads with purpose towards the western ranges. Mathew would like to move faster, and he'd like to be out ahead, but Billy is much better at following the tracks, so Billy sets the pace. Mathew dislikes this—it makes him feel as if Billy's colluding with the man they're trailing. What kind of man snatches a child, puts him on a horse, and leads him into the ranges? Discarding his boots, but keeping the laces? What kind of man allows that to happen to his son?

On the western edge of the plain, the ground begins to rise and the native pines to thicken. Billy and Mathew pass beneath she-oaks threaded with orange mistletoe and the seamed webs of orb spiders; a wind starts up and, blowing through the she-oaks, it sounds like the sea coming down off the ranges. The men ride in the shadow of the western cliffs. Rocks scatter underfoot, grey and plum and dun. They join a creek that's cut its way through a gap in a cliff—the trail follows the creek, and Billy and Mathew follow the trail. It leads them into the long, narrow valley that separates the first ridge of hills from the second. They're in the roots of the ranges now, and the plain is hidden from them—Mathew thinks of a heavy stone rolling and unrolling from the entrance to an ancient tomb. They're inside the tomb, and the stone has been rolled across the entrance. The sky above the valley is narrow and far. The tracks keep on beneath the valley walls, which ripple with their stripes of green, grey, red and white, like the flank of some ludicrous animal. Deep inside the tomb, Mathew starts calling Denny's name, and Billy joins him.

Further down the valley, they find a waterhole with one straight white gum growing out of it. There's some light left in the day, but the horses are exhausted, so Mathew agrees to stop. The water's low, but it's fresh and cold.

'What range is this?' he asks, looking at the broad cliffs rising above them. 'The Axam Range?'

'Yep,' says Billy.

Because they're looking up at the hills, they both see the smudge of smoke that begins to rise from a high, pale bluff: someone, presumably the man they're following, has just lit a campfire in the Axam Range. Seeing the smoke, Mathew understands that finding Denny is going to mean climbing into the hills. Mathew's body doesn't know hills. It knows flat land, wet land, and the black-frost wind coming straight from Russia over the fens.

'The very devil,' he says, but he feels a thrill run through him. There's a swarming in his limbs—he's ready to climb, fight, uproot trees, tear down mountains. 'Right then,' he says. 'All right. We'll have to leave the horses.'

Mathew tethers Bonfire, all the while shifting from foot to foot. He reaches up to scratch Bonfire's withers and says, 'We've got him now, girl.' They'll find Denny tonight and Mathew will have him home by early morning. And after that: the Shires, the carting, the mortgage, the wheat, and Mary will be pleased with him. He already sees Denny at the table: eating with his mouth open, trying to keep his elbows by his sides, and giggling when he hears his father burp.

When he steps away from Bonfire, Mathew sees that Billy hasn't tethered Virnu. He feels a surge of fury but finds himself laughing. 'Well?' he says. 'Do you plan to stand there like a sack of wet feathers?'

But Billy doesn't move towards his horse. He jerks his head at the Axam Range and says, 'I can't go up there.'

Mathew glances at the darkening scrub, then back at Billy, who looks unsure of himself.

Mathew says, 'It's not so steep,' but Billy doesn't answer. Mathew says, 'There's an hour left of decent light. And we'll see the fire in the dark.'

Billy says, 'I can't be on that country.'

Mathew looks at the hills, as if by studying them he'll understand why Billy is talking so back to front.

'It's law,' says Billy.

'What law?' Mathew shifts on his feet. His limbs are ready for action.

'Old law,' says Billy.

So he means what Mathew feels most comfortable referring to as 'blackfellow business'. Mathew says, 'Now's not the time.' He understands and appreciates the laws of property; every inch of the fen he grew up on was parcelled out, and you always knew just whose sod you stood on. But no one would begrudge a trespasser looking for his lost son. And Billy isn't even talking property—he's talking religion, which Mathew takes seriously, but thinks of as negotiable. He's accepted his sinful nature; along with it comes grace. There are always bargains to be made with God.

'All right, what happens?' Mathew demands. 'If you climb this hill, what happens? You're struck by lightning?'

Billy shakes his head.

Mathew can hardly breathe for rage and disbelief. He's protected this man for years—shielded him from George Axam's dislike when they worked together at Thalassa, and hired him away to safety when the Undelcarra lease came through. 'I order you,' says Mathew. 'What about that? You come up there with me, or there's an end to your job.'

Billy says, 'I can't.' He no longer seems unsure.

'All right, it's law,' says Mathew. He can hear the wheedling tone in his voice; it disgusts him. But he'll beg for Denny if he has to: for Denny's bootless feet. 'It's law. But who's to see? I'm not telling anyone. Who'll know? You'll know, I'll know. Not another soul.'

Billy says, 'It's dangerous. For you, for me, for Denny.'

'Dangerous how?'

Billy shakes his head; why won't he just explain? Mathew can't talk him out of something he won't defend. It's hurting Billy, too—Mathew can see that. Billy loves Denny and wants to find him. This, suddenly, is the greatest insult of all: that this man has the gall to love Mathew's son. Mathew could kill him for it. He could snap Billy's neck. He takes a step closer and says, 'I'm asking one more time.'

Billy bows his head with regret, and this gesture is intolerable. Mathew flies at him, wrestling him to the ground. Mathew's whole weight falls on Billy's chest—Billy wheezes, winded, and Mathew strikes beneath his chin, driving up with his elbow. Mathew can fight this way, too: not in their usual mannerly, upright style, but brutally. His father taught him by example. This is the kind of fighting that produced his cauliflower ear, that gave him a reputation on the fens and sent him slinking off to South Australia. Billy's body feels breakable beneath him. Ungrateful Billy—ugly, ungrateful, disloyal, stubborn Billy—he'll beat Billy's face to pulp. I'm stronger, thinks Mathew. Stronger and younger, and Denny is my son.

But Billy is faster, and he's moving. He rolls Mathew until he's lying on his back and digs a knee into his chest, pinning him to the ground. Mathew has never seen Billy look so determined. And he's stronger, somehow, unlike in all those fights they've had before, which Mathew now realises Billy must have lost on purpose. Billy is holding Mathew down so that all he can do is hit against his sides, trying to shove him off. What if Denny were here to see this? What if Mary were here to see it? The disgrace of being bested, and so quickly, by a black man, and an older one at that. He's crying, but not with pain—with surprise and anger. He cranes his neck to bite Billy's arm but, before he can, Billy strikes at Mathew's nostrils with the heel of his hand, hard and upwards, as if he'd like to shear the nose clean off.

Mathew feels the pain now. His nose is on fire, his eyes sting with sweat, and the distant sky is tilting. He tries to lift his head, but Billy stops him—gently. Then the stone rolls shut at the entrance to the tomb, and Mathew is inside it, in the dark.

The boy slept for most of the day in the shade of the acacia tree, and when he woke, the hills had come closer. His breath smelled awful, as if something were creeping up his throat and had nearly reached the dryness of his mouth. He lay beneath the tree until the arrival of a lizard with a blunt head and thick tail. The lizard opened its surprising mouth and hissed at the boy, so he stood up and began to walk again, looking for shelter from the sun. There would be shelter in the ranges. He moved slowly towards them, and when he was too tired he sat down, sometimes on the prickly ground and once on a downed tree trunk with thick, evenly spaced knots in it that reminded him of the teats of a sow. There used to be a sow at home, until

Dad killed it and Mam made sausages, bacon, salt pork and blood pudding. Sitting on the tree-sow, Denny saw the tracks of horses. He didn't know how many, but more than one. They were heading towards the ranges, so he followed them—that's how he found two more murky puddles, which he drank from.

Soon afterwards, the boy saw smoke go up in a thin line from a fold in the closest hills. Just imagining the sight of a person brought on a messy sob. He thought of hands above a campfire and the hands became his mother's. So he ran until he grew tired, which didn't take long. Then he walked, and as he came near to the smoke—the fire itself was hidden from him, in a gorge—he grew nervous and stood leaning against a rock near the gorge's entrance, thinking about what to do. Every time he tried to fasten on a thought it flew away. It was easier to think if he closed his eyes, so he closed them for a long time. When he opened them again he could see someone standing not far away. The someone hadn't seen him. It stood with its back to the gorge, and it was naked, with burning arms crossed over its burning chest, watching the setting sun. It looked as if it were made of the sun: it was big and gold and bright, and there was no shadow behind it. The sky was very red. The boy watched until the sun went below the horizon and the sky turned an even deeper red. Then the someone lifted its arms and raised its face into the redness.

The boy waited until the someone went back into the gorge. There was enough light left, and the cooler air helped calm the boy's mind. He climbed the rocky slope—he had always been a good climber, although today his legs were shaky—and he found a secure place from which he could look down into the gorge, which had a waterhole in it. Now he could see a campfire, and a lady beside it. The lady looked more ordinary than the someone. She wore a loose white shift that showed her knees. She worked over the fire, and the smell of the food she cooked rose to the boy and hurt his throat. When she called out, the someone appeared, dressed now and looking like a man. But he couldn't completely hide the sun that was inside him: he leaned down to the waterhole, dipped his hands, and when he shook the water off them, each drop turned red. Serving the food, the lady looked as if she were standing in the fire, as if its heat was nothing to her. The boy saw no sign of the horses that had made the tracks, and wondered if they'd been a trick.

The boy watched the man and lady eat. Afterwards, she went to the side of the gorge, hitched her skirt and squatted, then stood and kicked sand over the spot. The man put more wood on the fire. They covered themselves with blankets and spoke together. The boy, crouching cold in the dark, waited for the gods to fall asleep before going down to drink and look for food.

# THIRD NIGHT

Sergeant Foster is proud of his pipe, which was imported from London, is made of seasoned Mediterranean briar, and has an ebony mouthpiece. He takes pleasure in objects of quality, believing them essential to a worthwhile life. There should be great satisfaction for him, then, in sitting by a campfire in the Druid Range at the end of a long day of searching, in pulling out this handsome pipe, in smoking his strong Syrian tobacco with a practised pucker, and in thinking over the possible subject of his next book. Ordinarily, Foster relishes nights like this one: a waxing gibbous moon, cloudless, windless, chilly but far from frost, a light dew, sparks floating from the fire, and every inhalation fragrant with smoke, sweat, horse and leather. Foster has every reason to feel content, and therefore no excuse not to. But he's dissatisfied.

The fact is, he insisted on this north-easterly direction while only ninety per cent sure of it himself, largely because the Wallace girl was being difficult. In addition, Jimmy Possum—his native tracker, the one who won't be parted from his cloak—is sulking because he's been spoken to severely. There were, indeed, footprints leading up to the flat rock, but no clear prints leading away from it. There was a trail of some kind, however, which Jimmy followed, but the local man who reported the first tracks grew impatient—tracking can be a slow business—and went out ahead of Jimmy on horseback. The local did not, as far as Foster could tell, disturb the trail, but Jimmy was offended, the local man was offended, and the other local man took his neighbour's part. Words were exchanged. The trail, which Jimmy eventually returned to with a moody nonchalance, ran out in a rocky creek bed and Jimmy claimed not to be able to pick it up again.

Finally, the sky turned red and the sun went down and here they are, having made tense camp around a fire built large enough to attract attention, in the hope that the boy might see it and seek them out. Jimmy didn't seem to like the idea of attracting attention, which is, Foster thinks as he smokes by the fire, typical of natives; their every word and act is directed by some dreadful superstition. The local men produced a supply of rum and offered it around, and Foster refused for both himself and Jimmy. The men objected to this refusal on Jimmy's behalf, grew boisterous, then maudlin, and are now asleep and snoring—one with a courteous squeal, and the other like a church organ. Foster perches, disgruntled, in the front pew.

Jimmy sits beyond the fire, smoking cheap tobacco from a clay pipe. Foster worries about Jimmy's mood—he worries about both his trackers. He pays for their uniforms out of his own pocket. He knows their wives, their favourite foods, that Copper Bob is colourblind, that Jimmy loves a pun. Copper Bob claims to have learned from his elders how to weave vast, fine nets that can catch hundreds of fish, which seems unlikely. Jimmy's left arm is useless, but with a stockwhip in his right, he can break the back of a snake hidden in the grasses. Foster knows his boys and he's good to them. After all, he wants them to stay with him.

Foster, from his place beside the fire, notes the vigorous glow of Jimmy's bowl and is irritated with the man for not knowing how to smoke pipe tobacco at a proper pace. Aside from this glow, Jimmy is invisible, as if he's finally succeeded in merging with his cloak. But where Jimmy's forehead must be there is, sometimes, a glaze of light on the darkness, as he raises and lowers his head. Foster thinks, I should have forced that bloody cloak off him at Thalassa and sold the damn thing to the Axam woman.

Foster has ordered Jimmy to keep watch, but he'll stay awake a while longer himself, just to be sure. He knows you can't be too careful, even in these peaceful districts. It isn't that he fears attack from hostile natives (this hasn't been frontier territory for thirty years), but he's wary of being caught up in one of their tribal wars: someone desecrates a sacred site; someone carries off the wrong woman; some arcane, bloody, complicated law is broken and a whole family is wiped out. He's heard of bands of men spending years hunting, picking off their quarry one by one, and returning to their tribe as avenging heroes. Foster's other tracker, Copper Bob, saw his own father killed in the night by no one at all. By a movement in the branches. Well, it's to be expected, Foster thinks—any old bastard is going to have offended someone in the course of his long life. These people follow unwritten laws, which makes them unpredictable. As a result, they can't be trusted.

Look, here's Jimmy rising now—if it weren't for the visible pipe, you'd never know. Who can say what he's up to, wandering about in the dark? It occurs to Foster that Jimmy might take advantage of the darkness to remove his cloak; that this could be Foster's opportunity to see what's underneath it, once and for all. He doesn't particularly care what state Jimmy's arm is in—what's so unusual about a shattered limb? What bothers him, on principle, is the idea that Jimmy feels he's owed privacy. Foster distrusts privacy: when you live with honour, there's no need for secrets. He also considers Jimmy's obvious concealment of his arm to be a kind of vanity. Foster would be annoyed by this in a white man; in Jimmy, it infuriates him.

Foster lays down his own pipe, stands, stretches, and turns his back to the fire so that his eyes will adjust more readily to the dark. Then he sets out in the direction in which he saw Jimmy's little light move off. Foster aims to look like a man strolling out to take a piss; but, if questioned, he's prepared to admit that he's following Jimmy, who might be planning any kind of mischief. The two local men, however, are in no state to question anybody. The hostile one turns over and snores with renewed vigour.

In the dark, every rock and bush has a watchful quality. Foster knows this to be a trick of the moonlight: in reality, this whole region is dry and dead, and all the emptier for people's insistence on populating it and planting their doomed wheat. If anything ever truly inhabited this place, it left long ago. Foster prefers the genuine wastes of the central deserts, crossed by camel strings and Lutherans and ancient tribes, and no one else—out there, at night, a man can feel the lonely eye of God. But here, in the lesser landscape of the Flinders, he picks his way among clumps of spinifex, following a steep sandstone ridge that can have been Jimmy's only path.

Soon, Foster finds himself on a rocky outcrop studded with grass trees. There's no way to go further—the ground drops away from the outcrop in all directions except for the one he came from, and no one would attempt to descend these slopes in the dark. But Jimmy isn't here. The grass trees look larger than they should; Foster thinks for a moment that he can hear a faint chirping from within their verdant crowns. Their spears rise above them, long and straight. He disapproves of the popular name of these trees, which is 'black boys'; it feels lazy to him, as all metaphors do (he considers himself a naturalist and, therefore, invested in the precise description of the thing itself, without fanciful recourse to its similarity to any other non-related thing). But tonight, surrounded by the stalky flowers of the grass trees, their concealing leaves, and their low, thick trunks, Foster is unnerved: he feels himself to be the victim of a silent ambush. He stands motionless among the grass trees for some time, as if moving in their presence would be a kind of surrender. The thought occurs to him, as it often does lately, that it's been two years since he published his last book, and he doesn't have a new manuscript, a draft-in-progress, or even the inkling of an idea. Eventually, he hears the flat sound of a euro or kangaroo beating the ground with its tail as it jumps through the night; this breaks whatever spell held him, and he makes his way back down the ridge. When he reaches camp, the fire has turned to red embers and the local men are still snoring. Jimmy, smoking his clay pipe, is back in his position, as if he never left it. He breathes in through his nose, and yes, he is—Foster sees this clearly—he's taking pleasure in his pipe, the rest, the night. Apparently, Jimmy feels that he's done a good day's work.

Foster returns to his seat by the fire. He's gone so long without a book, he thinks, because he left the central deserts—a man like him can't write while settled in a town. He needs contact with the land, the natives; he needs the danger of the frontier while there still is one. But he also needs to not be disconcerted by a clump of grass trees. Foster takes up his beloved pipe and his Syrian tobacco, but can find no satisfaction in them.

Here is Constable Robert Manning, First Class, out on the plain. It's late at night; Robert is cold, hungry, tired, riding a tired horse, and following a girl. The girl is Cissy Wallace. If asked how he found himself in this situation, he wouldn't be entirely sure. All he knows is that, shortly after he and Cissy arrived back at the Wallace farm, delivered tidings of the footprints, and received the news of the handkerchief, Cissy came to him and said, 'Let's go.'

And Robert, who intended to talk her out of looking for her father, said, 'Wait a tick.' He had so many responsibilities: instructions to give, arrangements to make, bloodied handkerchiefs to inspect, a sunrise meeting at the scuffed rock, and Minna expecting him home tonight. God, Minna waiting for him in the dark—soft, tight, squealing Minna—breathless, sweat on her belly, biting her pink lip, bucking, rolling, laughing—and not leaving him even when he slept, but coming into his dreams with her hands and her mouth. My God, Minnow! Your goddamn mouth.

'Wait a tick,' Robert said to Cissy Wallace.

He went out into the wheat with the oldest Wallace girl, the one who found the handkerchief. When they returned to the house, someone came to him and said that Cissy Wallace had ridden off to look for her father—she couldn't be stopped—and would he go after her? He did. When he caught up to her she said, 'You were taking too long.'

He tried to talk her out of the pointless excursion: the day was getting on, her father knew how to take care of himself, they couldn't even be sure where to look for him.

Cissy said, 'You promised.'

'One hour,' said Robert, and they rode together, following Fairly Creek north-west. After half an hour, he announced that it was time to go home. When she refused, he said, 'I'm heading back. You can come with me or not, as you please.'

He turned his horse and set off for Undelcarra, sure that she would follow him. She didn't. So he turned again and caught up with her, mindful of Foster's injunction to keep her from getting lost. They had several arguments. He thought of forcing her off her horse and onto his—he would lead her horse and keep Cissy Wallace right in front of him in the saddle, where he could damn well see her. He thought of striking her, but he had never struck a white woman. When he ordered her to come with him in the name of the law, she laughed. He did pity her—her brother was missing, she wanted her father, she was a child. He imagined Minna out here alone. So he stayed with Cissy, thinking that she would tire as the day came to an end. When the sun set in the bizarre way it had been lately, he asked, 'Are you just going to keep on?'

Cissy scratched behind one ear and said, 'Yes, I am.'

So Robert kept on with her, and here they are, late at night, still riding. He's interested to see how far she'll go. He rides a few paces behind, watching the twitch of her horse's tail. She never turns to look at him. The moon is just bright enough to see by, and she rides as if she knows where she's going. Earlier in the evening, he allowed himself to fall into a kind of sleepy trance; for the last hour, he's been singing to keep himself awake. The girl doesn't join in with the singing, but when he finishes each song she recites part of a poem very loudly.

'*Into the valley of Death rode the six hundred!*' calls Cissy, and Robert sings, '*Poor old Jeff has gone to rest, we know that he is free! Disturb him not but let him rest, way down in Tennessee!*'

Making so much noise as they crash across the plain, Robert and the girl wake birds and send larger, unseen things scurrying through the scrub. They're getting close to the western ranges. Robert is curious: will she stop at the hills, or will she try to go on riding up and over them? He's impressed by her boldness. She seems less childish to him now, and he finds himself watching the sway of her hips as they move above her horse.

'*And like a thunderbolt he falls!*' Cissy shouts.

'*Who should I see but a Spanish lady, washing her hair by candle-light!*' sings Robert.

This goes on for some time, until a lantern swings amid the trees in front of the girl's horse and a man says, 'Whoa!'

Robert is ready for this, without being conscious that he's ready: he has his pistol, his sword and, more crucially than both of these, his uniform, which he's proud to wear. He's been under attack before. There was one evening, for example, some years back, when he was on patrol and surprised two natives slaughtering a cow. Robert had no choice but to kill one of them. If he thinks back on it, which he rarely does, he doesn't see himself shooting the man; rather, he feels as if his uniform did the deed. But he has, ever since, been ready for a situation like this: ambushed among trees at night. This man with the lantern is dark-skinned, too, and Robert's uniform is ready.

But it's all right—Cissy seems to know him. It's her father's farmhand, apparently, Billy Rough, who Robert has heard is clean and reliable, and hires himself out like a white man. Well, Robert will believe it when he sees it. The man doesn't look entirely reputable—he has a cut on his temple, and his curly hair is rather wild. He's saying now that he and Wallace are camped not far away, he came out to see what was making so much noise, and says that they should follow him—which could be a trap, but Robert is too tired, and the night is too odd, for this to feel likely.

The native leads them along the creek bed where it's cut its way through the western cliffs. Then they're in a valley and Mathew Wallace is here, looking bruised about the eyes. When Wallace sees Cissy, he stands and begins to shout at her; she slithers down from her saddle and shouts right back. Robert dismounts, lets Billy take his horse, and intercedes by placing one hand on Cissy's shoulder, which shuts her up. He squeezes her shoulder and is idly pleased by the way she shivers in response.

'Evening, Wallace,' Robert says. 'We've come with news.'

'What news, then?'

'We found the boy's tracks along Marsden's Creek, about six miles north-east of your place.'

'You found tracks,' says Wallace. It isn't a question—he's pondering this statement. He's purple about the eyes, and his beard looks a mess.

'Denny's footprints,' Cissy says, wriggling Robert's hand off her shoulder. 'And Joy found a handkerchief with blood on it in the wheat. So you need to come home with us.'

Wallace shakes his head, and when Cissy opens her mouth to speak, he says, 'Wait, girl.' He rummages in his pack, and look: a pair of boy's lace-up boots with no laces in them. Cissy cries out as if someone has struck her.

'But where'd you find them?' asks Robert. He's never seen a pair of boots look stranger than these ones do, although they're perfectly commonplace: scuffed heels, dangling tongues, with squinting eyelets where the laces should thread.

'Not five miles back from here.' Wallace tells them about a knife mark made on a tree; a scrambled trail left by a man (who might well have dropped a handkerchief) and his horse; and a fire in the hills tonight.

'A fire!' says Cissy. 'Where? Which way? Why'd you stop here?'

There seems to be some awkwardness about this question; Wallace looks at his farmhand before answering. 'It were too late for the terrain,' he says. 'And too dark to follow the trail. We meant to sleep and start early and catch him at his breakfast.'

Cissy throws her arms in the air and cries, 'You could sleep!'

'Ah, till two lunatics come along singing,' Wallace says. When Cissy makes a noise of disgust, he snaps, 'D'you think we're stopped here for the pleasure on it?'

'And they're Denny's boots for sure?' Robert asks.

Cissy and Wallace both answer: 'Yes.'

'Well, blow me,' Robert says. But he isn't truly surprised. It seems tonight as if anything might happen: as if the boy might have walked both north-west and north-east at once, have been carried away by phantom horses, have climbed onto multiple rocks and left boots all over the Willochra. He stifles a yawn and says, 'I'll get Foster. If I cut across country I can make the meeting.'

The farmhand asks, 'What meeting?'

'An hour past sunrise,' Robert says. He looks at Wallace. 'There's a big flat rock west of Ewart's Bluff, on Marsden's Creek. That's where they found the footprints.'

'I know the rock,' says the hand. 'I can go.' He seems uncommonly alert and sure of himself. Manning recognises him, now, as the black cricketer who used to play for the Thalassa team, and then for the town, and was so much better than everyone else that they all agreed it was preferable not to have him play at all.

'Yes,' says Wallace to his man, with a growl in his voice. 'Get on so I can't look at you.'

Robert is so tired that the next while takes on a muddled character: the cricketer rides off, carrying messages for Foster; Wallace wants to know everything about the tracks and handkerchief; Cissy, fretting, lies down beside her father and says she'll never sleep. She sleeps.

'You should have a kip yourself,' Wallace says.

'Just for an hour or so,' says Robert.

He goes into the dark to piss. Afterwards, holding his cock, he thinks of Minna. He could be buried in her right now. God, Minnow. Slick pulse, steady honey. His hand isn't enough but it'll do. He's quick about it: jerk and swell and spill. When he comes back to the low sparks of the fire, Cissy is lying with her head pillowed on her outstretched arm; her mouth is open, her breathing is loud, and her other hand is curled like a snail shell beneath her chin. Her father sits looking at her and frowning. The bruises around his eyes are even darker now—they'll be black by morning.

Robert says, 'Your girl's stubborn, all right.'

'Ah,' replies Wallace. 'She caps my arse.'

But the frowning way he looks at Cissy is also loving. She really is only a child, with a cross expression on her sleeping face and her fist pressed into her neck.

Robert settles himself for sleep. He does recall having sworn to Minna that he would be home tonight, but it doesn't occur to him that she will have taken such a vow seriously. Minna understands his obligations. If she knew where he was, he's sure she'd feel sorry for him: laid out to sleep on the dusty ground, dirty, tired, far from home, and still with an ache in his balls.

⁂

Tonight, Mary lies in her white bed and dreams she's on an ocean-going ship and has lost something: possibly a ring, or a watch, or her mother's hymnbook. She dreams of Denny. He's looking down into a gully full of scaly ferns at the body of a dead wallaby, and when she asks him what he's doing he says he's leaning over the edge of one day or another. She dreams of birds in houses, of combing lice from her hair, and of black dogs running through cornfields with trails of light behind them. Spilled salt. A lamp glass stained with soot in the shape of a coffin. The Devil living in the bottom of a boiled egg.

Mary is asleep or awake and sometimes both at once. She holds the blood-spotted handkerchief and is visited by all the dark dreams of her mothers and their mothers before them. These are not the lucid visions of the faith she was raised in; they're much older, they're long secrets stretched out over the centuries in which women have known death. She dreams that failure has left its habitual post in the corner of the parlour and come to stand above her bed. Failure is a stooped, pale figure with an open mouth and swollen eyes.

Mary dreams of a child born without ears, who will join her in a silent world and never grow and never leave her. She dreams that she is good at keeping sons. She dreams until she's no longer tired. Beside her, Lotta kicks and snorts and settles. Mary is afraid to open her eyes in case she finds that Lotta, too, is gone.

---

Bess, sleeping in the gorge, dreams of the wallaby. In the dream, it's a secret that she's kept from Karl, who believes her to be incapable of secrets. That isn't true. One year after they were married, Bess and Karl spent the summer in a small red house on an island in the Stockholm archipelago. Karl believed that a patron had offered them the use of the house, but in fact Bess owned it and hadn't told him. She'd bought it sight unseen the week before their wedding (a quiet wedding, with her father not invited and both her brothers gone to Australia) because Karl said he must do as the other young Swedes he knew were doing: leave Paris behind forever, return home, and paint Swedish themes in Swedish places. Bess was more than willing to leave Paris; she was only there because it was obligatory for anyone with painterly ambitions. She bought the island house with the modest amount of money she'd inherited when her mother died, and this may have been the reason she never told Karl she owned it: her mother, having married a man who turned out to be a gambler, had advised her daughter to keep a place that was hers alone, to which she could escape if necessary. Buying the house made Sweden feel feasible for Bess, and she kept it to herself. When they moved, not long after the wedding, it was to dark, stuffy rooms in Stockholm.

Months later, as the weather warmed those suffocating rooms, Bess invented the patron with a summer house. She packed a case with their clothes and books, arranged to have their painting materials sent after them, and they went out to the red house on the island. The house had big windows and, upstairs, a long empty attic room with good light. It came with a rowboat in which they could go back and forth between the island and the mainland, a trip of an hour in fair weather. Before the paints and canvases arrived, Bess and Karl walked in the woods, fished from a jetty they shared with another house not yet occupied for the summer, read, swam, spent hours in bed, sketched, and talked about the work they would do when their paints and canvases came: the best and easiest kind of work, that which is impossible at the time of the conversation but will become possible very soon. But not quite yet. And the sun is shining, the fish are frying. At night there's a fire in the small red house.

The painting materials came simultaneously with the occupants of the closest house, the house with which they shared the jetty. They were a family with five children. The wife was a blazing reddish-blonde who piled her hair on top of her head and looked, in the twilight, like a thick, pale candle; the husband had come with plans to build an extra room and paint their whole house white. Their name was Carlin. Karl befriended the husband, who went by Beppe, and spent all day with him, sawing planks and driving nails; the children ran between the two houses; the wife rose topless from the sea like Venus, the men applauding her breasts. She was generous, bountiful, with cheerfully crooked teeth.

Bess had no objection to Adi Carlin, although they had little in common. But Bess wanted to work, and the Carlins knew everyone on the island, knew how summer was to proceed: when sheets were to be washed and bilberries picked before the mainland people got to them, the best place to catch crayfish, nights of music, days in the sun, Karl shirtless on a ladder, Bess pressed into service with a tin of white paint, the children living between houses, the alliances newly formed every morning, the exhaustion in the evening after swimming, calling, scolding, eating. Karl going out most nights to drink with Beppe, visiting new friends, saying, 'Aren't you coming?', returning once with a wreath of flowers on his head and demanding that Bess smell them. Bess had been dreaming and the flowers smelled of nothing. It was five o'clock and already the day was fully light.

Only Bess was obstinate enough to resist the charms of the season. She fumed as she helped to paint the Carlins' house and herded their children; she fought for time to work but had barely anything to show for it—one small picture she was pleased with, a subdued seascape. She did make endless sketches of the Carlin children as they fussed and tumbled. Karl didn't work at all and was brown and happy. This loose, warm summer suited him, and he began to talk about babies.

'Why not a baby boy,' he said, 'who looks just like you, and a girl who looks just like me?' Karl knew how Bess felt about babies. So many of the girls she studied with at the Slade had stopped painting when they had children.

On the last day of that summer, while throwing white sheets over the furniture, sweeping, and packing trunks, Bess looked out of the window to see Karl and Adi Carlin sitting on the jetty, deep in conversation, and behind them the Carlins' freshly white house. Bess went out to join them when all the other Carlins did. They ate thick slices of bilberry pie as a farewell. The pie was warm; Adi had baked it, apparently, but when? Adi wept when they said goodbye. She was obviously in love with Karl, but she seemed also to be in love with her husband and each of her children, with Bess and with the summer, so that Bess was moved by the farewell—didn't cry, but might have.

Walking back to their house, Karl laid out the plan he and Adi had made together on the jetty: Bess and Karl would live in the Carlins' house, paying no rent, from the end of one summer until the beginning of the next. In the winter, they would eat vegetables and keep ducks inside for eggs; eventually they would build their own house next to the Carlins', paying for the materials but not for the land; this way they could be alone together and working, safe from the distractions of the city. Wasn't Bess always pointing out that Karl worked best without distractions? Winter would be for work, then summer would erupt and be glorious, as this one had been. They would go back to Stockholm now to arrange everything, but return in a few weeks and have the entire island to themselves. Bess said nothing and Karl became quieter too, asked her to think about it, then went to close and lock all the shutters. When he came back he said, 'It's a pity we can't just buy this house.'

They rowed across to the mainland for the last time and Karl said to her, 'You don't just identify obstacles—you invent them.'

Back in Stockholm, in another set of dark rooms, he poured sand from the beach near the red house into a jar. He painted a picture, quite uncharacteristic, in which a tall young groom and his thick, pale bride escaped laughing through a cornfield from the solemnity of their own wedding procession. Above the couple, birds carried garlands of flowers. His friends and admirers came to see him, and he began to work again in earnest and more quickly than before. His days grew full. Bess was, as usual, both proud and jealous of his talent. Mostly proud. The wind became wet, cold; the blue creep of winter covered Stockholm. Karl was often sick that season, sometimes dangerously; he had a child's fear of the dark and sleep, he needed reassurances of all kinds until he was well again; then he was grateful, adult, loving. The doctor, tapping at Karl's chest, suggested a sea voyage and a warmer climate. Bess reminded Karl that her brothers were always writing from Australia about the heat. Karl refused to leave Sweden—what use, he said, is a Swedish artist in any other place? They didn't speak about the red house.

Adi Carlin arrived at their door in April, very pregnant, announcing that she had run away from home, but only temporarily. She brimmed like spring itself. The baby wasn't Karl's—the dates didn't work—yet Adi became part of their household for the final month of her pregnancy. Karl's friends assumed a house of generous adultery, of a shared Karl, of a Bess willing to accept the tide of love Karl pulled after him like the moon. It made more sense of Bess: serious, English and not pretty, not at all Karl's type; and, as it turned out, not even rich (there had been talk, Bess knew, of her father's lost wealth). Adi was Karl's big, bright type. Actually, Adi spent all her time with Bess. Karl tiptoed around the women, passing them in rooms and hallways with amplified politeness, and went out with friends at night. Bess didn't ask Adi why she had left her family, but Adi offered explanations, different every day: the noise of her own house full of children, a dream she'd had, the need to be nearer doctors, Beppe's reluctance to have another baby, the love she felt for Karl and Bess.

The baby was born, a creamy boy, and within a week he died. Adi gave Bess her husband's address, asked her to tell him where she was, and stayed in bed waiting for him to fetch her. She wouldn't speak or eat or even sleep. Karl was made frantic by her implacable grief; he was used to being a consolation to unhappy people, who often smiled to please him. 'What can we do? What can we do?' he asked Bess.

Bess told him, 'Nothing.'

He wouldn't believe it. He sat by Adi's bed, held her hands, kissed her, told stories, and made plans and promises. Bess had never seen him woo a woman the way he did Adi Carlin. If Adi had risen from the bed and told Karl, 'To cure me you must never paint again', he might have agreed to it. Adi didn't rise from the bed. He painted her as she had looked in summer, and when Bess saw the picture she felt tremendous love and pity for both of them. She also knew the portrait would sell. Adi was quiet until her husband came; then she roared with grief and longing, and Beppe took her away.

'What more could we have done?' Karl asked, bewildered. He cried like a child and Bess calmed him. She had held the baby after it was dead and felt how Adi had made all of its parts and how they'd been taken from her. How do you console a mother for the loss of her baby? You return her baby to her. Bess knew of nothing else, and it couldn't be done.

'We'll see her again in the summer,' Karl said. 'At the red house.'

By the summer Bess had sold the red house and used the money to buy their passage to Melbourne.

And here they are, though not currently in Melbourne—they're in a mountain gorge far north of Adelaide. When Bess stirs from sleep and sees a boy crouching beside their campfire, it's Adi Carlin's baby she thinks of. This boy is much older, but his hair is bright in the darkness, the way Adi's was. And Bess can see that he, like Adi's baby, doesn't belong to this place and will have to leave it soon. She's also half asleep, so it may be that the boy is just another wallaby come down to drink at the waterhole. Of course he's a wallaby. She wills the wallaby not to be afraid. She thinks: never fear, little one. Look—no gun. Tonight I'm harmless. Then she sleeps again.

When she wakes a few hours later, not long before sunrise, Bess thinks she may have dreamed of a wallaby moving with cautious purpose among their things. But Karl is pacing by the waterhole and, seeing her sit up, says, 'Look—a thief! Someone's been here and taken all our apples.'

# VINDICATION OF THE RAMINDJERI TRACKER

***Port Augusta Dispatch*, September 1883**

**Open Column**
**To the Editor**

SIR,– The news that a boy has strayed from home in the northern town of Fairly, and that the native tracker Jimmy Possum has been dispatched to this region to assist in the search, prompts me to draw the attention of readers to the fact that the matter I discussed in my letter of June 15, regarding the unpaid balance of Jimmy's remuneration for previous work as a tracker, continues to go unresolved. For those of your readers who may have overlooked the abovementioned letter, I will, with your permission, Sir, explain its contents in as brief a space as possible.

Before I go further, let me state that, although I write on Jimmy's behalf, it is not at his request. Jimmy Possum is a simple man, and would never venture to make a complaint of this kind. It is for this very reason, is it not, that any white man ought to stir himself to be a champion for Aborigines of good character?

February last, a spate of fires menaced the township of Willoughby. My own cowshed was among the structures that burned. Suspecting arson, our Constable sent to Port Augusta to procure the services of a native tracker. Arriving soon afterwards, Jimmy Possum made efficient work of the tracks available, and, uncovering a number of deposits of redheaded matches placed on glass and covered with dry grass, led the Constable to the camp of the troublemaker, one George Pellow. For this excellent service, which saved a great deal of property and very likely many lives, Jimmy was promised a reward—over and above his regular payment—of £1/2/6, gathered by subscription from the grateful residents of Willoughby. This sum was forwarded, with instructions, to the Police Station at Port Augusta. We later learned that the sum had been withheld from Jimmy, although he was provided with tobacco valued at 2/6, in our name.

I can say without fear of contradiction that not one of the Willoughby men who subscribed to Jimmy's reward had any notion of his being paid in goods. There also remains the unpaid balance of the sum, which, we are assured, is being held in trust for Jimmy until such a time as he should need it. Despite requests, we have seen no evidence of the truth of this statement, nor do we believe Jimmy has ever been informed of his nest egg. I do not lay all responsibility for this outrage at the door of the Port Augusta Police. Indeed, petitions to the Sub-Protector of Aborigines were stalled until the close of the financial year (viz. June last), and requests sent since June have gone unacknowledged.

Aborigines of good character should be able to trust that in the white man they have both a champion and a sympathiser. The white man, in turn, must keep any promise he has made to the Aborigine. It is our solemn duty to protect these people while they remain under our care, regardless of their probable extinction. Any man of correct opinion would agree that this miscarriage of justice is a disgrace to a civilised society.

Apologies for trespassing on your valuable space.

I am, &c.,

P.R. Thompson

Eureka Hotel, Willoughby

# FOURTH DAY

The sun rises at half past six; by seven o'clock, the day promises to be warm. People tend to rise early on the Willochra Plain, whether or not a boy is missing. Already, Mary is stirring porridge clockwise with her right arm and wondering what has become of her telegrams.

Mathew, Cissy and Robert are climbing a limestone spur that rests against the broad red wall of the Axam Range, heading for the ridge where Mathew saw the fire last night. Both of Mathew's eyes are black.

Karl, whose head is full of his sunset painting, explores the area above the gorge in search of the apple thief while Bess prepares breakfast.

Billy stands beside the flat rock west of Ewart's Bluff, waiting for Foster's rendezvous; the only tracks he sees belong to Foster and his men.

The news that Joy Wallace found a bloodied handkerchief in her father's wheat has reached Fairly, prompting fresh speculations: murder, abduction, accidental death. Until now, the town has felt nothing but sympathy for the Wallaces, but that sympathy is curdled, slightly, by the possibility that Mathew and Mary may have been careless, secretive or dishonest; broken one of many unspoken rules; loved their children too much, or too little; had too many of them (the excessive number of daughters is noted), or too few; in a word, that they may have made some fatal error, for which they expect other people to pay. It could be that the Wallaces know exactly where Denny is—or what remains of him—and are sending searchers out to cover their own tracks; are, essentially, wasting the time of good men, who have their own children to worry about. After all, the boy's been gone three days—or is it four? How far could he have got, a boy of six, all on his own?

Others, more generous, are convinced that if a third party is involved in the boy's disappearance, that party will turn out to be an Afghan (either a cameleer or a hawker), or a Chinese (but not, they all agree, their own Chinaman, Sammy So, who has had years to prove that he's no murderer), or a native (not the local natives, mind, who are tolerably well behaved—the culprit, they believe, will be one of those northern natives who come down sometimes from the salt lakes or the central deserts, looking for trouble). But the handkerchief, which rumour says is of the finest linen, suggests otherwise.

Bear, who knows two useful facts—first, that the handkerchief belongs to him, and second, that the men of other Aboriginal nations only come into this part of the ranges to trade for ochre at Parachilna and would be very unlikely to enter the Willochra without honouring complex local protocols—hasn't heard the news about the handkerchief. Even if he had, he'd be unlikely to surrender these facts, despite his love of gossip, since neither would be popular. But Bear doesn't hear about the handkerchief and neither does George, because they're both out on the pastures of Thalassa, choosing which sheep should be sheared and which fattened for market: the shearers arrive tomorrow and shearing begins the day after.

Tal, hearing about the handkerchief, checks for his own kerchief—which he wears knotted around his neck, sailor-style—to reassure himself that it's still there, and can't be used against him. Nancy mentions the handkerchief to Joanna who, fussing over Bolingbroke, doesn't make any connection between the handkerchief and Bear out in the wheat with Minna Baumann (no one, not even Robert, seems able to think of her as Minna Manning). Minna herself lies in bed, missing Robert and in such a rage of longing that she thinks she may be going mad.

No one knows where Mr Daniels, the vicar, is; he hasn't been seen for days. But that isn't unusual—he will have gone out to Wilson, Cradock or Wilpena on his rounds, like a devout doctor.

A number of the town's men are still out searching for Denny, but life in Fairly continues all the same. Inge Schmidt, the German prostitute, takes her donkey to the farrier to have its hoofs trimmed. Miss McNeil hums as she sweeps the schoolroom, preparing to receive her pupils. A reporter, hungover, stirs in one of the bedrooms of the Transcontinental Hotel. He's come north from Port Augusta to write about the missing boy and is delighted by the information he picked up in the bar last night: blood-stained handkerchief, native trackers, blondness of the boy. Soon he'll go to the post office to file a report, in which he'll give Denny's name as Dennis Wallace, a mistake that will be repeated in every successive article. At the post office, the reporter will encounter Mr Blake with his green visor, who wonders if each telegram coming through might be a reply to one of Mary Wallace's messages, but is always disappointed.

In Goolwa, Mary's father is at his devotions. He reads and reflects on Isaiah—'Arise, shine, for thy light is come'—and he prays for his daughter, for each of her seven children, and particularly for Deniston, who is named for him and who, for this reason, the Southern Shepherd imagines as having hair as white as his own. Samuel Deniston is a long time at his prayers. He adores and implores and praises; he casts himself upon the mercy of God until sweat stands in droplets above his lavish eyebrows. He doesn't yet know that his wife Muriel, having interpreted Mary's telegram as a plea to have a parent by her side, left Goolwa early this morning in a hired conveyance; that this carriage took her to Strathalbyn; that she is now a passenger on the public coach to Adelaide; and that she should, if all goes well, reach the capital, where she intends to put up at a temperance hotel, late this afternoon. From Adelaide, she can take the Port Augusta train. Today is Tuesday. If the trains behave as she expects them to—and she has studied her husband's timetables—she will arrive in Fairly on Thursday. Mary's stepmother, rattling in the coach over the forty miles to Adelaide, retreats into the composure with which she endures each day. She is only faintly affronted, therefore, by the serial farts of the coach's other passenger, a man in a buff coat. Muriel Deniston takes comfort in the knowledge that she is in the hands of the Lord.

+

Karl discovers the apple thief sleeping in the sun by a large rock. He's not sure what, or who, he expected to find, but it wasn't a filthy, sunburned boy with bloodied feet. The boy is skinny and fair—his hair would be a thin wash of raw sienna, and rose madder for the paler flesh, with a dab of cadmium yellow. He has one hand in the pocket of his short trousers and the other flung, palm up, over his forehead. The apples have all been eaten deep into their cores, and what's left of them sits in a neat brown pile at the boy's feet. Well, Karl thinks, looking down at the sleeping boy, so much for rushing to Wilpena Pound today. It's typical, isn't it? You make plans, you promise to resist all distractions, and something undeniable happens: summer, for example. A newborn dies in your house. Pneumonia, resulting in exile to the Southern Hemisphere. A child appears in need of help. The world, as usual, has its ways of stepping in to keep you from your work, and Karl ignores the relief he feels at this salvation. Listen, he says to the sky, it's only a temporary delay.

Karl stands between the boy and the sun, expecting the sudden shade to wake him. It does—the boy opens his eyes and Karl thinks, oh, he's me. The boy looks the way Karl remembers looking as a child: the same thinness of hair and body, the same expression of hunger, fear and wonder. But it's more than that. There's something unhoused about the boy, as if he belongs in a shell from which he's been prematurely shucked. The boy licks his lips and rubs a wrist against his chin and *is* Karl, somehow, in all his grubby thinness.

There's no way to account for this sense of recognition. Karl simply knows that this boy has also stood for hours by the puppet show at Djurgården, watching Pulcinello argue with Death while the organ grinders sang of Stockholm's latest murder: 'He beat her, ladies and gentlemen, with a fire grate!' He has laughed at and been frightened of the Djurgården monkey dressed as Napoleon, and fed it pancakes. This boy has also been to church with Karl's mother, where the angels over the altar used to step down from the wall during the week and walk about, sleep in the pews, and rearrange the hymnbooks; you might see them at the windows as you passed by—though Karl never did. This boy knows that in the barracks down the street, an old guardsman made miniature churches all in wood, hinged to open on a congregation. The guardsman carved every candle flame and organ stop, children dozing on their mothers' shoulders, and cats stealing in from the vestry. He would work on a church for weeks, then dress in full uniform and go out into the city to sell it. Sometimes Karl went with him to watch the way he sidled up to well-dressed people as if about to pick their pockets. The churches always sold, and the guardsman was drunk for days on the proceeds. Then he returned to the barracks and began another church. Karl understood that the guardsman had made a beautiful thing, and that because the thing existed, it could be bought. The boy with the bloodied feet and the apples has also coveted the wooden churches but known that, because he has no money, he's not allowed to have them. Instead, he must make his own beautiful things.

The boy yawns and Karl is reminded of a Leda he saw in Paris, a da Vinci copy: rosy Leda, the chummy swan, and four babies tumbling out of big eggs. This hatchling stares at Karl. The apple cores at his feet are crawling with ants.

'Good morning,' Karl says.

The boy, properly awake now, sits up with a start. Then he freezes, much as the wallaby did before Bess shot it the day before yesterday.

'Don't be frightened, little one,' Karl says. He sees that the boy has laid a dirty sack out on the ground to lie on. 'What a nice morning for sleeping out of doors. Are you all alone?'

The boy squints as if Karl's face is difficult to see—and it must be. The dazzling sun is right behind his head. When the boy doesn't answer, Karl says, 'Are we near your house?' The boy just watches him. 'Well, then. Are you out for a long walk? Or could it be that you're an explorer? By the way, I'm an explorer also.'

Bess calls up from the gorge to say that breakfast is ready.

'Are you hungry?' Karl asks. 'Or are you already full of apples? Can you stand?' He holds out his hand but the boy doesn't take it. 'I'm called Karl. And you? Do you understand me? Don't be frightened. Nobody minds about the apples. I think you must be lost. What's your name?'

'Denis,' the boy answers, like a little Frenchman.

'*Bonjour*, Denis,' says Karl. 'I think you must be hungry, yes? Come with me. You can eat, drink, wash. Doesn't that sound nice?'

The boy stands slowly. He's taller than Karl expected. Karl continues to offer his hand, and the boy seems cautiously willing to take it, but he shies away when Bess calls again.

'It's only Bess,' says Karl. 'A kind and sensible lady who will take care of you. Come over here—look—can you see her? She's cooking the porridge. She's like a good fairy, the kindest in all the world.'

Denis turns around and peers down into the gorge, where Bess is moving about the fire.

Karl says, 'She'll make everything better. That's what she does.' He considers the wary set of the boy's shoulders, the cowlick that sprouts from the crown of his head, and the smudgy birthmark behind his left knee. Then he steps close and lifts the boy by the armpits. Denis begins to shout but, though he's full of conviction, he has no strength. He wriggles like a tired fish. Karl swings the boy's legs up and carries him, cradled, down the rocky side of the gorge. Bess meets them at the bottom.

'Allow me to present our apple enthusiast,' Karl says. 'His name is Denis.'

Denis looks stricken. Bess reaches out to stroke his hair and he begins to cry, gulping into one bitten fist.

'Bring him out of the sun,' Bess says, and leads Karl to the rusty gum nearest the fire, where he sets the boy down in the shade. He didn't think to pick up the boy's sack. Once Denis is settled, Bess smiles at the little thief in a way that Karl knows as private. It's the smile she often gave Karl during their final winter in Stockholm, when he was very sick, and it means that there's no need to be afraid, because Bess is here and she's going to take you into her room, where everything is calm and simple. She'll look after you there. Karl knows that Denis understands the smile because the boy's whole body relaxes. Yes, thinks Karl, go into her room while she allows it. Out here, where I am, the Djurgården monkey dances in his bicorn hat. But Bess's room is quiet. It opens on a hinge, like a wooden church, and Karl and Denis peer into it, full of longing. Karl would live there forever if he could.

Bess whispers with her head bent low over the boy, kissing his ham-coloured forehead. Denis wipes his wet nose with the back of his hand and gazes up at her. Karl knows that, in this instant, the boy feels like the most precious thing alive.

Bess looks at Karl and says, 'We'll need water.'

So Karl brings water, some of which the boy drinks. Then Karl watches Bess bathe the boy's face and neck; he watches the boy allow it. Bess unpeels the boy's shirt, and his trousers, and the vest beneath his shirt. She leaves him in his stained white underpants, and Karl feels his own dignity threatened by Denis's soggy, unclothed blinking. She cleans Denis's arms and legs and chest, and the boy leans forwards so that she can scrub his back. She washes his blistered feet, then produces, from her pack, the aloe leaf she had been so pleased to find on their way out of Fairly. The end of it is tied with string; she slices off this end and squeezes juice from the aloe, which she rubs over the boy's burned skin. Denis looks at the aloe as if he's never seen anything like it.

How does Bess know to do all these things? She takes the pot of porridge off the coals, stirs salt into it, and spoons it into Denis's mouth, which waits, open, like a chick's. Then she takes a darning needle and thread, pierces the largest blister on the boy's left foot, and passes the thread through it. Denis allows all this, barely flinches, and never speaks, although Bess doesn't seem to expect him to. She pops the other blisters, murmuring to him as she works, always telling him what she's going to do next. At one point, she looks up at Karl and says, 'Eat, if you're hungry.' He tries the porridge; he doesn't like the saltiness, but knows it's for Denis.

Bess is combing the knots from the boy's hair. His eyes, with their fringe of blond lashes, flutter open and closed—he's falling asleep, and Bess shifts until his head is resting in her lap. Karl is standing beside her in a stony gorge with the taste of salty porridge on his tongue, but he's also asleep in Bess's lap and he's also watching Pulcinello beat Death with his cudgel. The red rock of the gorge curves protectively overhead. Karl thinks of a Pietà, but he also thinks of the feeling he wants to capture in his sunset picture: the feeling of being both claimed by and exiled from the world. He feels it as he both sees and *is* the boy in Bess's lap. The absolute terror of childhood, and also the sudden shelter. The lost child out of doors, and the lost child returning home. How unbearable it all is, under the terrible, beautiful sun! Bess combs the knots from his hair. Then she looks up at Karl as if it's time for him to do something.

The thing to do is to love the boy and take him home: Karl knows this and can see its general outline. But he forces himself to think, as Bess would, about the specific, practical steps that will make this beautiful thing possible; he thinks of things Bess would do, then tells her he's going to do them. He tells her that he'll wash the boy's clothes in the waterhole and hang them to dry over the branch of a tree. He tells her that they'll let the boy sleep, and recover a little, then take him to the nearest house, where someone will direct them to his home. He studies Bess's map (seeing, and ignoring, Wilpena Pound to the north, where his painting awaits him) and, although he's not entirely sure of their location, says, 'We aren't so very far, in fact, from the town.' He brings Bess tea and porridge; she drinks and eats, then leans back against the tree with the boy still in her lap and sleeps herself, which is unlike her. Because he said he would, Karl washes the boy's clothes, which look rather meagre once they're clinging, wet, to a branch. He finds cut shoelaces in one pocket, and a very dirty sock in the other.

While doing these things, Karl thinks about the sunset picture. Everything he sees and does is part of the picture; Denis is now part of the picture, and so is taking Denis home. Wilpena is essential to him, but it will have to wait. He thinks of what he'll write to Alström: 'The boy isn't a distraction so much as an escalation.' And, 'For once, the world and the work demand the same thing.' This must be how Bess feels all the time. Karl goes to fetch the horses from where they're grazing deeper in the gorge and is newly struck by the startling angle of the veins in the red rock. It occurs to him that he's mischaracterised this vast, empty country by thinking of it as new and strange. In fact, it's old and half remembered, like childhood. It's ancient and awful and beautiful, like a civilisation you used to be a part of and forgot all about. You can only peer at a place like this, the way you look for the angels you know are walking in the church. Only a boy lost in the desert or on the streets of Stockholm could understand the ways in which it isn't safe to be alone under this appalling sun, and only that boy could know true shelter when he finds it. Karl leads the horses back to the waterhole, ready to be saddled and loaded, and wakes Bess by bending down and brushing the hair back from her forehead.

'Oh,' says Bess, looking at the boy in her lap. She gestures for a blanket, which Karl brings; gently, she lifts the boy's head onto the blanket. Then she kneels by Denis, inspecting him. Both she and Karl watch to see if the boy will wake. He doesn't. His eyelashes tremble against his blistered cheeks.

Karl waits for Bess to set in motion the business of packing up their camp. She's much better at this than he is; she'll issue instructions and he'll follow them; and she will, naturally, want them to get away quickly, so that this boy can be returned to his mother as soon as possible. Karl thrills with the urgency and mystery of it—a lost child returned to his mother! Yes, now is the time for action and haste, which Bess will facilitate. She'll know, as always, exactly what to do. And after that, Wilpena Pound.

Bess is still kneeling, studying the boy. Then, instead of standing, she takes pencil and paper from her pack, sits beside Denis, and begins to draw him.

Billy waits at the flat rock west of Ewart's Bluff until the two local men pressed into service by Sergeant Foster finally arrive for the rendezvous. Foster's man Wooding appears soon after, along with the native tracker known as Copper Bob. When Billy introduces himself to Bob, Wooding says, 'Don't you lot all know each other?' Wooding pulls out the bloodied handkerchief and is visibly disappointed to learn that it isn't news to Billy, but his mood picks up when he hears of the recovered boots and the fire in the western hills. Both local men thoroughly handle the handkerchief and theorise on its significance; it's never offered to Billy for inspection, but he studies it from where he stands and is grieved by the thought that this may be Denny's blood. The men, having exhausted the handkerchief, explain where Foster can be found, then set off for Undelcarra to locate themselves some breakfast. They have, overnight, become allies, and they ride away with the camaraderie of men who have grievances in common.

Now to find this Sergeant Foster. Constable Wooding defers to Billy in the matter of directions: 'You know the area,' he says. Yes, Billy knows the area. He knows the path the sun takes over the ranges in all seasons. He knows the signalling stars; which trees control the weather; which stories made which places and were made by them in turn. Where Wooding sees scrub and rock, Billy sees a language and can interpret it.

He leads Wooding and Copper Bob up a scree slope, around a stony crest, and through a folded gully golden with flowering *nguri*. As he leads them further into the eastern ranges, he rolls one aching shoulder—a souvenir of last night's fight. He thinks of the hurt and fury on Mathew's face, and he thinks of the laws he *has* broken in his long life. For example, he's helped Henry hunt *urnda*, the white-shouldered scrub wallaby, for sport. He's eaten red kangaroo that hasn't been prepared in the right way by the right people. But he's never killed his totem animal; or looked twice at a girl from the wrong kinship group; or been on forbidden country. If Henry had allowed Billy to be initiated into the second stage of the law, he could have gone with Mathew into the western hills; things being as they are, he can't walk on that country without risking the anger of old spirits, which might harm Denny. Denny would understand this, Billy thinks. Not the details of it, but its profound truth. Billy knows that Mathew will forgive him neither the refusal nor the broken nose.

Foster has made camp in a broad, level gully beneath a sandstone ridge. Billy, Wooding and Copper Bob find it deserted, but Foster and his other tracker aren't far away—they're standing among grass trees on top of the ridge, studying the stony open ground of the next valley. Foster's arms are crossed. Wooding whistles and Foster raises one hand, then starts down the slope towards the camp. The tracker follows in his skin cloak—when Billy nods at him, the man nods back. He descends the rocky slope with a lightness and control that suggest he'd make a decent bowler.

Foster looks and walks and speaks like a man who has always been in charge, but one who hasn't slept: listening to Wooding on the subject of the handkerchief, his face takes on a sceptical, harried look. He all but snatches the handkerchief from Wooding and holds it up against the sky, peering at it as if he might find something decisive in its fibres. When he hears the news of Denny's boots and the fire in the hills, he turns to the other tracker and punches him lightly on the shoulder.

'D'you hear that, Jimmy? The boy's not gone a-wandering—he's been abducted.' Foster shakes his head. 'Abducted!' He uses exactly the tone in which he might announce the name of a winning horse on which he failed to place a bet.

Copper Bob goes to stand beside Jimmy, as if awaiting orders, but Foster draws Wooding aside to confer. Billy watches him stamp his foot and say, 'Wasted! Wasted time!' Jimmy rolls his neck with audible cracks, and Bob whistles through his teeth like a man waiting for the mail coach.

Billy is afraid of two terrible things: Denny's death, and who will be blamed for it. He climbs the low ridge to look at the country beyond—country he's allowed to walk on. The sun is high now, and the shadow of a wedge-tailed eagle crosses the stony valley; walking down there, a horse's shoes would ring like a blacksmith's forge. Billy would like to pick up a stone and bowl it into the valley. But knowing, as he does, exactly where the stone would land makes the actual deed unnecessary; this is why he needs other players, who'll introduce variables. He longs to be evenly matched and to prove himself. Lately, Billy has been teaching Denny how to bowl. Denny has a natural understanding of the seriousness of games, and his aim is improving. Billy jogs back down to the camp without having bowled anything.

Here in the gully, Jimmy talks softly to Copper Bob, gesturing with his uncloaked arm, and Bob nods in agreement. Foster arrives, aloud, at the decision that he will go to the place where Denny's boots were found and take at least one of the trackers with him, but that to completely abandon this north-east trajectory would be reckless.

'*He* says there's a track,' Foster snorts, swatting a hand at Jimmy. 'It's no more than a day old, and there's no horse. *He* says. But bugger me, this boy can't have gone in two directions at once—so what's *he* following? Probably a wallaby for his bloody supper. But if there's a track, it has to be followed.'

Billy stands between the two groups of men, waiting to see what will be required of him. Foster strides and stamps and firms up his plans. Billy will take him to where they found the boots, and on into the western ranges. Jimmy, who's decidedly out of favour but is obviously considered the better of the two trackers, will come along with Foster and Billy. Wooding and Copper Bob will continue to follow these north-eastern tracks.

Billy wonders if the rest of his life will be spent crossing back and forth across the plain, which he has heard described as an empty wasteland but knows to be dense with motion: the motion of ancestors, spirits, the animals that should be here and the animals that shouldn't, songs, stories, people, goods, water, minerals, the railway, the roads, stock tracks, fire and the celestial bodies. When he crosses the plain, he both lives inside this density and passes over it. If Henry Axam hadn't singled Billy out, he would know how to speak to dust storms.

Billy makes a noise of assent when Foster issues his instructions, though he knows Foster neither expects nor needs it. Billy's tired and his horse is tired. When Billy approaches, Virnu swings his long head with its wide white blaze. He's a good horse—very calm. He used to startle when Billy bowled stones and wads of newspaper and imaginary cricket balls, but for a long time now he's shown no interest.

Cissy, Mathew and Robert, in search of last night's fire, have followed a goat track up the hillside, and Cissy is disgusted with it: she would like at least one piece of ground to be flat. She would like, also, to lie down on clean bedding in a cool room, flyless, antless and fatherless. With Denny at her side. Even once they reach the top of the ridge, they have to scramble over rocks and through thick mulga scrub. If her father reaches out a hand to help her over a gap or up a step, Cissy refuses it. There are multiple reasons for this rejection. They include Mathew's unexplained black eyes, his bewildering decision to stop for the night despite spotting the fire, and the fact that, as they set out this morning, Cissy told her father about the Training College and he scrunched his face and said there was no way to pay for such a thing. Then he tried to hurry Cissy—who had slowed her steps to match with his—by employing, in front of Robert, a phrase he often uses to move his horses.

Robert recommends sneaking up on the fire and has advised them not to call Denny's name as they go. Cissy and Mathew have agreed, but Cissy, who wants nothing more than to shout, finds this silence difficult. Mathew leads the group, sure he knows which outcrop to head for. Cissy, who walks behind him, has her doubts. Robert brings up the rear, but as they near their target, he hisses at Cissy to catch her attention, tells her to wait behind a boulder while he goes ahead, and draws his pistol.

'Don't come out until we call for you,' he says, momentarily wrapping one of his big, hot hands around her wrist.

Cissy, heart drumming, waits behind the boulder as she's told to. She prods a cast-off snakeskin with one toe, then leans against the rock, closes her eyes, and listens. A stray hair tickles the side of her face. She wants so much to call Denny's name. It's difficult to say how much time passes before she hears her father shouting. 'Jesus Christ!' he shouts. 'You must be joking! Jesus bloody Christ!' He isn't calling Cissy, but she still goes.

Mathew and Robert have found the remains of the fire in a shallow cave near the edge of a cliff. They've also found the man who lit it: Mr Daniels, the vicar, who's curled around a pack at the back of the cave, and fast asleep. He's lying by a large ant nest full of holes—the ants, each one as long as a fingernail, are busy at these tiny entrances. The top of the cave has been scorched black by centuries of campfires. There are wasp nests built into this sooty ceiling, and a dark moss crawls over the part of the rock that's most exposed to the weather; small red insects flicker over the moss. At the back of the cave, where Mr Daniels sleeps among the ants, there are shapes painted on the walls in yellow and white and ochre: tree shapes or maybe the skeletons of fish, and possibly the figure of a golden man standing many-limbed on a mountain. There's no sign of Denny.

'The vicar,' Mathew says. 'My arse. The bloody vicar.'

Cissy ducks her head, steps into the cave, and kicks at the sole of one of Daniels' boots. This is the second time she's seen him on the ground this week.

'Steady,' says Robert, who has put his pistol away.

Cissy kicks the vicar's boot again, harder this time, and goes back out to stand beside her father. Mr Daniels' camp stands at the eastern end of a long, narrow ridge, and commands a magnificent view of the Willochra Plain.

'I could wring his neck,' says Mathew.

Robert exhales loudly. 'He might still be involved.'

'Ha!' says Cissy. 'You think *he* made off with Denny? He couldn't kidnap his own trousers. Last time I saw him, he was waving a baby's napkin about.'

Mathew says, 'It goes some way to explaining the daft tracks. This idiot. Let him sleep, maybe the ants'll eat him.'

But Robert wants to see what the vicar has to say for himself, so Cissy goes back into the cave and kicks his boot again.

It takes Daniels some time to wake. When he does, he sits up and knocks his head against the cave ceiling. If he's surprised to find people looking down at him, he doesn't show it. He's groggy but courteous, as if he's opened his front door to see who's disturbed his afternoon nap. He'll receive them, as is proper, and when they leave he'll go straight back to sleep.

'Wallace,' says the vicar, with a nod of confirmation. 'Excellent. Wallace.' He's shuffled himself forwards to spare his head, but doesn't make any attempt to stand or leave the cave. His hair is darkened with dust.

Robert clears his throat and says, 'What are you doing, man, all alone up here? Where's your horse?'

Daniels turns his head towards the plain. 'Looking,' he says. Then he turns back, peering up at them. 'Looking. Hello, Cissy.'

Cissy is reminded of his expression when he fell at the wedding breakfast; also when she found him holding Lotta's dirty cloth. He's completely without guile. He holds out his palms as if to show her how empty they are, and begins to cry.

'Oh great God,' says Mathew. 'Spare us.'

Cissy is appalled by these humiliating tears, which are silent and streaming. Mr Daniels seems unaware of them.

She says, 'I think he's been out looking for Denny.'

Daniels nods. 'I didn't see him. He isn't anywhere.'

'This idiot,' Mathew says.

Cissy kneels beside the vicar. 'You've been looking for Denny, haven't you?'

'He isn't anywhere,' Mr Daniels repeats. He wipes with his sleeve at the wetness on his cheeks in exactly the way Denny would, and although this leaves a streak of dirt across his nose, there's still nothing muddy or complicated about his face. 'I've looked. From here I can see everything. I can see you, Cissy.'

'What about these?' asks Mathew, holding Denny's boots up.

'Aha!' cries Daniels, in apparent recognition. 'I lost my horse.'

'I've been following *this*,' says Mathew. 'How'd he get out ahead of us? This!'

Mr Daniels looks up at Mathew and says, 'Your eyes are hidden.'

'He's sick,' says Cissy. She presses the back of her hand against the vicar's forehead. 'He has a fever. Where's your food? Do you have water?'

Robert crouches beside Cissy. He's so close that his knee touches her back; the sensation reminds her that she's in love with him, but this only conjures Miss McNeil's dimples.

'Did you find a pair of children's boots, Mr Daniels?' Robert asks.

Mr Daniels says, 'I left them right where they belong.'

Mathew says, 'I'd knock his brains out if it were worth doing.' His bruised face is very ugly.

Now Daniels lies back down, but he continues to look at Cissy with peaceable curiosity. 'I see the shepherd,' he says.

'We have to help him,' Cissy says. But she doesn't want to. She wants, in fact, to kick the ashes of his fire over his face. She's so tired, and they've climbed so far, and now they'll climb down again, still without Denny. The ants continue their itchy industry at the many mouths of the nest.

Robert says, 'A wild-goose chase, then. And Billy's bringing the sergeant over here, all for nothing.'

Cissy considers. Or, she tries to consider, but she's distracted by Robert's knee at her back, and by the sickly tint of the vicar's face, which reminds her of the man in the post office, Mr Blake, and his green visor. Does he sleep in the visor? she wonders. Does he wear it as he strains on the privy, does he wear it while he washes his armpits on Saturday nights? Would Mr Blake leave a man to die on a mountain?

But Mr Daniels isn't dying. Cissy opens his pack and finds food and water—look, he has provisions after all. He's lying down, but she lifts his head and makes him drink.

'All right,' says Mathew. 'Let's get moving. He wanted water, and now he's had it.'

'We can't just leave him,' Cissy says, and looks to Robert, who is, after all, the law and will know what to do. But Robert shifts, his knee leaves her back, and he stands up, then walks over to the edge of the cliff. He lifts his hand to shade his eyes and looks across the plain as if he might catch a glimpse of Minna eating breakfast. Robert wants to be out of these hills as much as she does.

'He's made his bed,' says Mathew. He turns and begins to pick his way back along the ridge.

Robert looks at Cissy. 'He's only thinking of his son.'

Cissy is also thinking of Denny, who wouldn't leave the vicar in the cave. Her brother might even have helped the vicar, as Cissy failed to, when he fell at Minna's wedding. She hears her father roar her name along the ridge top. To Mr Daniels, she says, 'You have to eat and drink.'

The vicar smiles at her, but he's falling asleep again.

'Are you going to stay?' Robert asks.

Cissy doesn't answer him. She hears Mathew whistling loud and long, further away now.

Robert says, 'I should go with him, keep looking for your brother.'

Cissy wonders what the point of love is, if it's going to abandon her. Can she revoke her choice and disown Robert? Yes, she thinks she can.

Robert crouches again, although his knee doesn't touch her. 'Can you manage him?' he asks. 'Get him off this hill and home as soon as he's able?'

Another whistle, further off. Cissy nods, and Robert squeezes her shoulder. He says, 'You'd make a good policeman.' Then he's gone.

Cissy digs her finger into Mr Daniels' side; he responds by sighing and turning his face into the dirt.

'Up,' says Cissy, and pulls at the vicar's shoulders until he's sitting. He sways and puts one hand to his head.

'Drink.' Cissy pushes his pack into his lap. 'Eat. Will you?'

Mr Daniels nods: yes, he will.

'If I leave you here, do you promise to eat and drink?'

'Oh, yes,' says Mr Daniels.

'Could you get yourself home?'

'Oh, yes,' says Mr Daniels.

Cissy hears one more whistle. Go, she says to herself, or maybe to her father, and incidentally to Robert. Go, go, go. She squats at the vicar's feet, looks at his stupid face, and doesn't go.

---

Mary's other telegram, the one addressed to her oldest son, Joseph, has been received by the post office of a town in Victoria: a town of medium size, built solidly in brick, not particularly near the goldfields but with a gloss of gold upon it. The telegram is destined for a cattle station twenty miles from this town. The mail goes out to this district today, and Mary's message goes with it. When the mail coach calls in at the station, the driver draws the housekeeper's attention to the telegram, but not before she has fed him and plied him with strong tea. The housekeeper is all gruff efficiency until she sees the telegram; then she becomes confidential.

'Well,' she says. 'Who knew Joe Wallace had such a thing as a mother?'

'Why shouldn't he?' asks the driver, who doesn't know Joe Wallace.

'We've wondered,' the housekeeper says, 'since the baby was born. No one knew what to do with it, poor mite.'

'What baby's that, then?'

Joe Wallace, it seems, was a cheerful lad, bit of a rascal, and couldn't keep his pisser in his pants. He knocked up one of the maids—'a half-caste girl,' says the housekeeper, 'come from the missionaries, no family to speak of'—and when the girl started showing her condition, Joe moved on, no forwarding address. That was months ago.

And what of the maid?

She was let go, what else? The housekeeper shrugs. 'An ugly, sallow creature, though she did know how to scrub a floor. She went into town and the blacksmith took her in, though not entirely from the goodness of his heart. A dogsbody, she was, and a warm body at night, no doubt. People say he worked her so hard that the baby came early and the girl died, poor thing, in the delivery. Needless to say, the blacksmith didn't want to feed another man's son—not if the mother weren't there to make more kids on. No one knew a thing about her kin, nor

Joe Wallace's. And now here's Joe's mother sending telegrams from South Australia.'

'Where's the baby, then?' the driver asks.

'Vicar's wife took him,' says the housekeeper. 'She's none too pleased—got plenty of her own. She's one of them likes to do good and complain about it. Curly hair, he has, like his ma, and uncommon wrinkled when he came out. But his skin's pretty fair. They called him Arthur. Christened on his ma's coffin, poor lamb.'

'And there's no way to find this Joe Wallace?'

The housekeeper throws up her hands, then slaps them against her thighs—flour drifts from her apron—and by this gesture she means that men like Joe Wallace will always be disappearing, and that no one will ever be able to find them.

'Trouble is,' the driver says, 'I have to report on any telegram that's not delivered. And I don't like to report. Puts me to a bit of bother, you might say. And if there's no one goes by Joseph Wallace at this address . . .'

'Ah,' says the housekeeper, 'but you've come to the address, haven't you, and fulfilled your end of the bargain. So leave it with me, and no need to report.'

The driver, however, has been tempted by such shortcuts before and prefers to make things square. This is how news of the telegram is passed on to the overseer of the station; from him, word spreads through the stockmen, who carry it to the inn five miles away, where they drink with the man who's building a new outhouse for the rectory, who lets it slip to the vicar's nursemaid, who tells the vicar's wife that they have an address for Joe Wallace and can now send the baby. The vicar's wife begins to make arrangements at once, beginning with a telegram in reply. Baby Arthur's hair curls in puffs above each ear and he has recently discovered his feet.

The man who owns the cattle station on which Arthur's parents met lives in Melbourne and only visits this property, one of many in his possession, for a few weeks every year. If he ever learns of Arthur, or hears the name Joe Wallace, he forgets both within minutes.

A large camel team, on its way north to Beltana station, arrives in Fairly in the hour before sunset. The cameleers make camp beside the creek, and the town's residents walk down to look at them—Fairly sees camels reasonably often, but rarely quite so many all in one place. The camels cough and spit, and their Afghan drivers rebuke them, but with affection. 'Hoosh!' call the cameleers, and the camels bray and dance; 'Hoosh!', and the leading camel on each string tilts forwards and backwards on its foldable legs and sits down, followed by the camel behind it, then the camel behind that, and on until they're all seated. Then it's difficult to believe in their legs. They chew their cud, swallow it, bring it up again, chew their cud, and the drivers hobble the camels, remove their loads, and disconnect each animal from the string. Then some of the camels stand again, stretching their sinuous necks, and begin to eat from the willows by the creek. They scratch their flanks against the trunks of the trees, or piss for minutes, but none of them seem inclined to walk down to the creek to drink.

As the Afghans unroll packs, lay down carpets and pull cooking equipment from wooden trunks, they call to the camels. The local people, observing this, assume that the Afghans are calling the camels' names. These names sound like a spell to call down spirits, gods, the night. Some of the locals find this funny, or disconcerting, or both, and some of them recognise the way in which they call their own animals—Rover, Bessie, Florence, Clorinda—as if the names are a prayer, an incantation of safety and possession. So, the people of Fairly, watching the Afghans call out to their camels, and seeing the camels swing their heads or dip them in response, or just shift their sandy haunches, are reminded of their own flocks, and the necessary joy and worry of gathering them in. Children congregate at the camp, both wary of and fascinated by the camels, and the cameleers distribute boiled lollies, as is their custom. One man opens a pack to display patterned shawls and metal spoons with pierced handles; women come shyly to look, but no one buys anything. The sky begins to turn red and the cameleers build fires. The children, braver, move closer to the camels in order to inspect the swags and bells and necklaces they all wear.

The sunset this evening is the most violent yet. The sky rears up over the ranges, raw and red, broken in places by bars of bronze and pillars of gold. Mr Daniels, waking in the cave with a hammering head, looks at the sky and says, 'The sack of Jerusalem.' This doesn't startle Cissy, who has spent the afternoon watching Daniels wake up, say foolish things, and fall asleep again; to her, the sunset is nothing more than a marker that the day is ending and that her time has been wasted.

Karl stands at the mouth of the gorge, as he did the sunset before this one; he wants to repeat his promise to the sky that he'll get to Wilpena as soon as he can, but he feels uneasy, as if events are moving beyond his control and in ways he's not entirely sure he understands. Bess, still drawing the sleeping boy, racing to the end of the day's light, barely glances at the sky.

Billy, who feels he's been going in circles for days, rides behind Foster and in front of Jimmy Possum. He wonders what Denny makes of the boiling sky, and whether or not Mathew has found him in the Axam Range. Foster seems to rise in his saddle, as if this sky is, at last, a fitting backdrop to his struggles; in fact, he's impatient with the lowering light and sits higher in an attempt to see further. He wants to find the boy, ride into town, and visit each hotel, where the patrons will shout him to endless drinks.

Mary, sitting on the verandah at Undelcarra, finds that she can hear the roaring of the sky and, behind it, the sound of her father reminding her not to let the sun set on her wrath, for fear of giving the Devil a foothold (believing that anger only ever manifests in shouting and violence, Mary considers herself out of danger). Mathew, on his way to her with Denny's boots, feeling that he's failed, tries not to interpret the sunset as an extension of his personal catastrophe.

Robert Manning, riding towards Fairly, toys with the idea that his cock is a candle and the sky, therefore, his own flame; then he's embarrassed at having imagined anything so strange. Minna, looking down the road for Robert, thinks of the deep, swollen red of her mother's opal ring.

At Thalassa, the sunset reddens windows, water, stone, the slate of the roof, the damp tip of Bolingbroke's nose and

Joanna's scissors as she works in the garden. Henry's tall palm trees burn black and gold in the flaring light, as if they were planted especially for a sky like this one.

The sun sets behind the ranges. While the sky is still bright with colour, the cameleers wash their feet with water from the creek and begin their evening prayers. None of the locals are bold enough to stay and watch.

# FOURTH NIGHT

Billy, Sergeant Foster and Jimmy Possum make camp for the night by an old sand-filled soak, which Foster orders Billy and Jimmy to dig out for water. They're not far from the place where Billy found Denny's boots. Foster has been in a fury since an afternoon encounter with Robert Manning, who, empty-handed, was on his way back to Fairly, where he intended to change horses before setting out again. Mathew, he said, was further north, heading for Undelcarra. Upon hearing that all they'd found in the ranges (and left there, apparently) was a vicar, Foster fumed and said, 'Then why isn't he in custody?'

An argument followed, in which Manning insisted that the vicar wasn't capable of wiping his own arse, let alone making off with a child the whole town was looking for. What's more, Manning knew for certain that the vicar had been busy on the day the boy went missing: 'He was marrying me,' said Manning, 'to my wife.' The sergeant muttered something about accomplices, but by the time Manning left them, Foster had declared the following: Daniels couldn't be their first priority, but he was a person of considerable interest and should be placed in custody as soon as possible. Finding Denny was still their first priority.

'At this point,' Foster said, to no one in particular, 'we're looking for a body.'

Billy had already had this thought, but rejected it as both useless and unbearable.

Now, at camp, Billy is reminded of droving camps he's stayed in, in which the cattle gathered in a weary huddle and men rode around them in circles all night, singing to keep them calm. Those camps were full of hardened drovers who knew not to raise their voice or clang a spoon for fear of spooking the stock, and Billy shows the same caution around Foster's mood. Jimmy does the same. Billy is wary of Jimmy, who with his bushcraft and his uniform seems at once more like Billy ought to be, and far less. Jimmy doesn't speak much; at one point, though, he looks up at Foster and says, under his breath but loud enough for Billy to hear, 'Just like it bloody schoolboy.'

There's corned beef, tea and damper for an early supper. Afterwards, both Foster and Jimmy sit down to smoke their pipes. But Billy is restless, so he walks away from their camp and finds a stretch of level ground. Here, he presses a stick into the dirt to make a makeshift stump. Then he paces out the length of a cricket pitch and begins bowling stones at the stick.

Billy likes the feeling of using his arms for bowling rather than digging out sand or fighting Mathew. He likes the cool of the night, the moonlight on the pale acacia. He's bowled a full eight stones when he hears applause, looks for its source, and sees Foster, who calls, 'Bravo!'

Foster approaches. 'You're rather quick,' he says.

Billy can tell he's genuinely impressed, and that this has lightened his mood; but he could turn at any moment.

Foster bends down, picks up a stone, and tosses it thoughtfully from one hand to the other. He drags the toe of one boot across Billy's imaginary crease and positions himself to take his run-up. Billy sees that this matters to Foster: having been impressed, Foster wants to impress in turn. But he's moving now, and his form's uneven. Billy knows exactly what Henry would say: your run-up is too long, you're losing momentum in your delivery stride, you've brought your hip too far forwards and released too soon. Arm before hip, Billy! Watch the seam, Billy! Foster's bowled what would be a decent line if he were bowling to a left-handed batsman, but there was no weight in it. Still, Billy is prepared to be gracious. A stone isn't a cricket ball, and this would be a respectable line and length for a friendly match.

'Not my best,' Foster admits, and takes up another stone. 'When I apply myself to accuracy, I lose speed. The opposite is also true, of course. How d'you manage both at once?'

This question, too, is genuine, but Billy knows to be cautious. His skill has drawn the attention of men like Foster before. They might begin with admiration; they often end with wounded pride.

Billy says, 'What you want is weight. Don't trouble with speed.'

'And how do I do that?'

Billy must take real care now: Foster has explicitly invited instruction that he may resent receiving. Billy drops his gaze and says, 'First off, no need for a long run-up.'

'What, you mean I'm starting too far from the crease? Show me.'

Billy shows him.

Foster says, 'Damn me, you're one of those native cricketers, aren't you, who toured England? You've got to be.'

Billy shakes his head. 'Too old,' he says. He thinks of his young self in his cricket whites, truly believing he was training for Lord's. An Aboriginal cricket team did play in England in the late sixties, but Henry was dead by then and Billy was droving. In any case, all of those players had been recruited from the eastern colonies.

'Show me again,' says Foster. 'I want to watch your knees.'

'Watch the hips,' Billy says, and bowls again, but this time he goes deliberately wide.

'Ah!' cries Foster, with obvious relish. 'Bad luck, eh?'

There was no luck involved; for Billy, luck takes the form of a batsman waiting to meet his ball, who might send it in a number of directions. He hangs his head in humility, hoping that this deliberate error will end the lesson, and when he raises it he sees that Jimmy Possum has joined them. Jimmy is standing at deep mid-wicket, smoking his pipe, and just by looking at him Billy feels as if he's been caught out doing something dishonourable. Billy knows that Jimmy is a Ramindjeri man; he has heard those men, who live in the south of the colony, dismissed contemptuously as uncircumcised. The shadowy bulk of Jimmy's cloak makes him seem larger than he is. Billy doesn't think Foster has noticed him.

Foster selects another stone and positions himself behind the crease. 'Here?' he asks, and Billy says, 'Shorter.'

'Shorter!' Foster is obviously enjoying the novelty of it all. 'Any more advice?'

Billy glances at Jimmy Possum. He says, 'Wait a bit before you let go of the ball.'

'Listen,' says Foster, pausing before he bowls, 'have you ever thought of the police? We could use a talented man like you down at Port Augusta. The pay is good, the uniform's provided. A damn sight more interesting than things up here. What I wouldn't give to see you in a match against Port Wakefield! The looks on their faces.' He chuckles to himself. 'You could play as far off as Gawler, and there's a man or two in Adelaide I'd like to get their eyes on you. What was your name again?'

'Billy Rough.'

'Well, Billy, we could use a man like you. What d'you say to that?'

What does Billy say to that? He could say that he knows this story: a powerful white man admiring his skill, making promises, and disappearing. But it's true that Billy can't go back to live at Undelcarra—not after the fight with Mathew—and his choices are limited. Foster is waiting for an answer. Billy says, 'I'll think on it.'

'Good,' Foster says, apparently convinced that Billy's thoughts will lead him to the right decision. 'Very good. Just say the word.'

Foster bowls, and it's noticeably worse than the last time. Although visibly frustrated, he seems willing to try again. But as he looks about for a suitable stone, he spots Jimmy Possum, and bulky Jimmy and his pipe appear to startle Foster back into his bad mood. He calls out, 'You bugger! Who's watching the fire? Go on, now!'

Jimmy looks at Billy, turns, and goes. But Billy can see that Jimmy's presence, however briefly noted, has spoiled the lesson for Foster. The sergeant looks fiercely at Billy. 'And you too,' he says. 'What we need right now is sleep, not games.' He stalks back towards the camp.

Billy waits a minute or two before following. He relishes the silence and the darkness. He likes knowing how to bowl with both accuracy and speed. There are other things he could know if Henry hadn't kept him from the slow, demanding process of learning them. Tonight, though, walking back to the camp, Billy savours the fact that at least he knows things Foster doesn't, and among them: that Denny is smart and strong, and that he may still be alive.

⁂

Minna goes down to the Afghans and their camels after sunset, as the last of the local people are leaving. As she passes them, they greet her with some disapproval, although they themselves are coming from the creek. But now the sun has gone down, there's only a tinge of red left in the west, and it's time for decent citizens to be at home. Minna pays them no attention. She's a citizen of her body and of her marriage.

She's been asleep all day, because she was awake all night—waiting for Robert. Once, when she was a girl, wasps built a nest in the hollow brass frame of Minna's bed. Waiting for Robert last night was like lying in a brass bed full of wasps. She thrummed with the invisible diligence of the hive. Even now, approaching the camels, she's buzzing. Minna stands out of sight in the trees along the creek. She watches the camels: most are sleeping, but one of them, a big white one, hems and haws like an old man after a heavy dinner, and brays through blubbery lips. This noisy camel has tight curls beneath its chin, like a Greek in a picture book. It lets out a long, high-pitched wheeze until the camel beside it snaps at its haunches. The Afghans ignore it. Minna counts six men gathered around two fires, all dressed in loose white clothes, some with dark jackets or waistcoats. They all wear white turbans.

What does Minna know about the Afghans? Next to nothing. She knows that they're Mohammedans, like the Turks. At school she learned a poem about the Austrian army fighting the Turks, and every line alliterated on a new letter of the alphabet. Line number nine was, '*Ibraham, Islam, Ismael, imps in ill*,' and she'd pictured the Turks as dark little goblins swarming the Austrians, though these men aren't especially dark, or little, or goblin-like. She believes that the Afghans all come from Arabia, or possibly from India, where camels live—the Afghans were imported along with the camels, to look after them. The camels are necessary, because horses can't manage the true desert. She also believes the Afghans to be lustful, dirty and savage, and that they drink the urine of their animals, but if anyone were to ask her where she acquired this information, she would be unable to tell them.

Even asleep, the camels shift and chew. One of the men takes a kettle from the fire and pours its steaming contents into a pail. He carries this pail to the noisy white camel, which is decidedly not sleeping; when the man bends down to its face, the camel renews its complaints. The man takes the rope that hangs from the camel's nose and the camel, groaning, rises to its feet. The Afghan laughs and leads the camel along the creek, in Minna's direction. Minna sees that the Afghan is quite lean—boyish, although his beard is full. Minna would be afraid to step into the camp full of cameleers and animals, but she finds herself wanting to be near this one man and his camel with its beard like Alexander the Great. Only when the Afghan is closer to her and turns to encourage the camel forwards does she see the shotgun slung across his back. She knows she should be scared, but isn't.

The Afghan stops not far from Minna, puts down the pail, and ties the camel by its rope to a tree. He wears rings on his hands, and the long tail of his white turban rests on one shoulder. His face looks unguarded here among the trees—you could almost say pretty, even with his dark beard. This beauty, which surprises Minna, puts the Afghan in company with Karl Rapp and with Robert; she feels for him what she feels for them. She's unsure what she feels. She feels large and pure and loving. Her body is the beginning of everything.

It's dark under the trees, so the Afghan hasn't noticed Minna. She steps out from the shadows and says, 'Hello.'

The Afghan turns and is startled to see her, perhaps also frightened—he looks back at the other men by the fire, but they aren't watching.

Minna says, 'I didn't mean to startle you,' and smiles.

The Afghan smiles back. He puts one hand on the camel's flank, and the camel shifts on its feet. It wears a necklace of pink and green pompoms, hung with a bell, and there are three red pompoms on the bridge of its nose.

'May I?' Minna asks, holding one hand out to the camel. The Afghan nods. Minna hovers her hand close to his. 'Is this a good place?'

'Here,' says the Afghan, moving his hand towards the camel's head. 'He likes this.'

The camel lowers its head as if it understands, and Minna scratches above its plush eyebrows, as she would a dog. It has a sharp, rotten smell around its mouth, and the peg that attaches the camel to its rope is crusty in its nostril. The camel drools and nudges, closing its long, sticky eyelashes.

'It's lovely,' she says, and it is, but it also seems impolite to use this word about the camel when the Afghan beside it is lovely too. And very near her now, so that she can see the independent hairs of his beard. They both rub at the waxy wool of the white camel.

'What is your name?' she asks.

The Afghan, with a nod of his head, says, 'I am Charlie.'

Every man with an unpronounceable name becomes, eventually, a Charlie.

'And his name?' Minna indicates the camel.

'Also Charlie.' The Afghan laughs and she laughs with him.

'Hello, Charlie,' she says, nodding to both man and camel.

The Afghan stops laughing but continues to smile. 'No, no,' he says. 'Not Charlie. He is called Tukum.'

'You're Charlie,' says Minna, 'and he's Tukum, and my name is Minna.'

'Minna? Minna,' says the Afghan.

'It's German,' Minna says. 'Short for Hermina. A German name.'

'You are German?'

'Yes,' says Minna. 'You speak English very well.'

'You speak well also,' says the Afghan.

She doesn't tell him that English is her first language—she understands German, but hardly speaks it, and only calls herself German because her mother insists on it.

The Afghan leans into the camel's face so that their noses almost touch; he says a word in another language and the camel's head rises with a long, deep cry that makes the Afghan smile again.

'He is a beautiful camel,' Minna says. 'The most beautiful camel of all.'

'Yes,' says the Afghan. 'The white camel is the most beautiful. He is a noisy cloud.'

There's nothing in the world to do but laugh with this man beneath the trees. The world smells of pepper and smoke and dung and animal.

'Why did you bring him away from the others?' Minna asks.

'He is sick.'

'What's the matter with him?'

The Afghan seems embarrassed. 'He cannot pass.'

'Is there something wrong with his feet?'

'Feet? No, no.'

'What, then?'

'I cannot say.' The Afghan is so sweet in his shyness—he might be a boy hiding behind a beard. So Minna relents, and won't press him to explain what's wrong with Tukum if he doesn't know the English words for it. It makes sense to Minna that camels and their illnesses should belong to a language she can't understand.

She asks, 'Will you help him?'

The Afghan indicates the shotgun on his back, which Minna had forgotten about.

'But you won't shoot him!' she cries; Tukum, too, cries out as if in protest.

'No, no, not shoot,' says the Afghan; he reaches a hand towards Minna's shoulder as if in comfort, but draws it back before touching her.

'What, then?'

The Afghan looks at Tukum, who returns his look; they could be conferring. The white camel produces a gulping moan. It's as if they've decided on something together, and now the Afghan reports, 'I cannot say.' He spreads his hands and offers an apologetic smile. The shotgun glints on his back.

Still with one hand buried in the thick coat of the camel, Minna steps close to the Afghan and raises her face to his. The wasps buzz loudly in the bed.

The Afghan says, 'You are the one with the donkey?'

She realises that he thinks she's the prostitute, Inge Schmidt, who pretends to be German; an ordinary white woman would never approach an Afghan in this way. Inge Schmidt keeps a donkey at her door, and if a customer comes, she throws a blanket over the donkey so that other men will know to wait. The donkey swelters in the summer; in winter, if business is poor, it shivers in the cold. Could Minna do that to a donkey?

'Yes,' she says. What will he do now—and what will she? Will she let him touch her? Robert could pick him up with one arm and throw him across the creek. The Afghan averts his face.

'It's all right,' she says, moving even closer. 'Don't be frightened.'

But the Afghan shakes his head and steps away from her. His eyes, when he looks up, are pained, but it's not even that he's sorry for her. He's sad, she sees; and she sees herself as the latest in the series of strange things that have happened to him in this strange country, things that aren't quite real. But this lasts only a moment. Then she's Minna again, for whom the world was made. She wants to say: This is a game, and I love my husband. She wants to say: How dare you refuse me! Instead she says, 'Why not?'

Now he begins to speak in another language; it's the language, she assumes, in which he's eloquent in the diseases of the camel. He holds one palm up as if to ward her off. The camel nuzzles at his neck and he pushes it back. It steps sideways, away from Minna, and she pulls her hand from its flank. Her fingers feel gritty. The camel probably has fleas. Well, let the fleas come; they, at least, won't refuse her. The Afghan looks less pretty to her now. He has deep shadows under his eyes and a scar beside one ear; he's lucky to be allowed near her. This thought makes her laugh, and the Afghan stops speaking.

She says, 'The one with the donkey wouldn't even let you touch her. Do you understand? She doesn't take men like you.'

The Afghan says, 'God give you Heaven.'

'What did you say?' asks Minna, although she heard him.

'God give you Heaven,' he repeats, and adds a phrase in his own language.

Minna says, 'My husband is a constable. Police. Police.'

The Afghan looks left and right, as if there might be policemen hidden in the trees, and he pulls the white camel towards himself. It cries out and the other men at the fire look up.

Minna turns and walks away, through the willows and up from the creek. She feels fine and strong. But she walks to her mother's house rather than to the police station, because she doesn't trust herself to spend another night alone.

◆

It's fully night by the time Mathew reaches his own land. If anyone were to mention the recent red of the sky, Mathew would speak of it only in relation to what it might mean for the weather—and he isn't sure what it might mean for the weather, since these gaudy sunsets are unusual. Like all farmers, Mathew has a healthy distrust of the unusual. He distrusts his house tonight, too. He knows that it's full of people, because he can see them at the windows. He can also hear them singing, accompanied by an accordion; the tune is neither mournful nor exultant. There are unfamiliar horses in the yard.

Mathew dreads walking through his own front door and seeing people turn to look at his bruised face. He'd like Cissy to come out of the house and down to the gate, to take his horse and tell him how to arrive in such a way that no one will see or speak to him, but he's left Cissy in the Axam Range, and he hasn't found Denny, and all around him his own wheat is burrowing, it seems to him, back into the ground, so as not to hear what he's going to say to Mary. What *is* he going to say to Mary? That he's wasted days, that he shouldn't be here without Denny, that he doesn't know what to do now. That he hates failing her. That once you give a man a bad name, you might as well hang him.

Mathew turns Bonfire out into the yard and goes to the stable to check on the other horses, all of which look well but seem uneasy. He takes the bag with Denny's boots in it and waits on the verandah until he hears the people inside the house nearing the end of a song; then he enters the place quietly, as if it belongs to someone else. Mary sits with her back to the door. The room is full, mostly of women; he sees them see him and decide, collectively and without communication, that they will make no sign and continue to sing their hymn so as not to startle Mary. Ada and Noella are perched on the chiffonier, and they look at him with puzzled fascination—who's this man with two black eyes, dressed as our father?—and also a squirming concern that they should get down from the chiffonier, which he's told them isn't for sitting on. Mathew presses one shushing finger to his lips, then removes his hat and stands by the door with the hat cradled against his chest. Mopsy comes and whimpers at his knee. Mathew waits for the hymn to finish, which is when someone will touch Mary's arm and she'll turn and see him.

It happens just that way. Mary turns and sees him, and her face, as usual, is difficult to read. But the faces of the other women in the room say: what a shame, he's alone, he hasn't found his boy, and what a shame he's in that state, his face looks a fright, how can he show his face, what shame. Mathew feels this shame all through his long, tall form, in the bulby mess of his ear, in the knotty veins of his legs and the permanent ache in his back and in all the parts of himself that remind him he's getting old while continuing to disappoint his wife, who in choosing him has married down. Not that Mary has ever said, 'I'm disappointed.' But it's there, nevertheless, in the way she speaks and dresses, her insistence that the children wear shoes, the fact that she prefers souchong tea but would never spend the extra money on it. The disappointment also resides in the chiffonier, the embroidered cushions and her mother's clock on the mantel.

The faces of the other women in the room say: he's been gone for four days, you'll never find him now. The women smile and nod and gather their things together, knowing it's time to leave, and all the time they're saying: you should be ashamed, we hope you're ashamed, are you ashamed? Mathew smiles and nods and accepts the hands that squeeze his forearms and pat his shoulders. He could truthfully say: Yes, I am, I'm mightily ashamed. But won't.

The accordion player wheezes his instrument back into its case and leaves with the air of a fellow just stepping outside, no particular reason, don't mind me. Then it's just Mary, sitting in one of the dining chairs, and Joy, who's standing by the stove, and Ada and Noella, who have slithered down from the chiffonier, taking care not to scrape it with their heels. Mopsy, anxious, looks between Mathew and Mary as if deciding which of them to comfort first.

'Did you see Cissy?' Joy asks. 'She went looking for you.'

Mathew nods. 'It's like this,' he says loudly, stepping further into the room and addressing himself to Mary. 'We came across the minister fellow, Daniels, out of his mind with thirst and fever, and Cissy stayed to help him.'

'Is Cissy lost too, then?' Noella asks, taking her father's hat from his hand and putting it on her head.

'Shush,' says Ada. Noella removes the hat.

''Course she's not lost,' says Mathew. He crouches beside Mary and rests his hands on her knees. He can't think what to say. Mary reaches for his chin; holding it between her thumb and forefinger, she inspects his wounded face.

'It's nothing,' he says, leaning away from her. 'I fell and bumped my nose is all.'

Noella giggles.

Joy says, 'Did Cissy tell about the handkerchief? I'm the one who found it.'

'Ah, she did,' says Mathew. 'Can I see it?'

'The constable from Port Augusta took it with him,' Mary says. 'Do you have the boots?'

'How d'you know about the boots?' he asks, suddenly suspicious, though of what he couldn't say.

'Some men came back from the sergeant with the news,' Ada says.

'Where's my bag?' says Mathew. 'Fetch it for me, Ada. See here.'

He opens his bag, draws out Denny's boots, and places them in Mary's lap. Joy and Ada cry out, Noella bursts into tears, and Mary touches the boots all over with her hands—as if she's blind rather than deaf. Her hands are shaking.

'We followed the trail but all it got us was the vicar.'

Ada steps closer and places one hand on her father's shoulder. 'What does it mean?' she asks.

Mathew says, 'It means we found his boots, nothing more.'

Mary sets the boots down on the floor beside her chair, looks at Mathew, and says, 'You need a compress.'

'No need to fuss.'

But Mathew knows that Mary is relieved to have this task to do: it gives her a reason to stand up, to insist that he sit, to make preparations; it gives her a reason not to have to speak or listen. Mathew allows himself to be placed in his chair by the stove. Ada sits at his feet and Noella, with tears on her face, leans against his shoulder.

'All right, my lambs,' says Mathew.

Ada touches her father's knee. 'People are saying someone might have run off with Denny. But it couldn't be the vicar, could it?'

'I'm not so sure as someone's took him,' says Mathew.

Ada nods, but she looks sceptical.

Joy starts forwards. 'But the handkerchief?'

Mary says, 'Joy! Is that Lotta fussing?' And Joy, making a face, goes into the silent bedroom to check on sleeping Lotta.

Ada says, 'Billy was with the sergeant.'

'Does that mean he's arrested?' Noella asks.

Mathew shakes his head. He's watching Mary without looking at her—she glides about, fetching and preparing, as if someone has wound her up in the same smooth way as the clock on the mantel.

'Why aren't you with the sergeant?' Ada asks.

Mathew shakes her hand off his knee. 'Fetch me the tea box,' he says.

'What for?'

'Just fetch it.'

Ada scrambles up and, on tiptoes, reaches for the tea box on its high shelf. Mary stretches over her, takes the box, and passes it to Mathew. It rattles, full of bullets. He'd like Mary to ask why he isn't with the sergeant, why he's at home, what he needs the bullets for—but she turns away without looking at him. And how would he answer her? He doesn't know what the bullets are for. He's had his rifle and ammunition with him throughout the search. He could have blasted the minister with it today and Billy last night—Lord knows he wanted to. It may be that he just wants to run his hand over the wood of the tea box, which is proof that he once surprised Mary with a gift of souchong tea and she thanked him with a kiss.

Joy comes back into the room carrying Lotta, who sees her father and makes a happy whimper. Mary returns to Mathew's side, tilts his head back, and holds a compress over his eyes. It's cool and heavy and Mary presses it with considerable force against his head. He feels, then, that he's being punished, and that, by sending Joy to collect Lotta, Mary is making sure that all his children—all the ones he hasn't lost—are here to see it. He feels his cool, heavy responsibility for the humans in this room. He thinks of the mortgage, and the carting work that will pay for it. Mary makes him sit like this, with his throat bared, for half an hour, and at some point she shaves him. Mathew works not to shiver at every stroke of the razor's blade.

Later, when the girls have gone to bed and Mary has finished her chores and Mathew has seen to the horses and the only light in the house under the red hill comes from the coals of the dying fire, Mathew lies on his narrow cot in the lean-to. He smokes his pipe. Mary never allowed him to smoke when they shared a bed, and that was all right: it meant that he'd instilled in her the farmer's fear of fire. Will he sleep tonight, and does he deserve to? Should he have left Cissy in the Axam Range? Ah, Cissy, that mulish queen. And Billy, the two-faced bastard, what's he doing now? But what does that matter, when Mathew knows he'll never let Billy near him again.

Mathew's eyes hurt when he closes them. He opens them and there's Mary in the doorway, with Mopsy at her feet. Her braid rests on the shoulder of her nightgown. Mary only ever comes into the lean-to in order to sweep and change the bed, but here she is, entering the room, sitting on the edge of the cot, placing her hand on his knee, which jumps under the blanket. Mopsy follows, and sniffs at Mathew's empty boots. Then Mary pulls her legs up as if she's going to lie with him, and he shifts to give her room. She's further down the cot than he would like, with her right ear resting on his stomach; it makes a plaintive gurgle, at which Mary chuckles. He's always loved Mary's low, mannish chuckle.

'Cissy,' Mary says.

'I couldn't make her leave him. She has a horse, food, water. She'll be all right.'

'She will.'

'She's too stubborn not to be.'

Mary shifts on the cot, which creaks.

Mathew says, 'What is it, Mary?'

'What happened to your face?'

'I fought with Billy. It doesn't matter. What's he like, this sergeant?'

Mary considers for a moment. 'He's not a father.'

'What's that mean? Did you ask him?'

Mary doesn't quite answer this. Instead, she says, 'I didn't like his manner. But I could see how experienced he was, how able.'

Mathew's hurt by the implication that he isn't; he feels this hurt in his heart and in his belly.

Mary says, 'I've been thinking about the carting. You're expected.'

'I know.'

They sit without speaking in the smoky dark. He knows they're both thinking about the mortgage—a slower catastrophe than Denny's being lost, but a disaster all the same.

Finally, Mathew says, 'If we could just count on the harvest.'

And Mary says, 'The sergeant has so much experience.'

Before he married, it would never have occurred to Mathew that two people could make such an important decision in so few words. He says, 'I'll take the dray and set out tomorrow. I'll be on the road before dinner.'

Mary lies quietly for a minute. Then she kisses his stomach and stands. He assumes she's going to leave; instead, she lifts his blanket and climbs into the cot beside him. Mopsy follows her up, sniffs about their faces, and settles at Mathew's knee.

✦

The boy woke in the night, wrapped in a prickly blanket. His head hurt, his skin was hot, and he needed to piddle. He remembered some of the things that had happened: putting his face down to the waterhole and lapping at it, as Mopsy did; taking the first bite of apple and throwing it up again. He remembered waking up with the god standing over him. The skin on his feet felt raw and wet, and that reminded him that the lady god had sewn his blisters with a needle. Had she done something special to his feet? What for? Maybe the needle meant he could walk on the sun, as the gods did.

Denny freed his arms from the blanket. He looked around and saw the lady washing her face in the waterhole and the god stirring the coals in the fire. They looked ordinary, like somebody's mother and father. But then the god sang in a strange language, and the lady spat on the ground, which a mother would never do. Beyond the fire, the boy saw three horses tethered to a tree. They were like statues in the dark, except that their tails would sometimes twitch. The walls of the gorge seemed very high.

The lady came to look at the boy, so he pretended to be sleeping. She lifted the blanket back over his arms. Then she went away. When Denny opened his eyes again, the gods were lying down, wrapped in separate blankets, not talking. The fire burned low. Denny made plans to throw off his blanket, ignore the pain in his feet, run down the gorge or climb out of it, hide among the rocks like a wallaby, and wait for his father to come and find him. Or he would walk—for days and days, if necessary, all the way to Christmas—until he saw the red hill. But he found himself falling asleep again. During the remainder of the night, as he passed in and out of sleep, he dreamed of crossing the plain until he found a house, but it wasn't his own. He entered this house and saw someone else's family eating supper around a long table. The mother of this family pulled him onto her lap, kissed him, and told him to pray to God or she didn't know what would happen.

He woke up cold in the early morning. The sky was brightening, but sunrise was a way off and the moon hung above the hills with a funny light, as if it were caught in a thin green bag.

The blanket was damp and the boy realised that he had wet himself. He must have cried out without meaning to, because he saw movement from the corner of his eye—it was the god turning to look at him. The boy closed his eyes, but the god came and squatted next to him and said, 'What's the matter? Open your eyes. I know you aren't sleeping.'

The boy opened his eyes. Once again the god looked like an ordinary man, but the boy remembered his true form: glowing, joyous, and naked in front of the sun.

'Are you sick?' asked the god. 'Are you hungry?'

The boy didn't answer. He lay still in his blanket, hoping the god wouldn't notice that he'd wet himself. The god went back to the fire, picked up his own blanket, and returned with it. He laid it over the boy, right up to his chin. The blanket smelled of tobacco. The lady was asleep.

'May I sit?' asked the god.

The boy remained motionless under the fragrant blanket. His father would have stayed squatting on his heels, or found some low rock or branch to sit on. The god, however, sat directly on the ground and folded his legs beneath him, the way a child would, or a native. He smoked a pipe, and he didn't speak or look at the boy, but he seemed to know that the boy was awake and watching him.

Finally the god said, 'I don't believe you're French at all, are you, Denis?' He didn't seem to expect an answer; the boy, frightened because he didn't know what 'French' was, didn't provide one. A horse let out a soft whinny. 'Bess says your name is most likely Denny. Where do you come from, *lilla vän*? Perhaps you don't want to talk? You must tell me, you know. I'm going to take you home to your mother.'

The boy didn't believe this. He stayed silent.

'Very well,' said the god. He'd finished his pipe; he tapped out the bowl and balanced the pipe on his knee as he felt around in his pockets for something that he failed to find. He pushed his hair back from his forehead, which seemed to shine, as if he were wearing a crown that the boy wasn't quite able to see. 'If you won't tell me where you come from, I'll have to guess. That will be fun for both of us. But!' He looked suddenly and seriously at the boy, who shrank into his blankets. 'You must promise not to laugh if I make a guess incorrectly. Do you promise?'

The boy nodded. He felt sure that nothing the god could say would make him laugh.

'Very well,' said the god. 'I think, little friend, that you come from under the sea, where the whales sing. Yes?'

The boy shook his head. He didn't laugh.

'Could it be,' said the god, 'that you come from the moon? That's it! You are the son of the man on the moon, who carries sticks about on his back. But you're shaking your head. Well then, I think you come from a land far from here, at the top of the world, where winter is one long night and summer is one long day, and monkeys dress as soldiers and girls wear candles on their heads. Yes?'

The boy shook his head. He could imagine laughing at the idea of a monkey dressed as a soldier, but didn't.

'Do you come, perhaps, from a town not so far away from here, where the streets are all in straight lines, and some of the streets have no houses on them, just little flags to say where the house might one day be?'

The boy was interested in this description. He recognised it.

'There's a railway station in this town, and sometimes a train pulls in, *very* noisy, huffing and puffing—I think you know this town? But what could be the name of it? I can't remember. Fairy? Furry?'

The boy giggled in spite of himself and the god gave him a stern look. The boy composed his face. 'Fairly,' he said.

'That's it! How clever you are,' said the god. 'Fairly. Is that where you live?'

'Yes,' said the boy. It seemed safer to say so.

'Yes?' said the god. 'You wouldn't lie to me, would you? You don't look like a boy who lies.'

The boy shook his head. But he did lie, often, even to Mam. He lied to Mam about cleaning his teeth, about playing with his wee-wee, and about whether or not he had 'had a movement' that day. If there had been no movement, she would feed him Epsom salts before bed or make him sit on a steaming potty. So he would tell her, 'Yes, I did one,' and then he would have to pray out loud with his sisters listening, and all the time he knew that he had lied.

'All right, so your home is in Fairly,' said the god. 'By the way, since you're so trustworthy, I must ask you a question. May I?'

The boy nodded, though he was shy at the thought of not knowing the answer.

The god looked up at the sky and asked, 'What colour is the moon?'

'White,' said the boy.

'Now,' said the god, 'you must look properly at the moon before answering my question. Do you see it? Pay close attention. Is it white?'

'Yes,' said the boy, but cautiously.

The god gave him a friendly and disappointed smile.

The boy added, 'But it's in a green bag.'

The god seemed to like this answer. 'Very well, and what kind of green is the bag?'

The boy had seen this green, sometimes, in the glossy bodies of flies—it appeared when he looked at the flies from certain directions—but he didn't know how to explain this. The word 'housebound' dropped into his head and out again. He thought hard about it, then said, 'It's a hiding green.'

The god nodded thoughtfully, looking at the moon. 'Yes,' he said. 'It is.' They sat in silence for another minute. Then the god asked, 'Have you ever painted a picture?'

'No,' said the boy.

'Would you like to?'

The boy sank into his blankets. 'I don't know how.'

'I'll teach you. Nothing could be easier. We'll have a lesson now. I'll bring my paintbox.'

The god sprang up and hurried over to his things. The boy, feeling warm and comfortable, liked the idea of learning how to paint a picture. He had liked talking with the god so much that he had for a moment forgotten his mother and father. Remembering them now, he was ashamed of himself. He saw that the gods were clever, that they played tricks, and that unless he was careful, he could end up going to the red hill willingly, climbing it, and stepping off the hill onto the sun. The god was coming back now, carrying a battered box beneath one arm. He was shining at the thought of this painting lesson. The boy watched the god and rubbed his blistered feet together beneath the blankets so that they stung.

## DREAM OF THE PASHTUN CAMELEER

If you need to know what I was doing, if you're asking as the German girl asked, I'll tell you: the camel is constipated. Of course I won't shoot it for such a reason. The thing to do when a camel is constipated is to take a double-barrelled shotgun, open the action, place the barrels in the rear end of the camel, and flush with warm water. This may sound both simple and comical; believe me, it's neither. At home, we would burn the branches of a certain kind of tree so the camel would inhale the smoke. Here, we've tried other plant remedies, but none are so effective. Also, the shotgun is faster.

I couldn't discuss this subject with the German girl. I had already talked with her for too long. For her, I gave the camel a name, but we don't name each camel. We name herds. It also isn't true that the German woman won't do business with foreign men. Women like her say that because they know the Englishmen prefer it.

I'm explaining these things, but for what reason? Who listens, and why? That's unclear to me. I think I may be sleeping. I may be speaking to these willow trees. I don't think this is a true dream, revealing hidden things: in those I fly over vast encampments, I witness a furious wind full of dust, I see tent pegs struck in the sea. This dream is probably caused by indigestion—I have a habit of eating too fast. But what if I'm wrong, and the dream is true? I'll ask next time a mullah travels through our settlement, which is north of here, outside a town called Hergott Springs. We built our masjid there out of earth, with an iron roof, a channel of running water and a tree hanging with kettles, one for each man. We keep goats, we grow date palms. I live there with my wife, whom I haven't seen since Eid. My wife is a Dieri woman, and she knew, when we came to our arrangement, that I'd often spend weeks or even months away from her. She knows that's what men do.

My mother used to say: Gul Mohammed, if you don't marry a gentle woman, she won't bear you a gentle son. My wife isn't gentle. She has the scars of stockwhips on her skin. She brought one son with her—I take him to the masjid for prayer—and two shy daughters. Three children is a lot to feed, but we must be merciful to the orphans. Though my wife rarely disputes with me, I'm told she's fierce with the other women. I don't want a gentle son—not in this place. A gentle son might become lost, like the little one out in the desert.

When we came into the town tonight and heard that a boy was lost, we had a conference. We should leave now, one said, they'll be nervous; another said, We should offer to help, we might find him, *Inshallah*. No, said one, leave what doesn't concern you. And another: Aren't good deeds a better ornament than wealth? And another: How are they losing their children like this, all over the country? They aren't used to the desert. Neither are we—this isn't our desert. Godforsaken shithole. Do we lose our children? You don't have children. Not here I don't, I have daughters as beautiful as song at home, Allah be pleased with them. This is a boy we're talking about, a little one. They'll blame us. Well, what would we have done with the boy? Fed him to the camels? Where is your kindness, your mercy? And where is theirs? Enough, enough, his destiny is fixed by Heaven.

I listened, and then I said that I would go and help with the search. They laughed at me. On what, they said, your constipated camel? They said, We'll keep to our own business and we'll stay together, it's better that way. That's true: look what happened when I walked away from the fire, alone with my sick camel—there are dangers everywhere. The others said, These people won't thank you for helping them. Do you want to die in the wilderness, or return to Kandahar at the end of your contract? One said, He has a family now, he's sure to stay, contract or no contract. They all laughed. I'm the youngest. It's better to stay quiet.

The jemadar made the decision for all of us: we stayed at the creek. I'm asleep now beneath the willow trees, warm in the stink of the camels. And when I wake up, I'll walk with the others down to the creek to wash. We'll pray, I'll gather my things and tidy the camp and load my camels, I'll get them all up on the string. We'll pass out of here, going north, and this town, which exists because of men like us and camels like these, will fall back into a dream in which we play no part.

# FIFTH DAY

Minna wakes in her old room, in her old bed—the brass one in which the wasps once built their nest. She hears her mother calling out sharply to Annie Bell; she hears Annie scurrying about, and the wheels of Mama's chair passing in front of the bedroom door. Annie appears with breakfast to be served in bed—a married woman's privilege—but she makes it clear that Wilhelmina wants Minna up and dressed as soon as possible. When Annie opens the curtains, Minna is reminded of a saying of her mother's she's always considered lovely, though it's Mama's way of hurrying her out of bed: 'Morning has gold in its mouth.' She drinks her coffee slowly, picks at her breakfast, washes her face, dresses, and looks at herself in the mirror for some time before going to the parlour.

Mama raises her eyebrows at Minna and says, '*Morgenstund hat Gold im Mund!*' As expected, she looks cross and tired. She always is during shearing season, for reasons Minna has never quite understood. Apparently shearing used to be a great effort for Wilhelmina, back in the days when her husband managed Thalassa, and she seems to suffer, annually, from a vestigial strain. Minna knows that her mother will insist on sitting out on her verandah to watch the shearers pass, and that this will both delight and depress Mama for reasons—unfathomable to Minna—of pride and nostalgia. For now, Wilhelmina Baumann sits in the parlour with a blanket over her knees and wields a tight, forbidding smile as Annie frets and fusses. Oh, Mama, thinks Minna, why do you persist in being so unhappy in this full, free world?

'I feel a draught,' says Wilhelmina, her head cocked above the gleaming black slant of her arms as if she can detect breezes with her ears. 'Across my ankles, a draught.'

When Annie has adjusted the blanket and hurried away, Minna pulls out a dark, studded chair that has always made her think of a coffin, and sits.

'Try, Hermina, please, to be less noisy,' Wilhelmina says.

'Do you have a headache, Mama?'

'You know you are a married woman now,' Wilhelmina says, 'and "Mama" sounds like a word for little girls. I hope your husband won't call me Mama.'

'What would you prefer? "Mother"?'

'Is it important what I prefer?'

'Yes, Mama. Mother. You know it is.'

'I don't put my own wishes forward,' Wilhelmina says, and Minna's heart both breaks at and is bored by her mother's pious, sacrificial face. Minna has always assumed that marriage will liberate her from her mama's moods—and she does feel somewhat removed from them. But here she is, back in the same old house, the same old parlour with its paintings of muscular stags brought down by German hounds; the same fire screen with its pattern of embroidered cornflowers; and the same silver bowl with its palm trees and monkeys, which Minna knows is a source of special bitterness to her mother, without understanding why. In fact, there's something different about the bowl today—it's been half wrapped in brown tissue paper, as if it were to be put away. There were six candles in it on Minna's wedding day, but they're missing now.

'Why have you wrapped the Indian bowl?'

Wilhelmina grimaces. 'It is a thing of immense ugliness.'

'It isn't ugly,' Minna says. 'Mr Rapp admired it.'

Wilhelmina swats the Swedish painter's opinion away with one hand. 'I can no longer look at it. Now,' she says, 'we must speak as women do.'

Minna smiles mockingly at this, which her mother ignores.

'It's possible,' Wilhelmina says, 'that this marriage was too hastily undertaken, if here you are already back in your mother's house. But no.' She lowers her voice and glances over her shoulder as if Annie Bell might be lurking there. 'It could not be too soon.'

Weeks ago, when Minna first hinted at a pregnancy, Wilhelmina appealed to Heaven, represented by the ceiling; she spoke aloud as if the Lord, also a parent, would sympathise: 'One minute out of sight *und siehe da! Eine Mussehe.*' Minna likes the straightforwardness of the German '*Mussehe*': must-marriage.

This morning, Wilhelmina looks meaningfully at Minna's midsection and says, 'Not one moment too soon.'

Minna doesn't respond. Her trick with the baby is irrelevant now—what does it matter? She's thinking of the Afghan and the way he stroked the white, woolly camel; she's thinking of Robert's big red hands; of Karl Rapp, who kissed her in the garden; and also of Bear Axam, whom she made nervous. Minna leans forwards in the funereal chair and peels the paper away from the Indian bowl. She looks at her reflection in its curved silver and waits for her mother to chide her for her vanity by saying something like, 'The more one pets the cat, the higher it holds its tail.' Minna turns her head to inspect her profile in the bowl. She likes her tail.

'Look at me,' Wilhelmina says, so severely that Minna looks. Mama's fingers are laced together in such a way that her fire opal emerges as a fevered eye. 'I allowed you to stay here last night, but I should have turned you out. Next time, I will. Your husband may not come home—very well. That will happen. There is no end to the things that happen. Possibly he will drink, have a temper; who can predict such things? He may hit you. There may be other women. He may be angry at you because of other men. Whatever happens, you sleep in your husband's house. No one else's, not even your mother's. You sleep in his house so that he always knows where to find you. Do you listen, Hermina?'

Minna is surprised to feel herself near tears, which is inexplicable, and must be kept from Mama. 'Yes, Mother, I listen.'

'Good.' Wilhelmina leans back in her chair as if exhausted. This is an unusual posture for her; Mama has always been strict about a lady's need to sit upright. 'Now you will go to your husband's house. You will wash and tidy yourself. You will attend to the business of being a wife. Annie tells me you have already allowed things to become untidy. We must find you a maid at once.'

Minna presses one finger against the Indian bowl, leaving a print on the silver. 'I think it's rather pretty,' she says. 'The bowl, I mean.'

Wilhelmina sighs. '*Lieber Gott, hilf mir.* What does the bowl matter? Go home, Hermina.'

Minna stands up—slowly. 'I'll go,' she says. 'Look at me, I'm going.'

Wilhelmina makes a disgusted noise. 'You are a child,' she says. 'God help your little one.'

'There is no little one,' says Minna. 'Why do you talk like this? There never was going to be a baby.' Without daring to look at her mother's face, she leaves the room, and then the house.

The day, outside, seems ordinary—no sign of camels or Afghans. It's clear and warm. Minna has left her hat at her mother's; fine, she'll go hatless. The street is hers, anyway. Anyone can see that. The sun is hers: the hotter the better. Every man who looks Minna's way belongs to her, and every woman. There's a woman coming towards her—yes, it's the German woman, walking her donkey away from the farrier's, and Minna stops in the street to look at her. She's plump, and wears a lumpy hat. Her donkey is being stubborn. It lets out a comical bray, which makes Minna laugh. Now the German woman looks back at Minna—they look at one another. There's a shadow on the woman's upper lip that may or may not be the beginning of a moustache. Aside from this her face is fair; she must take care to stay out of the sun. Minna waits for the woman to speak, but she doesn't—she glances down at Minna's dress and back up at her face. Then she turns away and yanks at the donkey's lead rope as if she wants to both punish and protect it.

Minna continues on her way to her husband's house. When she arrives, it's as empty as she expected it to be, but when she finds that the kitchen has been used, the bed slept in, and that Robert has left a dirty shirt on the bedroom floor, she thinks of her mother sitting in her chair, her opal flashing, saying, 'There is no end to the things that happen.'

Bess is dismantling the camp by the waterhole. She slept later than she meant to and is cross at Karl for not waking her; this crossness manifests as brisk efficiency and a refusal to let him help pack up. As Bess works, Karl entertains Denny with an art lesson. Yesterday, Karl asked her, 'Why are you drawing him? Shouldn't we take him home at once?' Yes, of course they should have taken Denny home at once. A different sort of man would have insisted on it, but Bess knows that Karl trusts her judgement. She told him that the boy needed rest before the journey. To herself she said, Would it be so terrible to steal a day with him?

So Karl, yesterday, let her draw. He prepared the food and watered the horses, he went to see the sunset and returned without talking about it, and he didn't paint anything and barge into her head by being pleased or disgusted with the result. Karl might have been being thoughtful, or he might have been shirking the obligation of work. Perhaps both. Bess recalls his diffidence when Adi Carlin was in labour: never entering the room, hovering in the hallway, ready to fetch towels and water. As if attending, but in a minor role, some sacred rite.

This morning, as Bess glances at Karl and Denny, she's reminded of tidying the red house while Karl sat on the jetty with Adi, planning their future. The difference is that she wasn't afraid of Adi Carlin at the time, but she's unnerved by the boy. Two days ago, she sat by this waterhole and imagined a child, and then he appeared as if by expedient magic: this little pink Denny.

So yes, she kept the boy with her for one day, in order to sketch him and plan her book: a book about a lonely, lost boy with light hair who befriends a stripe-tailed wallaby. She's decided against the snake—no child would be convinced by it. The book will be poignant, sweet, and also it will touch on the wild, empty vastness of this place, its newness and its far-from-homeness—she'll just prod at that a bit, the melancholy of it, the terror, and this will lend solidity to the sweet story about the boy and the wallaby. If the book sells, Bess will use the money to establish their Melbourne household: she imagines a maid, a cook, a grey cat, two studios with good light, paints sent from England, and a garden with roses in it. The possibility of all of this warrants keeping the boy for just one day.

Besides, Bess tells herself as she shakes out blankets and fills waterbags, he needed rest; he really wasn't well enough to travel yesterday. And they'll soon have him home with his mother. Admittedly, his mother doesn't know this yet—she's been suffering the entire time Bess has been drawing the boy. Denny's mother, in Bess's mind, has Adi Carlin's face—Adi's face before the baby died: a tense, hopeful, frightened face. But the mother's distress will definitely end, so the extra day can be forgiven. There will be a happy conclusion. Bess has nearly finished the preliminary sketches for her book—another day with the boy would do it—but she thinks of Adi Carlin and knows they need to take him home.

Perhaps, though, not all the way home? Bess hopes to run into some trustworthy local people who know Denny and can get him to his mother. She does believe that it's acceptable—in the larger scheme of things—to delay the boy's return, but she'd rather not have to meet his mother and see the prolonged anguish on her face.

The camp is packed, the horses are almost ready. Bess instructs Karl to finish the art lesson.

'He has a way with colour,' Karl says. He holds out one of the boy's attempts at mixing tints, about which Bess sees nothing exceptional. 'Don't you think? He should learn properly. What do you say, Denny? We'll have to talk to your mother.'

Bess tells Karl that the closest house, according to the map, is on a property called Wilparra, and that they'll stop there first. They'll have to pass through this property on the way to Fairly, where Karl says Denny lives; Bess allows Karl to believe they'll take the boy all the way to town, but in reality she hopes to shed him at Wilparra. She looks at Denny, who's dressed in his wrinkled clothes—they seem to have shrunk since yesterday. He's crouched near one of those awful, lumpy lizards, the shinglebacks. He is watching the lizard and the lizard is watching him.

'It's time to go,' Bess calls, and Denny comes to her. When Karl invites the boy to share a horse, Denny steps into Bess's shadow and won't answer.

'So, my little friend,' says Karl, 'I hoped we'd have some more talk about colours.' He shrugs and laughs and turns away as if Denny hasn't hurt his feelings.

The boy rides with Bess, in front of her in the saddle. Looking down, she can see the way the sun has burned his scalp through his fine hair; when he turns his head, she sees the crust at his nostrils and the dirt embedded in his neck. When he gets home, his mother will have to scrub him vigorously. Every few minutes he leans forwards as if he's about to stroke the horse's mane, but he always sits back up without touching it. She considers the planes of his neck and shoulders, and she asks him questions: How are you feeling? Do you know the name of that tree? Where did you sleep before you found us? How common are those wallabies with the striped tails? He gives short answers. Bess is interested by the number of flies he allows to crawl on his skin and clothes before he shakes or swats them off.

Karl rides beside them, leading the packhorse. He sings cheerful songs in Swedish. He says, 'This would make a fine picture.'

Bess says, 'The flight into Egypt.'

Karl nods, but Bess knows he's unconvinced. He keeps looking over at her and the boy, and she suspects that he sees a woman and child riding together through a fir forest. There's snow on the ground, and the low winter sun picks gold out of the boy's light hair.

The ride to Wilparra takes much longer than Bess anticipated; it's early afternoon before they see the first fence and another hour before they spot any structures. A breeze has picked up, and there are distant clouds on the southern horizon. Bess wonders if this means rain, and if they'll reach shelter before it arrives. She wonders how much further they can push their horses, which definitely won't reach Fairly by dark. But that's immaterial, because here, having come to civilisation, they can hand over responsibility for the boy.

The Rapps ride towards the buildings of Wilparra and reach a sort of road. There are cartwheel ruts in the road, with grass growing in them. The horses pick up speed, as if they can smell water, and a flock of white cockatoos comes screaming out of a grove of gums in a nearby hollow: a spring, no doubt. The fence that runs alongside the road is broken here and there, and a lazy windmill turns in a broad, empty pasture. Bess studies the structures in the distance. Which is the house? It must be that long, low shape beside the long, low hill. Bess counts four chimneys. What will they find when they reach it? A maid, a cook, a grey cat, a garden with roses in it. Adi Carlin with her arms wide open.

'We're very close now,' she says to the boy, who leans forwards as if to pet the horse again. She realises he's unpeeling his sweaty back from her sweaty front. Kangaroos recline like odalisques in the shade of the acacias.

As they pass the outbuildings, Bess sees no sign of people, domestic animals, equipment or stores. Some of the doors are open and all the roofs appear to slump. Well, perhaps Wilparra has fallen on hard times. She looks back at the chimneys, hoping to see smoke. It's hard to tell—the house is in shade. But the homestead gate is open, which isn't a promising sign of habitation. Bess and Karl stop their horses and look up at the house, which stands at the top of a gentle slope. It's not as big as the house at Thalassa, though it's built from the same sturdy brick. The roof is slate, and someone has planted pepper trees against its windows. The windows are all shuttered and saltbush has crept onto the verandahs. Karl calls out, '*Hej? Är det någon här?*' Bess knows he would never call out in Swedish if he actually expected anybody to be there. The house is obviously deserted; although the structure is more or less intact, it announces itself as a ruin. It knows it's lost its purpose, and is anticipating a reduction to its constituent parts. Bess isn't sure why she's so perturbed by this: she's seen farms fail. Wealth disappears—her father's, for example. Maybe the Wilparra patriarch was also fond of baccarat.

Karl is tying horses to the gateposts. He raises his arms up to Denny, who allows himself to be taken from the saddle and placed on the ground, but doesn't join Karl as he walks up the slope towards the house. Karl looks back, sees that the boy isn't following, then claps his hands and begins to run as if heading out on some thrilling adventure. When he reaches the house, he bangs on the shutters and knocks at the door, calling, 'Hello! *Hej! Hej!* Hello! Good afternoon!' He's like a boy running up and down the long verandah, and sure enough, Denny can't resist him—he looks up at Karl and back at Bess, then back at Karl again. Bess takes his hand. Something about the uncertainty of that hand inside her own makes clear to her, for the first time, the palpable existence of this boy. If they'd set out when they first found him, he could be with his mother now. They walk up to the house together.

When Bess and Denny reach the front door, she opens it and steps inside. The boy releases her hand and stays on the verandah, bouncing on the balls of his feet. The rooms are dark and mostly empty—she walks through them and finds a few awkward pieces of furniture, evidence of mice, and not much else. Karl calls out to her, 'Is it safe?' She returns to the front door and steps with relief out of the house.

'It's perfectly all right,' she says. 'There's nothing here.'

But it's the nothing that horrifies her—the emptiness of the house, and also of the plain and ranges. This country is supposed to feel like virgin wilderness; instead it feels abandoned.

'We'll stay here tonight,' Bess says. She begins opening the shutters to let light into the rooms. She'd rather not sleep in the house, but it's the sensible thing to do, especially if it's going to rain. They'll light a fire in one of the fireplaces and find a well or pump, tomorrow they'll ride to Fairly, and for the rest of today and into the evening Bess will watch the boy and draw him. She hasn't stolen this extra time with him—it's been given to her. She need not judge herself for it. 'Do you understand, Denny? The horses are tired and it may rain.'

Denny picks up a stick and starts to make shapes in the dust by the front steps.

'Denny,' says Bess, 'did you hear me? We'll stay tonight.'

Karl says, 'We certainly will! We'll be warm and dry, and we'll wake up early, and tomorrow you'll see your mamma.' He lifts Denny and hoists the boy over his head and onto his shoulders. Denny's stick falls to the ground. 'Shall we give the horses a drink? Shall we watch the sunset? Do you think the moon will be green tonight, or will it become too cloudy to tell?'

Then Karl, still with the boy on his shoulders, jogs down the slope towards the horses. When he reaches them, he turns and grins back up at Bess. On a different day, she'd follow him, and together they would make up their own name for this place—they'd call it 'Wheelbarrow'. They could name the whole world, if they had the cook and the maid and the two studios with good light. The boy sways on Karl's shoulders with both his fists clenched in Karl's hair. He also looks up the slope towards the house, and Bess is surprised to see the terror on his face.

⁂

Ada knows from the women in the house that this afternoon's train will bring shearers with it. She likes to imagine them stepping down onto the platform of Fairly's railway station in a cloud of smoke and hair, their beautiful beards shaped to advertise their skill with blades, their arms so strong they could lean together to tip the train off its tracks. Most will go to Thalassa, but others, on their way to stations further out, will pass by Undelcarra. Last year, Ada took Lotta and Noella down to the gate to see them pass. The men tipped their hats and spoke as if the girls were ladies; when walking off, they called, 'Give my regards to—', without the girls ever knowing for whom the regards were meant. Lotta was most impressed by discovering that they carried their knives and forks with them.

The men always make a lot of noise. This year, when Mopsy starts barking at the sound of them on the road, Lotta begs Ada to take her down to the gate, and Ada agrees. Noella sniffs and shows no inclination to join them. They shut Mopsy inside the house—in the last few days, she's become a little crazed with strangers. Lotta is shy as she walks down the path to the road, but when she's near the gate, she runs ahead and throws herself onto its bottom rail. This frightens Ada; but the gate holds, and Lotta doesn't know how to open it. Ada believes in the power of the gate. Nobody will open it who isn't supposed to, and inside it they're all safe. Denny, though, is not inside the gate, and neither is Cissy, nor Joe, and neither is Dad, who left mid-morning with the cart.

Lotta squints up at the shearers.

'Who's this, who's this?' demands a man in a blistered black hat, with a loud, rolling voice. He stamps his foot in the dust of the road. Lotta seems to know that he's teasing her, and she laughs coquettishly, glances back at Ada, and hoists herself higher on the gate. Her mouth is open; she might be about to bite into the wood.

'It's a princess,' says a man with a thick red beard, and he winks at Ada, who places her hands on her sister's shoulders.

'What? What? A princess?' says the man in the black hat. 'And here's me without crown nor carriage.' He removes his hat and makes a deep, sweeping bow, at which Lotta titters. Then he returns the hat to his head.

The shearers step closer to the gate and Ada thinks that she can hear the rattle of their cutlery. There are six of them, all bearded, each with callused knuckles and sunburned faces. But when the man with the red beard puts his hand on the gate, his fingernails look clean and neat, as if he takes care of them. Lotta leans backwards so that she presses against Ada, and both girls look up into the hat-shadowed eyes of the men. The man with the black hat crouches so that his face is level with Lotta's.

'Tell me, princess,' he says, 'do birds fly?'

Lotta glances up at Ada, then back at the man. She nods.

'Say it—yes or no?' says the man.

'Yes,' says Lotta.

'Do seagulls fly?'

'Yes,' says Lotta.

'Do galahs fly?' asks the man and, when Lotta says yes, he asks, with increasing speed, if crows, eagles, magpies, swallows, cockatoos, ducks, dragonflies, bees, sugar gliders, flies and mosquitoes fly, and each time Lotta answers, with an anxious giggle, 'Yes.' So that when he asks, in the same brisk, business-like way, 'Do rabbits fly?', Lotta answers, 'Yes.'

The shearers throw their arms in the air and roar with delight at her mistake; all except the man with the black hat, who looks at Lotta as if full of regret—not at having tricked her, but at her having allowed herself to be tricked. He remains crouching at the gate. Ada wraps her arms around Lotta and kisses the top of her head. She wishes Cissy were here.

'Now,' the man with the black hat says to Lotta, 'isn't that a silly game? I reckon you're too grown up for silly games. And your sister'—he looks at Ada now—'is definitely too grown up, aren't you, miss? You're the oldest, I bet?'

Ada shakes her head.

'Second oldest, then?'

'Fourth,' Ada says.

'Well now,' says the man in the hat. 'So there are five of you altogether?'

'Seven,' says Ada, and the man whistles.

'All girls?' he asks.

'Denny's a boy,' says Lotta loudly, as if pleased to be able to contribute.

'And where's this Denny, then? Can we meet him?' asks the man. The flies on the brim of his hat look blue and green against the black felt.

'He's lost,' says Lotta.

The man's eyes grow large. 'He's never lost?' he says. 'Hear that, mates? A boy's gone and got himself lost!'

The shearers murmur and shake their heads. The one with the red beard says, 'More's the pity.'

Ada knows, now, that the men have already heard about Denny and have been talking about him as they walk along the road. They know Denny lives in this house, and they've stopped precisely because Denny is missing. The older Ada grows, the more she finds that she understands what people are thinking, and why they do the things they do. This morning, for example: Dad whistled in the stable as he greased the cartwheels; Mam packed food and tea; they smiled and kissed goodbye; Dad set out with the cart; and all the while they were angry at one another, and sorry, and sad, but pretending not to be. After Dad left, Mam told Ada and Noella that they needn't go to school today, not if they didn't want to; Noella was overjoyed and thought Mam was giving them a treat, but Ada understood that Mam, although she would never say so, didn't want to let them out of her sight. Ada doesn't find her ability to understand people remarkable, although as far as she can tell most other people don't have it. She thinks that the shearer with the black hat might, because he's studying her face, as if sizing her up.

'What if,' he says, 'what if *we* was to find your brother? What would you give us for a prize?' He looks from Ada to Lotta and back to Ada. Lotta, whose only possessions are the feathers she collects, washes and sorts into piles based on colour, length or shape, trembles at this question.

'We don't have anything,' says Ada. 'My father might . . .' But she doesn't know what Dad would or could give them, so she doesn't continue. She can hear Mopsy barking at the window.

'How's about a kiss?' suggests the man with the black hat. He's still crouched down at the gate and has to look up to see Ada's face. 'A kiss for whichever one of us brings him home safe?'

This makes Ada think of a fairytale that has long disturbed her, in which a king in need of help promises to give up the first thing he sees when he reaches his castle: his daughter, as it happens. The other shearers grin, but the man with the black hat cocks his head to one side and raises his eyebrows, expecting an answer. His lips look greasy behind his brown beard, and the thought of his mouth touching any part of her fills Ada with revulsion. But wouldn't it be worth it, if it meant having Denny safely back behind the gate?

'Well?' demands the man.

Ada nods noncommittally.

'Say it,' says the man, with a mild smile and narrowed eyes. 'Yes or no.'

'Yes,' says Ada. Lotta looks up at her in astonishment.

'How's about, then,' continues the man with the hat, rising now to his full height, 'a deposit? With the rest on credit, like. Just so we'll be extra thorough looking for your brother.' He tilts his cheek towards Ada and she sees, with relief, that he doesn't mean to involve his mouth at all; that he simply wants her to kiss him the way she might kiss her father. She rises on her toes to do this, trying to avoid his beard, but he moves his head and she ends up tasting his prickled mouth all the same. The shearer smells strongly of himself. The other men cheer.

'Fair's fair,' says Redbeard, presenting his cheek. 'It could be me that finds him.'

Ada, kissing Redbeard's cheek, is faster, but he doesn't even try to turn his head.

'And me,' says another man.

The remaining four shearers offer their cheeks in turn, and Ada kisses them, thinking all the time that she mustn't cry. Lotta has shrunk away from the gate, so Ada must lean over her in order to deliver the kisses. The gate remains closed.

The men, kissed, look oddly bashful; one of them pushes at the shoulder of another. The man with the black hat, though, who's older, looks at her with approval.

'Good girl,' he says. 'All right, mates, let's get looking for that boy.'

He stands up. The other shearers all straighten and settle their shoulders.

Ada sees now that they have no intention of looking for Denny—that they were teasing her as they'd teased Lotta. But she hopes that she's wrong. She's wrong sometimes.

When the shearers walk away, it's as a group. Almost immediately, though, they've separated and are strung out in a line, one walking in front of another: the man in the black hat leads the procession, and Redbeard brings up the rear. Lotta climbs back onto the bottom rung of the gate to watch them go. Ada has heard that Chinamen always walk in single file like this, stepping in each other's footprints, but she doesn't know if this is true. She's never seen more than one Chinaman at a time.

Later in the afternoon, out west on the Willochra, Sergeant Foster spots a kangaroo, aims his rifle, shoots, and misses. Neither of his Aboriginal companions react to any part of this. They're both getting on Foster's nerves. Billy, whose skill at cricket Foster is sure his exhaustion must have exaggerated (although he still likes the idea of adding him to the Port Augusta police team), rides like a western stockman—that is, with sloppy stirrups and his legs too far forward, not at all neat or upright; and Foster has had his eye on Jimmy since he snuck off and hid among the grass trees for no reason, presumably, other than to make Foster feel like a fool. He usually likes being alone with his native constables but finds himself desiring Wooding's company, which shows some desperation.

Foster longs for his days in the Northern Territory, where there was no one to object if he took a woman on his rounds. Ah, the books he'd have written and the women he'd have bedded if he'd never left the Territory. This whole affair is pointless; surely the boy is dead by now. They've spent the day riding in the direction of any unusual gathering of hawks—birds are usually the first sign of a body—and are now further south than Foster ever intended to go. According to Billy, they're not far from the northern pastures of Thalassa. The best outcome, now, would be to find this suspicious vicar so that the search, called off, can be seen to have produced at least one result. Rainclouds have rolled in and the sunset this afternoon only registers as a sour pinkish-grey above the hills.

So: the rifle, and the kangaroo. Some fresh meat for supper will cheer everybody up. But he misses, and swears, and the boys don't react, and what's the point of it all, anyway—this is settled country, he doesn't belong here, he should be up north where things are wild, the way they were when he rode through with the Telegraph. My God, the Telegraph! That long shining wire reaching from Port Augusta to Darwin. Sullen Jimmy, quiet Billy—look at them! They owned the country for so long, and never once did they achieve anything a hundredth as remarkable as the Overland Telegraph. Port Augusta to Darwin, then under the sea to Java, and on and on to England. Though the idea of England produces a derisive grunt from Foster, who firmly believes that the future of Australia lies in its native sons: men like him, proud to have been born right here, beneath the Southern Cross. It occurs to him, as he continues to ride south after his failure with the kangaroo, that he could write a book called *The Native Australian*. For a moment, he's full of eagerness, and envisions a preface that explains the distinction between the terms 'native Australian' and 'Australian native'. The book will put forward a strong argument for a federal assembly of the separate colonies; it might also include a chapter on necessary limits to immigration, and another on the role of the police force in protecting pastoral interests. But Foster feels the idea slipping away just as quickly as it came. The thought of writing it exhausts him. The hawks are still circling up ahead—he'll concentrate on them.

The hawks, it turns out, haven't found a dead body, but live sheep. Foster reaches the top of a rise and looks down at what Billy informs him is Thalassa's northern run. They're a long way from the homestead, but this is Thalassa land and those are Thalassa sheep. Men on horseback, aided by dogs, round the sheep into pens, where presumably they'll spend the night before being driven down to the woolshed for shearing. Foster observes the placid lumber of the pregnant ewes; soon enough, the hawks that fly above them will dive for their newborn lambs. Dust rises in clouds from the horses' hoofs.

'Down we go,' says Foster, more to his horse than to his men, and with a nudge of his heels he's riding onto Thalassa. There's a shepherd's hut by the pens, and a shepherd's hut is as good a place as any to spend the night, especially when there's rain about. Also promising: a dray stands beside the hut, bullocks in harness, with a few men gathered around it. Perhaps something has been delivered. Foster recalls the heavy, amber taste of the Thalassa madeira. Across the paddock, the stockmen swear at the sheep as their dogs wheel and yap.

Closer to the hut, Foster sees that the people standing at the dray are agitated about something. They're looking into the back of it with concern, and a smaller figure behind them is speaking with wild gestures. Closer still, and Foster recognises the speaker as a girl—and, yes, it's one of the Wallace girls, the belligerent one who tried to tell him, on the first morning of the search, that her brother was somehow unlike every other boy who's ever wandered off into the Australian bush. As Foster approaches, followed by Billy and Jimmy Possum, the men around the dray turn to look. There are three of them, one black and two white, presumably Thalassa stockmen. The girl behind them continues to wave her hands about.

Foster dismounts, ties his horse to a post, strides to the dray, and looks down at whatever is in the back of it: a body, scratched, filthy, not currently conscious, but definitely alive and certainly not that of a six-year-old boy. The Wallace girl seems to know more about the body than anybody else, but she addresses herself to Billy while the men try to explain to Foster what they know. Amid all the noise, he manages to glean that this is, indeed, the infamous vicar. The girl managed to walk him down out of the ranges (he was capable of walking earlier today, supposedly), but he'd lost his horse, refused to ride hers, and had collapsed some six or seven miles west of here. The girl, unable to lift him, left him where he fell and rode off looking for help (so where's her horse? Ah, behind the hut, and apparently it's thrown a shoe). She found these men when she saw their sheep, they went with her to collect the vicar, someone rode out to the road and found a dray on its way to Thalassa with a delivery of empty bales, the driver brought his dray here to the hut, they loaded up the vicar, and now the driver will take him down to the homestead. The girl wants him taken to town, but the driver is determined to go south: he has these bales, the shearing starts tomorrow (unless it rains, it looks like rain), and the bales are needed.

Foster quiets them all, leans into the back of the dray, and inspects the vicar. Foster isn't fond of vicars. He'll tell anyone who asks him that missionaries and men of God cause trouble in these remote places—they interfere with police work by being idealistic and impractical, and by lodging puerile complaints.

'His colour is good,' Foster says. 'All things considered.'

The driver nods. 'That's what I said. Didn't I say so?'

'Let me confirm,' says Foster, and turns to Billy. 'This is the man you were tracking from the boy's boots?'

'Yes,' says the Wallace girl. 'My father wasn't happy.'

'In which case,' says Foster, as if the girl had never spoken, 'I have some questions for our vicar.'

'Questions for *him*?' asks the Wallace girl.

'And you too,' Foster says. 'I'll want a statement from you. We'll accompany you to the Axam house.'

Now the girl objects, and once again it's Billy she addresses. She wants to go home, and she wants Billy to take her and her lame horse: Denny isn't found, the vicar is an idiot, and they're wasting time. Foster looks at the girl and says, 'You'll ride in the cart. You look worse than he does. Jimmy, walk round back and get her horse. Yes, miss, you'll get in the dray or we'll put you in it.'

The girl appeals to Billy, who's still in the saddle. She puts one hand on his boot—as if he has any authority here!—but he moves his horse, gently, until her hand is off.

Billy says to her, 'I'll go with you to Thalassa.'

The girl's skirts are dirty, her hair is snarled. She looks dog-tired. She turns her back to Billy and climbs, with childish dignity, into the cart.

The driver is seated and ready, the bullocks lift their heads in the yokes. Here comes Jimmy walking back with the girl's horse, and he's not handling it well. Ah yes, *this* horse, the ridiculous red mare, which slid and skittered over the plain two days ago. Jimmy, with his useless arm, can't manage it—the horse pulls at the lead rope, she pins her ears and switches her tail, and all Jimmy does is follow.

Foster looks up at the huge, hidden sun, and sighs. 'I'll take her,' he says. He jogs over to the horse with his hand out, takes the rope and tugs her forwards. She bares her teeth. Behind her, the driver raises his whip, ready to flick it over the backs of the bullocks—he's waiting for Foster's signal.

Now many things happen at once. Foster does or doesn't give a signal, which the driver does or doesn't misinterpret; the whip cracks; the bullocks bellow, lower their heads, and begin to pull; and the girl's horse, startled, leaps away and kicks out a hind leg. Jimmy is standing right there to be kicked. He's knocked back and down. He stands and falls again, groaning. Foster makes quick calculations: it'll be a hit to the thigh, hip or groin, and almost certainly serious. Did I give a signal? When did the driver crack his whip? He must keep track of all of this. Billy is off his horse now, on the ground beside Jimmy, keeping Jimmy's leg still. The stockmen and their dogs continue to bark at the sheep. The girl is white in the back of the cart; the cart's moving. They'll have to stop it, calm the horse, examine Jimmy, lift him and his cloak into the back of the dray beside the minister, make their way down to the homestead at Thalassa—hours away, two injured men. And who will have to write this up as a comprehensive report, who will have to swear by it and be held accountable? Foster will, because Foster is in charge of this situation, and the one in charge is the one who must report. It's these endless reports that prevent him from writing books.

Jimmy rolls in pain on the ground and a hawk lands on the roof of the shepherd's hut. When Foster takes off his hat to shoo it away, he feels the first spits of rain hitting the top of his head.

## FIFTH NIGHT

At one point during the night, the rain is so heavy that even Mary is woken by the sound of it on the iron roof at Undelcarra. She rolls away from Lotta in the bed, looks in at the girls' bedroom, and goes out to the parlour to check for leaks. Then she takes a lantern to the verandah and sits a long time with it, Mopsy on her lap.

Mathew, who has already picked up chaff and flour from the Fairly mill and is heading north with it, shelters under his dray and thinks that the rain is bad for bootless Denny but good for the wheat and for filling the tanks. There's no bargain here that he could make with God.

Robert, unimpressed by Sergeant Foster, has formed an independent search party with some local men and is spending the night out on the plain. He's used to bush patrols and is able to sleep, despite the weather. While sleeping, he needn't reflect on the terror he felt last night when he arrived home and Minna wasn't there. Even though he heard, from the Baumanns' groom, that she stayed with her mother, he can't shake the idea that she might never return, or that, if she does, he might prove to have no control over her.

Minna, in Robert's bed, doesn't sleep. She's hungry, because Annie Bell hasn't been sent with food—Mama, apparently, is sulking. Minna lies buzzing in Robert's bed, listening through the rain for the sound of him coming home.

Camped out in the Druid Range, Constable Wooding and Copper Bob agree to give up the search. 'He's not come this way,' says Wooding, miserable in wet wool; and Copper Bob agrees with him.

At Thalassa, the shearers hear the rain, turn in their swags, and think of the long and stinking stretch of hours without work tomorrow, crowded in with other men. The sheep that have already been brought to the woolshed huddle together in its pens; the rain will keep the fleece on their backs at least one more day. Bear wakes and thinks how much he'd like to piss if he weren't already falling asleep again. The rain wakes Joanna, and among the many predicaments that occur to her—the shearing, George's temper at the weather, the missing boy—she wonders if the possum-fur cloak is keeping its wearer dry. Nancy, in her room beside the kitchen, stretches her aching legs and notices that the rain seems to be leaving a greasy residue on the windowpanes. Tal broods in his shelter at the depot camp, having lost at cards to a man from Murray Bridge. Soon he'll hear the sound of a dray and bullocks, and that will be Foster, Billy and Cissy, all of them soaked, heading to Thalassa homestead with their patients.

Bess and Karl, dry and warm in the empty house at Wilparra, sleep through the rain. In the damp, the empty house releases its older smells of food and fire and bodies. Bess and Karl remain asleep as Denny drapes a blanket over his head, opens the front door quietly, and hurries away from the house. Outside, in the gums around the spring, the cockatoos spread their wings and shake their heads; they swing upside down from the branches in order to wash the undersides of their bodies. The frogs sing on the surface of the earth. The rain falls through the night and on into the morning.

# CONFESSION OF THE GERMAN PROSTITUTE

I'll be right with you, if you'll give me half a moment—it's been a busy day. A lot of customers, and each one brings me news of the missing boy: the laceless boots, the handkerchief, the fire in the hills. The story has run on down the railway line, so even men from elsewhere are coming to me with schemes and theories. I've been asking myself, why does this feel so familiar? Then I realised—I'm thinking of the goldfields: the feeling that we're close to something very precious, that nobody can find it, but that everything might change at any time.

On the goldfields I was French. I saw in Melbourne the way the French girls were favoured, so by the time I got to the diggings I called myself Odette. There was never once I told a lie beside my name: never came up with some family story, never tried to speak a word of French or change my voice to sound the part. It was enough, out there, to be known as Odette. There was money to be made and I made it in whatever direction.

And I met Nikolaj. Now, Nikolaj was a Dane, a sailor who jumped ship to come south for gold, the biggest man I ever met, all brown and wide, with a great flat nose. He could work eighteen hours a day at digging, and the only money he made was what his wife earned by selling rum and cognac on the sly. He had a genius for sinking shafts in unexpected places and finding just enough gold to get other people interested. They'd offer to buy him out for hundreds, he'd hold on fast, and a day or two later the seam would run right by and miss him by a yard.

His partner in all this was a Chinese, Li Longwei, almost as big as Nikolaj—the tallest Chinaman I ever saw, shoulders like a bullock, and the two of them together were a rare sight out in Castlemaine, that shithole. The goldfields made for peculiar friendships, the kind you'd not see elsewhere. Nick spoke no Mandarin, Long no Danish or German, both of them hardly any English, but they had their own language made of exhaustion and drink and optimism. For all their strength, they were such sloppy bastards: their shafts were always filling up with water and they'd spend a week or more bailing it all out; the beams they fitted would slip and half a tunnel would fall in; the seam ran by them like a golden train and they just shrugged and found another place to dig. Long had a dreadful fear of going underground, so he ran things up top while Nikolaj worked below. At night they went back to Nick's tent and drank rum till they were tight—which took some time, they were both so big—while Nick's wife cleared up around them, taking shirts to wash or scraping mud from boots. Their big drunk friendly voices were a way to explain the men who went into that tent every night, just to greet old friends, pass the time of day with those two lunatics, say hello to Mrs Nick. If the visitors left with a billy full of contraband rum, a flask of cognac, well, who's to know?

Once a week Nick's wife would send him on to me. She was a receptive woman, Mrs Nick, in the sense that babies planted in her right as rain, but she'd never brought one out alive, and she'd had well enough of losing kids. And Nick had needs—she understood. She also knew I wouldn't cheat him, I wasn't too young, I was an independent operator. I was busy out there in Castlemaine; there were women around, but they were mostly someone's wife or daughter, so I had my pick at the height of things and even then I preferred Nikolaj to the rest. Some of the blokes out there had rubbed their own pricks raw before they got to me, but nothing ever made Nick mean. Other men were horniest not when they'd found gold, but when someone else nearby had struck it rich. I think sometimes the only things that got them out of those mineshafts were their cocks. And even then, I'm willing to bet that there were men down there who whittled holes and fucked the rock itself, probably imagining their tips were touching gold. But Nick was solid, steady, and I appreciated that. There was no wounded pride to work on, no mess, no tears, he didn't take too long, and he was never over-rough.

Like all the miners, Nikolaj had bad lungs—too long underground—and every couple of months he'd be laid up with pneumonia. Then his wife would ask me to nurse him for a bit, since she was busy. She paid for this as well. Now, I liked Nick's wife—she had her head screwed on. She would have been down the shaft herself if she thought that it would pay. I don't know where she got her rum, which wasn't rotgut but good stuff;

I do know which troopers she paid off to make sure she wasn't caught. One of them bragged about it to me, so I squeezed his balls tighter than he liked and suggested he keep his mouth shut.

But Nick and Long were an unlucky pair, right to the last. Long fell, one night, into a disused shaft, and though he called and cried and sang enough to get pulled out, he'd broken both his legs and died six weeks later from infection. And the next summer, when the creeks and waterholes dried up and dysentery ran through the goldfields, Nikolaj was one of the first to go. Now, I've seen people die—my own mother and sisters, for example—but watching a body that large go out was another thing entirely. I sat on his left, his wife sat on his right, we all held hands. I cried as much as she did. Not long after, she started up in fright after looking at the fire and said, 'Did you see it? The Devil chasing Nicky through the flames.' I never took her for the superstitious kind. Two days later she'd packed the tent and was away, only the stone chimney left to say that they were ever there, and a box for me with two things in it: a sailor's dictionary and thirty pounds.

I had a comfortable few years on that money in Melbourne. Good living suits me: I fill out, I get a little lazy. Butter on bacon, my granny used to call it—I like things nice. But where I'm careful on a shilling, I'm stupid on a pound. And as Granny also said, money's quick, it's made to get away. So here I am again, too old now for the cities, and South Australia this time. I came out with the railway. I won't hang about in Fairly for much longer—the farms round here are failing, there's too much sorrow and more coming, and the railhead's moving further north. That family could find their boy and still lose everything.

But for now I'm here, and while I'm here I'm German. Well, why not? What would the men of Fairly know to do with a French girl? But call me Odette if you want to, or call me Inge Schmidt, it doesn't matter. Inge was Nick's wife's name. Actually, my name is Florence. My granny called me Florrie. Call me anything you like.

## SIXTH DAY

When George Axam wakes to the sound of rain, he sits up in his bed furious at everything: the weather, God, shearers, sheep, his exasperating brother, and the twistedness of his sheets. He suspects, as he always does when inconvenienced by rain, that the natives have brought it on to spite him. These are the only circumstances under which George would indulge such suspicions; he would never attribute to native magic a stretch of warm, dry, windless days for shearing.

George is a man who likes to make plans and keep them. He runs Thalassa like clockwork, or aspires to. He believes—passionately—in the Seven-Day Week, just as he believes in the British monarchy and Greenwich Mean Time: that is, as absolute verities. The difficulty, for George, lies in convincing most of his workers that days are counted in sevens, that the seventh day is the only one on which no work is done (unless it's a particularly busy time, such as shearing), and that these groups of seven days—these weeks—continue one after another with no interruption for weather, animal migration, personal preference, social gathering, or religious observance other than Christmas and Easter (days on which, lamentably, sheep must still be watched and cows still milked). It's inevitable, in this remote spot, that many of George's shepherds and station hands are Aboriginal; and he does prefer these employees, generally, to his white ones, who tend to be unsavoury characters on the run from something further south. He's come to understand that there are differences between, for example, a Nukunu man and a Yadliawarda man—though he would be unable to articulate those differences. Regardless, these people are simply not reliable when it comes to the Seven-Day Week.

That's why, when he finds his plans disrupted—even by a natural event like rain—George tends to feel that the natives are responsible. He thinks of them as disposed to laziness (they are, for example, disinclined to engage in hard physical labour during the hottest part of a hot day). This morning, he imagines that they'll be pleased to have a rainy day off, and that the atmosphere at the camp by the ration depot will be festive. George feels, as he often does, the loneliness of carrying this huge pastoral enterprise on his shoulders. He misses his wife. If Ellen weren't in Adelaide, but here, in bed, beside him, he would lay his head on her milky breast and feel the warmth of her breath in his hair.

George springs up, dresses, and looks in on his mother, who is sipping coffee in bed. This greeting is a morning ritual, largely rote, though George would be disconcerted if it stopped—it would be as if a number had fallen off a clockface. Mother, as usual, is fussing about all the wrong things. Apparently, Nancy delivered news with the coffee: Sergeant Foster arrived overnight, along with an unusual caravan including the Reverend Daniels, the sister of the missing boy, and a native tracker with a grievous wound. George dislikes hearing any news about Thalassa second-hand.

'You've noticed, I presume, the rain?' he says, which prompts his mother to ask him if a coat made of possum fur would keep off rain as effectively as an umbrella, and, come to think of it, does he know the whereabouts of one of those?

'Of one of what?' asks George.

'Of an umbrella.'

George says, 'Mother, can't this wait? It's rather a busy day.' And that's quite enough filial duty for the morning.

He closes his mother's door and heads towards the kitchen, running through the rainy yard. When he arrives, the first person he sees is a young white girl eating a soft-boiled egg at the kitchen table. She's curved one arm around her eggcup and is scooping furiously at the egg with a long spoon. Then he sees Tal, who's also sitting—his elbows are on the table, and he's resting his head on his hands in such a way that the back of his neck is visible, bound in its red handkerchief. Nancy is singing as she sweeps the room. It doesn't occur to George that Tal might be in bad humour (the result, perhaps, of a fruitless night at cards) and that Nancy is singing in an effort to make Tal laugh—that would be evidence of impulses unconnected to George and George's concerns. He sees only a man doing nothing when there's a lot to do, and a woman in a good mood when she should be in a bad one.

Nancy stops singing and says, 'Morning, Mister George.'

'Nancy,' George says, 'is there such a thing as an umbrella in this house?'

'Could be Mrs Ellen left one umbrella. What for?'

George pauses. 'I believe it's raining.'

Nancy laughs and says, 'So you wear a hat.'

It's true that George has never once used an umbrella at Thalassa—would, in fact, be ashamed to do so. Umbrellas are for town. He could explain that his mother asked after it, but why should he have to? 'A house this size should have at least one umbrella in it.'

'Maybe half one umbrella,' Nancy says.

George has not forgotten that, between the ages of three and ten, he would gladly have laid down his life for Nancy; but it's necessary, on occasion, to check the familiarity he allows her. So he says, sternly, 'Enough nonsense. Look about for an umbrella, Nancy. I want one.' Now he turns to Tal, who is bothersome, in that he's indispensable and knows it; this gives him a confidence that George detests, but has never managed to quash. 'And you can come with me to the sheds. Damned if I know what you're hanging about here for.'

Tal raises his head from his hands. 'There's a boy lost,' he says, and stands. He's taller than George, but this doesn't signify—George rarely looks directly at his face. 'And that Ramindjeri fellow's leg is bad. He can't get up.' He walks past George to the door of the kitchen and, addressing Nancy, says, 'That boy there, eh, that lost one. I'll go up and find him.' Then he steps into the rain, which has eased slightly, and crosses the kitchen yard without looking back.

George calls after him, 'If you don't work, you don't eat.' This isn't entirely true—not where Tal is concerned, anyway—but George often wishes that it were. He's tired of the arrogance of certain Aboriginal men. Not just Tal—he's also thinking of Nancy's brother, Billy, who returned to Thalassa when Otho Baumann left and acted as if he expected to be reinstalled as darling of the place.

Nancy hums the tune she was singing earlier. When George glares at her, she stops and says, 'You still want that umbrella?'

'It's still raining, isn't it?'

The girl eating the egg says, 'Hardly.' He'd forgotten about her; he wouldn't have said 'damned' otherwise. He has no idea who she is and, although strangers pass through Thalassa all the time, the mystery of her identity—along with the untimely rain—feels emblematic of a slight, but telling, slip in his authority. A shirtless boy appears at the door to shout at Nancy that Billy needs vinegar in the stable. Having shouted, the boy spots George, opens his eyes wide, and darts away. So Billy is here as well—a fact with which, notes George, his mother didn't see fit to acquaint him.

'Nancy,' he says, 'I won't have Billy interfering with the kitchen.'

Nancy looks hurt by this, which wrenches George's hidden heart. She says, without defiance, 'He's looking out for that tracker. The one busted his leg.'

'That's as may be,' says George, 'but unless Billy deigns to live and work here, he can't treat this kitchen as his own.' He shakes his head and heaves a sigh. 'Get me the vinegar. I'm going past the stable—I'll take it to him.'

Nancy sets the broom aside and leaves the kitchen, heading for the storeroom where the vinegar is kept. George, alone now with the girl and her shielded egg, says, 'And who might you be?'

'Cissy Wallace, sir,' she replies, and George says, 'Ah, the sister.' It strikes George that she is almost too old to be alone with. Nancy returns with a jar of vinegar. As soon as George leaves the kitchen, she sings as loudly as before.

George stops at the stable on his way to the woolshed, delighted, as he always is, by the way his horses nicker in greeting from their stalls. Their mangers are almost empty, so he calls for one of the stable boys. The stable is yet another part of Thalassa in need of his attention: it's much larger than it ought to be, now that they're no longer breeding ponies. George has been known to curse his father for having built so big, only to abandon all of it; he then invariably regrets being unfaithful to his father's memory. What memory? George has three distinct recollections of Henry Axam. He recalls a dazzling man with a prominent—but neat—moustache, who shook a newspaper and winked across the breakfast table. He remembers an instance in which Papa watched as Billy bowled a cricket ball at little George, and George, swinging his bat, missed. And he remembers a picnic at his father's absurd Greek temple, when one of the children in attendance pointed at Billy in his cricket whites, gave George a sly look, and said, 'Is that your brother?' At the time, George was unsure of whom, exactly, this was meant to insult: George for having a native brother, or Billy for being related to a useless boy like himself, who could neither bowl nor bat.

There's no sign of Billy in the stable. George, looking about with his jar of vinegar, hears footsteps overhead in the hayloft, then a shout. A trapdoor opens in the ceiling and hay rains down into a stall. The hay dust glitters in a shaft of light. Watching it, George has the feeling—as he often does immediately before shearing starts—that a man with more authority is about to come striding in, barking orders. George isn't sure if he craves or fears this man. Either way, he never comes, and George must pretend to be him. George hears a groan coming from the harness room, the door of which has been propped open with a stool, against his strict instructions.

Yes, a cot has been made up in the harness room and a man lies on it, covered by a blanket. George, peering in, remains half hidden in the doorway. He sees Billy, looking robust and wiry as he always does, poking at the fire in the cast-iron stove that George prefers never to light. A chair beside the stove has been draped with one of those fur cloaks the natives sometimes wear down south—presumably it's drying. The man on the cot groans again and Billy crosses to him, pressing at his forehead with a cloth. It's done, notes George, with uncommon gentleness, as if Billy loved this man above all else. Is that your brother? George can imagine, for a moment, how Billy might have been when Papa drowned: the sorrow and care he might have demonstrated. As he often does in Billy's presence, George feels a deep complaint, an undertow of grief. It's insufferable, so he presses it back down.

Billy looks up and his face is relaxed until he sees George in the doorway; then it neutralises. George holds up the jar of vinegar and places it on a table by the door. He nods at Billy. Billy nods back. They are civil and careful with one another. George stays for no more than three seconds, nods again, and backs away.

The boy had grown older overnight. He didn't notice this at first; he was tired and wet, the stolen blanket was heavy and smelled of piddle, and although he knew that the road outside Wilparra would lead him into town—the lady god had said so, yesterday—he had no sense of how long the journey would take. He was afraid to stop in case the gods caught up with him.

The road ran alongside a creek in which the boy saw shallow puddles of water. The rain wasn't as heavy now as it had been when he left Wilparra, but the boy knew to keep out of creek beds even in light rain—his father had warned him about the sudden rivers that could come pouring from the ranges. Even so, he climbed down into the creek to drink and take a rest. He was hidden from the road by the steep bank of the creek, and sheltered from the rain by the knotty, exposed roots of a red gum, and he slept without quite meaning to. He woke, hungry, when a pigeon flew down to drink from the deepest of the creek bed's puddles. The boy leaned across the water and cupped his hands over the bird, which began to hop and squawk and spread its wings.

The boy thought his hands looked bigger than they had yesterday. They were large enough that, if he wanted to, he could hold the bird down in the puddle until it drowned. Then he could build a fire, pluck and clean the bird, use his knife to gut it, and roast it on the fire. He couldn't have done all this if he were still the age he'd been yesterday. The boy had not, until this precise moment with the bird, understood or believed in time. The chime of his mother's mantel clock was only music;

how could it divide one day from another when every day was the same as yesterday, and would be the same tomorrow? And the sun was always shining, here or in some other place. But the boy looked at his hands holding down the pigeon's wings, and time presented itself to him. It said: then, and now. Before you were lost, and after. He could not have put into words this feeling that he had stepped aside from himself and was now just watching. The pigeon beat its bronze wings in the water. When the boy withdrew his hands, the bird skipped on its scaly feet, shook itself, and flew away.

The boy wondered if his mother would recognise him now that he was older. He climbed the bank, looked up and down the road, and saw that horses had passed while he was asleep: probably the gods'. So they were ahead of him, could reach Mam first, and if they did, what might they say to her? They might say that he had liked drawing with the god, had liked the god's stories of monkeys wearing hats, had liked the peaceful the way the lady combed his hair since she only had one head to comb and could take her time; they might tell Mam that he was their boy now, and that he wanted to go and live with them on the sun. And Mam might believe them. She might not care. She might say, 'Yes, take him,' and turn away to churn the butter.

So the boy needed to reach Mam before the gods did. This didn't seem likely, but he might manage it. The gods might get lost or fall asleep, their horses might run away. He followed the road, but kept to one side of it, darting from one damp clump of mulga to another—after all, the gods might have set a trap and be waiting for him up ahead. He watched himself stumbling in the rain. He'd gone a little way before he realised that he'd left his blanket by the creek, but there was no time to go back.

⁂

When Cissy finishes her egg in the Thalassa kitchen, Nancy offers her a second one. Cissy refuses it; she has never in her life eaten more than one egg at a time, and doesn't intend to start now. Then Nancy asks if Cissy wants a job to do and Cissy says yes, because if she's stuck at Thalassa, waiting for Sergeant Foster to speak to her and for June to be reshod, then she'd prefer to be occupied with something useful. So, on Nancy's instructions, Cissy sets out to collect the lamps from all the Thalassa bedrooms. She goes into the main part of the house and begins to march in and out of rooms, up and down hallways, refusing to look with any interest at anything. The house swims around her, vaguely full of glints and glosses: brass, wood, marble, china. It ticks with clocks. The floors are clotted with Turkey carpets. She will ignore this house as well as she's able, and she'll be useful—but only as it suits her.

There are so many bedrooms, and each has its own peculiar smell and oppressive wardrobe. In one room, the minister lies sleeping on a bed with his limp hair stuck to his forehead; Cissy is thoroughly sick of his face. In the final bedroom, Cissy finds Mrs Axam. She's sitting, dressed, in front of a mirrored dressing table, brushing out her hair. Her long, skinny dog lies at her feet and is indifferent to Cissy's arrival. Judging it best not to look at Mrs Axam, Cissy walks to the mantel shelf, where she's spotted a dirty lamp. She's poised and ready for the possibility that Mrs Axam will notice and question her, but Mrs Axam continues to sit in front of the mirror, no longer brushing her hair. Cissy can see from the corner of her eye that Mrs Axam isn't moving at all, just holding the bright brush against her shoulder. So Cissy dares to look at her directly, and she sees that Mrs Axam isn't aware of this room, or of Cissy in it—she's listening to some other part of the house, some part Cissy can't conceive of, with the air of someone entirely consumed by an idea. This interests Cissy, though she doesn't know what the idea could be. Mrs Axam interests Cissy—there, she'll admit it. Once, when a horse fell in an Adelaide street, Mrs Axam jumped from her own carriage and sat on the horse's head in order to keep it calm beneath her skirts while it was taken out of harness. Everyone in Fairly knows this story, which is among the most impressive Cissy has ever heard.

Cissy, interested in Mrs Axam, clears her throat. If Mrs Axam is startled, she doesn't show it—she simply returns to brushing her hair and looks at Cissy in the mirror. Cissy has the curious feeling that her mother is at stake: that every move she makes in this house, right or wrong, will reflect well or badly on her mother.

'Good morning,' Mrs Axam says. 'I think you must be Cecily Wallace.'

'Yes, madam.' Cissy finds herself making a curtsy, which she immediately—but invisibly—renounces.

'I'm truly sorry, dear, about your brother. And Nancy tells me you were extremely brave with Mr Daniels. Wasn't that clever of you.'

Cissy, unsure of the merits of cleverness, says, 'I'm here to fetch your lamp.'

'Is that so?' says Mrs Axam. 'I suppose Nancy is keeping you busy. You might stay here, then, and brush my hair for me. As you can see, I have only one useful hand.'

Cissy takes Mrs Axam's hairbrush. It's heavy and silver, and the silky bristles are looped with hair. Mam keeps a cleaner brush. Cissy tugs at the hair in the bristles and a mat of it comes out, brush-shaped.

'You're quite right,' says Mrs Axam. 'Disgraceful.' She puts her hand out for the hair, and Cissy gives it to her. 'Now, I prefer firm, even strokes, all the way from top to bottom.'

Cissy brushes Mrs Axam's hair in much the same way she would brush the coats of her father's Shires. She has to stop herself from making the hissing noise she does when grooming the horses—her father taught her this trick, which stops dust from their coats from getting into her mouth. Cissy can see Mrs Axam's pearly scalp through her thin white hair.

'Good,' says Mrs Axam. 'Nice, firm strokes. How old are you, Cecily?'

'Fifteen, madam.'

'Yes, I'm told you were very brave indeed with Mr Daniels,' she says again, then pauses. Cissy passes the brush through Mrs Axam's hair. 'There was another man brought in with you—a native tracker. Yes?'

Cissy is trying not to think about the tracker. He lay so quietly in the dray last night, as if asleep, but his eyes were open. He looked much more substantial than Mr Daniels, who remained unconscious beside him. Each time the dray jumped on the rutted road, the tracker narrowed his eyes as if waiting to see how much it would hurt. Sometimes he would begin to groan, then immediately stifle it. Sitting beside him in the cart, rain running beneath her collar, Cissy veered between feeling responsible for and revolted by his suffering.

'Yes,' says Cissy.

'Was he very badly injured?' Mrs Axam asks.

'I don't know. Nobody would tell me.'

Mrs Axam nods as if that's as it should be. 'Where did they put him?'

'I think somewhere in the stable.'

'And was he wearing that fur cloak of his?'

'Yes, madam, when I saw him last.' Suddenly, Cissy smells the cloak, as if it's just walked through the room.

'I wonder,' says Mrs Axam. She lifts her hand and places it on Cissy's—on the hand with which Cissy holds the brush. She looks at Cissy in the mirror.

Mrs Axam says, 'You're tall, aren't you, for your age.'

'Yes, madam,' Cissy says, colouring slightly; she's proud of her height.

'And brave,' says Mrs Axam, 'and helpful.'

Cissy sees that Mrs Axam has let her wad of hair fall onto the carpet; her skinny dog is sniffing at it.

'I wonder if you might help me, too,' says Mrs Axam. 'I want to give that poor man, the poor tracker, a new coat. I have it ready—there it is, folded on the chair.'

Cissy follows Mrs Axam's eyes and sees that on a chair by the door there is, indeed, an object that could be a folded black coat. It looks to be of sturdy quality—much finer than the tracker's mangy fur.

Mrs Axam turns in her chair to face Cissy, still holding Cissy's hand. 'It was my husband's, but he never wore it. Imagine how comfortable the man will be in a proper coat, with sleeves and buttons. What I would like you to do, Cecily, is take it to him in the stable. Can you do that for me?'

Cissy nods.

'But,' says Mrs Axam, 'I'm terribly worried that someone will see that old cloak of his and think it's just to be thrown away, or burned. Just a dirty old thing. That would be a dreadful waste. So when you take that nice new coat there to the stable and give it to the tracker, I'd like you to bring his old cloak back to me. Do you understand?'

Cissy is surprised by the request. She'd like Mrs Axam to understand that she, Cissy, is also the kind of person who would sit on the head of a horse. But she's horrified by the thought of having anything to do with the tracker's cloak, and this horror makes her pause. Why would someone like Mrs Axam want such a thing?

'And I, in turn, might be of help to you,' says Mrs Axam. 'Now, I can't imagine you're still at school.'

'I am,' says Cissy.

Mrs Axam lets go of Cissy's hand. The broken contact is a relief. 'Fifteen and at school? That's most commendable. And when you finish school? Will you stay at home to help your mother, or will you look for a position?'

Cissy says, 'I'm not sure, madam.' She thinks of Miss McNeil and the Training College in Adelaide.

'Very good,' says Mrs Axam, exactly as if Cissy had given a definite answer. 'A friend in town is looking for a maid and do you know, Cecily, I think you'd be just the thing. Yes, you would be most suitable. Do you know of Mrs Manning?'

It takes Cissy a moment to understand that 'Mrs Manning' means Minna. Mrs Axam is offering to help Cissy gain employment with Minna, so that Cissy will wash Minna's dresses, clean her outhouse, serve her dinner, and polish, forever, silver bowls with candles in them. She will sweep up after Minna Baumann, she'll inhale Minna's dust, smell her waste, scrub her plates, say 'yes, Mrs Manning; no, Mrs Manning' all day long to Minna Baumann. But, thinks Cissy, Minna would never sit on a horse's head. She remembers Minna kissing Robert in private on her wedding day; she remembers despising her for it, and wanting to be kissed herself. Cissy wants to be useful. She wants to *do, do*. But serving Minna Baumann cannot be her one idea.

Cissy hears the sound of Nancy singing. Mrs Axam hears it too; and Cissy sees that she would like a firm commitment before Nancy can interrupt them. Suddenly, Cissy understands that the cloak is, for today at least, Mrs Axam's one idea. It's an odd idea, but Cissy can accept it. And she's prepared to receive something in return, but that something can't be Minna. It seems to her that Mrs Axam might be prepared to offer almost anything in exchange for this trivial favour. The world grows larger, then, but so does the awfulness of finding the tracker and touching his cloak.

'Well, Cecily?' says Mrs Axam. 'What do you say to that? A position with Mrs Manning? I'm sure it would be helpful to your parents.'

Cissy takes a deep breath. 'No. No, thank you. Miss McNeil says I should be a teacher. She says I should go to Adelaide, to the Training College.'

'And who is Miss McNeil?'

'My teacher,' Cissy says.

Mrs Axam nods. 'You must be an intelligent girl. Would you like to attend the Training College?'

Cissy can't imagine being a teacher—she's not nearly as splendid as Miss McNeil, and is bound to make a fool of herself. She doesn't like the thought of spending all her time with children, teaching them simple things she already knows. But wouldn't it be better than sweeping Minna's floors? And if she went to Adelaide, she would have the opportunity to see the sea, which she's heard so much about. Cissy suspects that when she hears the rhythm of her Tennyson, she hears the sea. So, would she like to attend the Training College?

'Yes, madam,' she says. Nancy's singing grows nearer.

Mrs Axam studies Cissy's face. Cissy squares her shoulders and lifts her chin.

'I see,' says Mrs Axam. 'And can your parents spare you?'

Cissy understands that they're discussing money now, and that this requires some delicacy on her part. She swallows, conscious of the dignity of her mother, and says, 'I expect it would be hard on them.'

Mrs Axam narrows her eyes as if preparing for a negotiation; Cissy has seen her father do this when he's buying seed. The dog coughs like a little vicar. 'Well,' says Mrs Axam, 'if you were to bring me the tracker's cloak, and to do it inconspicuously, so that Nancy didn't see you, then perhaps we might discuss this further.'

Before Cissy can answer, Nancy is in the room.

'Too slow,' says Mrs Axam, but to herself. She turns back to the mirror, and it's as if Cissy no longer exists.

'Sorry, missus,' says Nancy. 'I said to this one, don't disturb you people. Didn't I say it? Where's that lamp? It's here.'

Cissy stiffens. She'll soon be old enough that Nancy wouldn't dare scold her.

Nancy lifts the lamp from the mantel, apologises again to Mrs Axam, and indicates with a tilt of her head that Cissy should leave the room. Cissy does; but just before she steps through the door, she takes the coat from the chair. Then she and Nancy are in the hallway, and the door to Mrs Axam's room is closed.

'What's this?' Nancy asks, indicating the coat.

'She said to take it.'

'What for?'

'I don't know what for,' says Cissy, and Nancy manages to look both sceptical and indifferent. 'I want to leave now. I want to go home.'

'Well, nobody will stop you.'

'The sergeant wants to speak to me.'

'Oh, that one,' Nancy says. 'Stay or go, suit yourself.' She offers the lamp to Cissy, who refuses it: no lamps, no chores. I am a lamp, thinks Cissy, and I am lit. Nancy shrugs. She turns and goes down the hallway, carrying the lamp ahead of her as if she expects it to provide light.

Cissy, holding the coat against her beating heart, resolves to go to the stable. If June has been reshod, Cissy will leave, and damn the sergeant. She walks through the dining room, and everything in it seems to shudder as she passes: glass and crystal, keys in cabinets, silver on sideboards. If Mam were here, she would feel the tremble produced by Cissy's footsteps and say, 'Lightly, Cissy, lightly.'

Out onto the verandah now, into the yard, around the house, past the kitchen and through the kitchen garden, ignoring everyone she sees: Cissy Wallace with her head held high, marching through a crowd of ruffled hens, carrying a woollen coat. Her skirts are clean—old Pearl washed and wrung them last night, aired them by the kitchen fire, and ironed them dry this morning while Nancy cooked Cissy's egg. She's washed her face and neatened her hair and saved, mind you, the minister from certain death. *Half a league onward, all in the valley of Death.* She's seen the way Minna Baumann kisses her husband—as if each kiss were a kind of plea. She's seen Minna's husband asleep by firelight and felt his knee against her back. She's loved Miss McNeil without ever deciding to, and she's a citizen of South Australia.

Striding down to the stable, Cissy feels the rain on her face and hands and in the parting of her hair. Stay dry, Denny, she thinks. Come home, Denny. She'll check on June and, while she's in the stable, well, it's possible she'll look about and find the tracker. Nancy said they had to cut his trouser leg open, because of the swelling. Cissy holds the coat to her chest as if to keep it from getting wet and thinks of the tracker rocking from side to side in the back of the cart, and the minister lying thin and long beside him. Cissy sat close to their heads with her feet drawn up so that she wouldn't touch either of them. Billy rode behind on Virnu with his head bent into the rain, for all the world as if he'd never met Cissy in his life. If she finds the tracker, then yes, she might take the old cloak (she hopes it will be folded, set in a corner, and ready for disposal) and leave the new one in its place, then deliver the awful, furry thing to

Mrs Axam. Imagine Miss McNeil's face when Cissy says, 'I'm going to the Training College.' Cissy thinks of Miss McNeil in the arms of her brown, happy Welshman. The body unfettered! Read this book, says Miss McNeil, think this thought; but Cissy has no time to read and think, she has to do. She recites poems while walking because it's a way to do two things at once. She marches through Thalassa and every second step is a stressed syllable: *My strength is as the strength of ten, because my heart is pure.* Sheep are being driven, bleating, through the wet, and Cissy waits for them to pass.

Here, at last, is the stable, cool and smelling of grain and hay, and here's June, still unshod. And here's Billy, sitting on a stool in the doorway of a smaller room. Cissy has known Billy since she was seven, old enough to know that her father pays him. She's secretly intimidated by him, because he's indifferent to her rages; she tends to treat him as a guest who's always on the point of leaving. But when she sees him here in the Thalassa stable, she could run to him, lay her head in his lap, and cry. She doesn't; she's too old for that. Billy looks at her with the same expression her father uses when he knows she's about to irritate him.

'I thought my horse might be ready,' she says. 'I mean, I know she's not my horse. But I thought she might be ready.'

Billy nods, then flexes his hands to crack the knuckles. Behind him, a window pours dusty light into the smaller room. Cissy can't see any sign of the tracker, but she knows he must be in there. She makes a half-hearted attempt to peer over Billy's shoulder.

'Is he very badly injured?' she asks.

'We'll see,' says Billy. 'The doctor's due from Quorn.'

Cissy tightens her arms around the coat, takes a step forwards, and says, 'I need to go in there.'

'What for?'

Cissy finds that she's ashamed to say. With Billy here, sitting on the stool in the doorway, the harness room seems forbidden. 'Does he have his furry cloak?' she asks.

Billy looks at the coat in her arms, then back at her face. 'Yes. He never takes it off.' A pause. 'Unless he really has to.'

Cissy shudders. 'Why not?'

'It's part of him,' says Billy, but Cissy doesn't understand. 'What's that you've got?'

'It's a coat from Mrs Axam,' Cissy says. She looks down at the dark bundle in her arms as if she's not sure how it got there. 'A new one for him. I'm supposed to give it to him.'

Billy looks at her for a long moment, then says, 'Better leave him be.' There's nothing unkind about the way he says it, but Cissy understands that he will never rise from his stool or let her into the room, though Mrs Axam might sit on the heads of a hundred horses. And June isn't ready, Denny is lost, Cissy will finish school and look for a position, she'll go away from Mam and Miss McNeil. She has no power at all over her own heart.

Cissy, afraid she's going to sob, thrusts the coat at Billy, and he takes it without a word. Then she runs out into the stable yard, where it's still raining, light and steady, as if it will never stop.

⁂

Minna is reading the one interesting book she can find in Robert's house—the memoir of a shipwrecked sailor—when she hears horses and the low voice of a man outside the police station.

She's sure that it's Robert, and debates waiting for him in the bedroom—she likes the idea of him finding her in his bed. But Robert knocks at the door, which is unexpected, and when she hurries to open it, she finds the Swedish painter and his wife. They're both quite wet. Karl Rapp looks astonished to see Minna standing in the doorway. Mrs Rapp seems less surprised, as if every door her husband knocks at opens on an informally dressed woman. They announce that they've come to the police station in order to report a missing child.

Minna says, 'But this is wonderful! We've been looking for him for days.' She finds herself ushering them into the parlour with her mother's graceful gestures, and sitting in an armchair as if bundled in black silk. The parlour is more untidy than it should be. It occurs to her that she should offer tea, but there's no one to prepare it—other than herself.

Karl Rapp tells her about a waterhole, some missing apples, and a place Minna doesn't catch the name of. It begins with 'w'—ah, Karl means Wilparra, which he pronounces as if it's spelled Wilporough. Something about the boy wandering off from there last night? The painter's not what he was last week: there's something dimmed about his face. But he's still very beautiful. His damp hair is the colour of late-summer grass.

Minna, in turn, tells the Rapps about the search for Denny Wallace; her heroic husband features prominently in her account. She describes Sergeant Foster, although she's never met him, and reports his statement that children, when lost, always walk in a straight line, while adults wander in a circle. To this, Mrs Rapp responds, as if quoting somebody, 'Anything that embodies itself with freedom seeks a rounded shape.'

'Gosh,' says Minna.

Karl says, 'We must go to these Wallace people and tell them we found their son.' He glances at his wife. 'And lost him again. How far is their farm? Our horses are tired.'

'It isn't far,' says Minna, who has never been good at judging distance. 'You take the road by the church, going north, and follow it until you see the odd hill that sticks up out of nowhere. Theirs is the house beneath it.'

'Hill?' says Mrs Rapp.

'Yes,' Minna says. 'You might have seen it as you came in from Wilparra. You wouldn't have passed the house, that's on a different road, but you will have seen the hill in the distance. It's quite striking.'

'Then we know the place,' says Mr Rapp. 'We stopped there, yes, for the piece of aloe?'

Mrs Rapp nods. How drained she looks. She has, at some point, removed her riding gloves, and she slaps these lightly against one knee. 'I wonder,' she says, and apparently what she wonders is whether someone ought to be sent out looking for the boy along the Wilparra road.

With pleasure, Minna says, 'I'll raise the lads.'

Neither Karl nor his wife seems to understand what Minna means by that; she isn't sure herself. But since she's offered to take action of some kind, she goes into the hallway and opens the front door. Having stepped with purpose onto the verandah of the police station, she stands helpless for a moment. The rain has stopped, the air feels sticky, and the flies hover as if dangling on gummy threads. There's no one on the road but a tall, dark native man, heading north; he'll have to do.

Minna calls, 'Hello there! You!'

The native doesn't stop.

'You! Boy!'

He looks over his shoulder.

'Yes, you! Come here!'

Slowly, the native comes back down the road and stops in front of the police station. She knows she's seen him in town before—he's from Thalassa. He stays on the road and she stays on the verandah, but even like this he's taller than she is. No part of her body is interested in him.

'What are you called?' she asks.

The man tugs at the red handkerchief around his neck. Then he says, 'Tal, missus.'

'Very well, Tal,' Minna says, and draws her purse from the pocket of her skirt. 'I'll give you sixpence now if you run over to the hotels and find able-bodied men to help with a task. And sixpence later, when you've done the job.'

He considers this possibility and says, 'Can't do that, missus.'

'I know you can't enter the hotels, but you needn't. You can call through the door, or ask someone outside. Tell them I'll pay well.'

'How much?'

'Ten shillings,' says Minna. 'At least. If they carry out the task.'

'What task?'

Minna is growing impatient with him. 'They're to look for the missing boy on the Wilparra road. That's where he is.'

'What for Wilparra?'

'Never you mind,' Minna says. She takes sixpence from her purse and holds it out to him. 'Quickly, now,' she says. 'Go longa hurry hurry. It's very important.'

He takes the money.

'And another sixpence, Tal, when I know you've done the job.'

He nods, but doesn't move.

'And no drunks,' says Minna. 'Respectable, able-bodied men.' She waits for him to move away in the direction of the hotels; when he does, she goes inside and returns to the parlour.

Karl Rapp is alone in there, standing with his back to the unlit fireplace as if to warm himself.

'The rain has stopped,' she says.

'Ah,' he responds, as if she's just revealed something surprising.

Only last week, he was in her mother's house finding excuses to touch Minna's arms and waist and hair. He drew a picture of her wearing a crown of flowers. He spoke German with Mama and admired the silver bowl, and he suggested a walk in the garden, managing things so that he and Minna found themselves alone. Mrs Rapp stayed with Mama, inspecting a piece of lace or a bed of lettuce, while Karl led Minna to a shady tree, pressed her against it, and kissed her mouth. The kiss was almost chaste. As he drew away (his face still just an inch or so from hers), she thought, Oh! A man can be beautiful. He told her that he could see how much she loved her future husband, and that she was the kind of woman who, in loving one man, loved all men. He kept looking at her mouth, and she felt how Robert had been included in that first kiss; she leaned forwards to find Robert's presence in the second, which was less chaste.

Now, in the parlour, she steps closer to Karl Rapp and flattens her hand over his heart. He looks down and sees her wedding ring.

'Ah,' he says again. 'Of course, you're married now. So much can change in such a little time. My most heartfelt congratulations, dear Miss Minna.'

'Mrs Manning,' she corrects him, smiling.

Karl lays one hand over hers where it rests on his chest, presses it, then returns her hand to her as if bestowing a precious gift. He moves away.

Minna's longing rushes at her with renewed force. Yes, she thinks, this desire I feel all goes back to Robert. She wants her husband very badly. She *demands* her husband. It occurs to her that, were she to take the Rapps out to the Wallace farm, she might see him. She could be the one to tell him where to find the boy. And when the boy is safe, Robert will come home and make her a bride again.

Mrs Rapp returns to the parlour—who can say where she's been? To use the privy, to wash her face, to attend to the mess of Minna's kitchen? What kind of woman wanders, uninvited, in another woman's house? Karl goes to stand beside his wife. They both look sad and weary.

Minna says, 'You said your horses were tired? I'll drive you out to the Wallaces. We can take my mother's pair and buggy.'

Mrs Rapp agrees to this plan, and Karl agrees with her. They seem hesitant, though, as if they dread the trip. As Minna prepares to leave them, to arrange the buggy, it occurs to her to wonder why the boy, having found the Rapps, would choose to run.

⸻

At Thalassa, Sergeant Foster sits outside the door of the room in which the vicar is sleeping. The vicar has slept through both breakfast and dinner, completely unaware that he's in police custody. Foster has tried to wake him; the man was groggy and unintelligible every time. A doctor has been sent for, but he's not expected until later this afternoon, so there's nothing to do but wait. If Foster hadn't parted from Wooding two days ago, then Wooding would have been given the task of guarding the vicar's door. As it is, Foster has no one to rely on but himself. He's commandeered a writing desk and chair, had them carried into the hallway, and here he sits, working on his damn reports. Before dinner, Foster wasted his time on questioning Wallace's man, Billy Rough, who answered with pleasing efficiency but had nothing useful to say. Then, a light meal of roast bantam and steamed cabbage. Afterwards, he questioned Cecily Wallace, who glowered at him, gave vague responses, and asked if *now* she might go and look for her brother. She appeared to have a smear of lampblack above her left eye.

From Mrs Axam, Foster has gathered that this Daniels is considered a harmless fellow. She explained that when her husband established the Fairly church and living, he put in an order for 'an extremely mild clergyman'; Adelaide has obliged, since then, by sending a series of innocuous young men, none of whom have lasted long in the north country. The younger Axam son, whose name Foster has already forgotten, dropped in after his mother. He was freshly sunburned on the neck—remarkable, given the rain—and only said, in response to Foster's questions, that he supposed Daniels was a self-sufficient sort of gentleman, which presumably means he doesn't dine at Thalassa often. Mr Daniels' profession recommends him, as does the colour of his skin, but the discoveries of the handkerchief and boots both tell against him.

By the middle of the afternoon, Foster's reports are up to date. He's sleepy himself, and bothered by both a persistent fly and the thought that his time might have been better spent locating the boy's body. His thoughts also dwell on Jimmy Possum, who he thinks has probably broken his femur, and for whom he feels responsible. Foster has insisted on Jimmy's being kept under guard so that none of the natives will attempt to set the bone, and has left Billy there with instructions to stretch the leg manually every hour, no matter the patient's objections. Jimmy is lucky the kick didn't rupture the artery: Foster has seen a native die within minutes of a shot to the thigh, and for this reason, he recommends that his men always aim for the calf when they're bringing down a runner.

But Jimmy is likely to survive—barring an infection—and it's just as well, because Foster's made a vow to take Jimmy's body, should he die, all the way to Encounter Bay, where it will be involved in elaborate mourning rituals. Jimmy will be a long time healing, though, and Foster will need another man. Well, he'll repeat his offer of employment to Billy Rough. Usually, it's best not to hire a local man for police work; but this disadvantage would be offset by Billy's prowess with a cricket ball.

From where Foster sits, he can see into the Thalassa dining room: good furniture, polished silver behind polished glass, a table draped in white damask, a wedding portrait of the lady of the house, and a candelabra fluttering with wax-paper shades. A dining room isn't at its best in the afternoon, when it's never needed; there's something cringing about it, thinks Foster, leaning forwards in his chair to make a note of this observation, which might prove useful (that is, if he ever manages to write another book). From this new angle, the room reveals an unexpected treasure: most of one wall is taken up by a vast cabinet of honeyed wood. The cabinet is adorned with etched glass and brass knobs and veiled, in its upper half, by a pair of faded velvet curtains. Foster enters the room to take a closer look.

Yes, of course—he heard tales of this object when he was writing about Henry Axam in *Forging the Path*. It's the Thalassa orchestrion, a spectacular piece of foolishness imported from Switzerland and installed by a madman on an isolated sheep station in the Australian bush. Axam, presumably, considered it a witty oddity. Yes—here, behind the velvet curtains of the upper cabinet, are the silver pipes, just like an organ's, and above them two flat drums; and here, behind the lower doors, are the big brass cylinders that produce music when they turn, a giant's pianola. Here is the place to put your chosen cylinder—Foster notes one sitting ready, sharp with steel teeth—and here's the crank you turn to wind it up to the top of the cabinet.

Foster rubs his hands together: this is just the thing to wake the vicar. The mere winding of the crank produces such a racket that he's amazed no one comes to see what he's up to. Ah, he thinks, there'll be noise enough when the music starts, and attention with it. He releases the crank, the cylinder begins to descend, and the whole absurd object wheezes into life.

Well, it's tremendous. At first there's the tinny sound of the steel teeth; then the pipes join in, and finally the drums are thumping, the floor of the dining room begins to throb, and everything in the room strikes up a rhythmic rattle. It's as if a tiny, angry brass band has taken up residence beneath the house and is now marching its way out. And here it comes, a surge of sound: fierce, triumphant. If music could be considered athletic, this, thinks Foster, is that music. Weight, not speed! He hears people coming towards the room with their voices raised, but the march can't be stopped, even if Foster wished it: the cylinder has been wound to the top of the orchestrion, and as a result it must wind its regulated way back to the bottom.

No one could sleep through this. How puny Foster feels inside the muscle and blood of it; but he made it happen! There are women on the verandah, the kind of native women who, on every bush property all over this fine country, sit for hours every day on verandahs grinding corn or sorting rice; they look in at the windows. The music thunders. It sounds like a cathedral organ played underwater, and Foster could give himself up to its sheer magnificence. He sways his body, taps his feet and moves his arms as if conducting the apparatus; for five terrific minutes he's in charge of all the noise in the world. Then the mechanism winds down, the cylinder stops turning, and the house settles back into itself. The orchestra beneath the floorboards packs away its brass.

There are figures in the doorway—one of them may be the Wallace girl—but they retreat when Foster looks at them. There's no sign of any Axam, although the wedding portrait on the wall seems to pulsate with disapproval. Even the women on the verandah have gone back to their tasks. He's tempted to wind the orchestrion and do it all again: repeat the grinding of the cylinder before it starts, repeat the hiccups in rhythm and skips in melody where a tooth has worn down or a pipe become buckled.

The novelty of perfect repetition! But he leaves the orchestrion be. The audience he wants is captive, anyway, and lying in the room across the hallway.

Foster, entering the dark bedroom, finds himself walking lightly on his feet, as if afraid to wake a sleeper. But the narrow bed is empty. In a clear admission of his guilt, Mr Daniels has up and fled.

⁂

Noella is on the front verandah when the Transcontinental dogcart arrives at Undelcarra, bringing clear skies with it. The naked sun begins to dry the plain. Noella watches an old woman alight from the dogcart, all large skirts and small bag, and calls for her mother as loudly as she can. When Mam appears in the doorway, she seems surprised by this new arrival; then she's welcoming. She asks Noella to run down and carry the woman's bag, which Noella is happy to do because it looks as if it won't weigh much. It doesn't, and Noella shakes it as she walks up the path behind the woman, trying to guess what's inside. She hopes its rattling noise is produced by tins full of boiled sweets. If it is, thinks Noella in a fit of impetuous generosity, she will save half her share to give to Denny when he's home.

Once she and the visitor reach Mam, Noella learns that the woman's name is Muriel, that she arrived on the afternoon train, and that she's here to be a grandmother. At least, that's how she's introduced: as Grandmother Deniston. She produces a photograph of Grandfather Deniston, who looks much older and thinner than he does in the picture on Mam's bedroom wall. Mam studies the photograph, then goes inside to prepare tea. The woman sits down on one of the chairs that live on the verandah, removes her hat, and holds it in her lap. Noella sits on the chair next to the woman's, and together they look out at the moisture rising off the heating plain. Soon, it will be as if it had never rained. The afternoon sky burns white, readying itself for another blinding sunset.

Noella sits alone with this woman, her new grandmother, whose face reminds her of a pudding on a plate—folded, squashy. The grandmother opens her mouth to yawn behind a crinkly hand. She smells as if she's made of the fine dust that collects in the seams of the chiffonier drawer where Mam keeps her violet hair powder. Noella is interested in the dark stuff of the grandmother's clothes. Recently, she has learned that people can wear clothes made from the fleece of unborn lambs, and that the difficult, delicious name for material of this kind is astrakhan. She wonders if the new grandmother is wearing astrakhan.

Still studying the grandmother, Noella observes, 'You don't have any hanging parts on your ears.'

The grandmother nods. 'Those are called earlobes.'

'I don't have them either.'

'Neither did the Lord.'

It seems appropriate to leave a bit of silence after this revelation. Then, judging the time to be right, Noella says, 'I was born at Christmastime. That's why I'm called Noella.'

The grandmother smiles, but not at Noella—the smile slides off towards the gate, though it's nice nonetheless.

Noella asks, 'Did you come because of Denny?'

'Yes, dear,' says the new grandmother. 'It's a time for family, and the love of God.' She says it as if she's soothing someone who isn't feeling well.

'Why didn't Grandfather come?' Noella asks.

'He's far too ill to travel.'

'Is he dead?'

'He's ill.'

'What sort of ill?'

The grandmother pauses, then says, 'Neuralgic diarrhoea, duck.'

Noella doesn't know what neuralgic diarrhoea is. 'Does he sleep a lot?' The grandmother nods. 'All day? Does he eat?' Noella, a middle child, has a tactician's interest in food.

'Aye, he eats,' says the grandmother; this seems to be a cause of satisfaction to her. And then, with some wistfulness, 'Mostly beef broth and oats, on account of his teeth.'

Noella presses a finger against her own reassuring front teeth. 'When will he die?' she asks.

'It's not our business to know when he will enter the Kingdom,' says the grandmother, but not sharply. There's nothing but mildness on the creased flannel of her face.

'Whose business is it?' Noella asks.

'The Lord's.'

Oh yes, the Lord again. 'Should we pray, then?' asks Noella, pulling at the part of her ear that, on another sister, would extend into a lovely plump lobe.

The grandmother blinks slowly and says, 'No thank you, duck.'

Noella sits frozen in her chair. Nobody has ever refused to pray before, not even politely. Nobody has ever called her duck.

She thinks that she could curl herself into the soft lap of her soft, new grandmother, and she might—it seems possible—grow feathers and cluck herself to sleep. She sits vibrating with the possibility that this grandmother might be hers alone; that she, Noella, might be gathered up and taken to a place where there are no sisters, no brothers, and only a toothless old man with whom to compete for food (it's unlikely the grandmother eats at all). But I would miss Mam, Noella thinks, and lets out an accidental sob, which prompts the grandmother to make a cooing noise. This noise startles Noella into further tears and, although the grandmother makes no more sounds, Noella leans her head against the old woman's shoulder and burrows into her side. Now the grandmother's hands are moving: one of them finds Noella's hair and pets it. The hand is bony and crab-like, her dress is scratchy, she smells of water that's been in a vase too long, and the grandmother who Noella thought would be so soft is actually stiff like an old broom, or a doll you expect to be spongy in the body but turns out to be made of wood.

Mam returns, carrying the tea tray, and Noella slips off her chair. She sits on Mam's knee as Mam serves the tea. Noella eyes the thick slices of fruitcake until Mam takes one, breaks off a corner, and gives it to her.

'This is a very fine place,' says the grandmother, smiling, but not at anything in particular.

'Thank you,' says Mam.

'Your father would have liked to see it.'

Noella, who never thinks of Mam as having a father, looks at Mam's face to see how she reacts to this news. She seems pleased. Noella knows, or thinks she knows, that the grandmother isn't

Mam's real mother; nevertheless, she notices the similarity of their smiles. They're the same gliding kind of gentle.

'Speaking of your father,' begins the grandmother, and reaches into a fold of her skirt, which must contain a pocket (the depth and darkness of this pocket, the way it would smell, both thrill and alarm Noella). Drawing out an envelope, the grandmother says, 'My dear, I have a letter from him.'

Mam takes the letter and tucks it into the waistband of her apron.

'And here,' says the grandmother, reaching into another pocket, 'is a telegram I promised to deliver.'

It will turn out that, while she was at Fairly railway station arranging transport to Undelcarra, the grandmother managed to meet all sorts of people, especially once they learned that she was Mary Wallace's stepmother. One of them was Mr Blake from the post office, without his green visor and with a newly arrived telegram for said Mary Wallace. Now the grandmother's hand emerges from the pocket holding a folded piece of paper, which she passes to Mam.

Noella, being eight, can read—but not as quickly as Mam. On the paper, she sees the words 'baby' and 'kindly arrange'; then Mam closes her fist around the message and it disappears.

'So there, you see,' says the grandmother. 'Another little boy, dear. Isn't it a mercy?'

Mam is quiet for a long moment. Then she nudges Noella off her knee, stands, and goes into the house. This behaviour is so unlike Mam that Noella waits for her to return with a forgotten plate of scones, or more milk, or some other offering that will explain it. When Mam doesn't come back, Noella sits in Mam's vacant chair and looks at the grandmother, who smiles her equable smile.

'I hope,' says the grandmother, 'you are being good for your poor dear mother.'

Noella ponders this. Is she good? And is her mother poor? In Noella's experience, anyone whose name is preceded by the word 'poor' is usually dead. She watches the grandmother a little longer, and waits; then, when it's clear that Mam isn't going to reappear, Noella eats the rest of her slice of cake.

⁂

For the eleventh time today, Billy stretches Jimmy Possum's leg. The pain is terrible—Jimmy's pain, that is, which he expresses through a series of low, contained cries. Billy places one hand on Jimmy's hip and, with the other hand, presses on his knee. Then Billy eases off, and presses again, as Jimmy bites into the greasy leather handle of a stockwhip. The leg is swollen from the groin to just above the knee. Early this morning, when Foster cut Jimmy's trousers off, he said, 'One thing I'll say for you fellows, you know how to hide a bruise.' But Jimmy's injury is highly apparent now: the point where the hoof hit the top of the thigh is a mottled, raised yellow and the brown skin around it has deepened into purple.

Billy stretches the leg as much as he thinks Jimmy can bear, then pulls the blanket back up to his waist. The room is hot and smells of vinegar, which Billy has been warming on the stove and applying to the outer edges of Jimmy's bruising. The tracker breathes heavily, his eyes closed and his face slick with sweat. Each stretch perturbs Jimmy's hair, which he evidently likes tidy, so Billy combs it for him. He's wearing his cloak, which is mostly dry—he asked for it, and Billy, helping Jimmy into the cloak, tried to imagine a life in which he could wear it. He made sure not to look at Jimmy's injured arm.

Billy allows Jimmy the privacy of his pain by returning to the stool in the doorway of the harness room. He's kept this post all day. Nancy has brought him food and drink and the news that Tal is now out looking for Denny. Cissy has come and gone, leaving behind a coat Billy recognises as having belonged to Henry Axam—a coat Henry rarely wore, because he disliked black clothing. He used to say that the fashion for wearing black had turned all men, even princes, into northern schoolmasters; he blamed the French Revolution and refused to raise black sheep. Billy, sitting on the stool with Henry's coat folded on his lap, is aware of both the busyness of the stable and the suffering of the man on the cot in the harness room. He thinks of Henry Axam's body laid out in the homestead parlour.

More than thirty years have passed since Henry insisted on riding into the rushing yellow water of a flooding creek. Billy was a young man when it happened, and knew not to ride into high water, or that—if you absolutely had to cross—you should coax the horse in and follow it on foot, gripping it by the tail. Billy knew this because Henry had taught him. But Henry and Barabbas entered the creek in full splendour. Henry was dressed, that day, in the red shirt he called his Garibaldi; Barabbas was bright black, and so were Henry's boots. The horse lost its footing when the flood rose over Henry's knees, and Henry simply slipped out of the saddle and disappeared. Barabbas swam for a brief time against the current before he was carried down the creek, managing to hold his head above the water. He bared his teeth and his white eyes rolled.

Billy cried out as he ran down the riverbank. Ahead of him, Barabbas, swept against a tree, found his footing; Billy stepped into the edge of the tugging creek, reached out, took Barabbas's lead rope, and pulled. Billy pulled and wept and the horse screamed. The terror, the terror of the horse. And when, finally, Barabbas rose up, came clear, and scrambled—somehow—onto the bank: there was Henry beneath his horse, his boot still in the left stirrup, his leg still in the boot, his shirt still red and his head broken open. Barabbas was trembling all over.

Laid out in the parlour, Henry was tidier and smaller than he had ever seemed in life. Billy might have been allowed to sit with the body, but he didn't ask to; he took a stool from the kitchen and sat on the verandah instead, under one of the windows, as if on guard. From this position, he heard the strangled sounds of Joanna Axam's grief and, later, the bewilderment of little George's questions. Baby Bear growled and giggled from his mother's arms. Visitors arrived to pay their respects, and Billy heard them comment on Henry Axam's eccentricity, his various appetites, the probable ruin of his family, and the likelihood that he'd been killed by the black boy who played cricket. By the time Billy left, taking the stool with him, Henry had been declared a visionary. His like would never again be seen on the Willochra, in this colony, or in any other part of the globe.

Now Billy sits on the stool in the door of the harness room and thinks of Henry and doesn't think of Henry, which, for Billy, is the same thing. Two white stockmen pass through the stables. One of them, tossing his head in Billy's direction, says to the other, 'He's been there all day. What's so precious it needs a watchdog?'

Late in the afternoon, the doctor arrives from Quorn carrying a dingy black bag. He's a plump, pink fellow, and he stops short and squints behind his spectacles when he sees Billy on the stool. Foster, behind the doctor's shoulder, says, 'Not him! Keep on, keep on,' and Billy stands and steps away from the door. The doctor enters the harness room, followed by Foster; behind them both comes Bear, who has never lost his look of a small boy peering over a tabletop. Bear is so intent on what's going to happen that he's entered the room before he registers Billy; then he peeks back around the door, says, 'You're here! Good man!', and disappears inside again. Billy remains out in the stable with his back to the harness room door. He hears Bear's exclamatory whistle as, presumably, the blanket is pulled away from Jimmy's leg. The doctor speaks too quietly for Billy to hear, Bear makes audible noises of sympathy and assent, and finally Foster says, 'Listen, the sooner the better, I've an escaped convict to hunt down.' Then he calls out, 'Get in here, would you!'

Billy imagines the daily hell of working for Sergeant Foster, taking orders and being trotted out onto the cricket pitch. He waits until Bear calls, 'Billy!' Then he lays Henry's coat on the stool and goes into the harness room.

Jimmy Possum sweats on his cot. The doctor presses at the injured leg with attentive courtesy, pausing whenever Jimmy takes a sharp breath through bared teeth. Looking up at Billy through his glinting spectacles, the doctor says, 'Who's this, then? A family member? Brother?'

'Not at all,' says Foster.

Nevertheless, the doctor offers Billy a smile of consolation. In a voice designed for reassurance, he says, 'He'll pull through. We'll set this leg right in a flash.'

Foster says, 'If anyone's responsible for him, it's me.'

The doctor nods affably.

'And I'll pay,' Foster says, 'from my own pocket.' He turns to Billy. 'I broke my forearm as a boy, and who do you think set it for me? A cockeyed blacksmith. Never could bowl straight after that.'

Billy knows not to react. The doctor gives orders—Billy at the shoulders, Bear holding down the hips, Foster pulling from below the knee. Billy takes up the stockwhip, taps it against Jimmy's shoulder, and, when Jimmy opens his mouth, places the whip between his teeth.

'Will it hurt like the blazes?' asks Bear, who has removed his jacket and is rolling up the sleeves of his shirt.

'Yes, terribly,' says the doctor. He takes off his glasses, breathes onto them, and rubs them with a cloth he's taken from his pocket. 'Quite aside from the break, the muscle is torn through. The pain will probably knock him out. It's a good thing you've been stretching the leg, Foster. A damn good thing.'

Billy crouches behind Jimmy Possum's head. He adjusts the cloak, arranging it so that he can hold it down along with Jimmy's torso, keeping the injured arm concealed. Bear leans over Jimmy's middle, flexes his fingers as if he's about to play a piano, then presses his palms against Jimmy's hipbones. Billy lowers his head so that his mouth is next to Jimmy's left ear. He doesn't watch the bone-setting, although he feels and hears it—Jimmy's body twists and buckles, the doctor grunts, Jimmy hisses through the whip and beats his head back against the cot. Billy stays by Jimmy's ear. He doesn't know Jimmy's songs or speak his language, but he says steadily throughout, 'All right. All right. All right, now. Yes, brother, all right.' The veins rise and pulse at Jimmy's temples, the tendons of his neck stretch taut, Foster growls, Billy bears down on Jimmy's shoulders with all his weight, the doctor grunts, and with a loud, crisp crack the bone is set. Jimmy's body goes limp, but he's conscious. The pain hasn't knocked him out.

Bear draws back from the cot. He's sweated through his shirt and his face is pale. 'Bless me,' he says, laughs, and looks about as if he's been caught at something naughty.

The doctor gently palpates Jimmy's leg. Foster stands with his hands on his hips. 'A clean set?' he asks.

'Time will tell,' says the doctor, but he looks satisfied.

Foster says, 'It can always be broken and set again.' He bends at the waist, reaches out one solid hand, and pats the ankle of Jimmy's uninjured leg the way he might the head of a child or the flank of a familiar horse. Billy rises and steps away from the cot. Foster, nodding as if in the acceptance of some regrettable truth, tells the doctor to send the bill to him at the Port Augusta Police Station and strides out into the stable. The doctor pulls splints and bandages from his bag.

'Bless me,' Bear says again. He tugs at his collar, looking as if he's both witnessed something and been witnessed. 'Why not,' he says, 'why not find Nancy and ask for the Scotch. Eh, Billy? He's earned it.'

Billy isn't sure if Bear thinks it's the doctor or the patient who's earned the Scotch. He nods. He'll find Nancy, find the Scotch, bring it back to the stable, and in this way become a person at Thalassa with a task to carry out. He could become absorbed by this again, no different from anybody else.

When he walks into the stable, Billy sees Cissy, holding her borrowed horse by the bridle. The horse has been shod and is saddled. Cissy's face is very white.

'Is he dead?' she asks.

'You heard it?'

'I heard.'

'He's all right. Better not to listen.'

Cissy draws herself up. 'Oh,' she says loftily, 'I've helped Mam with two babies.'

Billy nods at the horse. 'Leaving?'

'I'm going home,' Cissy says. She does look out of place here. Around her, the stable moves and settles and moves again. It won't accommodate her. 'Are you coming?'

'No,' says Billy.

Cissy controls the hurt in her face. This restraint is uncharacteristic, and Billy is reminded of her father. Like Mathew, Cissy has the tall, set stance of a person ready to bargain with the Almighty. In her, Billy sees Mathew, and also Mary, Joy, Ada, Noella and Lotta, and Joe who went droving and never came back. Billy sees the shepherd's hut among the she-oaks and big, bad-tempered Treat stamping in his stall. He sees the red hill and he sees Denny bowling stones at the hollow tree, then stopping to ask if the tree might mind having stones bowled at it. But Denny—if he's found—will grow older and care less about the moods of trees. He'll enter into time, into something else that's waiting for him, and Billy won't be able to follow. Billy thinks, I'd like to be there when Denny is brought home. But he knows he won't be.

Cissy says, 'Tomorrow, then? Dad will want to know when you'll be back.'

'Your father knows. Tell him I'll send over for my pay.'

Cissy looks scandalised. 'You're leaving us,' she says. 'Is that allowed?'

'Yes,' says Billy. 'It's allowed.'

Cissy waits a moment, thinking. Then she points at the coat where it sits on the stool. 'Did you give it to him?'

'Not yet,' says Billy. 'When he's more himself, I'll ask him if he wants it.'

Cissy considers this. She says, 'He might not want it.' Billy can see that this possibility has just occurred to her.

'Take care with that horse of yours,' Billy says. 'Keep her on the road.'

Cissy, proud, doesn't answer. She tugs at the horse's line and leads it out into the late afternoon, and she takes Undelcarra with her.

The stable settles back into its purposes. As a child, Billy was never allowed to play with cricket balls in here—Henry warned that they would upset the horses. Now he steps outside, where the sky has gathered itself into a bright band of red, with green at the horizon and pale purple high above. Billy, crossing the stable yard and, following the road towards the house, watches Cissy ride ahead of him on her fussy horse. The dust of the road has been flattened and pressed by the rain, and it feels firm and good beneath his boots.

When Henry and the other pastoralists first came to the Willochra, they broke up the dams in the creeks and banned the use of any language beside English. Their men shot at anyone who came near the permanent water they'd claimed for their sheep and cattle. Billy's father was gaoled for trespassing while on a hunting expedition; officially, he died in custody of dysentery. Billy was a child then: he stayed in camp with the women and children and wasn't present at his father's murder. Some of Billy's mob had already left the plain for the safety of the northern ranges. From there, they attacked stations, raided shepherds' huts, and herded cattle into narrow gorges. When the Thalassa ration depot was built, his mother said that the people in the northern ranges might come back from their safe places, but she said this as if she hoped they wouldn't, for their own sakes. More recently, there's been talk of bringing scattered groups together up there so they can all have ceremony again. Billy has considered the possibility of going north himself, to recover some of what Henry took from him. He might do it, one of these days. He could go tonight—what's there to stop him?

Up at the house, Billy sees Nancy walk into the kitchen garden and throw a pail of dirty water over a bed of greens. He knows that at night, when Nancy finishes her work, she goes down to the camp to see their mother, but that Joanna makes her sleep up at the house. Nancy has her rhythms, her liberties, her obligations. If he asked her to go north with him, he knows she wouldn't.

Seeing Billy, she stands with the empty pail at her hip and waits for him to join her.

The sun is walking down by the time Karl, Bess and Minna approach Undelcarra. It took Minna some time to secure the buggy and horses, because her mother refused to see her—Karl has gleaned that they're having some kind of quarrel. Also, the Wallace farm is further out of town than Minna estimated. Karl is grateful for all of these delays. He wants the sun to sink, the darkness to fall, and for there to be some reason not to go to the house with the aloe by the gate. He dreads their arrival: how the family might behave, what Bess might say or do. He noticed, at the police station, that Bess didn't lie outright, but she did imply that they'd only had the boy for one day and night, and therefore that they'd lost no time in trying to get him home. He's never known Bess to be deliberately deceitful.

Minna apologises once or twice for how long the trip has taken; otherwise, no one in the buggy speaks. Ahead of them, the lonely hill rises from the plain, and Karl remembers that the French word for this kind of solitary hill is *mamelon*, which means 'nipple'. To paint its red, he would need a tube of madder lake—but he also notes the low bushes that climb the slope, that from a distance resemble lichen, and would require both emerald green and mummy brown. At the very top: one of those native pines, tall and narrow, like a leafy column. It looks as if someone has plucked a cypress from a Swedish graveyard and deposited it here, at the end of the world.

Studying the hill, Karl thinks that this place has a childish sense of humour, with its outlandish animals and surprising trees. And, he wonders, how would this ride out to the Wallace farm feel if Denny were with us? Like a blessing from the sky; an ancient exile coming to an end; a walled city thrown open, pierced with lights. Karl feels the way he did when, as a boy, he ran away to watch the puppets at Djurgården, knowing he'd be whipped when he got home. Karl thinks of his picture, still. It beckons from the future.

The Wallace house, when they reach it, is smaller than he remembers. He can't imagine Denny living here. As the buggy draws up to the aloe gate, Karl observes an old woman sitting on the verandah; as he jumps down from the buggy and secures the horses, he sees a steady stream of girls coming out to join her. Bess opens the gate and steps onto the path. Karl's hands are shaking.

Another woman appears on the verandah, tall and neat—it's the woman they spoke to last week about the aloe. She must be Denny's mother. As Bess walks up the path towards her, the mother tells the girls to go back inside. They go, with obvious reluctance, and the old woman follows them, shooing and clucking. The mother comes down from the verandah, walking towards Bess, and this is what Karl has been waiting for. How will Bess present herself to the mother? Will she confess and beg forgiveness? Or will she lie? Will the mother assume that Bess is always right, just as he has all this time? From behind, Bess looks as composed as ever. Karl and Minna stay a few paces back. Minna, Karl can see, has recognised Bess's seriousness and deferred to it, as people tend to. Bess meets the mother on the path.

'You found him,' the mother says. Bess nods. Karl sees that this woman is ready to hear any terrible thing: her city fallen, her husband killed while seeking shelter, her son dragged behind a chariot.

'He's alive,' says Bess. She favours the woman's left ear and speaks loudly, just as Minna instructed. 'He was alive last night. But we don't have him.'

The mother takes a deep, shuddered breath. It hurts Karl to see happiness flicker across her face, then hide itself.

Bess says, 'We were bringing him home to you, but he ran away.'

'When?' the woman asks.

'We put him down to sleep last night, but he was gone when we woke up.'

Karl wishes that he could see Bess's face. He thinks that, after this is over, when they're alone again, he'll insist that she explain to him why it was acceptable not to bring the boy straight home, and to conceal the delay from his mother. Surely she can explain.

The mother moves forwards, gazing steadily at Bess, and the women grip one another's forearms. Bess says, 'I wish we could have brought him home to you.' In response, the mother draws her arms away from Bess, touches the back of one hand to Bess's forehead, then presses that hand against her own heart, as if to steady it. The effect is regal, gracious, and strangely Catholic—Karl thinks of a benediction. Above them, the red sky rings like a struck gong.

Now Minna speaks up. 'Mrs Wallace, we know he's near the Wilparra road. Men have gone to look. Is my husband here?'

'Why don't we go inside,' says Bess. She means inside the house, but she's also entering her room, and taking the mother with her. In they go. The door closes, the key turns in the lock.

Next to the women, Minna is agitated. 'Mrs Wallace,' she says, 'my husband—Constable Manning. Is he here?'

Mrs Wallace shakes her head. Bess takes her arm and leads her towards the house. Behind them, Minna raises her voice and says, 'Where is he, then? If he's not at home and he's not here, where is he?'

Mrs Wallace looks back over her shoulder and says, 'I couldn't tell you.'

Bess and the mother go into the house. Karl isn't needed. Minna, too, is surplus—she's stranded in the absence of her husband. But they follow Bess—what else is there to do?—and then they're also stepping inside. The house is full of girls and furniture. Karl looks for signs of the boy, but doesn't find any.

Bess has led the mother to the hearth. Karl knows not to join their conversation—his allegiance is to Minna now, because they're adrift together. The old woman who was sitting on the verandah enters from another room and speaks to him from inside her fortress of dark clothes. Karl introduces himself and Mrs Manning, and is forced to listen to Mrs Muriel Deniston as she wonders whether she and Minna are related, because Muriel has a cousin by the name of Manning. It doesn't seem to matter that Manning is Minna's married name: the woman pursues the connection through South Australia, an unexpected second marriage, Victoria, smallpox, two shipwrecks, Portsmouth, and on to a mill in Glasgow.

All the while, Bess is talking to the mother. There are so many girls in the room—well, four, to be precise—and they all seem to be paying attention to the old woman, but in truth they're doing just what Karl is: trying to hear what Bess is saying.

Minna is also trying to hear Bess, and even the old woman's eyes slide towards the hearth, but she continues to talk about her maternal great-aunt and the nephew who invented a new kind of soup spoon. Every relative of the old woman's seems now to be standing in the crowded room, gathering about her so that no one but the mother can hear what Bess is saying. This, Karl realises, is the woman's intention. When, finally, Bess calls Karl's name, the old woman shrinks back, exhausted, into her stiff clothes.

Karl stands and reluctantly approaches the women at the hearth.

'Mrs Wallace, this is my husband, Mr Rapp,' says Bess.

Karl greets her, unsure of where to put his hands or what to say. He says, 'We're both very fond of your son.' He knows this is inadequate. The mother looks up at him, but her face is blank. Karl leans towards her ear. 'He will be found. I'm sure of it. And when he is, you must tell him that his friend Karl says hello, and that I'll keep my word and teach him how to draw and paint.'

Bess touches his forearm with one finger.

He says, 'We really are so very sorry.'

The mother holds her hands tightly together in her lap. Bess takes Karl's arm and guides him to the door, where Minna joins them. Once he and Minna have passed through and are standing on the verandah, Bess stops, remaining inside the house.

'I'll stay,' she says.

'What for?' asks Karl. His voice whines like a boy's.

Minna says to Bess, 'If my husband comes, will you tell him I was here? Tell him I'm waiting for him at home.'

'But why should you stay?' Karl asks Bess. 'There's no need for it.'

Bess smiles from inside her room and says, 'I can be a help to her.'

This feels grotesque to Karl—he wants to enter the house and tell them all that Bess kept the boy because he was necessary to her work. But then he'd have to admit that he let her do it.

Bess says, 'Come back with the horses in the morning.' She closes the door, and Karl and Minna are alone outside.

The sun is still a little way above the ranges. Surely it should have set by now—but here it is, reminding him with various reds and greens of their arrangement. This sky, to Karl, seems raided, rotted, near its end. He can't imagine painting it. Its weird, infected light turns Minna's hair a surprising red. He remembers kissing her in the shade of an ugly tree, telling her she was in love with all men, and believing it as he said it. He remembers promising the sky that, for the sake of the picture, he would never touch a woman who wasn't Bess. Karl and Minna, both abandoned by their spouses, walk together to the buggy.

⸻

The boy saw the red hill just before sunset. It was a long way in the distance, but he left the Wilparra road and began to cut across country because the hill meant home and Mam, and there was the possibility that he would reach her before the gods did. But it wasn't likely—he was forced to move slowly because the ground was scratchy with stones and with dry, prickly grass, and his bare feet hurt him. He felt tiredness creeping up on him with sneaky steps.

The hill never grew any larger, and the sky turned red in the broad, bright way it seemed to now. The sky roared over the desert like the Red Sea. There was Pharaoh's army, drowning in the waves; and there was the Hooky Man, reaching his long, bent arms out of the red water. There was the great snake, the Akurra, swimming behind the sun. When the sun dropped behind the western ranges, the boy realised that it would be dark before he reached the hill. The hill was already hard to see, because it was evening and because the boy was crying. The snot dripped to his mouth. He wiped his face with his sleeve and squinted and walked and the hill seemed to move away from him, then jump about, and finally to dissolve.

Once the sky was dark, he continued for a while in the direction that seemed right to him. Then it no longer seemed right, so he stopped. He understood, as he hadn't properly until now, that he was lost. He observed this feeling, *lost*: it was bowling a stone at the hollow tree and missing, and never going to look for the stone. It was someone asking you the colour of the moon, and you looked at the moon and saw that no one had ever taught you the word for its colour. Lost was the sun gone forever, and the hill gone, and Mam and Dad and Billy and all the sisters gone, and nothing left but the dark. He sat down in it.

# SIXTH NIGHT

The Reverend Mr Daniels isn't sure where he is. He knows it's night, because it's dark, and the darkness of the desert is permanent, blazing, and deep deep deep; it's the well of God, awful and inapproachable. This darkness is so without light that it produces its own radiance. This is the darkness Daniels was dismayed by when he saw it in Spanish paintings: an altarpiece darkness, against which a crucifix hangs suspended, and the hills are black, every doorway and window of the painting is black, the heart of the lily is black and the eye of the angel; the stable, the star; every saint wears black; and there in the dark you can see the dark mourning of the monks. Daniels thinks of papist churches as being full of gold, but the gold is grubbed and sooted, even when it shines, as if the black light has cast a fine dust over everything—almost invisible, and deadly. And here, where Daniels believes there are no churches, no ruins, nothing old enough to have been ruined, nothing that has been destroyed and might be mourned, not enough fires and factories to produce soot, and a treasury of gold still hidden in the ground—here, a black light has spread out into the night, over the hills, across the plains, until the landscape and everything in it is buried in black, and it's always night, and Mr Daniels is always alone in the desert.

He's thirsty. His tongue is a mystery to him—it's larger than it should be and can find no proper position for itself. He's misplaced his horse and seems to be wearing a nightshirt: more mysteries. But Mr Daniels has chosen, as his profession, the most profound mystery, and he knows how to live alongside the inscrutable. Once, as a young man full of doubt and education, he listened with scorn as his father said: 'If we understood the Gospel, we would not believe it.' Later, as he stood on the deck of the ship that was taking him to the Australian colonies, watching fish fly from the water with their bronze fins outstretched (he thought of a Greek fleet upon a wine-dark sea), he conceded that his father had been right. There is no way to fathom the strangeness of God's creation. There's no way to understand it now, in the darkness of the desert. He's almost sure that he did, at one time, have a horse with him; he also has a memory of seeing, or perhaps carrying, a pair of boots.

Mr Daniels so wants to love and be loved that even here, in the darkness, he looks for a pulpit or a piece of raised ground, so that he can preach God's loving word. The song of the angels might return, then, and shake the earth; by this he means the vast music that hoisted him from his bed—whose bed? someone's bed—and sent him out into the light. The music sent him in one direction and another. Then the sky poured with red, the red burned backwards until the darkness came, and that was the well of God. But there's no pulpit or raised ground here, just the low plain, and anyway the darkness, audible everywhere, is a sermon.

Daniels' feet are bare and the saltbush cuts them, so he finds clearer ground that may be a river or a road. It's a road—at some point he hears rumbling and shouting behind him and he waits for the music of the angels, but the rumbling and shouting are only a bullock dray advancing up the road with sooty lanterns swinging. Daniels doesn't intend to hide from the bullocks and their driver; he merely draws back to the edge of the road, where the darkness is as black as a black feather is black. The darkness hides him. It speaks in his ear and flicks at the hides of the bullocks, but it doesn't reveal Daniels to the driver of the dray. The bullocks stink and sweat. They walk with their heads low, as if participating in a funeral procession, and the driver hunches over the reins. Perhaps he's whispering 'memento mori'. The dray rolls by and Daniels thinks to follow it. Again, he doesn't mean to hide from the driver. He walks quite openly behind the dray, but the darkness never tells the driver to turn around and see that he's being followed by a pale man in a pale nightshirt.

Daniels hurries to keep up with the dray, and is not always successful at avoiding the fresh deposits the bullocks leave in the road. But he's awfully cold, and the dung does warm his toes. The dim lights of the lanterns on the dray take on strange, star-like properties—they wink in and out, and disappear if he looks at them directly. He remembers a horse and water and also a girl—yes, Cissy Wallace was the girl, she held his hand, he leaned into her shoulder, and together they came down from a mountain.

He remembers, even further back, finding a small pair of boots among the roots of a tree; he remembers wandering with the boots, feeling as if he was being followed, and taking a crazy path to throw off his pursuers. He thought to set the boots beneath a bush as some kind of lure. He was looking for something, hoping to trap it, although he can no longer recall what it was. He waited near the bush, but nothing happened. What was he expecting? And the sun—which he remembers as dark—was beating against his head. Then he thought that he would find a hill or a mountain, a natural pulpit, and look down at the boots from there. He would see what could be seen.

So he left the boots and walked his horse directly at the hills. At some point, he was climbing and had no horse. At some point, he lit a fire outside a cave. There was a yellow man painted on the side of the cave. He had his arms outstretched as if delivering a sermon, and another yellow shape floated near his head. Daniels understood this to be an image of Joshua stopping the sun. But who had painted it? In the morning, ants on his neck; later, Cissy Wallace sitting beside him. When did the bed come, and the nightshirt, and the music of the angels? He isn't sure.

Ahead of Daniels, the driver is calling, 'Whoa!' and slowing the bullocks. He's turning them off the road onto flat, grassy ground. Daniels stops in the darkness and observes the beauty of this: the man unyoking the bullocks, building a fire, smoking a pipe and opening a tin of meat. Daniels doesn't mean to hide; the darkness hides him. He watches and loves the driver and his camp—the lowing bullocks with their faces in the grass, the smoke hanging above the fire. His body feels as if it's risen an inch above the ground. Could this be the second blessing?

He steps forwards into the light with his arms outstretched. The driver, startled, yelps and reaches for a pistol that lies beside him. Daniels jumps at a loud noise. Then he thinks that he may be on the ground, that something may be wrong with some part of his body, that the light of the fire is warm and red, and that the driver, standing over him with a frantic face, is saying, 'Christ Almighty, it's the vicar. Jesus. Jesus Christ.'

⁂

Mary's house is full: the girls (except Cissy, of course), her step-mother, the Englishwoman. But Mary is outside, raking the dirt in her garden. The girls watch from the windows. She's carried a lamp out with her and has set it on one of the broad stones that mark the garden's edge. These stones have been moved recently, because Mary has been preparing a new bed in which she intends to plant spinach and turnips. Mary, out in the night, lifts stones and roots with the prongs of the rake. Each of the girls comes in turn to the door of the house and calls out to her. She doesn't hear what they call, but she knows it's always a variation on, 'Mam? What are you doing?' Mary stands straight and smiles—although she's not sure if they can see her smile—and says, 'Go back inside.' Mary can't be inside. Denny is alive, and he's out here.

When Mary was born, her father opened his Bible and gave her the first female name he encountered. Her siblings were named in the same way. For the Reverend Deniston's girls, God consistently guided Samuel to the New Testament: Mary, Lydia and Elizabeth. The boys were baptised by the Old. Mary was given to understand that she was not named for the mother of

Christ, but for the sister of Martha: the Mary who sat at Christ's feet and listened to His Word while Martha, in another room, prepared a meal. Mary was taught to admire her namesake's humility and reverence, but she has always worked like Martha, and been praised for it. At a young age, she realised that she was expected to embody both of the sisters—to work in the world, and live beyond it—and she has dedicated herself to this task. She wonders, as she rakes her garden, what her mother would have named her if she'd had the choice. Mathew gave Mary the choice. She opened the Bible for her first child, and he became Joseph. She didn't open it for her second, and this child was named what Mary felt at the birth of a girl: Joy. Cecily was named for Mary's mother and Ada for Mathew's. Noella was born on Christmas Eve. Deniston was named for Mary's father. There's no particular reason for the name Charlotte. It would be difficult for Mary to admit, even to herself, that she simply likes it. But what is the name of this new baby, Joseph's son, which she must 'kindly arrange' to have sent to her? The telegram didn't say. It didn't even mention the baby's mother.

Mary's father taught her that there's a point at which grief stops. It's something akin to raking the dirt: you rake so far, and stop. Grief comes this far; also beauty, love, and happiness, and pain. They all reach a point and stop, and beyond this point the believer trusts and rejoices in the will of God. Mary believes this to be true and has often been consoled by it. She's comforted herself with the knowledge that she needs only to be still and know that He is God. But tonight, she can't seem to be still; she can't even stay in the house. Denny is alive and outside. He needs a light to guide him home. So here she is, outside, with her lamp, just as Mary, the sister of Martha, might be. But also raking her garden, as Martha would. Mary's left ear aches in the cool night air.

Joy comes to the door. Mary straightens and smiles. 'Help your grandmother feed your sisters, dear,' she says.

Ordinarily, Joy would fuss about this—claiming not to know what food was in the house, or how to prepare it, or how much to serve—until Cissy would flare up and say, 'I'll do it!' But Cissy isn't here tonight, and Joy only nods, turns inside, and calls her sisters away from the windows. Lotta stays the longest, peering out at Mary with her hands cupped around her eyes. Then she, too, jumps down from her perch, and the windows are empty. Mary feels an immense, impatient strength inside her tonight; she's unsure what it's for, but she knows it's not for them.

As she rakes up the stones and roots, she reminds herself that the fig tree shall not blossom, and the labour of the olive shall fail, and the flock shall be cut off from the fold; knowing all these things to be true, she will yet rejoice in the God of her salvation. She has lost Joseph, possibly forever, and perhaps now Denny too. This new baby will come, with the stain of illegitimacy on it. Mary, who had been promised an end to babies, will exhaust herself for another one. Be still, be still, Mary reminds herself. She can't be still. Denny is alive. She lays the rake down in the dirt, takes the lamp, and walks out of the garden.

This is the first time Mary has gone beyond the fence since the day Denny was lost. She walks away from the house and its attendant buildings, its children and its chiffonier, the snakeskin that hangs from the northern eave, the crouching fear of failure. This baby, she thinks, has been sent to me as a consolation. The

Lord has taken, and now He will give. When will she reach the point at which grief stops? Is it here, at the foot of the red hill? No, and Mary begins to climb.

The lamp attracts moths; they accompany her up the hill. Mary thinks: store up no treasure, send no word, and have no fear—always be ready to enter into the life to come. Halfway up the hill, she's not at all ready. She looks down at the house. It has four of her seven children in it; and her stepmother, who believes that she's done the loving thing by coming; and the Englishwoman, who lost Denny all over again, and who must think that staying here to help will absolve her of it. Mary looks for the lettuce plant by the gate, although she doesn't expect to see it in the dark. The lettuce plant contains the name of every person she loves, and she allowed the Englishwoman to cut it with a knife. She turns away from the house and resumes climbing.

What if Joseph's baby is deaf? There came a point, with all her children, when they learned to speak and so stepped out of the enclosed world in which they were her babies and she their mother. What if one baby stayed? She's near the top of the hill now, and can see the silhouette of the cypress pine on its peak. Should she be still, and rejoice, and let the Lord work out His purposes? What if she has purposes of her own?

Mary reaches the top of the hill and leans with one hand against the cypress pine. Its lowest branches are just above her head. The moon is fat but not yet full and Mary stands beneath it, thinking of the strawberry birthmark on the back of Denny's knee. She really did crave strawberries while she carried Denny, and Mathew had done all that he could to get them for her. How to make it clear to Mathew that she knows he's doing his best? Even so, there comes a point at which everything stops.

Mary's breathing is uneven and her heart beats in her aching ear. Her boy is alone in the dark, frightened and wanting her, with a stolen blanket and bare feet. He needs a light to guide him home. She lifts the chimney of the lamp and holds the flame to the thick foliage of the cypress pine. Its needles smoke and kindle, but don't take. Of course they don't: it rained today, for which she should be grateful; rain, to a farmer's wife, is always heaven-sent. It's the Lord working out His purposes. Mary removes her apron, drenches it in oil from the lamp, and bundles it among the branches. Then she lights the apron. It burns, the needles catch, and fire takes hold of the tree.

---

The burning tree is visible for almost eleven miles. Inge Schmidt sees it from the upper verandah of the Sheaf of Wheat Hotel, and raises the alarm in town.

Robert Manning, out with his local search party, sees the fire in the distance but can't tell that it's on a hill. His first thought is that his house is burning with Minna inside it.

Minna, driving the buggy, doesn't see the fire until Karl looks back along the road and points it out to her. He feels a clenching in his gut. Here, finally, is his pillar of fire. Here's the sun come back to laugh at him. He's lost the boy, and he'll never paint the sunset. He puts one hand on Minna's thigh. Minna assumes it's a bonfire, and is delighted by it. It feels like a correspondence—as if something in the world is answering something inside of her. She whips the horses to make them run.

Mathew is too far away to see the fire—he won't hear of it until late the following afternoon when he reaches town with his first load of wool.

The fire isn't visible from Thalassa, where the shearers drink rum and play euchre in the bachelors' hall. At the house, George frets, Bolingbroke coughs, and Bear, walking past the dining room and seeing his mother sitting by the orchestrion, thinks to ask her if she's feeling quite well. Joanna says, 'Of course I am.'

Billy sets up a cot beside Jimmy's in the harness room and settles down to smoke, pulling Henry's coat up to his chin. Jimmy is asleep, but earlier he laughed while Billy imitated Foster, even though the laughing must have caused him pain. He makes strange movements in his sleep, as if someone is throwing him a rope that he can't catch.

Cissy, riding June, is also too far from home to see the fire on the hill. She sees a different fire: a campfire beside the road between Thalassa and Fairly, and, next to the campfire, a dray, a bullock team and three men. One of the men is the driver of the dray—she recognises him as the man who drove them all to Thalassa the night before. He sits by the fire, smokes, and looks both sullen and embarrassed. Cissy slows her horse. One of the men lies asleep on the ground beneath a blanket; his hair is light, and she isn't immediately sure, but yes—it's Mr Daniels, with his head on a folded jacket. It's always Mr Daniels. And beside him is Sergeant Foster, sitting on the ground. It must be his jacket that's beneath the vicar's head, because Foster is in shirtsleeves. He looks happy. Cissy pulls back on June's reins and is surprised to feel the horse obey her.

Cissy looks down at Mr Daniels, then at Sergeant Foster, and says, 'What happened? Wasn't he in bed?'

Foster grins. 'He ran off from the house. I followed him.'

Cissy is grudgingly impressed. 'Is he all right?'

'He's been shot,' says Foster.

Cissy looks at the fair head showing above the blanket. There's more colour in Mr Daniels' face than there was this morning. She shakes her head in disbelief. 'Who shot him?'

'I did,' says the gloomy driver. 'Nicked his shoulder. He showed up out of nowhere and scared me half to death.'

'Shouldn't he see the doctor?' Cissy asks. 'Again?'

Sergeant Foster says, 'I've bound the wound, he's in no danger. Just feeling the shock.'

Foster stands and comes over to June. His manner is jovial and obliging, as if Cissy is an old acquaintance and, if not his equal, then at least a member of the same wide congregation.

'He's in police custody,' Foster says. 'The minute he comes to, I'll arrest him for the abduction of your brother.'

'He didn't abduct my brother,' says Cissy. One look at the minister's flushed, silly, gentle face should confirm that fact.

Foster gives an indulgent chuckle. He thumps June's flank, says, 'Walk on,' and June, suddenly utterly docile, obeys him.

Cissy could object. The vicar is, after all, her responsibility. She has saved his life, fed him, cleaned him, and heard him talk in his sleep. She turns in the saddle and observes how cosy they all look by the fire: the bullocks, the driver with his pipe, and Foster returning to his seat by Mr Daniels' head. They already look very far away. She could make a fuss on the vicar's behalf, but she chooses not to. She'll go home to bring them news, then do what she always meant to: find her brother.

In the house at Undelcarra, Ada is the first to see the burning tree. She notices a flicker through the window and runs outside with a cry. Her sisters follow her. The fire is contained on top of the hill—it's well beyond the safety of the gate, but Ada knows how quickly fire can spread. And Mam is up there still. At Ada's side, Lotta stumbles, and Joy catches and rights her. They all stand, stricken, looking at the hill.

Bess runs through and past them, calling, 'Mary! Mary!' She fears she's made one calamitous mistake and now will have to go on making it. Muriel Deniston emerges from the house making hushing sounds of comfort and regret. Noella runs to her and grips her hand. Bess turns to the sisters, shouting, 'Water! Pails! Water!' She climbs over the low garden fence, tearing her skirts, and starts running up the hill. She can see Mary walking near the fire, which roars above the cypress pine. Tongues of flame taste the air around the tree, burning seedpods fly into the grass. Bess, in her panic, thinks of Moses and the burning bush, but can't remember the proper name for it; the term that occurs to her instead is 'God-struck'.

Mary paces by the God-struck tree. She's shouting Denny's name inside her head, and the tree is her shout made visible in the world. Has Denny heard it?

Yes, the boy heard it. Seeing the burning tree, he understood that the gods had reached Mam first and brought the sun down to the hill.

# NOTES OF THE AUSTRALIAN WRITER

Get this down, Foster. Whether or not we find the body of the boy, there's a book in this. Set the scene: a desperate search beneath the scorching sun. Emphasise the size and fairness of the boy. Mention, more than once, the strawberry-shaped birthmark on the back of his knee. Heroism of the father. Quiet dignity of the mother. The bloodied handkerchief and the boots are gifts! The vicar, driven to madness and murder by the desert, wandering the night like a wretched ghost. Wherever there's a desert, there's a man sent mad by it. A man such as this Daniels, a little cock-ant, pale and skinny, all ribs and prick like a drover's dog, straight off the boat and sent up to the north country, which scares him silly. Yes! *Wandering the Wilderness*, by Sergeant Stephen Foster. *Under the Desert Sun. In a Desert Land*, by Stephen Foster.

But not only a book about the shit-stained vicar. No, include dramatic accounts, based on true facts, of all the men who weren't strong enough in mind or heart or body for the cruelty of the

Australian bush. The true story of Henry Axam, with his temple and his music machine, riding full pelt into a raging creek as if he could handle it—a peacock like Henry Axam, not fit to carry offal to a bear. The befuddlement of the blue blood who comes out to the colonies and finds himself on a level with every other man. A lord heads out bush, and what is he lord of? Nothing but sheep, flies, blacks, wife. If he encounters any force of nature (viz. a flooding creek), he must assert himself. And thus, and hence, and accordingly, into the valley of Death rode Henry Axam.

I must have a hundred stories of desert madness. Think, Foster, think. The Naked Prophet of Bedunda Run. The whole family who just up and left—stew cooking on the stove—and walked out into the bush without food or water. A chapter on the deaths at Evers Creek: husband kills wife because wife kills children, or so he claimed. All he'd say was, 'It just seemed for the best.' The surveyor in the tea-tree, stretched like Christ. Every damn explorer. There's almost too much for one book.

Discuss causes. Isolation, solitude, distance from anywhere that looks like home. Sunstroke bringing down fine officers, nostalgia turning proud men into hypochondriacs. For the fairer sex, prolonged lactation in a dry climate. Excessive masturbation in the homesick—why not? This book will tell the truth to the city folk, who think it's all boiling billies and the Milky Way. This is bloody country for those who aren't prepared—the weak, the nervous. The true pioneers, true children of the bush, are always masters of themselves.

And end with this: the raving minister bleeding in the night, and I keep vigil. This is the climax of the drama, the great set piece: the lowing of the bullocks, the sparks and embers of the fire, the deep dark night and the sky full of twinkling stars, the lonely road, the officer waiting to bring the murderer to justice. The sound of a mopoke in the lonely night. The aroma of a good pipe, smoked well. The sergeant's jacket keeps the vicar's head out of the dust. The sergeant's horse makes quiet sounds. Get it all down, Foster. This book is your reward for years of waiting. Wings heard in the darkness, beyond the light of the fire. Everything known contained in the light of the fire; beyond it, the whole vast, empty country, ready, after years of waiting, for us to love her in her wildness. The bleeding vicar, the watchful officer, the long and lonely vigil in the night. End with this.

# SIXTH NIGHT, STILL

The night isn't over. Cissy thinks it must be, riding into Fairly, but the hotels are still open. She doesn't look at the ladies' entrance of the Imperial, afraid of seeing Miss McNeil; and, further on, she doesn't look at Minna's house. If she did, she might see two figures in the dark of the verandah: Minna unlocking the front door with Karl standing close behind her. On the edge of town, Cissy does see a smudge of fire in the distance, but doesn't connect it to home until she's passing the house with the donkey, hears a voice addressing her, and is startled into thinking that the donkey has spoken. The voice comes again, and turns out to belong to the woman who lives in the house, the seamstress: she's climbed the peach tree and, half hidden in its branches, she calls out to Cissy, 'You're a Wallace, aren't you?'

'Yes,' says Cissy, slowing June, but the woman in the tree says, 'Don't stop—it's your house on fire. Go, go.'

Cissy leans forwards in the saddle and urges June on with her heels. The horse speeds up, just as she's been told to, and goes flying down the road. Cissy holds tight, sure that June will throw her. But the horse, who's been so silly, is steady now—she likes a road, as Billy said she did. Closer to Undelcarra, Cissy sees that the fire is higher than the house—it's on the hill, the bulk of which is burning. Above it, the sky is lightened by the smoke.

Nearer the house, Cissy sees horses in the yard and people moving. They're rushing to and fro, between the house and hill. As Cissy reaches the gate, amazed to have arrived so quickly, she sees that men are running to pumps and tanks and troughs with pails and bags, collecting water, and running back to throw it on the hill. She recognises Constable Manning—Robert. But no, they aren't all men. There's Joy, carrying the washtub full of water—how heavy it must be! Joy carries it all alone and, nearing the hill, throws its contents onto the fire. And there's Ada and Noella by the hollow tree, stamping out embers that have drifted from the blaze. Men with shovels dig a ditch—the dirt fills pails and boxes and is also thrown onto the fire. And Cissy, watching as she secures June, her hands trembling so badly that she finds her fingers hard to use, sees another person dashing about in skirts and thinks it's Mam. But, running towards her, Cissy sees that it isn't Mam—it's a younger woman Cissy doesn't recognise, who calls out orders in an English accent, who shouts and points, whose dark hair is falling loose, who's stripped down to her petticoats, and whose face is streaked with soot.

Cissy reaches Ada and Noella. A spot fire has begun in their patch of ground and they've drawn away from it with shrunken faces. Without much thought, Cissy steps out of her skirt and uses it to smother the blaze. From this point on, Cissy is everywhere: on all sides of the hill, with tubs and pails, wielding a shovel, tossing dirt and water. White ash drifts down, and Cissy recites, *Full knee-deep lies the winter snow.* Her body works as if the poem, rather than her heart, propels her blood. She sees Mam working at the pump, drawing up water. She sees Lotta at the window, crying with her face against the pane. She sees an unfamiliar old woman carrying packs and baskets onto the verandah. She sees Robert with bare arms, whipping at the fire with wet sheets, Mopsy snapping at his heels.

And everywhere she goes, she sees the magnificent woman in her petticoats, fast and strong. As they work together, beating back the fire, it feels to Cissy as if the fire is theirs—hers and this woman's; that they have power over it; that they will never grow tired and never let it reach the house. She will turn out to be partly right: they will grow tired, but the fire won't reach the house. Cissy fights beside the woman, who is—and Cissy doesn't know it yet—the Swedish painter's wife, and also the heart's decision, the amazed arrival, the headlong fall.

Tal sees the fire from where he walks east of the Wilparra road. He's carrying a blanket. He found it in a creek bed earlier this afternoon, along with a set of tracks belonging to a child: a bootless child, moving slowly, dragging its left foot slightly. Tal is an excellent tracker. He knows the plain's particulars and also its entirety, so that he can see it as the moon would, looking down, and also as a mouse would, running through the saltbush. But even he can't track reliably in the dark; he has resigned himself to waiting until dawn. It's then he sees the fire, which looks like the sort someone would light to warn of an arrival. Walking towards it, he sees the silhouette of a child. The boy is close, then closer—now the boy is here, in his own patch of stink. Tal looks down; the boy looks up. The boy has cried so hard he's forgotten how to do it.

'Can you stand?' Tal asks.

If the boy tries to stand, Tal can't detect it. Tal picks him up and holds the boy across his body, as he would a lamb. Then he runs towards the burning hill.

## STATEMENT OF THE ENGLISH ARTIST

E. RAPP, known as 'Bess', stands charged before the undersigned, Justice of the Court of Both Private and Public Opinion, for that she, the said E. Rapp, wilfully did prolong and make use of the suffering of others in order to facilitate the execution of her art. This charge is read to the accused and to the witnesses for the prosecution (some of whom are living, some dead, and some not yet born). The accused is now addressed by me as follows:–

Having heard the evidence, do you wish to say anything in answer to the charge?

Whereupon E. Rapp says as follows:–

'The execution of my art' has an unfortunate ring to it, don't you think? I never intended harm. However: yes, I freely admit my guilt and throw myself upon your mercy. Yes, I made use of a thing that wasn't mine. I didn't ask for it; when it came to me, in the manner of a birthright, I simply didn't resist. In fairness, however, I also didn't take the boy from his home, or lead him over the plain, remove his boots, set him in the sun, or deliberately lure him with apples. But, those things having happened, I kept him with me longer than I might have, knowing I could make use of him. It was a timely opportunity, nothing more.

I intend, your Honour, to write and illustrate a book for children in which a boy of this child's age and appearance loses his way in the Australian desert and is rescued by a wallaby. Based on the days I spent in Denny Wallace's company, I have preliminary sketches for at least two-thirds of the illustrations. Once complete, I'll send the manuscript to London, where I hope it will be accepted by a publisher, printed and distributed, and sold for at least three shillings per copy. Sales of the book will allow the purchase of a property in Melbourne, pay for a buggy, horses, a gardener and a maid, and fund my husband's first Australian exhibition, the success of which will bring in further funds. These will in turn make possible other plans and other funds, which will beget more plans; and so on, in the haphazard way that people of our kind earn money when we don't receive it from our families.

In addition, the book will reflect the beauty of the country, so that when uncles give it to their nephews in damp, dull London, those boys will dream of the Australian colonies; eventually they'll emigrate and become useful members of this fair-weathered society.

In addition, the book's natural themes will inspire nostalgic sentiment that may, some years from now, save the specific species of wallaby in its pages—*Petrogale petri*—from sure extinction (at present, it is over-hunted for its attractive pelt).

In conclusion, the book will serve the personal and public good, at very little cost.

Yes, your Honour, I will outline the cost: a needless day's extension, or perhaps two, of a family's uncertainty and distress. One burned hillside. The terror of a boy, apparently unconvinced that we would truly take him home, which prompted him to run out alone into the rain. Each additional bruise and blister he acquired on that extra day. Also, one should note, his discovery of time. But I can't be blamed for all of that—it's the natural way of things. All children encounter time, some earlier than others; it's melancholy, yes, but unavoidable.

Having told you more than I should, by all rights, know, I might as well continue. More costs: afraid of us, the boy left the road and could easily have been lost forever—swept off in a flood, parched in the saltbush, or injured in a ditch. Also, if it weren't for us, the boy would have seen the fire on the hill and known to run to it, because it called him to his mother. Instead, he found himself unable to move either towards or away from the burning hill, which signalled to him that my husband and I had reached his home, lied to his mother, and were preparing to take him with us to the sun.

When spoken aloud like this, it does seem most unlikely, and in my defence I couldn't have known that he perceived my husband and me as greedy gods. He couldn't explain such a thing himself—not at the age of six, and probably not later. We were, I suppose, the figures of his greatest fear: maternal abandonment. But it's still the nineteenth century, and we don't yet have language for that. Our language is more sentimental.

It asks your Honour to imagine being a boy of six, alone in the dark. You're tired, hungry, shoeless, burned and blistered, cold, and witness to the coming of another, awful world. Look at your tummy, round and taut! Your fears are real to you, all of them; every fear has taken form.

This won't be in my children's book, of course. Neither will the dark-skinned man who carried him towards the burning hill. By the time they reached it, the fire had been smothered by a miniature militia of girls and men and women—and one dog. Smoke rose from the blackened hill. People rested, covered in dirt and ash and water, some sitting on the ground and others leaning against the house. Some of them were coughing, and one girl cried. It seemed as if the world had only ever smelled of smoke.

The man, who wore a red handkerchief around his neck, carried the boy towards the house until someone saw him: that's when one of the girls called his name, and the boy heard her. Even when he saw his mother, even when her face was above his, crying, and she took him in her arms, he thought he must be dreaming. He thought he must have climbed into the sky, walked across it, and arrived in a strangely familiar life. His limbs were tugged, his face was kissed. The man who carried him spoke to the constable, then left—and I can't follow. Not even I would dare to keep *him*. The boy was mute until he saw me—then he began to scream, and wouldn't stop until his mother took him into the house. I stayed outside.

I won't write that. But all is well. The boy is safe. He met his wallaby, who brought him home. I'll write my book, we'll buy our house, and no one will know I kept the boy when I shouldn't have. Except my husband—he'll know and be uneasy with me for a while, and trust me less. But he depends on me entirely and will be, for that reason, a lenient judge. To whom do I answer, if not to him? Certainly not to you.

# SEVENTH DAY

The sunrise this morning is a gritty pink, as if stained by the remnants of last night's sunset. Minna wakes to a dreadful stink in the house; later, she'll discover it's coming from the butter she's left uncovered in the kitchen for days, which has become flyblown and rancid. She needs a maid. For now, however, she stays in bed and inhales deeply through her nose, as if the awfulness of the smell demands continual examination.

'Do you smell that?' she asks, and Karl Rapp, who is sitting on the edge of the bed as he pulls on his boots, turns and smiles and says, 'Good morning.'

She asks again, 'Do you smell that?'

Karl lifts the blanket, puts his face between her naked thighs, and sniffs. 'You smell like me,' he says.

Although this delights her, she scowls and says, 'I certainly don't. I washed.' But she brushes her hands over her thighs, to make sure there's no dried semen left.

'Pretty Minna,' says the Swedish painter. 'Go back to sleep.' He was an angel last night, winged and dazzling; this morning he's a man again, yawning as he finishes putting on his boots. He kisses her forehead; he leaves.

Minna, in love, rolls in the bed and thinks of Robert. She kicks the blanket off, lifts one shapely leg, points her toes, and thinks of Robert. When she hears Robert's voice out in the yard, she hurries to the window and sees him with his horse, looking thoroughly filthy. She's never noticed how steeply his shoulders slope, so that he hardly has a neck. Minna sees that there is no end to desire.

Chemise first, then dressing-gown, and now she's in the hallway—the awful smell is stronger here—she's at the open door, her feet are bare and cold, but what does it matter? Robert is home. He sees her, says something she can't hear, and comes to meet her. The greasy red of Robert's hair, his big golem hands, his Faustian freckles and his dark, stained uniform have never been more beautiful to her. She flings herself at him—he laughs and says, 'Steady, Minnow!', but she can see that he's pleased and will go on being pleased. She pulls Robert, blushing, into the house. Before she has a chance to kiss him, he stops, sniffs, and says, 'What's that rotten stink?'

Minna laughs until her stomach hurts as he goes looking for the source of the smell. Marriage is new enough to her to be adorable. When Robert shouts from the kitchen—he's found the butter—Minna leans against the closed front door, laughing still, and quite sure that she'll always find his shouting funny.

The sunrise this morning is the soft but sturdy pink of a cat's paw. Mary wakes with Denny in the bed beside her, grubby and burned, thinner than ever but lovely, sweet, her own sweet boy. She holds him and his heart feels near. This wakes him and he looks about, frightened; then he relaxes. He allows her to cuddle him for a few minutes. Then he draws away and sits up with a look of suspicion on his face.

'Who's out there?' Denny asks, and, although Mary hasn't heard anything, she infers that her stepmother is making noises in the parlour. Infers this because the stepmother shared the bed with them last night—her nose, while sleeping, whistled in a minor key, right in Mary's good ear—and is gone from it this morning.

'It's your grandmother,' Mary says. She sits up beside him and combs her fingers through his hair. Her arms ache, as they should—she worked the pump for hours last night. Her throat feels hoarse from shouting. Denny remains rigid, as if listening for more sounds. She remembers the way he screamed last night when he saw Bess Rapp.

Mary asks him what he'd like for breakfast, and Denny thinks about it before shaking his head and saying, 'I don't know.'

'Anything at all,' says Mary. 'Porridge with as much sugar as you like. Bread and treacle. Pickled ham and runny eggs.'

Mary licks her thumb and rubs at a smudge on the side of his face; normally Denny would squirm away from this, but he doesn't even seem to notice. Finally, he says, 'I don't want anything.'

She touches his forehead with hers and cups his cheeks with her hands. 'No sugar!' she says. 'No treacle! Who is this boy? He mustn't be my Denny.'

Denny whimpers and pushes her away.

Mary, horrified at herself, says, 'But of course you're my Denny!'

He shakes his head, just as he did when he decided against breakfast, and says, 'I'm not anybody.'

⁂

The sunrise this morning is a muted, lazy pink. Joanna Axam sits in bed, propped against pillows, waiting for Nancy to arrive with coffee. Bolingbroke sits beside her, his paws arranged in front of him—a civil sphinx. Since the orchestrion wheezed back to life yesterday afternoon, the house has been full of Henry. Joanna is thinking of him and also of Jimmy Possum's cloak, which, like Henry, is beyond her reach. The cloak seems somehow enchanted, in the same fairytale way that Wilhelmina's opal does, but this makes no sense: Willie's ring is valuable and the cloak is worthless. But if I owned it, Joanna thinks, there would be strength in knowing that such a thing had pledged itself to me.

There's a knock at the door but it isn't Nancy—it's George, who's carrying a package. Her sons have taken to dropping by her bedroom every morning; before her accident, she was always up earlier than they were. George is much cheerier than he was yesterday—the weather is fine, the shearing can begin. He looks so like Henry, though he lacks his father's confidence; he always walks into a room as if someone just outside it has made a glib remark about his character.

George brings the package to her bedside, leans down to kiss her forehead, and says, 'This came for you last night, apparently, from Wilhelmina Baumann.'

It's a heavy, roundish bundle. Even before Joanna pulls away the string and paper, she knows it's the Indian bowl. Yes, here it is, with its silver monkeys and its natives in their turbans. There's no note. Joanna places the bowl on her lap, still nestled in its leafy paper, like a ripe cabbage head. She waits to see if the bowl will come to life, now that it's hers again.

'Why would she send you that?' George asks.

'I'm not sure,' Joanna says. 'It used to be your father's.'

George responds, as he always does to mentions of his father, with a mixture of reverence and affront. 'Another knick-knack,' he says. But he picks it up and, just as Henry would have done when he first bought it, checks underneath it for a mark, breathes on it, and polishes it with his sleeve. He sets the bowl back down on Joanna's lap.

'Well, I mustn't dawdle,' says fretful, efficient George, and off he goes into the world for which he feels responsible.

Joanna sits with the bowl, waiting to see if it belongs to her again.

Another knock, and this time it's Bear, who's dressed and ready for his day. Bear comes into his own at shearing time: he's a better, faster wool grader than his brother, and for a few happy days a year he occupies his station in the woolshed with the pride of a prosperous shopkeeper. He hesitates in the doorway.

'Good morning,' he says.

'Well, come in, dear,' Joanna says. 'Don't creep about.'

Bear walks towards the bed. He looks both pleased and nervous. This is the sort of moment, Joanna thinks, in which I should say that his father would be proud of him; and Henry would indeed be proud, but he was also pleased by anyone, and at the same time took no one seriously, least of all himself. She's reminded, for some reason, that Henry was always talking about their future as ostrich farmers: always mentioning the ostrich operations he'd seen in South Africa and telling visitors that ostrich was an important impending industry of the colony. All this while keeping a family of emus in a pen, as pets. She'd never quite known if he was sincere or teasing. On one occasion he'd told a guest at dinner that ostriches will eat anything, even iron—Shakespeare said so. She sat across the table waiting for him to look at her, waiting for the wink that would invite her inside the joke. He never winked. The bowl does belong to her—it's ornamental and exasperating. It's beloved. She will send away for a new shawl, dove grey and done in sturdy, silky wool.

Bear, at Joanna's side now, pets Bolingbroke's head.

'I'm headed to the shed,' Bear says. 'But I wanted to tell you, we've had a telegram: a bonny boy, ten pounds four ounces, full head of hair. Mother and baby fine and well.'

'Oh,' Joanna says. She takes Bear's hand in hers and presses it to her cheek. 'Oh, my darling.'

⁂

The sunrise this morning is the soft, glossy pink of Bess Rapp's neck when she washed at the basin last night before going out to sleep in Mathew's cot. Cissy, hearing Lotta fuss, dresses quickly. In Mam's room, she sees Denny in the bed and goes to cover him in kisses, but Mam shakes her head to warn, 'Not yet.' In the parlour, Grandmother Deniston is cutting the rind off a slab of bacon. When Cissy doesn't see the Englishwoman she hurries outside—and here she is, here's Bess Rapp, dressed in her sooty clothes and sitting in the sun on the edge of the verandah. She has a bowl of tea beside her.

Bess looks up at Cissy and smiles without dimples. 'Good morning,' she says.

Cissy is too shy to answer, but she sits down next to Bess. This silence doesn't seem to perturb the Englishwoman, who is so contained, so self-possessed, whereas Cissy—fussed at and fussy—is always leaking away. Bess Rapp's one idea is her own perfect, useful self. Cissy knows that the Swedish painter is due to arrive this morning, that he'll take Bess away, and that Cissy will never see her again. All the same, she has this moment on the verandah. She can't think of what to say, but talking isn't necessary. It's enough to sit in the sun, sometimes looking at Bess's face and sometimes at the blackened hill where they fought together.

Denny cries inside the house. Noella appears at the front door and says to Cissy, 'He won't come out from Mam's room till the lady's gone.' Sly and triumphant, she glances at Bess—who has closed her eyes as if to ward off a calamity. Noella giggles and disappears inside. Cissy takes the Englishwoman's hand.

---

The sunrise this morning is a tender, mottled pink, a little like the skin of Minna's inner thighs, a little like the marzipan peaches in the bakeries of Stockholm, but truly a precise combination of rose madder, white and yellow, which Karl knows he could reproduce with ease. He has no interest in reproducing the sunrise. He feels emptied out this morning—as if a pure fire has burned him up and then moved on. As he rides out to Undelcarra, leading the other horses, he imagines writing to Alström: 'My dear fellow, ignore my previous letter,' (a letter Karl hasn't yet sent, and never will) 'which was nothing more than the ramblings of a man deranged by a crisis of scale. Quite simply, this country and everything about it is too large, and no man—certainly no artist—likes to be reminded of his smallness by comparison. I'll continue to work at the sunset picture, but with humility: I have broken my arrangement with the sky, and I feel better for it.'

Does he feel better? Not at all. Not yet.

He arrives at a sooty Undelcarra and finds Bess sitting on the verandah, holding the hand of a tall young girl. This girl, on seeing Karl, issues him a look reminiscent of Caravaggio's Judith: scornful, queasy and unsure. Bess lets go of the girl's hand, comes to Karl at the gate, and tells him that the boy's been found, which Karl already knows; he heard the news from Robert Manning, who he passed on the road just out of town. She tells him that she wants to leave the desert right away, to return to Melbourne—she has a book to finish. They'll go immediately into town to make arrangements, leave the horses with instructions, and take the first southbound train.

Karl could say, 'But I'm not ready to leave the desert. I have to see Wilpena Pound. I have to paint the sunset.' He doesn't. He does ask to see Denny, but the tall girl—lingering on the verandah—calls out to say that Denny is ill in bed and won't see anyone. So Karl decides to leave a letter.

'My dear Denny,' he writes, 'I'm overjoyed to know you're safe at home. When I reach Melbourne and we have a new address, I'll send it on. We'll arrange lessons for you. Please don't forget your Swedish friend.' Then he draws a picture of a monkey wearing military medals.

Karl and Bess don't speak on the ride back to Fairly. Karl assumes that Bess thinks it's unnecessary: she knows Karl so well, knows what he'll have done with Minna, and needs neither his apologies nor promises. Karl looks at her from time to time, wondering about her private room. If he could find its hinge and open it, what would he see inside?

There's not much to arrange in town. The next train is due tomorrow, so they take a second-floor room at the Imperial. They both wash thoroughly and nap through the afternoon. When he wakes, Karl goes out onto the hotel's balcony, where the sky is just beginning its evening business.

Soon Karl will learn that his remarkable sunsets haven't been limited to the Flinders Ranges: they'll continue as he and Bess make their way down to Adelaide and back, by ship, to Melbourne. Karl will attempt to paint the desert sky, but later in the year he'll see newspaper articles about unprecedented skies in London; in the New Year, he'll receive a letter from Alström—'My dear Kalle'—with reports that the winter sunsets in Stockholm have been inconceivable, horrifying, as if nature herself were screaming.

Later still, Karl will learn that his demanding sky was the direct result of an immense volcanic eruption that tore apart an island in the Dutch East Indies. He'll be consoled by this news, by such obvious cause and effect. The blazing sunsets were simply elemental and, artistically, he can manage the elemental. He'll be able to look back at the work he produced in the months immediately following the Flinders trip—good work, very good—and see that he didn't fail to capture the large, dark idea behind those sunsets, because there was no idea, they were an atmospheric disturbance, and thank the Lord for that. It will become easier, then, to label anything for which he's worried his talent and courage are insufficient with one glorious word: Krakatoa.

For now he studies what he thinks may be his final true desert sunset. The sky burns and leaps, it gilds and candles—every drenched inch of it, until the sun falls below the ranges. Then the sky darkens. The red returns, stealthy now, with green above and lilac higher still. It deepens into purple. Here's the strange new cloud, hovering in its own grey light. Then night comes in, black and blue and grey and white, and the moon in its green bag swings heavy over the red nation of the ranges.

## SEVENTH NIGHT

Oh, Denny is home, and Lotta watches him eat bread in milk. Mam sweetened the milk, she crumbled the bread, she stirred it in the best blue basin, she even sprinkled nutmeg across the top—puff! puff! A tiny dust storm. Denny's hair is wet and combed because Mam heated the copper and washed him, even though it isn't Saturday. First she let him sleep all day, then she washed him. Then Mam dried him and combed his hair, then she made bread and milk for Denny and not for Lotta, and this, to Lotta, doesn't seem quite fair. Denny isn't the littlest, it isn't Denny's birthday, he was only lost, and being lost is not the same as being on a birthday or being poorly.

He does look poorly, though, red and flaky, and his eyes sit deep in his head. Maybe the Hooky Man came and pressed Denny's eyes into his head—oh, oh, give a shiver, run to Mam, but Mam pushes Lotta away—gently. So Lotta goes to Ada, who will always cuddle. Ada accepts Lotta onto her knee, but even Ada is watching Denny eat from the best blue basin. Mam is crying, but no one will say so or say why or tell Mam to stop. She's quiet when she cries. Why should Mam be crying if Denny isn't lost anymore?

Now Mam is preparing another basin, it's chipped and white—what will she put in this one? Hot water and soap, that's all. She brings it to the table with a cloth and the scissors. Is she going to cut Denny's fingernails? Yes, and Denny hates to have his fingernails cut. Look at him! He shrinks away from the basin as he eats the last of his bread and milk. Lotta can see a dark line of dirt under each of his nails.

Mam sits beside him, waiting for him to finish eating. If he doesn't want to have his fingernails cut, he'll have to eat forever. It's the same when Lotta says her prayers at night: prayers mean staying out of bed, so holy Lotta takes time to bless everyone she knows. But Denny does finish the bread and milk. He pushes the empty basin across the table. Noella takes it up and carries it away; behind Denny, she tilts the basin and drinks the last of the sweet milk. Lotta licks her lips.

Now Denny must give one hand to Mam, who takes it. She's holding the small scissors, they're shaped like a long bird called a stork. Lotta can't look. She watches Denny's twisting face instead. His mouth opens as if it wants to make a noise, and Lotta knows it hurts, so she squeezes her fingernails into her palms. Sometimes Denny's hand jumps away from Mam, who always catches it with the shining stork.

Mam, finished with one hand, puts it in the soapy basin. Now she's at Denny's other hand, he holds his shoulders up at his ears, there are tears on his face—his hand jumps and Mam catches it, the stork opens and closes, oh, the pink parts of the fingertips, oh, ow, the skin beside the fingernail, the soft bed beneath the fingernail. Lotta crosses her arms and hides her fingers in her armpits. Then Mam is finished and Denny's other hand goes into the basin. Mam sweeps the bits of cut nail into one cupped palm, and Denny sits with his fingers in the basin. In a moment, Mam will pass him the cloth to dry his hands.

But first, here's Dad at the door, shouting. Mam jumps up from her chair and her hand opens—there go the pieces of fingernail over the floor, little crescent moons that bounce and scatter. Denny lifts his hands out of the soapy water. Lotta watches as Denny looks at his clean, pale fingers. He's waiting for something—yes, here it is, a bit of blood is coming out on them, Mam has cut nearly every finger, she's trimmed each nail back so far and Denny's hands have jumped so much. Denny puts his hands back in the water. Lotta watches him while Dad shouts.

What's Dad shouting about? Fire, the hill, what was Mam thinking, the risk of it—has she ever seen a hayfield burn? So close to the house, the children, the horses the wheat the house—what bloody why, what possessed, bloody fire, of all things! We're lucky we'd had rain! Is it that Mam wants, to see it burn? Does she want to lose it all? He shouts at Mam's left ear. She stands at the table and he shouts. Even Cissy is quiet. Bloody burn the hill! 'Bloody' is a Bad Word. Do you want to ruin me! he shouts. Do you want us all ruined! Then you can pray for us! Then we'll need your prayers! The pieces of fingernail lie in curls on the floor. Three of them have bounced onto the pink sheepskin rug. What did I do! Dad shouts. What did I ever do to you!

Mam says, 'Mathew,' and she moves aside. Behind her, Denny sits at the soapy basin.

Now Dad lets out a funny sound—a sort of moan. He's standing, shouting, and then he's moaning, and somehow he's at Denny, on Denny, he's kneeling by Denny and putting his arms around Denny's shoulders and he makes this new moaning sound. He's upset the basin of water and it runs across the table, but when Mam goes to set it right he takes her hand and pulls her over to where he crouches with Denny. His arms go round both Denny and Mam now, his face is bent to Denny's, Mam's face as well, and the moans become more organised—thank God, Dad says. Ah, ah, thank God. His voice sounds something like the cow the time she had her calf that died. Thank God, thank God.

Noella and Ada and Joy all look at one another. The old lady who's called Grandmother sits by the fire with a handkerchief pressed to her lips. Mopsy whimpers by the stove. Cissy goes to the table and takes the chipped white basin; she uses the cloth to mop the water. Denny blinks up from between Mam's and Dad's faces. His own face is red, he looks muddled, everything is muddled—then he pushes his head against Dad's shoulder and Dad says, again, Ah, thank God, thank God.

Lotta sinks to the floor and crawls to the sheepskin. She picks one, two, three pieces of fingernail out of the rug. Ah ah ah. She extends one hand to sweep up the other bits of nail from where they lie near Dad's shaking foot. Above her, such strange noises. Her father's face, seen from underneath, is twisted: he's crying. He makes the same sort of gulps Denny does when he cries. Ah, ah, thank God. What will she do with the fingernails, now that she has them? Lying there on her hand, they look like grubs. She goes out of the front door and flings the nails off the verandah. She checks to see if the red hill is on fire again—it isn't.

On the verandah, she sees the feather she found this morning, the long brown feather with yellow at its tip. As she picks it up, she hears Mam calling her name. 'Lotta!' calls Mam, and Mopsy barks. Mam has a soft voice but Lotta will always hear it.

Things are calmer inside, but they're still not right. Denny and Dad both sit at the table with blotchy, slippery faces. No one is crying—now it's Lotta's turn. She runs to Mam and sobs into Mam's leg and her chest feels opened wide, feels empty, there's not enough Mam to put back inside it. Lotta gives herself over to her grief. Mam picks Lotta up, she cradles Lotta; this is close but isn't close enough.

Then, all at once, Lotta feels sleepy. She slackens in Mam's arms. She presses her face into Mam's neck while Mam moves about the kitchen. Mam is taking the jar with the sherbet powder down from the shelf. She's putting the powder in the brown jug, she's mixing it with water. She's making Lotta's favourite drink: lemon kali. Mam sets Lotta down at the table and gives her the first cup. Denny gets the second. Lotta is happy at the table. In one hand, the cup of lemon kali; in the other, the brown feather with yellow at its tip. She lifts the feather up to show it off.

'What a pretty feather,' says Mam, who is passing cups to Joy and Noella.

The lemon kali is sweet but also makes you want to suck your cheeks together. Lotta and Denny both suck their cheeks together. Something small—a louse or a flea—jumps off the feather and onto Lotta's finger.

# THE STATE OF SOUTH AUSTRALIA, FEBRUARY 1901

The boy is now a man of twenty-three, and he stands with his fiancée in a crush of people at the Ocean Steamers Wharf in Port Adelaide. Yes, Denny will be married soon, to a young woman called Dotty. They're a well-matched pair, Denny and Dotty: he settles her, and she encourages levity in him. They can be alone together without talking. Dotty would like to be known as Dorothy, and she would like Denny to be known as Deniston; she thinks these names are more dignified, more useful in the world, and, as it isn't so much to ask, Denny has begun to introduce himself as Deniston. Each time he does it, he feels slightly less as if he's impersonating someone. Also, Deniston Wallace is preferable to Dennis Wallace, which is the name of the boy who was lost in the desert and found again, who continued to appear in newspapers for years, particularly around the anniversary of the whole episode, and was the inspiration for a celebrated children's book. Deniston, however, can't seem to train his mind to think of his bride-to-be as anyone but Dotty.

This excursion to the wharf was Dotty's idea—the troopship *Ormazan* departs for South Africa this afternoon, and Denny's nephew Arthur is on board. Arthur is seventeen and off to fight the Boers. Dotty read that the ship was expected to receive a warm send-off, and wanted to see it for herself: she's the type to relish ceremonial events, particularly when she feels some personal connection. Arthur Wallace is her personal connection to the *Ormazan*, although they've never met. It's enough, she says, to know that he grew up in the same house as her Denny. Dotty knows Arthur simply as Denny's cousin; no need to mention his illegitimacy, to her or to anyone. Or the persistent speculation among their neighbours wherever they've lived that Arthur, with his dark eyes and hair, might not be impeccably white. Cissy once asked outright for the name and history of Arthur's mother, but Mam didn't know it. Perhaps it was better not to.

The crowd on the wharf heaves around Denny and Dotty—Deniston and Dorothy—and instinctively they link their arms and lean together in the shuffle. Dotty must stand on her toes in order to see anything of the ship other than the plume of steam from its funnel and the flags strung between its masts. She asks Denny, continually, to describe what's happening, but the truth is that nothing seems to be happening at all: whatever activity is preparing the *Ormazan* to sail is occurring deep in the bowels of the steamer, which, according to a friendly fellow standing beside them, has been outfitted with blankets of unrivalled quality, provided by the firm of one Mr William

Durrant, the fellow's brother-in-law. The fellow wears a black band on his arm, for Queen Victoria.

'But you must spot Arthur,' says Dotty, who can't stand the idea of a boy going off to war without seeing a friendly face. 'And he must see you. You wrote and told him you'd be here.' She rises up on the balls of her feet and cranes her neck, steadying herself on Denny's arm, and Denny feels, as always, the insistent current that passes between their bodies.

But he can't see Arthur. There are hundreds of troopers on the deck of the *Ormazan*. Some of them call and wave to the crowd, others push in bashful fun at one another's shoulders, and others grip the railing and look with prophetic dread at the rooftops of the port. How to distinguish Arthur from among them? He has dark hair, dark eyes, and skin just a shade or two darker, perhaps, than he should, but really he looks like any other boy. Weeks ago, when Ada passed on the news that Arthur had volunteered for the South Australian Imperial Bushmen, Denny said, 'But why should he want to go to war?'

And Ada replied, 'That boy has been at war since the day he was born.'

Denny, who's in love with safety, can't conceive of choosing to leave South Australia and risk his life in a place he's never been. He spent his childhood terrified of the summons he was assured would come, someday, from the Swedish painter and his wife, of whom he has only a vague recollection.

'You'll go to Melbourne,' Cissy would say sometimes, 'and learn to be a painter.'

And Joy would say, 'Think of the money she must have made from that book of hers!'

Denny's signed copy of that book, *Tom and the Wallaby*, took some time to reach him. It arrived in Fairly by mail in 1886, addressed to Undelcarra, but Undelcarra had been abandoned by then, like all the other wheat farms on the northern Willochra Plain. Even Thalassa had only three years left before the drought would end it, the Axams would retreat, and the homestead would begin to crumble around its immovable orchestrion, which, once exposed, made eerie noises in high winds. After Undelcarra, the Wallaces moved south to Murray Bridge, where Mathew sold his Shires to buy an orchard. Fairly's postmaster, Mr Blake, tracked Cissy via Quorn—she'd spent a year in service at the doctor's there, and the doctor could say which hospital he'd sent her to, to start training as a nurse.

So Cissy, finally, was the one who brought the book to Denny, and even she was impressed by his likeness in its pages. There was one picture, in which he slept beneath a tree, that caught him quite uncannily—Cissy has been heard to say so on more than one occasion. The Rapps never sent for him, but Denny still imagines that word might come and he'll be obliged to step out of his life and into another. The thought, now, isn't terrifying—only tiring. He's worked so hard to inhabit this life of his, to feel at home in it.

Now the *Ormazan* sounds its whistle, loud and deep. 'Look!' cries Dotty, pointing at the ship's stacks. 'The steam changes shape when they blow the horn. How marvellous!' She claps her hands together and smiles up at him, so pleased, so dear, that he would like to kiss her.

The whistle blasts again. Around them, the crowd begins to cheer—even the women who have, until now, been weeping.

The fellow beside them, brother-in-law of Durrant, raises his hat and shakes it in the air.

'Quick,' says Dotty. 'You must spot Arthur.'

Denny is able, then—for just a moment—to see Arthur on the deck, not from this position in the crowd but as if the two of them, Denny and Arthur, are standing side by side, shipboard, beneath the flags. They call each other cousin, as they always have. Arthur is the one of Denny's family members who might understand if he were to say, 'For as long as I remember, I've lived outside myself.'

Arthur, serious and imposing in his trooper's hat, would nod his head. 'Of course you have,' he'd say. 'Is there another way?'

Dotty bounces on her toes. Denny thinks, it's only because I got lost that we ever even learned of Arthur. That's why he's real to us. That's why he's on this ship. What would Mam say about her grandson in uniform, sailing for South Africa? Mary is two years dead of meningitis—a complication from an ear infection. Denny's sisters are married, except for Cissy, who is matron of a private hospital, and Lotta, who Mam always seemed to hold close in a particular way, as if she were afraid of something terrible happening to her youngest daughter. Lotta, who unlike Cissy is still young enough to marry, keeps house for Mathew, who has managed better with fruit trees than he did with wheat. Joseph—Arthur's father, the firstborn Wallace—died in 1884, a farm equipment accident in New South Wales. By the time the family learned this news, Arthur was six years old—the same age Denny had been when he spent his week in the desert. Still holding the telegram, Mam had taken Arthur on her knee, pressed her face into his neck, and wept without a sound.

'Oh, hurry! Find him!' Dotty says, and Denny sees that the ship is moving. He scans the troops. He'd like to spot Arthur for Dotty's sake; otherwise, Denny feels how little difference it would make. He already perceives his love for Arthur as something remembered rather than felt. But memory, in Deniston's experience, can be peculiar. For instance, he remembers hardly anything of the week he spent in the desert. He knows he was afraid, which seems natural, but the fear he recollects takes strange shapes and forms. He can't explain it, even to himself. He has some sense that the stories he heard as a child—the Bible stories, the fairytales and myths, Billy's native tales, his father's Hooky Man—all jumbled in his head and became some other, much more alarming thing. Of that desert week, the fear is really all that's left.

But there are times when being a boy on the Willochra does come back to him, in vivid detail, almost as an assault: the smell of Mam's braid, the rubbing together of the feet when happy, the sun through hot eyelids, the loose tooth rocking, the closing of one eye and then the other, the swallows above the stunted wheat, the wind in the she-oaks, the urgent stirring of the pot of blood for pudding, the shed hair of the sisters, the wet foot of the lizard on the wrist, and the wave until the guest is out of sight.

'I see him!' Denny says, though he doesn't. Dotty gasps. He points at the steamer, and she looks beyond his finger. She's beaming. Denny raises his hat, and Dotty her small, gloved hand, and together they wave at the ship as it moves out onto the river.

# ACKNOWLEDGEMENTS

This novel was written with generous support from the Australia Council for the Arts, for which I'm enormously grateful. Thanks, also, to the Santa Maddalena Foundation for a writing residency in the autumn of 2018.

In South Australia, I'd like to thank the State Library of South Australia and Iga Warta. I owe a particular debt in my research to the work of Lily Neville, Dorothy Tunbridge, Peggy Brock and C. Warren Bonython.

Thank you to Stephanie Cabot, my agent and friend, for her patience and loving support; and to everyone at Susanna Lea Associates. In Australia, I'm indebted to the insight and enthusiasm of Jane Palfreyman, Angela Handley and Ali Lavau, and everyone at Allen & Unwin. Thank you to Mitzi Angel at FSG and Carole Welch at Sceptre for their wisdom, grace and continued faith. And to Ben Ball, who has believed in me since the beginning.

Thank you to Jack Ellis, Fatima Kola, Namwali Serpell, Mykaela Saunders, Mimi Chubb and especially Michelle de Kretser, who all read versions of this novel and made it better. Thanks to dear Prue Axam for being generous with her family name; and to the Reeves/Muszkiewcz family, in Texas, Rome and Montana.

I've talked a lot about writing novels with my students on both sides of the Pacific, at The University of Sydney and UC Berkeley; now is my chance to thank them for all the ways in which their curiosity, enthusiasm and intelligence have fed this particular novel. Thank you also to my colleagues in the English departments at Sydney and Berkeley, especially Beth Yahp.

Gratitude beyond words to my beloved parents, Ian and Lyn McFarlane, without whom I would never have been to the Flinders Ranges or met the von Axle family; to my sister, Katrina McFarlane, who has helped me out of many puzzles of my own making; and to my Perth family: Evan and Bonita McFarlane, and my darlings, Rowan, Anneka, Archie and Jemima.

And finally, thank you to Charlotte and Giamaica, who dozed beside me while I wrote sections of this novel; and to Emma Jones, always.